I0761107

ALSO BY CHRISTIE GOLDEN

WORLD OF WARCRAFT

Sylvanas
Before the Storm
Lord of the Clans
Rise of the Horde
Beyond the Dark Portal (with Aaron S. Rosenberg)
Arthas: Rise of the Lich King
The Shattering: Prelude to Cataclysm
Thrall: Twilight of the Aspects
Jaina Proudmoore: Tides of War
War Crimes
Warcraft: Durotan: The Official Movie Prequel
Warcraft: The Official Movie Novelization
Exploring Azeroth: The Eastern Kingdoms

STARCRAFT

The Dark Templar Saga, Book One: Firstborn
The Dark Templar Saga, Book Two: Shadow Hunters
The Dark Templar Saga, Book Three: Twilight
StarCraft II: Devils' Due
StarCraft II: Flashpoint

STAR WARS

Star Wars: Fate of the Jedi: Omen
Star Wars: Fate of the Jedi: Allies
Star Wars: Fate of the Jedi: Ascension
Star Wars: Dark Disciple
Star Wars: Battlefront II: Inferno Squad

ORIGINAL NOVELS

On Fire's Wings
In Stone's Clasp
Under Sea's Shadow
Instrument of Fate
King's Man & Thief
A.D. 999 (as Jadrien Bell)

STAR TREK

Star Trek: Voyager: The Murdered Sun
Star Trek: Voyager: Marooned
Star Trek: Voyager: Seven of Nine
Star Trek: Voyager: The Dark Matters Trilogy, Book One: Cloak and Dagger
Star Trek: Voyager: The Dark Matters Trilogy, Book Two: Ghost Dance
Star Trek: Voyager: The Dark Matters Trilogy, Book Three: Shadow of Heaven
Star Trek: Voyager: No Man's Land
Star Trek: Voyager: What Lay Beyond
Star Trek: Voyager: Homecoming
Star Trek: Voyager: The Farther Shore
Star Trek: Voyager: Spirit Walk, Book One: Old Wounds
Star Trek: Voyager: Spirit Walk, Book Two: Enemy of My Enemy
Star Trek: The Next Generation: Double Helix: The First Virtue (with Michael Jan Friedman)
Star Trek: Hard Crash
Star Trek: The Last Roundup

BLOOD TIES

BLOOD TIES

CHRISTIE GOLDEN

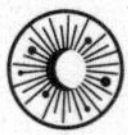

RANDOM HOUSE WORLDS
NEW YORK

Random House Worlds
An imprint of Random House
A division of Penguin Random House LLC
1745 Broadway, New York, NY 10019
randomhousebooks.com
penguinrandomhouse.com

LIBRARY OF CONGRESS CATALOGING-IN-PUBLICATION DATA
Names: Golden, Christie author
Title: Blood ties / Christie Golden.
Other titles: At head of title World of Warcraft midnight
Description: First edition. | New York : Random House Worlds, 2025. |
Series: World of warcraft
Identifiers: LCCN 2025036194 (print) | LCCN 2025036195 (ebook) |
ISBN 9780399594243 hardcover acid-free paper | ISBN 9780399594250 ebook
Subjects: LCGFT: Fiction | Fantasy fiction | Novels
Classification: LCC PS3557.O359268 B58 2025 (print) | LCC PS3557.O359268 (ebook)
LC record available at https://lccn.loc.gov/2025036194
LC ebook record available at https://lccn.loc.gov/2025036195

Printed in the United States of America

1st Printing

First Edition

BOOK TEAM: Production editor: Jocelyn Kiker • Managing editor: Susan Seeman • Production manager: Kevin Garcia • Copy editor: Laura Dragonette • Proofreaders: Emily Cutler, Vicki Fischer, Judy Kiviat

Book design by Jo Anne Metsch

The authorized representative in the EU for product safety and compliance is Penguin Random House Ireland, Morrison Chambers, 32 Nassau Street, Dublin D02 YH68, Ireland. https://eu-contact.penguin.ie

This book is dedicated to my mother,
Elizabeth Colson Golden
(March 25, 1925–July 22, 2024)

Who instilled in me a love of reading and respect for writing;
never judged me when I wept for characters;
and never, ever stopped being curious about the world.
I love you, I miss you, and I wish you could read this one.

THE BROKEN ISLES

HIGHMOUNTAIN

VAL'SHARAH

STORMHEIM

SURAMAR

AZSUNA

Suramar City

The Tomb of Sargeras

THE BROKEN SHORE

BLOOD TIES

PROLOGUE

Felsoul Hold Ruins, Suramar

THE BROKEN ISLES

"You're having second thoughts."

"No, I'm not," Dionaar lied. He winced inwardly as he heard his voice quivering. "I just think . . . we may be pushing our luck. That's all."

The nightborne youth craned his neck to look up at the demonic structure. It was broken, a ruin created by a long-defeated foe. Dionaar knew it ought to have signified nothing more than a reminder of the past—a reminder, in fact, of a great victory.

But the stories of what had happened here were not easily forgotten, and this unnerved him.

"You're certain no one followed us?" Corentyn stood up a bit straighter. He was taller than Dionaar, slim, almost bony. He had all the recklessness expected of his seventeen years, a confidence that Dionaar could only dream of possessing. The flickering orange glow of the torches played over his frowning, knife-sharp features, casting a capering shadow of his profile.

Confident and clever, but not too wise, Dionaar thought. Two weeks ago, in an act of rebellion, Corentyn had carved a protection glyph onto the back of his hand, bragging about it to all the students who would listen. If he'd spent even a little time studying, his bravado would have been productive. But he hadn't, so of course he'd messed it up, and now the glyph etched into his very skin meant nothing. When his parents discovered it, they'd been furious with him, told him he'd simply have to wear it until he could earn enough coin to have it removed himself.

He's all talk, Dionaar thought, though his stomach clenched. He shook his head vigorously. "Not that I saw, but . . . a patrol might come by here. Eventually."

Corentyn gave a careless shrug. "We can just hide—wait until they pass."

"If we were noticed . . ."

Corentyn laughed and prodded him in the chest with a forefinger. "I'll just shove you out in front of me. You'd take the fall, right?"

Dionaar looked down and didn't answer. It wasn't fair, of course; Corentyn was always out in front showing off, and Dionaar was just his lackey, spreading the stories of all the great things Corentyn did or the creepy abandoned places they'd checked out together. Even now Dionaar was expected to convince the others that they needed to sneak out, see for themselves if the horror Corentyn warned them about was real.

Corentyn slapped him on the shoulder. "Ah, cheer up, I'll get you out if your parents lock you up. But I need you at your best tonight because I have something special planned." He toed the large sack he had brought. Its lumpiness shifted slightly, but Dionaar had no idea what might be inside it.

"What's that?"

"Can't reveal the trick." He sniffed. "Don't be too scared; *you* at least know it's all fake."

Even though Dionaar was in on every prank, sometimes Corentyn's antics still scared him. "You sure about all this? Vanaur and the Mystralin girls are coming, and their uncle is part of the Duskwatch. What if they tell—"

"They won't, or they'll get in trouble, too." Corentyn rolled his eyes. "Don't be such a baby. Go on, get going. Oh, wait—tell them before they come that orc warlocks used fel magic to steal years of life from their own children so they would be old enough to fight!"

"What?" Dionaar had never heard this. "Cor, you're making this all up. And no, I'm not going to tell them that."

▪ ▪ ▪

"They did what?" Renae's voice was a horrified whisper.

Dionaar nodded sagely. "They drained their lives with fel magic so that they grew years older in seconds!"

"I want to be older," Julyan said.

"Not like that," Vanaur said.

Each of the teenagers carried a torch, except for the youngest, who clung tightly to her sister's arm. "Now, remember," Dionaar said, "we have to be very quiet. No talking, not even whispering. Demons have excellent hearing."

Their faces were turned up to him, their eyes wide, and they nodded. "I'm going to take you to where I last saw the fel magic, but we have to be careful to not attract any attention. Because if they find us . . ."

"They'll eat us," whispered Renae.

"No," Vanaur said, rolling his eyes. "Haven't you been listening? They'll drain your life and make you *old*!"

"Oh, they might eat you *afterward*," Dionaar said. "Probably shouldn't stick around to find out, right?"

Energetic nods. "And one more thing. You can't tell anyone what you saw here. Not a word. Ever."

"But shouldn't we— I mean, if there truly is a demon in these ruins . . ."

"I've, um, already alerted them," Dionaar lied. "This is our last chance to see it before the Duskwatch takes care of it."

They agreed silently, and Dionaar lifted his torch, stepping into the darkness.

It was a short, easy path, and Dionaar knew it well by now. He gasped and pointed at a puddle of "demon blood" (water thickened with luminous mushroom gills), a "victim's bone" (which Corentyn had salvaged from a birthday celebration featuring roasted stag), and a "demon horn" (which had also belonged to the unfortunate stag).

The Mystralin sisters were properly alarmed, but Vanaur was growing bored. "You promised fel magic."

"There's only fel magic when they've fed souls of the innocents to the machinery," Dionaar replied.

That was Corentyn's cue, but nothing happened.

"And if we see that, we've stayed too long," Dionaar said louder. "And we *don't want THAT.*"

Nothing.

What's going on? Corentyn had said something about a surprise, but maybe his trick didn't work. This wouldn't be the first time one of his pranks backfired. Still, by now he should have at least activated the lamp with the green glass, started the smoke . . .

"I *knew* it," Vanaur said. "Just another one of your stupid pranks, you and Corentyn. You really shouldn't—"

He broke off with a strangled sound, his mouth open, staring behind Dionaar, who exhaled in relief. *Thank goodness.* The audience was bathed in the familiar eerie green of the filtered light. But there was a smell . . .

Rotten eggs. Fel was supposed to smell like rotten eggs! So *that* was the surprise!

It was then that the sensation of fear struck Dionaar so powerfully that his knees buckled. The others shrieked, the promise of silence utterly abandoned, and they ran back the way they had come, the wildly bobbing orange flames of their torches growing smaller and smaller, then devoured by darkness.

Dionaar had dropped his own torch and made no effort to find it, his breath catching as he covered his head with his hands and curled into a tight ball. He tried to gulp air, but he could taste the awful odor, and there was another smell laced with the reek of rotten egg, a smell less innocently explained. The smell of something *dead.*

Then came the scream.

It was coming from right behind the rock, high-pitched and pure in its perfect terror, a sound that Dionaar had never heard issue from Corentyn's throat but that was undeniably his. Dionaar squeezed his eyes shut against the green glow, but it seemed to penetrate his very skin. His throat hurt so badly, was so raw, and he realized it was because he was screaming, screaming to drown out Cor, whom he was sure was dying back there, *dying*—

And then there was silence, except for Dionaar's panting and the pounding of his frantic heart.

"Are you all right, Dio? Looks like I scared *you* more than them!"

The voice belonged to Corentyn. He sounded . . . normal. Excited, even.

Dionaar's body shook violently, but he slowly lifted his head to see his friend grinning down at him. "Good prank, huh?"

Emotions flooded Dionaar: Relief, anger, confusion. But most of all *joy*. He got to his feet and threw his arms around his friend.

"It's all right," Corentyn said, hugging him back awkwardly. "I'm fine. I'm fine."

Dionaar pulled back and then swung at Corentyn, cursing him, but the young man ducked and laughed, fending him off easily. As Dionaar's adrenaline ebbed, Corentyn explained what he'd done. He'd been hanging on to the rotten eggs and meat for a while, and he'd practiced his shriek several times near the shore, where his voice would be drowned out by the tide.

"I did too good of a job, though," he said, relighting Dionaar's torch from his own. "I suspect the Mystralin girls are going straight to Uncle Duskwatch now, to tell him they saw fel magic down here." He flashed a grin. "Party's over, but at least I went out on a high note . . . so to speak."

"We should tell our parents the same thing," Dionaar said. "So they won't blame it on us."

"Good idea. Let's get going. Do you need to change your pants?"

"Oh, shut up!" Now that Corentyn had officially ended the hoax,

Dionaar could laugh about everything. Even if his parents found out they'd been behind it, he was just glad that it had been a foolish joke.

Corentyn placed a hand on his friend's shoulder and gently started to turn him around, but then Dionaar froze.

A hand was sticking out from behind the boulder.

A hand with a half-healed, miswritten rune carved into it.

Corentyn laughed, following his friend's line of sight. "Looks pretty real, doesn't it? I was going to wave it like I was trying to climb out, but those kids ran before I could even use it! What a waste."

"Y-yeah," murmured Dionaar, staring at the hand. "A waste."

"Come on," Corentyn said, "let's get out of here." He had already begun talking about their next prank before they reached the exit.

But as Dionaar glanced behind them, searching the green, unnatural glow, he could have sworn he saw the hand twitch.

CHAPTER ONE

Light's Hope Chapel, Eastern Plaguelands

THE EASTERN KINGDOMS

Clang. Clang. Clang.

The sound of hammer against steel was a familiar one outside Light's Hope Chapel. But this time Master Craftsman Wilhelm—who usually repaired the weapons and armor of the Knights of the Silver Hand—was not the one producing it. The gruff dwarf was instead leaning back against a grassy hillock, peering up at the brown-gray sky of the Eastern Plaguelands and belting out a smithing song between swigs of Thunderbrew lager. He paused long enough to pose a question to the half-elf champion who had offered to take his place.

"How long can that skinny little arm of yers keep this up, laddie?" Wilhelm's eyes twinkled, his mustache wet with foam. The "laddie" in question, Arator the Redeemer, grinned at him as he wiped his brow.

"Yet again I lament that I do not possess the dwarven musculature," he said with an exaggerated sigh.

Wilhelm guffawed. "Ah, well, we cannae all be so fortunate."

Arator's arm was certainly up to the task, but it was hot work, and neither his human nor his elven blood gave him the innate dwarven ability to long withstand the heat of the forge. He removed his upper body armor and laid it to one side, revealing a pair of dragon tattoos on his muscled upper arms. They were identical in style, both outlined in gold, but filled in with different hues: one bright as the White Lady moon and the other a shade of charcoal.

A human boy of about ten, Winthrop, sat beside him. Winthrop was the newest squire to the famed paladin Lord Grayson Shadowbreaker, a position that Arator himself had held when he was new to the order. It was the boy's task to which Arator now plied his own efforts, working on cleaning and hammering dents out of the great man's armor. Today marked young Winthrop's first visit to Light's Hope Chapel, and he was far too dazzled by the elite company he presently kept to have made much progress in mending his lord's gambeson.

"I can't believe you're bothering to help me," he told Arator. "I mean . . . you're the son of High Exarch Turalyon and Lady Alleria Windrunner! They've statues in the Valley of Heroes, *songs* sung about them. You were practically *born* famous!"

Arator had heard all this before and had tired of it years ago. Still, it was hardly Win's fault, and he meant well. Although Arator was much older than Winthrop, the years of a half-elf did not keep pace with those of humans. It was one of many challenges bequeathed by his unique parentage. For all Arator's experience and all he had seen, in many ways, he felt more kinship with the new squire than with his lord knight.

Arator turned his smile on the boy. "As I said, I enjoy being of assistance." Arator well remembered how many tasks had been assigned during his own time as Grayson's squire. It was important to learn skills like armor repair, of course, but young Win seemed buried beneath mundane chores. Arator felt that there was no task so small it was beneath him, if he could help someone by performing it.

Winthrop's brown eyes narrowed, and he glanced toward where Lord Grayson and another of his former squires were engaged in conversation. "I hope he doesn't get angry at us," Winthrop murmured.

Arator couldn't blame the boy for being concerned. Tall, muscular, having lost his right eye in battle long ago, Lord Grayson could seem intimidating even when out of armor and chatting casually. As one of Stormwind's foremost paladins, he'd trained many among their number, had even brought Arator with him to their order's war council a time or two. It was hard not to see him as intimidating, formidable—certainly an enemy Arator would not want to meet in battle. Simply sparring with the man was hard enough. But Grayson had made a firm commitment to others in the order, and he'd served the Light longer than most.

"Don't worry," Arator reassured the boy. "He'll know it was my idea, not yours, trust me."

"I don't want *you* to get in trouble, either."

"I won't."

Winthrop sighed. "Everyone says I'm lucky he picked me, but . . ." The boy looked down. "He's so . . . strong, and confident, and can knock me to the ground in seconds when we're sparring. I've heard a lot of the stories—he's a real hero! He's more than just a knight, he's a *lord*! I've got to make sure I don't disappoint him." As he spoke the words, Winthrop reached for the gambeson and set to mending it with renewed purpose.

Arator felt his smile fade slightly. Even though he might be the son of legends, he was, in Winthrop's innocent words, *just a knight* of the Silver Hand. Many would say that was honor enough, but Winthrop's easy dismissal of it only echoed Arator's own thoughts. He had earned that rank for himself long ago, had even been recognized with a title. Now and then, the Light would grant a paladin inspiration regarding another's destiny. Arator's own father had been so moved to name the famous Uther "the Lightbringer." Arator had been named "the Redeemer." But whom or what exactly he would one day *redeem* eluded him. And until that moment came, it seemed the order was content to let him chase accolades without ever receiving them.

He tried not to let it bother him, but others younger than he, still panting and bloody, had received battlefield promotions. Their companions, weary but buoyed by victory, had cheered them with hoarse voices. Usually when he had such thoughts, Arator rebuked himself, as he did now, for being envious—and, perhaps, overly imaginative. He had joined the Knights of the Silver Hand to lend his strength to a worthy cause, and while acknowledgment of his efforts was nice, he certainly didn't require it to continue his course.

Arator had fought well and valiantly in several wars already, but his efforts had been insufficient to attract much notice. At least, he thought ruefully, notice of the *good* kind. There seemed to be no end to the order's rules, and Arator had bent, if not fully broken, most of them. He'd concerned himself too much with the locals here, hesitated there, gotten information from a questionable source another time. His methods were always a topic of discussion among the order, but Arator noticed that no one raised concerns with his results. Some had voiced, obliquely or bluntly, that his disregard for protocol and rules would one day harm his standing in the order, but Arator dismissed the idea. To him, it was simple: If he could not change his world, improve the lives of common folk, what purpose was left for a Knight of the Silver Hand?

In truth, it had been more than a willingness to be helpful that had prompted Arator to help young Winthrop. He had been summoned to Light's Hope by Lord Maxwell Tyrosus, one of the central leaders within their order. Arator understood that Lord Tyrosus was an extraordinarily busy individual, and while he was not surprised he had to wait for an audience, he did need something to keep his mind off the meeting. Arator knew exactly why he had been asked to come here today, though he did not know what the outcome of the conversation would be.

Abruptly, Winthrop sprang to his feet, dropping the gambeson.

"Lord Tyrosus!" he exclaimed, his voice climbing a half octave with excitement and delight.

But Arator felt only knife-sharp disappointment as he beheld the expression on the knight's weatherworn face. An ominous clue as to the tone of the conversation. Arator schooled his own features lest Lord Tyrosus see how hard the blow had struck. Rising, Arator placed Lord Grayson's armor down next to Winthrop, who was still gazing up at Tyrosus with wide eyes.

Lord Tyrosus glanced over the boy's progress. "Good work, young man! But best pick up the pace, eh?"

Winthrop gulped and nodded furiously, unable to speak.

To Arator, Tyrosus said merely, "Come. Let us pay our respects together."

They fell into step, heading toward the Sanctum of Light, the scent of stone and its coolness enveloping them as they descended. This had been the headquarters for the Knights of the Silver Hand since the Burning Legion's invasion, and Arator knew it well. He had come here many times on Silver Hand business, but he often found himself at the sanctum for no other reason than to simply be with the Light, to draw inspiration from watching others perfect their skills, and to pay respect to the many who had gone before.

They paused before the tomb of the legendary Tirion Fordring. Tirion had been one of the five original paladins—the first in Azeroth's history. Archbishop Alonsus Faol had called upon these five to lead the order long ago. Faol's vision was to marry the Light's compassion with the power of the hammer, knights who would be priest and warrior both. But where the Light had a tendency toward order and rigidity, Tirion knew it to be flexible and kind. He saw the Light's reach in all he met, famously held empathy for his former enemies, and yet never feared raising hammer or sword when he saw injustice . . . even when it meant standing against his fellow paladins. Even when it meant exile from his home and this very order.

It had been the honor of Arator's life to fight beside Tirion at the

Broken Shore, a bleak and bitter fight that held catastrophic losses for their kind, including Tirion himself. The knight had died as he had lived, serving the people of Azeroth until his final breath. It was the kind of legacy Arator hoped to leave. Not a list of victories achieved by following every archaic convention to the letter, but a tapestry of service to his world, every thread a deed, a word, a thought.

"Heroism has never been commonplace, and yet it has never disappeared altogether," Lord Tyrosus said quietly, as if speaking Arator's thoughts aloud. "Even if it goes unremarked by history, it dwells in the hearts of good people. Some are trained for war. Others are ordinary folk who discover it in their souls and rise to the challenge when heroism is asked of them. Fordring taught us that heroic deeds need not be confined to the battlefield. They are also found when holding firmly to one's faith and ideals, even if it costs one everything."

"I know all of Tirion's stories," Arator said. "He ever fought for peace. I am glad he lived to see the Horde and the Alliance working together, however briefly, before the end."

Lord Tyrosus nodded. "Charging into battle takes far less courage than enduring so much loss for doing the right thing. It is our most admirable, and rarest, quality. Compassion, a true understanding of justice, bravery . . . *all* these things make a paladin. But heroism transcends even that."

Arator's heart sank. This was starting to sound like a prelude to bad news. He turned, not looking at Lord Tyrosus, his visage a model of neutrality, hands lightly clasped behind his back. Part of him—likely his mother's blood—longed to simply interrupt and be done with the conversation, but he held his tongue.

His superior continued. "In recent years, paladins and champions have risen to the demands of their order, and many have performed extraordinary acts. And even so, few have earned the right to accolades beyond knighthood."

With uncharacteristic informality, Tyrosus placed a hand on Arator's shoulder, turning the younger man to face him. "We have had our eye on you for some time, Arator. How could we not, given your lineage? We find you consistently remarkable both in battlefield skills and in the gentler aspects a paladin should embody. Like taking the time to help young Winthrop today. But we have not yet seen you rise to *truly* heroic heights. Therefore, we will not be considering you for lordship."

Arator nodded. "I understand, Lord Tyrosus. I shall continue to strive to be better, so that I may more effectively serve those I am sworn to protect."

Tyrosus squeezed his shoulder briefly. "I do not doubt that for an instant. I hope to be there when the truth of your title is revealed to us. I know you will astound us all."

Arator felt the genuine warmth of these words, but then Lord Tyrosus continued. "After all, with the blood of High Exarch Turalyon and the legendary Alleria Windrunner flowing through your veins, you were practically born to heroism."

There it was. The stone that inevitably dropped in every conversation he had with another of his calling. The comparison he could never escape. He summoned his rote response. "My lord, thank you. It is a high calling indeed. An honor and a responsibility both."

The older man seemed pleased with this. "You are dismissed, if you'd like to rejoin your young admirer outside."

"I believe Lord Grayson's gambeson is, justly, consuming Winthrop's attention," Arator deferred. Tyrosus chuckled. "I'd rather stay here awhile, if you don't mind, and meditate on what we discussed."

"Of course. It is a lot to think about, and there is no better place to ponder than here."

Arator listened until he could no longer hear the sound of boots, then turned to regard another image carved in stone: High Exarch Turalyon.

For Arator's father, like Tirion, had been one of the original five paladins.

You were practically born to heroism, Tyrosus had said with complete confidence.

Was I? Arator wondered. *Was I, truly?*

Ever since he was old enough to understand the concept, he'd been introduced and spoken of as "the son of Turalyon and Alleria." He had never asked for—nor accepted—anything that smacked of favor due to his parentage, but the fabled couple were so universally known that it had been impossible to conceal his identity among his fellows. Lord Tyrosus's rejection stung in part because, although Arator worked harder than most to prove his worth and skill, his accomplishments were ever weighed against or eclipsed by those of his famous parents.

Alleria and Turalyon had lived through an extraordinary era. Arator's own lifetime had certainly been fraught with danger, from demons to the undead to the shattering of Azeroth itself. So many had risen to join those battles, people from both the Horde and the Alliance who fought with skill and dedication and passion. But acts and feats that had been remarkable in earlier times were so no longer, and while Arator was glad that his companions on the field of battle excelled at what they did, he could not help thinking of the deeds of his parents, not just on Azeroth but on other worlds, performed so consistently and successfully for so very long.

Arator had grown to realize that, although he was a blend of humanity and elvenkind, rather than straddling both worlds, he increasingly felt that he belonged to neither. The rejection today also brought home other truths, other struggles. He had become an adult, his own person, long before his parents had returned. In many ways, he was still getting to know them, even as his life had been indelibly shaped by their legacy, by the *idea* of them. Arator wanted nothing more than to be with and learn from them after they had been so long away . . . but he also longed to stand apart, to contribute in his own ways and not be judged against their standard.

How long he knelt ruminating, in the shadow of his father's statue, Arator did not know, but when he stood, his legs were stiff, and his heart was, perhaps, even heavier than it had been.

He emerged, blinking, into the daylight.

"Perfect timing," said a friendly, familiar voice. "I've only been waiting a few moments."

"Liadrin!" Arator exclaimed, surprise driving away the cloud for the time being. "What are you doing here?"

"I come bearing a special delivery," she said, indicating the small, cloth-wrapped package she held.

Lady Liadrin led the sin'dorei paladins, an order called the Blood Knights. She had been the first of her order, a former priestess who turned to the tools of war to fight for her people. Though Liadrin and his father were quite different, Turalyon had done the same thing.

After his parents had been lost beyond the Dark Portal, Arator had been raised by his aunt Vereesa and the many friends who had loved his family. While his aunt Sylvanas had been kept busy by her duties as ranger general, her second-in-command, Lor'themar Theron, had taken Arator under his wing.

After the Scourge decimated Quel'Thalas, it was Lor'themar and Liadrin who had been at the forefront of the kingdom's reclamation, but they had not forgotten Arator. From Arator's youth, Lor'themar had trained him in the tradition of the Farstriders. And Liadrin had been a confidant, easy to talk to, who held his friendship close and his secrets closer, speaking both kindness and truth when he needed to hear it. He had remained fond of and grateful to her all his years.

"You're a hard fellow to catch up with," she continued. Her brow furrowed as she regarded his expression. "Don't tell me you had a dressing-down."

"No," he replied quickly. "It's nothing."

"I see," Liadrin said, her tone implying she knew quite well that it was not *nothing*. "Perhaps this will sweeten your mood." She extended the package to him, untying the bow that held the cloth closed. Arator recognized the item instantly: honey from the Breezeblossom Apiary. He accepted the jar and dropped it into his satchel.

"Thanks."

"You didn't even ask which twin sent it." At Arator's listless shrug, she sighed. "Come on. I brought a bottle of Suntouched wine, too."

■ ■ ■

Liadrin and Arator sat on the dried, yellow grass of a hillock a short ride from Light's Hope Chapel. His gaze was fixed upon the chapel as he took a decidedly inelegant swig from the excellent vintage. Then, in a quiet, flat voice, he told the Blood Knight leader what Lord Tyrosus had said.

Liadrin grimaced in sympathy and extended her hand for the bottle.

"I understand his point," Arator continued. "But I was . . . frustrated. Disappointed."

"Disheartened?"

"That, too, yes."

Liadrin took a swig of wine, then handed him the bottle. "And now?"

A smile that had nothing of humor about it twisted his lips. "Frustrated, disappointed, *and* disheartened."

She chuckled at that. "Would it surprise you to know that I am quite familiar with all of those emotions?"

It did. Liadrin had always struck him as confident, undaunted. She led the Blood Knights with passion, inspiring them to excel by modeling excellence and courage, a commander seemingly as bright as the Light she wielded. Her next words startled him even further.

"You know well that my path to knighthood was quite the winding road. Looking back on it, I welcome the false starts, the dead ends, the misconceptions. Without each of those, I would not have developed the strengths that got me to where I am. You're on your own journey, Arator. It's as unique as you are."

"No shortcut through the farmer's field, huh?"

"I'm afraid not. You must walk every step of it. And it might take you places you don't want to go."

"For a priestess, you're doing quite poorly at cheering me up."

"I cast that vocation aside long ago. I'm just telling you, now is not the time to imagine what might be written on a plaque beside your statue."

He thought about what he'd been doing before Liadrin showed up and had to laugh. "Well, the words 'The Great Failure of Two Great Peoples' did come to mind." Arator lifted the bottle to his lips, but Liadrin's arm stayed him.

"Arator," she said quietly, "look at me." Reluctantly, he did so. Her gaze was steady and kind. "I've known you for many years now. I watched you grow into someone strong and kind and sincere. Lord Tyrosus's denial is not the end of it. You will be acknowledged as exceptional with time. Or . . ."

Liadrin paused, seeming to reconsider the words she had been about to utter.

"Or . . . ?"

She was silent for another moment, then chose her words carefully. "Yesterday, I met with the regent lord and the first arcanist," she said. "Thalyssra has received some reports regarding possible demonic activity near the ruins of Felsoul Hold."

Arator raised an eyebrow. He'd heard that, during Azeroth's most recent battle against the Burning Legion, the demon Azoran had made Felsoul Hold his base. The place contained a soul engine, a fel machine designed for harvesting souls to convert into fel magic. Azoran had planned to use the engine to fuel his command ship, which he would turn against the armies of Azeroth. Azoran had been slain, and the attack, thankfully, foiled. "I thought the nightborne led strikes to ensure the Legion's soul engines were all disabled."

"They did. And they were. At least . . . they *thought* so," Liadrin replied. "But local inhabitants have reported witnessing what they said was a fel glow coming from the area."

"That's alarming."

"Indeed. Thalyssra requested a small team of Blood Knights to conduct reconnaissance and report back to her. But I think you're more than capable of handling that by yourself."

"Just . . . scout and report back? Winthrop could do *that.* Well," he amended, "almost."

"Arator," Liadrin said, sitting up straight and looking him in the eye, "think for a moment. If you go to Suramar City and volunteer, this puts you in an active role. You're no longer waiting around, hoping for the Silver Hand to give you a task. And . . . it puts you in front of the First Arcanist of Suramar, and, very likely, the Regent Lord of Quel'Thalas, too. They think far differently about things than the Silver Hand does when it comes to what's important. I can't make any promises, of course, but if you do a good job for them, they might be inclined to write to the order about you in a positive light. The Silver Hand may be taking you for granted. It wouldn't hurt to have other leaders remind them how lucky they are to have you."

"I appreciate you saying that," Arator said, moved.

"I wouldn't say it if I didn't believe it."

He knew. "Do you really think she'll do it?"

Liadrin extended her hand for the bottle and took a final drink. "Well," she said, "there's only one way to find out."

CHAPTER TWO

The Nighthold, Suramar City

BROKEN ISLES

Since childhood, Alleria Windrunner had yearned to make her own path in the world. It did not take long before she realized that yearning would fling open the door to a life filled with the unexpected, and tonight was no exception.

For most of her life, the land of Suramar had been the stuff of legends. Its enigmatic magical shield had isolated it for more than ten thousand years, and—as the world learned when they ended their isolation during the last Legion invasion—the inhabitants had changed over millennia, eventually becoming the nightborne. Simply stepping foot in Suramar had been beyond Alleria's practical imagining, let alone forging a friendship with the nightborne's present leader, their first arcanist. Yet here Alleria was, supping with Thalyssra and her husband. The fact that said husband was none other than Regent Lord Lor'themar Theron was another thing she could never have imagined.

Lor'themar had once been one of Alleria's dearest friends, and he was certainly her oldest. She remembered many a sun-drenched morning in her childhood home of Windrunner Spire, where Lor'themar inevitably turned up to brief her ranger general mother on some Farstrider matter or another. Ever relied upon by her mother and later named her sister's second-in-command, Lor'themar had known well the pressures Alleria experienced as the reluctant successor to the post of ranger general.

But Alleria had left Quel'Thalas, called to her own mission. After she had spent a thousand years battling demons in the Twisting Nether and heard tell of all the trials, changes, and upheavals that had reshaped Azeroth in her absence, she had been grateful to know that Lor'themar Theron, at least, remained. That he had provided a steady hand in training her son, had helped reclaim Quel'Thalas from the Scourge, and now stewarded their people was welcome news to her indeed.

And then, as it had with so many facets of her life, the Void had changed things. During a visit to the Sunwell—the center of Holy Light and arcane power for her people—Alleria's mere presence had summoned creatures of the Void. Catastrophe had been narrowly averted, but her folly had come at a high cost: exile from her home and estrangement from her people, including Lor'themar.

But years later, an invitation had come . . . to the wedding of the regent lord and the first arcanist. It was a step toward mending a bridge, and while Alleria spent more time alone than ever these days, a part of her still desired Lor'themar's friendship. He had witnessed so much that few around her could understand. Though Alleria was disappointed with what had transpired in the depths—that Xal'atath had again evaded her—her brief triumph over the Dark Heart continued to affirm to many that Alleria had mastered control of the Void. And while she was still not allowed back in Silvermoon, Thalyssra had kindly extended a dinner invitation to Alleria and her husband.

Her *husband* . . . That, too, was something the Void had wedged itself in the middle of. She and Turalyon had never formally wed.

They had overcome much in their millennia together, but mastery of her powers, facing down the Void threats still at large in their world . . . these matters would always come first—even before him.

Turalyon knew that, but she still felt his pain every time she pulled away. She wondered how long they could continue like this, how long she could bear growing increasingly distant from the man she had once loved with all the passion that fueled her in battle and in life.

In truth, Alleria had felt at war within herself about this very dinner. Mending this bridge with Lor'themar came at the price of an awkward, formal meal, the kind she had long detested. That she and Turalyon would need to discuss matters beyond the most recent battles—laugh, exchange loving glances, pretend that their relationship was clear and uncomplicated—served only to increase her tension. But the time came when she realized she'd put the invitation off for too long and the offer was at risk of being rescinded. So, here they were.

Alleria brought her attention back to the present, as an honored guest of an intimate supper hosted by Thalyssra and Lor'themar. Their meal was being served outside, in one of the open, graceful courtyards, at a low table where the diners reclined on pillows rather than sitting in chairs. With only herself and Turalyon as guests, the two powerful leaders were quite different from what their people usually saw of them. The pair had shed their armor, both literally and figuratively, at least in their behavior to each other. While Lor'themar greeted the guests pleasantly, Alleria, who knew him so well, could still sense his reservations. Thalyssra's welcome, though, felt so warm and genuine it served to put even Turalyon—who could be stiff in the best of circumstances—at ease.

"I still marvel at your willingness to have members of the Alliance as guests," Turalyon said, taking a sip of arcwine.

"I believe the armistice is best served by Horde and Alliance regularly sitting down together over something other than strategies. It's part of what inspired us to invite both sides to our wedding," Thalyssra said. "Although there always seems to be some kind of distraction at weddings."

Lor'themar nodded. "Quite true," he said. "We were more fortunate than Thrall and Aggra in that regard. At least our disruptor only exchanged harsh words with Wrathion."

"You *did* lose the cake," Alleria pointed out, deadpan. "That was a tragedy."

"It could have been, had we not prepared far more than enough."

Turalyon looked a bit sheepish. "I confess . . . I *did* have seconds."

"My husband had thirds." Thalyssra's voice was teasing as she mock-scolded Lor'themar.

"They were *small* pieces," Lor'themar protested, matching her playful mood.

Alleria smiled a little. These two thrived when they were together, as if each amplified the best in the other without taking anything away. Lor'themar's wit was less biting than Alleria recalled from her upbringing in Silvermoon, and in these informal surroundings, Thalyssra's fierce intellect and boundless curiosity ensured the conversation never ran dry.

The warmth of their genuine love and respect for each other, along with the potency of the deceptively drinkable arcwine, loosened Alleria's tongue. She found herself saying, "You've been back from your honeymoon for some time, but it doesn't seem to be over. How do you do it?"

"Portaling," Lor'themar quipped, but added more seriously, "and prioritizing."

"And poetry!" Thalyssra reminded him. "Though I must say, before we met, we were married more to our duties. It was . . . a problem that persisted even after we'd exchanged vows."

Lor'themar reached silently for her hand as she spoke.

She curled her fingers around his and continued. "We were so single-minded of purpose that we lost sight of the very reason those duties existed: so that our people would be prosperous and peaceful. The sin'dorei and the shal'dorei did not need *only* protection and physical nourishment. They deserve the chance to spend time with loved ones, on joyful pastimes. All the things that nourish a soul."

A memory swam into Alleria's mind, vivid and sweet, of the many simple hours spent with her sisters while their beloved little brother plucked at his lute and sang for them. How deeply the family had lived for those moments of peace, together in their cherished spot. It was impossible to reside there forever, of course, but it was a scene Alleria returned to often in her mind. Lor'themar was studying Alleria closely now, his guarded expression softening as he noted the hints of pain that doubtless flitted across hers. When he spoke, it was as if her old friend had read her thoughts.

"We sacrificed, so that they would not need to. So that they could remain as untouched by pain and loss as possible. We forwent lasting friendship, peace of mind, love, all in the name of duty . . ." He sighed. "One forgets the energy such pursuits provide. Love becomes stale, your home simply a structure, rather than a refuge."

Alleria kept her features neutral so that the too-perceptive regent lord would not see how deeply his innocent words had cut.

She and Turalyon had leaped from battle to battle, partners in love, yes, but perhaps even more so in combat. War and violence had brought them together, had bound them as they spilled blood enough to fill an ocean. Demons did not rest, and so *they* did not rest. There had been barely time for food or sleep, let alone tenderness, or the simple act of lying on green grass and gazing up at a blue sky.

Or had there? The two leaders sitting before her had also faced terrible, tragic events. Their people had suffered greatly. But they had found the time. Or . . . had carved it out with the same determination with which they fought and cared for those in their charge. Alleria thought somberly that while all four of those seated here tonight had waged war for their people, only their hosts had waged it for themselves as well—against all the things, little and large, that seemed to pile up and fill a lifetime.

"How arrogant of us," Thalyssra said, interrupting Alleria's musing, "dispensing advice to you two. You have been married for a thousand years! We should be asking *you*!"

Alleria froze. Not only were she and Turalyon unmarried, she realized . . . she *had* no wisdom to dispense. Why take time for songs or poetry or stargazing when demons were burning their way across the Great Dark Beyond, searching for your world, for your *child*? Why spend a few hours in quiet conversation when one could seize such time for sleep or smithing or nourishment?

Even now, in a time of relative peace, she and Turalyon filled their days with all things martial, not marital. They had spoken of it, of course, from time to time, in the moments when they could catch their breath. *When we return. After the war is over. Let things settle down.* There was always something more important than a wedding to occupy themselves with. Now they moved in separate spheres, encountering each other infrequently, making time for intimacy even less. Was he content with only that?

Was *she*?

"Oh, I think you're doing well enough," Alleria said lightly.

"Indeed," Turalyon agreed. "But I don't think you asked us here just to enjoy good food, wine, and conversation."

"We've tried before," Thalyssra quipped. "The only way we could get you to accept tonight was by promising to discuss—"

"Fel activity," came a voice.

Alleria's heart quickened at the sound, and she made no attempt to hide her delight. She rose at once from the comfortable purple pillows to embrace her son. Turalyon wasn't far behind her, his hand on Arator's shoulder. Alleria turned to her hosts with the first genuine smile of the evening.

"You could not have thought of a better surprise," she told her hosts gratefully.

The pair exchanged glances.

"I'm afraid we cannot take credit," Thalyssra said.

"Arator!" Lor'themar exclaimed. "Your presence is a welcome surprise to us all."

"Yes, please join us!" his wife invited. "We are only on the first course. How lovely to have the whole family for dinner!"

Arator bowed. "First Arcanist, Regent Lord, I apologize for the interruption. I'm afraid I'm here on business. I spoke with Lady Liadrin this afternoon, and she informed me that her Blood Knights had been tasked with a mission. I humbly offer my services to this endeavor in their stead, if it pleases you."

At this, Lor'themar and Thalyssra laughed, shaking their heads. "You are truly cut from the same cloth as your parents," Thalyssra said. "We had been about to speak to them of these very reports. Please, sit, and we will brief . . . well, *all* of you."

Alleria listened with half an ear as Thalyssra outlined the sightings. The first arcanist seemed delighted to turn the task over to Arator and not the Blood Knights, thinking Liadrin's idea sound. Although the orders were those of his wife, Lor'themar was visibly pleased that Arator had expressed interest in aiding Suramar.

It seemed simple enough: a routine scouting mission to investigate the rumors. It did not require the time and attention of several Blood Knights at this juncture, as Arator could certainly do it with ease by himself.

And yet . . . the arrangement still gave his mother pause. She had conquered the Void whispers in her mind; their fears and thinly veiled manipulations rarely troubled her these days. But Alleria had spent a millennium in the Twisting Nether, sometimes hunted by demons who sought to hurt her, her lover, or even their son. The Void could conjure any number of terrible ends Arator might meet on this mission, but there was another anxiety gripping her heart, one that gnawed at her and surged to the forefront thanks to the recent conversation and her son's unexpected appearance.

Most parents made sacrifices for their children in the hopes of ensuring a better life for them. Certainly she and Turalyon had, sacrificing not just body but heart, spirit, and ideals. Hopes. Innocence. Things that had been ripped from them or deliberately laid aside in the pursuit of duty.

They sacrificed all these things so that their son would not need to.

But Arator's decision to become a paladin put him on that road despite their efforts.

Perhaps that path can be altered, Alleria thought. *Lor'themar,*

Thalyssra . . . they have found a way to fulfill their duties while still making a place for joy and love to flourish.

"Given that we have neither seen nor heard anything of this nature in years, we should treat the sightings with caution," Alleria heard herself saying.

Turalyon did not respond. He was scrutinizing Arator, searching his son's eyes as if seeking the answer to something.

Alleria could not speak her heart in front of Thalyssra and Lor'themar, so she rose, keeping her voice quiet and calm despite the tempest of emotions inside her.

"Turalyon, a word?"

He accompanied her as she stepped away. Alleria spoke quickly, before he could say anything. "We have nothing but a few reports to go on—he could be walking into a trap. Our son may have fought demons, but he doesn't *know* them. Not like we do. No one in this or any other world does."

Turalyon seemed pensive. "Arator is a grown man. Not a child. But . . ."

Alleria stared her love up and down. Something was amiss. "What do you know that I do not?"

"Arator has striven for years now to be promoted within the order. He met with Lord Tyrosus earlier today. I don't know for certain, but I don't think it went well."

Alleria turned to look at Arator. He was chatting amiably with their hosts, but now she could see some of the disappointment in his body language. Alleria thought of her own struggle to prove herself when she was younger than her son was now, to find her own way against her strong-willed mother's determination.

"Our son is a superlative swordsman and strong in the Light," Turalyon continued. "And he's a good, kind person. I think the only thing standing in his way is his readiness to bend the rules and bypass protocol. Which, by the way, he did moments ago by talking to Liadrin and then approaching Thalyssra directly."

Alleria bridled slightly. "Had *I* obeyed protocol, we would never have met."

"Oh, we'd have met," Turalyon said, with the rock-solid surety he always conveyed when it came to their bond. For a moment, she let it warm her.

"Arator chose to join the Silver Hand knowing there would be established, respected methods he'd need to follow," Turalyon said. "I'd like to observe him on a mission. See how he makes his decisions, what action he takes. Maybe guide him a bit."

"He may not want to be analyzed by his father," Alleria said.

"He may not want to feel coddled by his mother, either," Turalyon pointed out.

Alleria sighed and placed a hand on his arm. "He may not want his parents," she said, "but . . . he needs allies."

Her love smiled softly. "I think we might, too. Let's ask him."

They strode back to the gathering. "Now that Thalyssra has briefed the whole family," Turalyon interjected, "Alleria and I are wondering if perhaps the whole family should go. What do you think, Arator?"

Arator looked a bit startled. "*All* of us?" he said, frowning a little. "That . . . seems a bit excessive."

Turalyon looked at him uncertainly, but Alleria pressed her lips together against a smile. "*Completely* unnecessary," she said.

"A waste of resources, truly," Arator continued. "I'm in."

▪ ▪ ▪

Their hosts appeared delighted with the decision, though Thalyssra was surprised that the family had chosen to leave almost immediately. She could not argue with Arator's dedication, however, and had equipped them with magnificent manasabers to bear them to Felsoul Hold. The large cats were purple, their pelts covered with runes. They had evolved with an innate connection to Azeroth's leylines, drawing power from them, and they had a nose for arcane energy. Plus, as

Thalyssra told them, once they were out of their tack and rein for the day, they loved to be scratched behind the ears.

Felsoul Hold was not a great distance away from the city, and the short trip afforded Arator opportunity to think on the upcoming mission. The knight had been pleasantly surprised to encounter his parents in Suramar City. The warmth of his mother's embrace and his father's genuine, broad smile cheered Arator more than he would have thought, and he looked forward to having more time to spend with them doing something they all excelled at.

Even so, the three were quiet initially, as if, after anticipating a chance to get to know one another better, they were all suddenly hesitant. When the silence started feeling uncomfortable to Arator, he searched for a topic to get a conversation started.

Unexpectedly, it was his father who fired the opening volley. "I can't help but feel at a disadvantage, starting a reconnaissance mission in the middle of the night. Both of you have much better vision than I do."

"Ah, but it's a beautiful night," Alleria said, "and both moons are in the sky now."

"But we're going to go into . . . caverns. Where it's dark anyway," Arator pointed out.

"Perhaps *you* can light our way, dearest?" Alleria said, with exaggerated sweetness. Arator tensed, wondering how his father would react to a direct jab at his calling.

To his surprise, his father's eyes twinkled, as if at a private joke. "Oh, like this?"

And then the high exarch's armor began to glow, bright as a beacon. Cautiously, Arator said, "Great! We'll just stand there and shine, and if there are any demons in Felsoul, they'll run out to say hello."

"That's the plan," Turalyon said, so earnestly that for an instant, Arator thought he was serious. At their son's expression, Turalyon and Alleria started laughing, and Arator joined in. It was as if a door had been opened, and Arator was glad.

The manasabers were comfortable to ride, and their paws were silent as they ran. Arator guided his manasaber between those of his parents so he could speak easily with them both.

They spoke of ordinary things at first. Turalyon expressed his pleasure that Genn Greymane had been willing to mind Stormwind for a while so that Turalyon could come to the dinner—and, fortuitously, thus be present to join Alleria and Arator on this mission. Anduin had returned but had not yet formally reclaimed his title or his seat on the throne.

"How are they? Both of them?" Arator asked.

"Genn is glad to have Tess ruling Gilneas, but he seems to miss ruling himself. And *I'm* pleased to have someone willing to look after things in my stead every so often."

Arator refrained from further comment on that issue. Turalyon was an excellent general and leader of troops but a bit too rigid to adapt well to the fluid and flexible nature of politics. The high exarch, from what Arator had heard, had rubbed many common folk the wrong way, and Arator knew he hadn't enjoyed it much, either. But his king had asked this of Turalyon, and the paladin was nothing if not dutiful.

"I'm glad you were able to come with us," Arator said, and the words were true. "And Anduin?"

Turalyon went quiet for a moment. "War is never without its costs," he said. "And everyone is affected differently by it. Anduin was wise to realize he would best serve his people by stepping away for a time, and he made sure his kingdom would be protected while he did so. It took courage and faith to do that, and I respect him all the more."

Arator told them about Lord Grayson's wide-eyed squire and his excitement and apprehension about serving such a famous man. He did not, however, mention his meeting with Lord Tyrosus, and when he caught his parents exchanging glances as he spoke, he realized that Turalyon probably already knew—and had told his mother.

It was not a topic Arator cared to discuss, so he steered the conversation back to the present event.

"It was good to hear how Lor'themar spoke to you, Mother," he said. "I hope the situation is thawing."

"It seems to be," Alleria replied. "I knew he would invite *you* to the wedding, but we didn't expect an invitation after what happened."

"Thalyssra said it had been her idea, and I think it a sound one," Turalyon said. "It's not what I would expect from a Horde leader, but it shows her commitment to keeping the peace. I found it surprisingly pleasant . . . other than, of course, the quarrel."

"And the cake loss," Arator said with a grin.

"Hey now, the regent lord had *three* pieces," Turalyon said. "Your poor father can have two."

"Maybe it's all the cake that's sweetened Lor'themar," Arator mused. "He's been different ever since he and Thalyssra finally admitted their interest in each other. And after the honeymoon, he's almost unrecognizable in some ways."

"He and Thalyssra talked about that very thing, before you arrived," Alleria said. "How *both* of them changed. They decided to . . ."

Her voice trailed off and she drew her manasaber to a halt, staring at what was up ahead. Alleria shifted from mother to hunter, her body taut and ready to respond in an instant.

"What is it?" Turalyon asked quietly.

Alleria didn't answer, but she did smile slightly. And a moment later, first Arator and then Turalyon saw it, too.

Demonic corruption withered and twisted everything it touched—flora and fauna alike. In areas that played host to demonic machinery and architecture, it even pooled into sludgy, glowing green goo in a bright, unnatural shade with which the three were deeply familiar.

The landscape before them, however, revealed the work not of demons, but of *druids.* Upturned rocks and craters revealed scars of battles past, but every rift was being overtaken by a different kind of green—soft mosses, creeping vines. Azeroth healed where her people tended. There was even a recent trail through the lushness, more evidence that Felsoul Hold was no longer feared by those its inhabitants had once terrorized.

Even so, despite the care of druids and the gentling blue-white glow of moonslight, they could all see the distinctive smudge of fel green. As their manasabers drew closer, the characteristic destruction of the demons became more apparent. The ground here was barren, and shortly they beheld stone shaped into terrifying form, a land violated rather than explored or even plundered. The expected sickly radiance, however, was dim. No fel fire burned, and the gooey lakes had long ago sullenly subsided.

The moons continued to light their path as they approached the edge of the hold. A few yards away, Arator signaled his mount to halt, slipped out of the saddle, and gently scratched the great beast's neck. With a low, happy rumble, the animal moved to carefully headbutt Arator, indicating he should continue the pleasant sensation.

He chuckled. "You really *are* just oversized cats, aren't you? Don't worry, I'll give you more when we come back." Arator gave the manasaber a final pat, adjusted his sword, and went to join his parents while the manasabers, accustomed to waiting for their riders, plopped down and curled up like any house cat.

They stood for a moment, peering down into the chasm below. "I guess we won't need you to light the way after all, Father," Arator said. Glowing green fel would provide sufficient illumination for their travels. They could glimpse structures that, in this darkness, appeared undamaged—curving archways, which would have looked almost pretty had the three assembled not known what they did.

"Unfortunately," Turalyon said, and he turned to Alleria. "This is starting to look more familiar, isn't it?"

She nodded. "It still looks . . . lifeless. Not as seething with malice as we're used to. Follow me. I think I see a good way down."

Alleria walked a short distance along the rim, assessing, analyzing, and dismissing possibilities, then paused. She pointed.

"There's our route."

"What are your thoughts, son?" Turalyon asked.

A little surprised to be asked, Arator said, "If Mother thinks this is the way we should go, we should follow her lead. She knows more about this sort of thing than either of us."

"Good answer," Alleria said.

Turalyon looked amused. "Indeed."

Without further conversation, Alleria jumped down, landing as lightly as the manasabers might on a small area of flat stone. Arator did not attempt to emulate her. Although both he and his father moved comfortably and lightly in their armor, it was still bulky. And despite Arator's teasing, it *was* dark. Arator glimpsed the narrow path winding downward into the shadowy depths—not easy, but accessible. He was comfortable that his mother could see its twists and turns even more clearly than he. She had chosen well. Of course.

"You haven't thanked me," Arator said as he jumped lightly but carefully from perch to perch.

"For rescuing us from dinner?" Turalyon asked, moving as easily as his son.

Alleria, in the lead, paused and looked up at them. "Was it that obvious?"

"No, I don't think so." They were almost at the bottom, and before he leaped the rest of the way to the path proper, Arator gave his mother a reassuring smile. "I just know that chitchat through a seven-course meal is not your preferred way of spending time."

"Quite right," Turalyon said. "We'd both much rather tag along with you."

Arator had a feeling that Turalyon might do more than just "tag along." Even so, he knew the other paladin was sincere, and the thought warmed him. Even if a lecture was in store, Arator would much rather be fighting a real enemy alongside his father than simply training.

"I'm glad things worked out this way," Arator said.

"I as well" was all Alleria said, but Arator could tell she, too, saw and appreciated the burgeoning harmony.

It was an unusual family outing, but then again, they were a most unusual family. Arator thought of the last time they'd been together, briefly, when both parents had separately come to visit him in Silvermoon City. Turalyon, in a still-hostile land, had seemed out of place and uncomfortable. But Silvermoon had been his mother's home once, and when she had walked with Arator through the city, she declined Turalyon's offer to accompany them. Thinking back on it, Arator felt the whole encounter had been awkward.

Now, though, the pair looked at ease, and . . . happy. Maybe this was how they could really be themselves. If the three could not find a little time between their duties to be together, maybe those duties themselves could bring them all closer.

The path continued. As the three descended and the moons' light no longer penetrated the darkness, the fel energy that yet lingered on the Broken Isles increasingly closed over them. At one point, Turalyon glanced up at a curving dark green structure.

Alleria spoke quietly. "It was so . . . *strange* as we approached. The areas tended by the druids were comforting, but the dark ruins seemed even more unwelcome by contrast."

Turalyon nodded. "It's clear that the energy is slowly ebbing on the surface. It will take longer to fade the deeper we go. It's certainly not what you and I are used to seeing."

"A fel-corrupted land, *healing*? We never stayed long enough . . . We were always on to the next battlefront."

"So many changes Azeroth's been through," Turalyon said. "Imagine being a mapmaker after the Cataclysm."

Arator listened without interrupting, a little smile growing on his face.

Alleria caught it and teasingly challenged him. "What's so funny, my son?"

"Well," Arator said, chuckling, "you returned to Azeroth nearly a decade ago. Yet you seem to be constantly surprised at the changes. Not just this, but so many things. It's a bit . . . endearing, honestly."

Turalyon clapped a hand to his breastplate as if stricken. "You wound me, son. Don't look now, Alleria, but it would seem that after a thousand years, we've suddenly become . . . *old.*"

"No, no, that's not what I meant!" Arator said, still chuckling. "It makes perfect sense that you're unfamiliar with the landscape after the demons have been gone for a while! You and Mother have been so busy chasing them that you've never had a chance to see the aftermath for yourselves. The good things. How the land can heal."

"Well," Alleria said, still smiling but growing more serious, "if we're lucky, your knowledge about all things *post*-demonic will be exactly what is required here."

"Ah," Arator said, "but where is the fun in that?"

They turned a corner, and their levity vanished. Before them lay an enormous pile of rubble blocking what had once been an entrance. At the top, a defiant piece of demonic architecture was still visible, though cracked.

"The damage is from the nightborne attack," said Arator. "They hit it quite severely after the invasion was quelled." He pointed to a cluster of dust and rubble. "That's not from a cave-in."

"No sign of disturbance in the dust," Alleria said.

Turalyon's gaze roamed the huge pile of fallen stone chunks, and he nodded. "With the place in this shape," he said, "it makes the reports of fel magic seem less likely."

Arator had another suspicion, however, one that had gnawed at him from the moment he heard about fel fire being glimpsed in the hold. It had been growing with each step they had taken, and now he felt compelled to speak.

"There's one thing we haven't yet discussed," Arator said, reluctant. "It could be that these 'sightings' are nothing more than pranks."

His mother frowned. "Demons are not to be joked about."

"I agree," Arator said. "But have you ever been around a group of bored young people? Trust me, Giramar and Galadin may look innocent, but they made a lot of mischief growing up."

"*Just* them?" Turalyon said.

"I can neither confirm nor deny any involvement."

"You get that from my side of the family," Alleria said. They both looked at her, their faces, features so similar, showing the exact same expression of surprise.

"What mischief did *you* get up to, my love?" Turalyon asked.

"Oh, not from me. I was boringly serious when I was a child. But Sylvanas *loved* to pull pranks when she was young. Nothing hurtful," she added quickly. "Some of them backfired spectacularly, but . . . I must admit, some of them were quite funny."

"I remember Vereesa telling me about a few of them," Arator said. "Now that I think about it, she said you did a few less-than-perfect things yourself."

"What did she tell you?" Alleria demanded.

"No, no, I made a promise, and I keep my word," he said.

"We're going to have a talk later," Alleria said, hoping she sounded light. Thinking of the middle Windrunner sister always made her a bit melancholy. She took a deep breath and returned her attention to the rubble. "I wonder what this sealed in."

At her words, the other two sobered, regarding the area with fresh seriousness. There were few gaps in the fallen stone. Imps might have been able to escape easily enough, but anything larger would still be buried. While she and Turalyon craned their necks to look upward for disturbances, Arator crouched down, regarding the stone floor of the cavern.

"I can't imagine much is intact," Arator said. "Not with this supporting—"

There was a rattle, and a few stones began to roll down.

Alleria's bow was nocked, and the men had their swords at the ready. Silence fell for a moment, then another little shower of stone.

Alleria almost let fly at once but then paused and lowered her bow. Arator followed her gaze, squinting slightly, then grinning.

"Go in peace, little friend," Alleria said. "And boast of your escape to your family."

The rat chittered at her, as if affronted, then slipped back inside.

"It doesn't seem properly grateful," Turalyon observed. "Seeing him is a good sign, though," he added. "Our unappreciative friend wasn't imbued with fel."

Arator couldn't help but roll his eyes. If Turalyon had seen the rat well enough to discern it wasn't corrupted, he had to have known it was obvious to Alleria and Arator. *School's in session, all right,* he thought.

The path descended more sharply now, and the damage from the nightborne assault was visible only in places where there had been cave-ins. Several areas remained structurally intact but had long since been gutted, monuments to a defeated army. There were many such places in Azeroth.

There's nothing here for us to find except for rats and debris, Arator thought. "Well," he said, a touch of irritation creeping into his voice despite his best efforts, "I'm sorry that I dragged you along with me."

Turalyon spoke even before Alleria in replying, "We're not."

"I mean to say," Arator said, "it's great to have your company, but . . . I wouldn't mind a *little* more excitement."

Alleria had opened her mouth to protest but froze in place, lifting a hand to silence them.

All three stood as still as stone, following her gaze toward the dim but unmistakable flicker of fel fire.

CHAPTER THREE

Felsoul Hold Ruins, Suramar

BROKEN ISLES

The trio flattened themselves against a large, jutting boulder. Alleria glanced at the two paladins and lifted a finger to her lips. Turalyon and Arator nodded; stealth was their friend until they knew what they were dealing with.

Father and son waited and watched as Alleria moved swiftly in all but complete silence, slipping from stone to stone, then disappearing behind the now-dark ruins of what had once been fel cannons. She emerged a few moments later and beckoned them to follow.

Together, they moved past a pool of fel goo and around another curve in the wide road. The turn revealed more glowing puddles and another, brighter light, wafting upward like steam. It was what they had all dreaded discovering. The bright, misty light was emanating from the innermost chamber of the hold, its source obscured for the moment.

"I do not think it is occupied," Alleria whispered. "But it could be a trap."

Arator was furious with himself. "How did we not notice this on our approach?"

"The stream is weak," Turalyon observed, his deep voice soft. "We're used to encountering things like this at full power. It was likely not strong enough for us to see it from a distance."

"I should have," Alleria said bluntly. Her color was high. "My sight is better than yours."

"We see it now," Turalyon said. "So. Let's do something about it."

The soul engine was the only structure they had seen illuminated from within by yellow-green light. Although the path to the entrance led downward, the building itself rose up—the lone sign of life, such as it was, amid the chaos of rubble, wreckage, and old skeletons left where the demons had fallen.

Standing beside Alleria, Turalyon said, "With all the other areas dark, the light—it looks like the stained glass in a cathedral." He still spoke quietly, but his voice simmered with anger. "Demons pervert every norm of decency and goodness."

Arator could hear the slight creak of armor as the older man tightened his grip on his sword. Alleria laid her hand on his arm. He took a breath, embracing her steadiness as they moved down toward the entrance, separated by a section that allowed the fel within to be glimpsed through a filigree of either carved stone or metal.

Arator suppressed a shudder of revulsion. His father was right. It *did* look like stained glass.

As they approached, Arator heard the telltale deep thrumming, a twisted parody of a living heartbeat, the sound so deep as to be almost more sensed than heard. Though he needed no further confirmation that the soul engine was active, he could now glimpse the engine's heart and the glow of fel it emanated. The design of the dreadful receptacles varied, but their purpose was the same: to contain souls and use their energy toward advancing the Burning Legion.

He did not linger too long upon the vile thing, letting his gaze flit from it to his surroundings, alert for danger. His mouth was set in a grim line. He disliked how little they could see, but it could not be helped. He and his father murmured soft words, invoking the Light's blessings before this possible battle. He felt himself settle, his mind clear. Alleria looked and listened for a moment more, then nodded. Weapons at the ready, they stepped forward and together entered the chamber.

It was empty of demons, but their obscene handiwork was on proud display.

For unlike everything else the three had seen in the hold, the soul engine was not in ruins.

Any detritus from the nightborne attack had been removed. Empty cages hung from the ceilings of alcoves; Arator thought it likely they served to hold the demons' victims. Winding stairs led to an upper area.

And in the center, an inactive control board arching in front of it, was the soul well.

Every pulse of fel energy the engine produced was fueled by the souls contained within it. Atop the simple basin perched something Arator had never seen used in such a way. It was a metallic cage, but it looked more like an insectoid creature with long, spiky legs that gripped the lip of the well. The design was, fittingly, the stuff of nightmares, a construction extraordinarily complex and yet brutally simple.

They had seen demonic creations like this cage before. They were designed to hold powerful souls.

"What is the point of trapping the very souls you're trying to use?" Turalyon asked. "It makes no sense."

Arator agreed, but then he looked more closely at the runes that glowed on the unsettlingly spider-like legs.

"Cages work both ways," he said. "It keeps something in—"

"And keeps something out," Alleria said.

"Take a look at this," Arator said. "This rune looks different from any I've seen or heard described. Does it look familiar to you?"

His parents both stepped closer to the engine and regarded it. "Sharp eyes, son," Turalyon said. "This is slightly different. I don't recognize it." There appeared to be small runes in Eredun carved into each of the curved legs, and there were other small but possibly significant differences as well.

"They could be wards," Alleria said. "But this device has extra pieces, and I do not know their function."

Arator did not yet move, but his gaze roamed over the construction, and his heart lifted slightly. Breaking the shocked silence, he told his parents, "Don't celebrate yet, but . . . the well's level is very low. I think it's only barely charged."

"Then we have some time," Turalyon said.

Alleria nodded. "True, though we do not know what 'barely charged' can do."

Arator could not help but notice his parents stepped toward each other instinctively. How many times had they done so, bound by purpose and experience?

"Well, we've found demonic activity, so our scouting mission is complete," Arator began. "Given these wards, we shouldn't try to disable or destroy the soul engine until we know what we're dealing with." He looked to his mother. "We could wait, attempt an ambush of the demon, or see if there's a trail we might pick up. If the engine is activated, innocents have already died—more may be at risk."

Turalyon's response was instant. "That's not what we were ordered to do."

Someone once joked that Arator was "allergic" to orders. Arator laughed along with the rest but didn't deny it. It was one of many words he particularly disliked hearing uttered in his father's voice, so he turned away and began to examine the machinery while his mother and father spoke. Out of the corner of his eye, he glimpsed an alcove.

"Love," Alleria said with a sigh, "all Thalyssra is going to do is send us back out."

"She could have received new information," Turalyon continued doggedly. "She may want to dispatch troops, given what we found here. She may know these runes, may know how to disable it."

The dust near the alcove had been disturbed, just as it had been in the main control area. And there was something else. Arator continued moving slowly, careful so as not to disturb any evidence. An unpleasantly familiar scent reached his nostrils, telling him what he was about to discover, and he closed his eyes for a moment before going the rest of the way into the alcove to face what awaited him.

His parents continued their polite but strained argument. "No offense to either the Duskwatch or the Blood Knights," Alleria said, "but I would venture to say the three of us will accomplish more than three contingents of either."

"Alleria, that's not the point."

"Come over here," Arator called out before squatting down beside the bodies to examine them.

It hurt every time. It was no longer overwhelming, of course; familiarity with death had done its implacable, merciful work. But Arator grieved at lives cut short, at the pain of those who missed them. Both victims were nightborne. One was an adult woman, but the other had been young, still in his teens. Arator's eyes went from the cruel gash across his throat, recently made, to a symbol the victim, or someone else, had carved some time ago into the back of his still hand.

He heard his parents enter.

"Is that . . . some kind of rune?" Turalyon asked.

"It looks like someone *thought* it was, but it's nothing I recognize. Mother?"

Alleria shook her head. "If those two lines there were vertical, it would be a rune of protection. Someone didn't know what they were doing."

"How long have they been dead?" Turalyon asked.

"Less than a day, judging by the pliability of the bodies."

"No one has reported anyone missing yet. We would have been told," Alleria said, reasoning it out. "Arator, are there any established villages near here?"

"None that I know of," he replied. "Last I checked, no one wanted to live anywhere near this place. Understandably." Abruptly, Arator remembered what he'd observed earlier. "But . . . I spotted a trail on our approach," he said. "In the restored area." There was nothing they could do for the fallen nightborne, but they could still help the living.

"Let's go," said Alleria.

■ ■ ■

The three hurried back the way they had come and climbed out of the hold. The trail Arator had noted was easy to locate, worn enough to mark the passage of several people, new enough to not be overly trampled.

"Leave the manasabers," Alleria said. "I would prefer to scout on foot, so we don't miss anything."

They did so, walking in silence until they glimpsed the outskirts of an encampment. From here, the makeshift tents looked unharmed, and the earth yielded no clues to indicate anything other than the ordinary marks of daily life.

"Something's wrong," Arator said. "They let their suppers burn, there are children's footprints, but it's too quiet . . ."

They approached cautiously. The few campfires had burned to embers, and any food was blackened beyond identification. While there was no sign of violence, there was evidence of disarray. A child's discarded toy here, an overturned bench and spilled goblet there. Yet the place appeared to be completely empty.

Arator pointed to the first tent, a fairly large one, and raised an eyebrow in question. His parents nodded, but as Arator made to approach, Turalyon put a hand on his arm, pulling him back gently. Arator let him. This was the time not to protest, but to prepare for an attack.

Turalyon called the Light, cupping it in his left hand. With his right, he used the tip of his sword to flip back the canvas door. He peered inside, then turned and waved them forward. "No occupants," he said. "Looks like a whole family lived here."

Arator took in the simple but well-made furnishings: two bedrolls . . . and an empty cradle. Cushions on the floor, fruit in a woven basket, an extremely large, sturdy chest covered by a blanket. A doll and other toys were scattered on the fabric floor.

The wind picked up, shifted, and a gust blew in through the door. Arator caught the unmistakable, familiar scent. One hidden by the reek of the fires.

Fel.

Thump.

Something was inside the trunk. Radiance exploded into the room as father and son called upon the Light in the same instant. Alleria's bow was nocked and ready to release.

Then, a different sound: the sharp wail of an infant.

Adrenaline ebbed from Arator. He lowered his sword, approaching the trunk.

"You're safe," he called, in a reassuring tone. "We won't hurt you. I'm going to open the trunk now." There was no response. Slowly, Arator eased the lid open.

A terrified nightborne woman clutching her baby looked up at them.

He smiled at her. "You're safe."

She shrank back, covering the squalling infant's mouth, and said in a harsh, frantic whisper, "No, no, be quiet, they'll hear you—"

The next shriek came not from the infant but from beyond the tent.

Felbats!

The woman looked up at Arator in horror. "I told you!" she cried.

"We'll be back," he promised, and closed the trunk.

His parents were already outside. Two felbats were on the ground, arrows protruding from their eyes, and a bolt of shimmering golden radiance struck another out of the skies. It dropped, flapping erratically. Arator was there, lifting his sword. As his weapon descended, Turalyon's joined it. Light flared as the two powerful, blessed blades simultaneously plunged into the creature. Then Arator pulled his sword free to leap upward, cleaving another enemy in two.

Slighter than his father, less powerful but faster and with his mother's agility, Arator darted from place to place, sometimes leaping to strike with a cry, or moving away from his parents to draw the felbats to himself. Like Turalyon, he was strong in the Light, and it came when he called it.

The demonic beasts exploded, emitting a horrible screeching sound as a merciless blast destroyed them. The shimmering golden image of a hammer crushed another, caving in its skull. Arator paused for a moment as he quickly assessed the situation and chose his next target.

He was not too concerned. Felbats were easily dispatched by those as experienced as he and his parents were. He'd even ridden one once. The ground was littered with them now; Arator did not bother to count their number. His only concern was for how many more would come.

His gaze caught that of his mother. They smiled at each other. Hunting together felt good. He only wished they had arrived in time to—

Four of the demons swooped toward Alleria in a perfectly choreographed attack. Two dropped straight down, wings folded for speed. The second pair darted out from behind the cover of a row of tents, one on either side of her.

Arator didn't know if it was her instincts or if she'd caught the whiff of fel the creatures emitted, but Alleria sprang upward, tucking in her knees and arcing her body into a high backflip, firing the entire time. The Void arrows thunked satisfyingly into their targets, killing one of the descending felbats and wounding the other.

Arator began running the second he saw the danger, focusing on the demon his mother had wounded. He used the momentum of his speed to hurl himself toward the falling, flapping creature and sliced it in two before it hit the ground. Alleria had just brought her slender body into landing position in preparation for engaging the two at her sides, when the one on her left unexpectedly swerved—not to attack, but to knock her off-balance.

Alleria twisted, unable to completely avoid the impact. The felbat on her right seized its opportunity—and Alleria. Its talons dug into her calf and its fellow grasped an arm, both sets of leather wings beating in an attempt to abscond with her.

A voice, deep and rumbling like booming thunder, spoke. The two felbats shrieked as they burst into sun-bright flames of Light, and Alleria began to fall. Arator realized she wouldn't be able to adjust her injured body in time to land safely.

Arator thrust out his left arm, palm extended and fingers splayed hard.

Light. Heal her . . .

Catlike, Alleria twisted and landed gracefully on the balls of her feet, nocking her bow, ready for the next wave. Catching his breath, Arator looked up, gripping his sword. There was a small cluster of felbats hovering, and the paladin opened his hand. Even as Light formed in his palm, though, the felbats darted off to the west. The ground was littered with demonic corpses, but Arator made note of the direction in which the demons fled. If this was indeed a larger demonic plot, a swarm of felbats was just the beginning.

He turned to his father, smiling a little. "Good teamwork there. Not bad for an old man," he teased affectionately.

But when Turalyon turned from Alleria to regard him, Arator saw that he was not amused.

"Teamwork is being aware of what others are doing and working in concert with them. That's how you turn luck into strategy. We were lucky here—next time, I'd prefer to be strategic."

Arator blinked, remembering his rush out of the tent, two paladin blades in perfect harmony dispatching an enemy together. "You brought it down, and I—"

"A paladin *must make contact,* however briefly, with the senior paladin before just . . . jumping in, unless someone is in mortal danger."

Arator's brows drew together. "Mother needed us! Did you expect me to—"

"You distracted her in battle."

"Turalyon. Arator." Alleria's voice was cold and clipped. "Discuss this later."

"Mother's right," he snapped. "You want to talk? I'll talk. But let's get the survivors to safety first."

Without another word, Arator turned and stalked back to the tent. He could hear his parents speaking in low voices outside, but he took a breath and his own advice, pushing his heated emotions aside.

"I'm back," he said as he opened the trunk lid. The woman trembled, her infant wide-eyed and eerily silent. "They're gone now. You're safe, and we'll take you to the first arcanist in Suramar City. She'll take care of you. What's your name?"

"M-Mauvara."

Indicating the baby, Arator asked, "And hers?"

Mauvara smiled, just a little. "Trinette."

"May I?"

The mother hesitated, then nodded, wincing as she handed her child to him. Arator was sufficiently older than his cousins to be well familiar with the handling of infants. He whispered something softly and felt the Light warm his arms. Little Trinette did, too. She murmured, yawned, and fell into a restorative slumber. Arator placed her down gently on the bedroll, then turned to help her mother.

He heard the canvas flap being lifted and glanced up to see his mother standing in the entrance.

Alleria addressed Mauvara. "We're glad we found you," she said. "Is there anyone else in the encampment we should look for?"

Mauvara's eyes filled with tears. "I . . . do not know," she said. "We have not left this trunk since the bats came yesterday. I did not dare risk my child."

A look of deep understanding flitted across Alleria's face, then was gone. "This encampment, how many people were here?"

"There are forty of us." The woman paused, then amended somberly, "There . . . *were* forty. Have you found anyone? Any . . ." She bit her lip, unable to speak the word.

"No," Alleria said. "But we're still searching."

Had the bats taken *everyone*? Arator wondered. He had discovered only two corpses in Felsoul Hold.

"Alleria," came Turalyon's voice. Alleria glanced at Mauvara one more time, then let the flap fall.

"Can you stand?" Arator asked, returning his attention to the nightborne, who was, he was starting to suspect, not going to be receiving good news.

She tried to move her arms and hissed, as she had when handing him the baby. "Here," he said, leaning in. He helped her put her arms around his neck, moving the limbs gently, then eased his arms underneath her. She cried out as he lifted her and bore her to the bedroll, and Arator placed the sleeping Trinette in her arms.

"I'm going to talk with my companions," he assured her. "Try to move, just a little bit. I'll be back shortly."

"You checked everywhere?" his mother was saying when he approached.

"Of course," Turalyon said, his deep voice sorrowful. "I made a circuit of the area. No new paths. They're all gone."

Arator resisted the urge to take up their prior argument, his irritation tempered by the quiet melancholy in his father's voice. Whatever his issues with his father, Arator would never say he didn't care about others. It was more that Turalyon's empathy was too often eclipsed by his affinity for orders and protocol.

"I think it's safe to say they were abducted alive," Arator said.

"The demons cannot harvest their souls if they are dead," said Alleria, "but that doesn't mean their prisoners are well treated."

Arator understood that his mother was a hunter. A soldier. And he knew from experience that sometimes one needed to harden in order to function appropriately. Even so, it felt so strange to see this in his mother, she who had, not two hours ago, been warm and kind and smiling. He understood it. Valued her ability to do it, even. But he did not like it.

"The survivor says the attack occurred yesterday," Alleria continued. "Let us assume the rest of the encampment was taken and kept alive until they were sacrificed. If we also assume they died alongside the other two we found, then we know that at least forty souls have been fed to the soul engine."

Turalyon glanced back at the tent. "Think there could be other encampments?"

"It's possible. The demons intended to take everyone and leave no witnesses to inform Thalyssra of the attacks."

"They miscalculated," Arator murmured.

"They will soon regret their oversight," Alleria said.

"Indeed they will," Turalyon said, an undertone of righteous anger in his voice. "But you were correct earlier, Arator."

Arator was confused. "I was?"

"We should get these two safely to Thalyssra. They need food and care, and we need to report to Thalyssra. She needs to know everything, including anything this woman—"

"Mauvara," Arator supplied.

Turalyon nodded. "Everything Mauvara can tell us. Thalyssra will, I hope, wish us to continue the investigation."

Arator returned to the tent, calling over his shoulder. "I hope so, too," he said, "because I have an old friend who may be able to help."

CHAPTER FOUR

The Nighthold, Suramar City

BROKEN ISLES

Returning to the city of Suramar, it was difficult for Turalyon to believe that only half a day had passed since he and Alleria had discussed poetry and love while sipping arcwine at a table piled with delicacies. Unlike Alleria, who had appeared uncomfortable since they arrived, Turalyon had been enjoying a chance to sit with those who had once been his enemies and discuss topics other than the weather and politics.

Indeed, it was politics that had plagued him of late. When the king of Stormwind had temporarily vacated his throne, the mantle had fallen to Turalyon. Anduin had surely believed one of the founding paladins of the Knights of the Silver Hand would rule with a vision both devout and wise, and Turalyon had done his best to be worthy of the king's trust.

Privately, though, Turalyon had felt himself ill-suited to the great honor. Nothing had prepared him for its unique challenges. It was true he came from a noble line, and perhaps if his parents had lived, they would have taught him the diplomatic arts. But they had died when he was an infant, leaving their orphaned child to be raised by the church. He had reached adulthood bathed in sunlight filtered through stained glass, with no aspiration other than to humbly serve the Light and cleave to its teachings. Instead, the Second War had forced a weapon into his hand, and ever since then, he found that he made his greatest contributions to Azeroth on the battlefield.

He'd spent a thousand years in the Twisting Nether, led the Grand Army of the Light. He was familiar with dispensing orders on the battlefield but never at court. He was fortunate to be surrounded by friends and allies, nobility with more experience than himself. But Turalyon disliked the ever-shifting, unpredictable nature of politics. He preferred the orderliness of the church and the martial chain of command, the orphan who had been uplifted to heroism by chance and wandered into greatness. Anything outside it, well, the conversation with Lor'themar and Thalyssra was proof enough of where his comfort lay.

It was not uncommon for people to assume he and Alleria had married long ago, but the paladin and the ranger had met during war, fallen in love during war, and lived a life of battle until recent years. Even then, in an alleged time of peace, Turalyon had the throne of Stormwind to contend with. There had been a few years' time when he and Alleria had felt settled, somewhat at peace. But then Xal'atath had surfaced, and with her all the burdens of the Void Alleria now bore. Alleria had vanished off and on for months then, thinking to protect Turalyon and Arator from her power, worried it might endanger them.

Turalyon knew not what lay ahead, but he was glad they were together as a family now, even if on a dangerous mission for only a small span of time. But as he helped Mauvara from the manasaber, he felt a flush of shame. Over the last several hours, he and Alleria had known the luxuries of regal fare and spending time with their healthy adult son. Mauvara, her body cramped and contorted, had been hiding her child from demons that had abducted and slaughtered her entire community—no small feat. She didn't speak during the ride back, and Turalyon had not pressed her.

When Turalyon set her on the ground, Mauvara was so weak that her feet and legs melted bonelessly beneath her, and she nearly fell.

After a long moment with Turalyon steadying her, Mauvara nodded, and he released her. She was unsteady but could walk, and she quickened her pace as Arator approached with her daughter, clasping Trinette tightly.

Thalyssra and Lor'themar had been given word of their approach and hastened toward the family, their expressions shifting from curiosity to alarm. Thalyssra slipped an arm around Mauvara as Turalyon delivered the dire news.

"The reports were, unfortunately, all too accurate," he said. "The soul engine at Felsoul Hold is functioning."

"But we destroyed it—reduced it to rubble," Thalyssra said.

"You could hardly tell," Arator said grimly. "Someone has gone to great lengths to rebuild and augment it, even ward it against further interference," Arator said. "We found two sacrificed nightborne in an adjoining chamber."

Turalyon noticed that Mauvara had gone very still, listening intently. *The fate she escaped,* Turalyon thought.

"That said, the engine still seems far from fully operational," Arator continued. "We also discovered that demons have been abducting travelers from nearby encampments to fuel it. Mauvara and Trinette were the only survivors we found."

Lor'themar tightened his jaw. "I had hoped it was nothing, but in this life, that is most often wishful thinking."

Simple words, true, but they struck Turalyon harder than Lor'themar had likely intended.

"Mauvara," Alleria said kindly, "the first arcanist will take excellent care of you, but first we need to ask you some questions."

Mauvara nodded and let herself be assisted to the cushions at the table where Turalyon and Alleria had so recently dined.

"Your baby is beautiful," Thalyssra said. "And a sound sleeper!"

"She had a little help from the Light," Arator said. "She'll sleep for at least another hour, I'd imagine."

"You paladins do come in handy," Thalyssra said.

Arator's eyes darted to meet his father's.

"We try," Turalyon said, hoping his son would hear what he didn't say.

He didn't regret reprimanding Arator after the fight. His son had gone against protocol in a dangerous situation. This particular rule had been designed to prevent inadvertent harm from the worst possible source—a fellow paladin. But Turalyon *did* regret the harshness of the words. He was angrier than he should have been because for a moment, he'd known a stab of fear—fear for the two people he most loved.

The food, fresh and hot, and plenty of clean, cool water arrived quickly. While they ate, Lor'themar and Thalyssra summoned the Duskwatch. Turalyon recognized Victoire, the first blade and a leader of the order, but he did not know the officer who stood next to her, who also appeared to be high in rank. The paladin was glad to see how seriously Thalyssra was taking the matter.

She and Lor'themar settled in to listen as Mauvara repeated what she had told her rescuers. "We had no warning," she said. "The felbats simply arrived in numbers so great we were overrun."

She glanced at Trinette's small face, then resumed in a quieter voice. "Few among us knew how to fight, and they were mostly hunters, not soldiers. My husband was one of the only ones who had martial training. He told me to take Trinette and hide in the trunk, and he would get us when it was safe. When he did not return . . . I didn't know what to do. So we just . . . stayed."

Since reuniting with Arator, Turalyon had been belatedly plumbing the seemingly bottomless depths of the bond between parent and child. He was fiercely grateful that his family could more than defend themselves and ached to imagine how he and Alleria would have felt had they been in Mauvara's position.

Alleria had always been someone who closely guarded her emotions, continuing to do so even recently, when Turalyon felt there was no need. But now he saw the same expression in her eyes that he imagined his own held.

"We had heard nothing about such attacks," Thalyssra said. "In recent years, the druids of the Cenarion Circle have worked hard to restore what the Legion sundered, such that my citizens have felt safe to travel about our lands freely. I deeply regret that such was not the case for you and yours. I will have the entirety of Felsoul Hold scoured, and send word to those in the area that they will have safe harbor here, until we have once again purged the demonic threat." She indicated the nightborne who stood beside Victoire. "Patrol Captain Niandar will take you to my own estate. It's private and restful and nearby."

"Thank you," Mauvara whispered, bowing her head to hide fresh tears.

Turalyon had guessed correctly. This soldier was indeed an important figure. The patrol captain had the stance and muscled body of a warrior, but he spoke gently, and his scarred face was kind.

"I have two children of my own," he told Mauvara. "I will make sure there is always someone available to tend to you, and if not, I will enlist myself and my kin. You need not want for anything."

"You are in good hands with him," Thalyssra said. "Whatever you wish, if it is in my power to grant it, it will be yours." Her words were sincere and kind, but she knew, as all did, that Mauvara's only wish was that none of this had ever happened.

"Is there anything else we should know?" Thalyssra asked Alleria once Mauvara and Niandar had gone.

Arator gave her a full description of what they'd discovered, including the cage over the soul and the runic wards. "We don't know what is at play there. They could be wards of protection, or self-destruction. If you count an expert in Eredun among your citizens, First Arcanist, I'd suggest they be summoned. If the engine is rigged to explode, it could impact Suramar City."

"But we bought some time for investigation—if not much," Alleria added. "In the encampments, the demons had a source of fuel they will now be denied."

Souls, Turalyon thought but did not say. *Souls, not fuel.*

"Once they can no longer prey on smaller, temporary settlements close to the hold, it will take longer for them to scout and harvest what they need. Their attacks may grow farther ranging, or they may make a move on Suramar itself. I would tighten all entry points to the city."

Thalyssra frowned. "It would not be the first time the Legion has targeted Suramar, though at least the power of the Nightwell has faded and cannot be used against us. What worries me further is whether this is an isolated incident or a vanguard for some larger incursion."

"With the trail somewhat cold, I've a source I'd like to check in with next," said Arator. "He is in a position to know much more than we do about current demonic activity. And if he isn't aware of this particular incident—which he may not be, given how recent and contained it is—then he will be grateful for the information."

"And just who is this mysterious source of yours?" Turalyon asked.

"Kayn Sunfury."

"That sounds like a blood elven name," Turalyon said. "Do you know him, Lor'themar?"

The regent lord paused for a moment. "I do," Lor'themar replied, but his tone of voice indicated he had reservations about the other blood elf. "So does Thalyssra."

"Sunfury is a strong personality," Thalyssra said, "but he helped the nightborne greatly in our previous conflict regarding Felsoul Hold."

A fighter who knows more than we do about current demonic activity—and one whom Lor'themar views with caution. Surely his son didn't mean . . .

"Arator," Turalyon said slowly, "is your friend . . . an Illidari?"

"He's a leader within their order, actually, and I'm sure he'd be glad to help us," Arator said.

Turalyon looked to Alleria. As she so often did, Alleria knew what he was thinking.

Alleria had been there with him when Illidan Stormrage, paragon of the Illidari, had killed the prime naaru Xe'ra. She was one of the oldest naaru in existence, had led the fight against the Burning Legion from time unfathomable. Turalyon had served under her for centuries; it was she who raised him up, made him Lightforged. But Xe'ra was also convinced that Illidan was prophesied to defeat the Legion, and when he refused to submit to his destiny, the naaru had forced her will upon him . . . and Illidan had destroyed her.

The act had been so unexpected, her loss so great, that for a moment, Turalyon had felt nothing but righteous, adrenaline-fueled wrath. He had tried to kill Illidan on the spot, shattered with grief for his mentor and believing that Illidan's arrogance rendered their cause utterly lost. His attack had failed, and Illidan and his followers proved to be key players in the Legion's eventual defeat.

Over time, and with much reflection, Turalyon had come to realize that the Light, while compassionate, could also harden into implacability. Even the Prophet Velen, a close friend and the leader of the draenei, had informed the paladin that Xe'ra had deliberately kept things from him.

Yet Turalyon remained haunted by the thought that there might have been some other way, and while he understood Illidan's reaction, he could not forgive the demon hunter. Turalyon did not fully trust Illidan, and he did not trust those he had molded to serve him.

Like Illidan, the Illidari thrived on fel energy, wielding the powers of the demon they'd defeated and consumed, taking on some of their features in the process. They became the thing they hated most to destroy it more efficiently.

And his son—his bright, brave, good-hearted son—claimed one of their leaders as a *friend.*

The silence stretched out tautly, then at last Turalyon spoke.

"How well do you know him?"

"Very well," Arator replied promptly. "Our paths crossed during the most recent Legion invasion. He fought valiantly in the battle for the *Exodar*, helping to slay High General Rakeesh."

"After . . . what Illidan did, I wanted to know all I could about his followers. They consume a demon as part of their transformation into one." Turalyon's voice was calm, but only by force of will. "Did your friend tell you that?"

"I knew," Arator said.

"This demon is held at bay inside them for the rest of their lives. It is *always* trying to escape. Did you know that, too?"

Arator glanced at Alleria, then back at his father. "We have many valuable Illidari allies in the Alliance. And I would think, Father, that this family, of all people, would respect those who choose to accept constant vigilance over themselves for the power to fight the very darkness they contain."

A wave of shame washed through Turalyon, dousing the fire of anger that was simmering inside him. Alleria regarded him steadily, expressionlessly, and he reached out a hand to her. He sighed deeply as she took it.

"I do respect such people," he said to both of them. "But not everyone who makes that choice has your mother's strength."

"Kayn does," Arator said.

"You may trust him, especially if he knows Arator well," Thalyssra said. "His friendship is no small thing."

"May I remind you, our order has protocol regarding knights meeting with Azeroth's various leaders," Turalyon told his son. "Bypassing this once, as you did when asking Thalyssra to assign you this mission, is pushing it. Twice . . . let's just say they won't be happy with you."

"They won't be happy if there's a Legion invasion in the works and we didn't contact someone I know could help. Besides, I still have the regent of Stormwind in my party. Surely you don't seek the Silver Hand's permission for every diplomatic meeting you have, Father?"

He had him there, but Turalyon felt there was a lesson to be learned, one his son needed to grasp sooner or later.

"Look," Arator said with a sigh. "I'll keep track of all the times I violate protocol and submit it to Lord Tyrosus if this turns out to be nothing."

There was nothing for it. Arator was right. "I'll double-check that list," Turalyon grumbled, trying to lighten the mood.

Arator relaxed and gave a cautious smile, unsure if his father was joking. Turalyon was, but just barely. "Fair enough," said Arator.

Turalyon squeezed his beloved's hand, and she squeezed back. He prayed he was doing the right thing.

"Very well, son," Turalyon said to Arator, "we shall go meet your friend."

▪ ▪ ▪

"When I would bring a new friend home to meet my mother, it would usually be for a nice meal and conversation," Alleria commented as the trio stepped through the portal.

"Well," Arator said, "you've already had a nice meal—or most of one, anyway—and I *promise* you there'll be conversation. Besides, you two don't exactly have a house where we can sit down for dinner."

"While it's not technically *my* home, I'd feel much better near my chambers in Stormwind Keep, with the guard at my back," Turalyon mumbled. "Besides, I'm not sure I'd call a Legion war vessel a *home*."

Turalyon and Alleria were all too familiar with demonic ships, though the memories they evoked were not of arcwine and roasted stag. Instead, they recalled prisons and torture chambers, monuments to obsession and hatred, and the stench of suffering. As they reached the hall of the Illidari, the former Legion vessel named the *Fel Hammer*, Turalyon couldn't help but tense in anticipation, and he rather badly wished he could be holding his sword.

Figures approached at the entrance to the citadel: elven, but only to a point. Their torsos were either completely bare or only slightly covered, the better to reveal the green, glowing swirls of fel runes on their bodies. Unlike their leader, Illidan, they did not have hooves, although they did have curving horns jutting from their skulls. In place of eyes, fel green glowed through the black bandage covering empty sockets. Turalyon knew that, while they were blind physically, they saw not with eyes anymore but with magic. Beyond them, Turalyon could see into the vast heart of the ship, peopled with Illidari, Broken draenei, shivarra, and likely other demons. The space was lit by massive braziers burning with green fel fire. In the distance, others turned toward them as the two who had spotted them initially drew closer.

"They don't *look* pleased to see us," he murmured to Alleria.

"No, but there are only . . . fifty, sixty at most, if it comes down to it."

Standing beside them, their son scoffed under his breath. "Please behave, both of you."

For an instant, Turalyon imagined himself in an ordinary home, teasing an ordinary son with ordinary friends, and hearing a very ordinary exasperated response. The charm of the thought was quickly replaced by a small pang of regret. Nothing about any of them was ordinary nor ever would be.

"Arator," said one of the Illidari in a cordial tone. "It is good to greet you again. Sunfury will be pleased." She turned to Turalyon and Alleria, conspicuously looking them up and down with sightless eyes. The faintest of sneers curled the Illidari's lips.

"You must be the high exarch," she said.

"What gave me away?" he said innocently, thinking of his shining plate and wondering if he shone as brightly in the Illidari's fel vision.

"You attempted to slay our leader," she said. "We should slay *you* for that."

"Salira," Arator said sharply.

Chuckling coldly, Salira lifted a hand. "Do not worry, Arator. We have no desire for you to be without your parents . . . again," she said.

The dig cut Turalyon more sharply than the murder threat had.

"Our son and the first arcanist assured us we were all on the same side," Alleria said. "And that Kayn Sunfury was honorable."

"He is." The second Illidari sighed. "And you are fortunate that this is so. Come."

Turalyon glanced at Arator as they followed the pair down into the vessel's heart. He leaned toward his son and said quietly, "Are you sure Kayn *knows* that you're friends?"

"We are," Arator said. He looked more annoyed than troubled.

Turalyon nodded, taking everything in, once again face-to-face with Legion technology and structure. Years at war could never permit him to feel anything save pain and anger in places such as this, yet he could not help but delight in some small bit of irony. The Legion enjoyed twisting its fel magic about every world, being, and place it touched, though here, aboard the *Fel Hammer,* their sworn enemies had taken a Legion vessel and perverted it for their own uses—namely, destroying demons.

He glanced over at Alleria, wondering if she was thinking the same, but her face betrayed nothing. There were uneasy moments, more than a few, when he was unsure of where he stood with his lover or his son. That he loved them and would die for them if need be—and they for him—was beyond question. But Turalyon, high exarch, often found himself at a loss in these uncertain times.

They were approaching the command deck. Below was a large, flat area where several trainers were giving individual lessons to grim-faced Illidari. But what drew Turalyon's eye was an enormous chain link, high in the vaulted ceiling, from which a demonic body was suspended.

As the group progressed, one by one, conversations halted. At the edge of the deck's precipice, an Illidari, a blood elf taller than most of the others, paused mid-conversation with perfect stillness. He faced away from the newcomers, his broad back partially obscured by long, dark hair. He cocked his head as if listening and then turned, nostrils flaring, before facing them squarely.

"Arator," he rumbled, the deep voice surprisingly warm. "It has been too long since we hunted side by side. Your presence gladdens me."

Arator relaxed. "Kayn," he said, with pleasure. "I'm glad to see you. I've brought—"

"I know exactly who you've brought." Just like that, Kayn Sunfury, one in command of the Illidari, was as cold and supercilious as ever his leader had been. "One of the few who have dared raise sword against Illidan Stormrage and survived such an offense."

Turalyon pressed his lips together. This prickling hostility was starting to annoy him. But this was Arator's friend, not his, and so he waited.

"And Alleria Windrunner," Kayn said. "You know a little something of darkness and rage, do you not?"

Alleria may not have shared Turalyon's aversion to the Illidari, but she certainly shared his impatience with them. "My son spoke highly of you," she said. "We have come in good faith, with information you will want to know. If this is how the Illidari receive us, then we are wasting our time here."

Arator stepped forward, reaching out to his friend. "Kayn, please—"

"You wish to be properly received, Lady Alleria? High Exarch?" Kayn drew himself up to his full height, and all the Illidari snapped to attention. Turalyon's fingers twitched in preparation to hold the Light. For his son's sake, he would wait until the last possible moment, but if his family was in danger, the Illidari would pay.

"Then by all means, let us show Arator *exactly* how we receive such guests."

Their tattooed arms snapped up in a uniform salute. In the silence, Turalyon heard a suppressed snort of laughter. He realized it was coming from Arator.

"I *can't believe* you messed with them," Arator said, halfway between anger and humor, punching the demon hunter playfully in the arm. "Honestly, I at least know to expect it."

The Illidari dropped the ruse and started laughing.

"And now they do, too," Kayn said, shaking his head with a smile, then he spread his arms. "You are both well and truly welcomed here, for your own courageous selves as well as for the friendship and debt I owe your son. Few who are not Illidari have devoted so much of their lives to the destruction of demons. You have been doing so for centuries."

Kayn did not ask for forgiveness for the trick, nor did Turalyon expect such from him. He was mildly annoyed that Alleria was smiling a little.

"Well played, Sunfury," she said.

Turalyon nodded. "You had me reaching for the Light."

"It was not so great a gamble," Kayn replied. "You trust your son. Therefore, you would never strike unless you were certain our intention was hostile."

Turalyon did not reply.

"You're still lucky, and you know it. Do not think for a moment that I'll forget this," Arator said, feigning anger.

"Good," Kayn said. "You must always be on your guard, my friend. You are still a bit too trusting. But much as I enjoyed our little jest, you did not come all the way to the *Fel Hammer* simply to provide me with entertainment. I am greatly curious to know the business you bring. Come, let us adjourn."

Kayn turned and leaped off the deck, his wings snapping out, permitting him to float easily down to the training area. He smiled up at them and beckoned.

"Show-off," Arator muttered, but he was grinning as he jumped. His parents exchanged glances, then followed, landing only slightly less gracefully than the Illidari.

"By the way," Turalyon said, pointing up to the suspended demon body, "interesting choice of décor."

"Ah, yes," Kayn said, smirking. "That is Brood Queen Tyranna, the *Fel Hammer*'s former occupant. She was so very reluctant to abandon ship. Now . . . she never will."

Turalyon was repulsed but did not show it. He tried to remind himself that the brood queen was a fearsome and merciless enemy, and many Illidari had died to win this ship from her and halt the Legion's invasion. He respected their dedication and their sacrifices, and certainly he himself loathed demonkind and found satisfaction in executing them. But that was not the same as displaying their bodies in such a fashion.

And my son is Kayn's friend.

"Most of the ship is open area, but there are corners here and there for conversations. I commonly hold private discussions in one of these. We will not be interrupted nor overheard." He indicated an area set back from the training floor that had small tents, each roomy enough for several people. Thick hide rugs covered the floors, and there were cushions and low tables. A few scattered parchments indicated that some aboard the *Fel Hammer* used these small nooks for study.

It was unexpected, almost cozy, more of Azeroth than the Twisting Nether, and sharply at odds with the harsh design of the vessel and the demon hanging from a chain. Turalyon struggled to reconcile the two images as he and his family sat down on the green pillows. When everyone was seated, Kayn took a breath.

"Now. Tell me."

Arator described what they had seen at Felsoul Hold and at the encampment. Kayn listened with complete attention, interrupting now and then to ask a question. The younger paladin spoke clearly and succinctly, yet no detail that might be of import was omitted.

Turalyon thought back to the soul engine, how quickly he and Alleria had taken the lead in making decisions, issuing, if not quite orders, directives to their son. Yet here he was, creating solid alliances with people so very different from himself, a far better diplomat than Turalyon could ever hope to be.

I wish I could claim some credit for raising you right, my son, Turalyon thought. *But perhaps you are better for the many hands and hearts who helped shape you.*

"I had thought Felsoul Hold scoured clean, but demons are persistent wretches," Kayn said. "There is a debt between you and me, my friend, and I do have something that will help you. Then we shall consider it even."

"Agreed. Although," Arator said, "I still do not consider it a debt."

"You have a good heart, young one, but I prefer to act of my own choosing and have obligations to none." Kayn turned, now including Arator's parents as casually and easily as if they had been old acquaintances. "As you may imagine, we have recovered a good many demonic artifacts. Some are too dangerous to use and must be destroyed at once, or secured until such a means can be found. Others we have turned against their creators, to most satisfactory effect. One such item should suit your needs perfectly. It tracks demons—and can be attuned to the unique energy of a specific one. Once it has been trained to find a singular demon, it will track *only* that demon, until it is in its presence. At that time, it becomes inert and can be reactivated with a new target."

"That sounds ideal," Alleria said. "What does this artifact demand in return?"

"It does not require a soul or a blood sacrifice to function, if that is your concern. At least, not *yours.*"

"How rare and refreshing," Turalyon said drily.

Arator frowned slightly. "So, what's the catch?"

"Someone left with it a few days ago." At his friend's groan, Kayn added, "But . . . this may be to your advantage. I do not know if you made the acquaintance of Lyana Darksorrow, Arator. She knows Felsoul Hold well, having fought her way through it years ago. Lyana was among those who helped destroy its initial overseer, Azoran. She has attuned the artifact to a demon she suspects was one of Azoran's associates—the last one she hasn't slain. With the connection to Felsoul Hold, this demon may well be the very one you seek. You'll find her in Outland."

Outland. The place they'd gone . . . the choice they'd made that had preserved their world and cost them a thousand years away from their son.

"Well *that* narrows it down," Arator said.

Kayn shrugged. "I have no tracking device for *her*, alas. But both Lyana and the artifact are distinctive. She is a kaldorei of average height, with blue hair. The runes on her body are green. She wields a pair of glaives with exceptional skill."

"Oh, *that* narrows it down," Arator said sarcastically. The description matched at least eight Illidari they'd encountered in the guild hall.

"What does her face look like? Any distinctive markings?" Alleria asked.

"I cannot say. She has always worn a veil. I do not think she cares to show her face."

Turalyon nodded. "Very well. That's distinctive, too. And the artifact?"

Sunfury grinned suddenly. "A very large tooth."

"All right," Arator said, "there's got to be a story here."

"There is, and a fine one," Sunfury replied. "It is the Fang of Haa'zuun, faithful companion of the great demon Golgoroth the Hunter. Felhounds can sense magic, of course. The stories say that Golgoroth, with the patience of the undying, trained Haa'zuun over untold millennia how to also sense a demon's unique fel essence. Golgoroth kept his power for so long because the moment he suspected an underling plotted against him, he would send Haa'zuun after that unfortunate demon. No matter where it was, the devoted felhound would track it down and drag it to the Twisting Nether, where it would die a permanent death."

"So . . . good dog?" Arator said, amused.

"Very. Haa'zuun was killed while defending his master, but Golgoroth was not about to let his efforts go to waste. He transferred the beast's ability into a single fang."

"I am annoyed with myself that I'm impressed by all this," Turalyon grumbled.

"Do not be," Kayn said. "It is important to acknowledge when our enemies are brilliant, so that we do not make the mistake of underestimating them."

"How have the Illidari been using it?" asked Alleria.

"In a similar fashion as Golgoroth. At the beginning of the hunt, the fang looks like an ordinary tooth. To give it the scent, as it were, you'd place it near something the target has touched recently."

"As you might give a mortal dog a whiff of someone's clothing," Alleria said, nodding.

"Precisely. The runes Golgoroth inscribed on the tooth will begin to glow. After that, it is little more than a compass, but Lyana is very fond of it, and it's served her well, or so she tells me."

"Is there anything else we should know?"

"I would exercise caution in Outland," Kayn said. "I do not know when you last ventured there, but the defeat of the Legion saw an explosion of fel activity in its reaches. Unbound demons found refuge there, many throwing in their lot with diabolists. These threats have remained largely unchecked in the ensuing years. Tread carefully."

"Appreciate the warning," Arator said.

Kayn nodded. "When you have found your demon and slain them, return with the fang, and tell me what you have learned." Throughout most of the conversation, the Illidari commander had been unexpectedly pleasant, and at times almost jovial when interacting with Arator, but his face hardened now. "We would be honored to assist you in thoroughly ending any hint of a demonic incursion."

"I will convey that to Thalyssra. Thank you," Arator responded.

Turalyon still could not bring himself to say he had changed his mind about the Illidari. Anything with a demon inside them had a better-than-average chance of falling to temptation. But he had to admit, he now understood why Thalyssra, Lor'themar, and Arator had spoken so highly of Kayn Sunfury.

"We are grateful for your help," he said, and meant it.

He turned to his beloved. He could not have guessed this "adventure"—which was supposed to be little more than a pleasant outing with his family—would take them to the place where she and he had once expected to die. Where the rest of the Sons of Lothar had stayed for years with no way home. But they were soldiers and hunters and would follow wherever, and to whatever end, that trail led.

"So," Turalyon said, turning to Alleria. "To Outland?"

She squared her shoulders. "To Outland." Then, allowing herself a small smile, she said, "And this time, our son comes with us."

CHAPTER FIVE

Suramar City

BROKEN ISLES

"Captain?"

Patrol Captain Niandar opened his eyes immediately, fully awake and reaching for his uniform as he spoke. "Has the scouting party returned?" he asked the younger lieutenant who'd roused him.

"Yes, sir. The first blade apologizes for disturbing your rest, but she requested you specifically."

No emergency, then, the captain thought. *Likely just a debriefing, for the moment, at least.*

Still, he'd wear his armor and take his sword. Just in case.

Niandar and his officers had been instructed to discourage rumors about demons returning to Felsoul Hold when speaking with the public until the reconnaissance was complete. Niandar was in complete agreement, as panic would accomplish nothing. But the Duskwatch knew that the first arcanist was taking the reports seriously, even though they came from terrified students who, Niandar thought privately, had likely been victims not of demons but of some fellow youths with more mischief than wisdom.

Victoire, the first blade and a leader of the Duskwatch, nodded at him as he approached the small gathering, stepping beside her and standing at attention. As he perused the group, he realized two things. First, Thalyssra's caution had been warranted. Second, he now understood exactly why she'd wanted him, specifically, present.

The scouting party had indeed returned . . . but they had not come alone.

Food and beverages had been provided for the group. The two paladins and the hunter had partaken, but the nightborne woman they had brought with them had only picked at the fare. As Niandar regarded her, she looked up, seemingly sensing his gaze.

He knew that expression all too well and could guess her story before she even spoke. Niandar was a hardened fighter, no healer in the traditional sense of the word. But few in the Duskwatch had a way with children like "Captain Nee," as the youngest ones called him, and he possessed a deep understanding of the unseen harm that violence, fear, and loss could wreak.

Victoire, who'd known him for millennia, nodded as he stepped beside her and stood at ease but attentive. She confirmed his deductions, murmuring, "The rumors were true. The soul engine has been rebuilt and is being fed from nearby encampments. Mauvara and Trinette were the only survivors of an attack."

Niandar listened with his odd combination of compassion and detachment as the woman spoke of a peaceful encampment of civilian families and a quiet evening brutally interrupted by a swarm of felbats. Of a beloved husband who had gone to fight but was lost trying to keep his family safe.

The news was not only a tragedy but an enormous setback. Thalyssra had worked tirelessly with the Cenarion Circle to heal the wounded land, and she had the Duskwatch conduct patrols to ensure those settling outside the city remained safe. As Niandar had expected, she offered the woman and her infant sanctuary—in her own former home, no less—and placed them in his charge.

"I'll brief you later," Victoire said as Niandar stepped forward. The patrol captain was aware he presented an intimidating visage. The children always saw through it, but some of the adults needed to be convinced. He made his deep voice as gentle as possible when he spoke.

"I have two children of my own," he told Mauvara. "I will make sure there is always someone available to tend to you, and if not, I will enlist myself and my kin. You need not want for anything."

Mauvara rose, clasping her sleeping child close, and they departed. Before they had gone too far, he said, "Is walking comfortable for you? I can get manasabers for us if you prefer."

She nodded. "I'm all right. Walking was painful at first, but it feels good to stretch my legs now. You are all being so kind to me, thank you."

"You are most welcome."

"Are . . . are we really staying in the first arcanist's home?"

"Her old estate, yes. Now she lives here in the Nighthold. She and her husband and other guests return to her estate from time to time, to escape the city for a while."

Mauvara was silent, continuing to hold her baby close as they walked through the splendor of the Nighthold, looking at the lavender gardens, the graceful statues, and the members of the Duskwatch. Quietly, she said, "I have never been here before. It is as if it was never occupied by . . ."

Her voice trailed off.

"The nightborne have defeated demons once before," Niandar said. "We will again, do not worry. You will be safe at the estate. Thalyssra keeps her word. I am deeply sorry for what you have endured. I lost my wife in the fight against the Legion, so . . . I understand, at least somewhat."

They had reached a docking area, with three or four small boats. Niandar pointed. "Can you see that building over there?" She nodded. "That's where you'll be staying."

She grabbed his arm suddenly, gripping hard. "*Outside* the city?"

"Only just," he reassured her. "And someone will be there all the time."

Her grip lessened, but she did not let go. "Will you be staying?"

"I'll check in on you both, but I have other duties as patrol captain." She clutched tighter for a moment, then released him. The gondola rocked gently as he stepped in, extending a hand to her and getting her settled before casting off, and they began to move.

"Your duties," Mauvara said. "Will . . . will you find the demons who attacked us?"

"Yes, we will," he promised her, as certain of that as he had ever been of anything in his life. "And prevent any from entering the city." He was anxious to see Mauvara settled and to speak with Victoire about everything she'd learned, but he also found himself reluctant to depart. Mauvara reminded him of his daughter, Veviene, and his granddaughter Renni. Renni had been a handful, all curiosity and adventure. As soon as the Legion had been defeated at the Nighthold, she was ready to leave Suramar and explore the world.

"Why do you smile, Patrol Captain?" Mauvara asked.

"Because you and Trinette make me think of my own children, and one of my granddaughters in particular. Her name is Renni."

His charge gave him a tentative smile. "That's a pretty name. Tell me about your family?" Her voice was wistful, and he knew she was thinking of her own.

So, Niandar did. Of his feisty granddaughter, and her gentle mother. Of his son, who was also in the Duskwatch. And he found himself speaking, too, of his wife, Juliere, and his friend Victoire.

"When Victoire told me she was going to support Thalyssra and the rebellion, I knew it was time for me to do so as well. It felt wrong to be disloyal to Elisande, but it felt worse to carry out her orders against her own people. I've never regretted my choice."

As the gondola approached the landing dock, Mauvara asked, "How long will you keep me here?"

"Keep?" he asked in surprise. "No, no, Mauvara, you're not being held! Do you wish to leave? Do you have any other friends or family you could be with?"

She shook her head. "Viel . . . my husband . . . and Trinette are my only family. And our friends were in our encampment. Are you sure they are all . . . gone?"

"I would be glad to be proved wrong, but yes, I am. I will not lie to you."

Mauvara swallowed hard. "Thank you. Now I know I can trust you."

He tied the gondola to the post and helped her up. "Then stay as briefly, or as long, as you like. Others will be joining you until the danger is over. Which I anticipate will be soon."

Her mother's movement had roused Trinette, who began to fuss. Mauvara tried to soothe her, but the baby only wailed the louder and started to kick. Niandar stepped quickly onto the dock, removed his gloves, and extended his arms. "May I?"

"She's usually a very calm baby," Mauvara said, hesitating.

"Both she and her mother have been through much today."

She searched his eyes, then gave Niandar her child.

Without even thinking, he shifted to a position he had held countless times before. He had cradled his own children, theirs, and great-great-grandchildren. The children of other friends, and babies who had lost their parents. Niandar was proud to serve his people as patrol captain. He would fight and die for the nightborne. But this duty, the care of one little soul, gave him the most joy. Trinette sensed it, as the other children had, and peered up at him, waving a hand. Niandar shifted position slightly and extended a forefinger. The little girl gripped it strongly.

"Working your magic again, I see, Papa."

Niandar looked up, delighted. "Veviene!" he exclaimed. He had planned to request this particular priestess to tend the survivor, but either Victoire or Thalyssra herself had preempted him.

His daughter smiled warmly, then turned to Mauvara.

"I am so, so sorry for your loss," she said. "I have prepared a bath and fresh clothes for you, and a soft bed." To Niandar's surprise, Mauvara stepped back slightly, looking from Veviene to him, fear creeping over her face.

"Can you not stay?" she asked him.

It seemed as if, having given her trust to Niandar, Mauvara was unwilling to transfer care of herself and her child even to his daughter.

"I must go," he said. He deliberately handed Trinette to Veviene, hoping to reassure Mauvara that the infant would be in safe hands. "I need to be briefed, and we are likely to act quickly."

"Will you come tomorrow?"

"I will try," he said. "As soon as I can." To Veviene, he said, "The child is restless, and I think Mauvara needs her sleep."

"I'll give her a sedative, and I will be happy to amuse little . . . ?"

"Trinette," Mauvara said.

"Rest well," Niandar said, and stepped into the gondola. He was only halfway back to the Nighthold when he heard the infant, again, begin to wail.

▪ ▪ ▪

"First Arcanist, I must thank you for sending my daughter to tend Mauvara," Niandar said, inclining his head as he stood before Thalyssra and Victoire. "I'm very grateful."

"I'm certain Mauvara is, too," Thalyssra replied. "Veviene is both knowledgeable and caring."

"As is the first arcanist, if I may say so."

Thalyssra knew that to truly win over Elisande's Duskwatch, she had to gain their trust—and give them hers in return. She found it easy to care about her subjects, and she made a point to know all who served her to at least some degree. Some were easier to connect with than others, and getting to know "Captain Nee" and his family had been a joy.

"How are they?" she asked.

"I think both mother and child will need time," he said. "My duties permitting, of course, but I'd like to continue to visit them."

"Duties are what we are here to discuss," said Victoire. Thalyssra listened with half an ear as the first blade brought Niandar up to speed, thinking first about the lone survivor, then about those who had not been so fortunate, and estimating how many others might be out there right now—future victims who had no idea of the danger.

"So," she said when the other woman had finished, "we have three masters of demon hunting searching for the one behind this. I have faith they will be successful. In the meantime, we have four priorities to manage on the home front. One: Establish a perimeter and tighten security around the city. We do not yet know what we are up against. Two: Scour the hold and kill any demons there. Three: Summon an expert in Eredun to examine the wards and supervise destruction of the soul engine once the hold is cleaned. And four: Prepare the city for refugees."

"If I may," Niandar said, "a fifth, related to the most vulnerable. We'll need to anticipate where the demons will strike next and get there before they do—augmenting the ranged patrols. Each of these tasks requires a sizeable number of soldiers. We must allocate our resources wisely."

All were quiet, thinking. Then Victoire spoke. "Here is what I suggest. We *know* the encampments nearby are under immediate threat, and we know we must begin preparing to house refugees. We *know,* once those populations are safely relocated in the city, that the demons will assault other areas. And we know that the soul engine is not yet fully functional. We should focus on finding and housing those in danger and warning others. The soul engine isn't going anywhere just yet, especially if the demons can't fuel it."

Thalyssra wanted to think—to hope—that there were several survivors hidden in the depths who yet lived, and could be rescued, but she knew better. They would have been killed as soon as they had been brought to the hold.

Had been brought . . .

"Captain," she said, "how few troops do we need stationed at Felsoul Hold to accurately monitor activity?"

His lips twitched in a slight smile. "I think I see where you're going with this. I'd recommend regular, frequent aerial patrols as well as several units of four—three at the minimum, to establish a perimeter. If we do need to go into the hold, of course, that number would need to increase, perhaps quickly. But if a mage is assigned to each unit, then movement wouldn't be a problem."

Victoire was nodding. "Speaking of teleportation, there is a possibility that demons are opening portals inside the hold to transport victims to the soul engine. They could use those portals to bring reinforcements and attack here."

"Agreed," said Thalyssra. "They *could* attack us from the hold. But they *will* attack elsewhere . . . and the city is better equipped to fight them off than lone encampments."

Niandar leaned back in his chair. "The Duskwatch will be spread thin," he warned. "Three arenas with three different needs."

"We are the shal'dorei," Thalyssra said. "We will find a way. We will enlist the aid of the citizenry, ask for volunteers to open their homes for a short period of time."

"We should begin at once," Victoire said. "There is much to do, and we need to move quickly." She sighed. "I wish we had more information, but until Alleria, Arator, and Turalyon return, we shall do what we can."

Thalyssra gave Niandar an apologetic smile. "I fear I have asked for a year's worth of patrol schedules for the next few days, Captain. You may need to let Veviene take care of Mauvara for the time being."

"I may indeed," he said, but privately, he knew he would make time, even just ten minutes if it was all he could spare, to make sure she was settling in.

■ ■ ■

The perimeter around Felsoul Hold was established swiftly, a visible sign to the populace that their leader was taking action. Niandar and

Victoire assigned those Duskwatch already familiar with the patrol patterns to this task in order to speed things up even further.

Niandar was going through the rosters to compile three lists—to start—of Duskwatch guards to deploy to encampments and other evacuation areas when a note arrived from Veviene.

Papa—

Would you be able to spare a few minutes from your schedule to visit Mauvara? Both she and the child are agitated and she keeps asking for you. I attempted to explain that you were leading efforts to repel further attacks, thinking the news would please her, but she continues to ask. Even a quick visit might settle her mind.

—*Vev*

Niandar leaned back in his chair and rubbed his face. His lieutenant was sharp and a good judge of character and abilities; she was more than capable of compiling a list of solid candidates, and he could make the final decision.

He chuckled; Victoire was always telling him he should delegate more often, and Sidonae was itching to feel useful. Niandar called her in, told her where he would be, instructed her to work until he returned, and headed to the estate.

As he had last night, he heard the infant crying piteously, and his heart ached at the sound. Worse, though, was that as the gondola approached the dock, he could hear Mauvara's raised voice, laced with frustration and fear.

He tied off the rope as Veviene hurried to meet him, Trinette clutched in her arms. "Tell me," he said, reaching for the baby. Trinette's little face looked up to him, wet with tears, as the sobs subsided.

"Mauvara slept all night, and I rocked Trin to sleep for her. I had hoped both would be better today, but instead—" She shook her head. "Mauvara is terrified demons will find her and says she only feels safe with you."

"Hardly unexpected, given what she's been through."

"Of course, Papa. But . . . well, come see."

She grabbed his hand and practically pulled him behind the house to a small area set aside for reading and relaxing. Mauvara lay on the beautifully woven rug, shaking with sobs. A decanter of arcberry juice had been knocked over, staining the pillows dark purple.

Niandar knelt beside her. "Mauvara, I'm here. You're safe."

She lifted her head and stared at him. "I'm not," she said. "The demons . . . I think they know where I am."

"What makes you think that?"

Mauvara beckoned him close and whispered in his ear, "I heard one outside last night."

Poor child. "I think it much more likely you had a terrible nightmare."

"No, I heard it, I—"

Niandar glanced over Mauvara's shoulder at Veviene, who stood behind her. His daughter shook her head.

He returned his attention to Mauvara. "Veviene was here all last night, taking care of Trinette and protecting you," he reminded her.

"It's just Veviene," Mauvara murmured.

"I assure you, any demon that tangles with 'Just Veviene' will be very sorry soon after. It's important that you understand I can't visit as often as I'd like because I'm trying to help others just like you. I'm organizing the patrols to bring people back from the encampments."

"But the hold . . . are the demons . . ."

Niandar chose his words carefully. "If there are any still there, we will take care of them."

"What will you do? *I need to know, please!*"

He sighed and sat down, preparing to give Mauvara's daughter to her, but Mauvara shrank bank.

"She is afraid of me," she said. "She won't nurse, she starts to cry . . ." Her own eyes filled with tears.

Niandar considered, cradling the baby. He'd seen this before.

Children, even as young as Trinette, often picked up on and were affected by their parents' emotions, particularly in violent, tragic situations. "Let us make a bargain. If I tell you things, you must promise me that you'll listen to Veviene and do what she says. I don't want to distress you or Trinette further. If you are calmer, she will be, too."

"I think . . . if I know exactly what you are doing to stop the demons, I think it will help us both," Mauvara said.

"Very well. We're working on many fronts. We've already set up a perimeter around Felsoul Hold . . ."

She listened, wiping her face, and he could see she felt better already.

▪ ▪ ▪

At his next briefing with Thalyssra and Victoire, Niandar informed them of Mauvara's distress.

"It is only her fear speaking," he told them. "Veviene has reported no signs of any such thing. But we do know that some demons can disguise themselves in order to infiltrate a secure location. I would urge everyone to stay alert."

"Agreed," Victoire said at once. "I will do so. No one should hesitate to report someone, even a friend or partner, if they begin acting unlike themselves."

"It is better to offend and apologize than to dismiss unusual behavior," Thalyssra replied. "Every nightborne will understand what must be done. But with luck, we may have nipped this in the bud."

Niandar listened with growing confidence as they filled him in. Reports from the perimeter around Felsoul Hold were coming in regularly with no activity reported. None of the patrols sent to the first found of encampments had been attacked. Two groups of refugees had already arrived and were being safely relocated in Suramar City, and a third was expected later in the day. As more folk were accounted for, the focus could shift to scouting in other areas of the kingdom, which required far fewer people.

"We located a few scholars who have studied Eredun from prior Legion invasions," Thalyssra said, when Victoire finished. "They are eager to help, soon as the hold is safe for them."

"Once this third group has gotten settled, I suggest we proceed with conducting a proper patrol of the hold," Niandar said to Victoire. "Give the soldiers a hearty meal, a hot bath, and a good night's sleep, and they'll be ready to go tomorrow first thing," he said.

Victoire nodded. "Speaking bluntly, I think they'd be thrilled at the potential of seeing action after all the evacuation work," she said.

"While I suspect you are right," Thalyssra said, "hopefully, there will be nothing to discover in the hold other than the soul engine. Once that's secured, we can call in our scholars. With luck, they will determine how to safely destroy it."

With the plan settled, Niandar went from the meeting straight to the first arcanist's estate. The place was oddly silent as he approached, but the young patroller he'd assigned to watch duty, Officer Etain, saluted correctly, if without urgency.

"Report?"

"All quiet, sir. Veviene took the child to the Artisan's Gallery. She told me to inform you that Mauvara hasn't been eating much, and your daughter hopes to tempt her with some delicacies. She says she'll bring you some snowplums."

Niandar's sweet tooth was legendary, but he was disturbed to hear that his charge was not eating. "Did Mauvara not want to go?"

Etain hesitated, then said, "It's the strangest thing—she's the one who asked Veviene to take the child somewhere."

"What?"

"Mauvara, ah . . . believes she'll be snatched by demons if she leaves the estate. She wanted the baby to be safe. Veviene thought it best to humor her. Can you wait until she gets back? She wanted to speak with you."

"I can see why," Niandar said. He sighed heavily. "I'm sorry to hear this. I'm taking a team to scout tomorrow morning and clear it out, if there are even any demons still there. Hopefully when I return, Mauvara will feel much better about everything. Where is she?"

"She's either in the study or behind the house. Those are her two favorite spots. Veviene should be back soon."

Niandar nodded, thanked Etain, and went around the back of the estate. He found Mauvara pacing, wringing her hands. She looked up as he approached but kept moving anxiously.

"Captain!" she said. "Oh, it is good to see you."

"It is good to see you, my dear. I hear you're not eating."

She stopped abruptly. Her eyes narrowed. "Who told you that?"

"Etain," he said. "Veviene told him to tell me, because she knew I'd be worried about you. She'll be back soon and I'm certain she'll bring you something delicious."

"I'm not hungry," Mauvara murmured.

"Are you at least drinking some arcberry juice or wine?"

"You sound just like her."

"The fruit doesn't fall far from the tree," Niandar quipped. "Is Trinette sleeping better?"

Mauvara turned away and began pacing again. "She still screams when I hold her. I can't . . . Veviene has made something she can eat with mana juice." She wiped at her wet face. "I'm not good for her, Captain. I'm putting her, and your daughter, and you in danger."

Nonsense," he said. "Veviene and Etain—"

"That's not Etain," she said quietly. "He tried to poison me. That's why I'm not eating."

Niandar considered trying to reason with her again but decided against it. He would calm her down tonight, and once he was back from the hold and he could show her that her fears were unfounded, she would begin to heal. "Come with me," he said. "Let us walk a little bit. There's a trail here that should take us to the Twilight Vineyards. They're quite beautiful."

She shrank back. "I can't leave the estate," she said. "They'll take me!"

"We won't leave the grounds. Just a few steps along the trail. After all, you'll have the patrol captain protecting you."

For a moment, Niandar thought he had pushed too hard, but then she nodded. He held out his arm and she clung tightly to it as they stepped onto the trail.

He didn't press her for conversation, and she offered none. Her first steps were hesitant, then, more certain, and soon they left the house behind them. The path was easy to follow in the moonslight.

Mauvara took a deep breath and exhaled, relaxing.

"How are you feeling?" he asked.

"Better," she said, and seemed surprised.

"Good." Niandar felt his own tension ease. He'd made the right call. "We should probably head back."

"Oh, no, let's keep going," she said. "Just for a bit. It feels good to walk."

"All right," he replied, pleased. "But Vev will be back soon, and I have work to do before I see my bed tonight. Tomorrow will be a big day."

"Why?" she asked, halting and looking up again, fear once again upon her face. "What happens tomorrow?"

Niandar berated himself. He should not have mentioned it. But they would be prepping in the open tomorrow, and it would be public knowledge. *Perhaps,* he thought, *this will reassure her.*

"We're going to patrol Felsoul Hold," he said. "And if we find any demons, they'll be sorry they ran into us."

Her grip on his arm became painful.

"We'll be leaving in the morning. All seasoned soldiers," he continued. "We will scour it clean. And you won't have anything to be afraid of anymore."

"I'm afraid now," she said, and he could feel her shaking. "Please . . . don't go."

"I must, my dear, but I'll be back before you know it."

"Tell me," she begged. "How many of you? Only Duskwatch?

Healers, you should take healers . . . and weapons, what kind . . . please . . ."

Mauvara wept openly now, in a full panic. And so, as he was betraying no secrets, Niandar told her in a steady, slow voice, holding her hands in his, exactly how they would be attacking and defending themselves, how they had planned for ambushes, and where their path would take them. He emphasized how experienced everyone would be, and how carefully and thoroughly they would progress. How very safe they would all be. She calmed with each point he addressed, and when he had finished, she sagged against him, all her anxious agitation spent. Niandar patted her on the back, gently, relieved.

"Let's go back now, hm?"

She pulled back and wiped her face. "Thank you," she said. "I believe you. You'll be safe."

"I will," he said. "I promise." Niandar started to turn around, his arm around her shoulders to guide her, when suddenly she stiffened.

"They're here," she whispered. "Can't you feel them?"

"Mauvara," Niandar began, "you—"

He smelled it then, the reek of rotten eggs.

"Run," he said, shoving her in the direction of the estate. She stared at him, frozen in terror.

"*Run!*" Niandar shouted.

She did, fleeing toward safety as Niandar whirled around. He drew his mace, the gentle father gone, the soldier on full alert now, scanning the area. Nothing appeared to be disturbed on the dirt path, or in the grasses to its side. He strained to listen; only silence. Even the scent of rotten eggs was gone.

If indeed it was ever here, he thought.

Niandar lowered his weapon slightly, turning in a slow circle a final time. He took a deep breath, irritated with himself. He had let himself get too caught up in Mauvara's worries, obviously. He must not allow that to happen again. Sighing, Niandar began to stride back toward the estate when the wind shifted.

The sulfuric stench. Familiar.

Real.

Slowly, too slowly, Captain Niandar of the Duskwatch began to turn, lifting his mace far too late to be of any use. He did not see his assailant, but the air of its movement stirred his hair as its weapon descended upon him. And in the fraction of a heartbeat before the blow struck, Niandar's only thought was that Mauvara had been right after all.

CHAPTER SIX

Shattrath City

TEROKKAR FOREST, OUTLAND

Shattrath City.

The ogres who had built the city hundreds of years in Draenor's past called it Goria, "Throne of the King." It had been the violent heart of the ancient Gorian Empire, but the ogres had doomed themselves with their own arrogance. In a single harrowing night, the city was reduced to rubble by the furious elemental spirits who sought to protect themselves from the ogres' greed. The draenei lovingly rebuilt it centuries later, imbuing it with their powerful technology. Instead of boasting of a king's throne, the city was now a "Dwelling of Light," open yet protected, and graced with crystals and lilting architecture. It, too, fell, but this time to the fel-fueled orcish Horde. Once again, the streets of this beautiful city ran with blood, and it was abandoned.

The Sons of Lothar had come in later years, and eventually the armies of Azeroth had poured through the reopened Dark Portal to drive back the Burning Legion. It became a sanctuary, and even now, after that victory, it welcomed denizens of Outland and Azeroth.

Alleria was the first to step through the portal, onto the stone floor of the city's Terrace of Light, and she instantly sensed the power of A'dal, leader of the naaru who dwelled in the city. It was powerful, bright almost beyond bearing, enormous as it hovered high above those arriving. She peered up at it, eyes squinted against its radiance. It was not hostile, but neither was it inviting. It recognized her, and the Void within her, and accepted that she would respect it but not obey. That was fine with her.

"I was greeted by Khadgar here, more than once," Arator said, pointing to a spot directly beneath the naaru. "He would speak often with A'dal, or he would want to be present when he knew certain people were arriving. He told me that A'dal thought of him and Velen as friends, and that A'dal was certainly the largest, shiniest friend he'd ever had."

Alleria chuckled at that, then glanced at Turalyon, also large and shiny in his radiant armor. He was not listening to Arator but focused on the luminous being, smiling softly as it brushed his heart and restored him, then bowing his head. Its sounds, which her ears heard as chimes sufficiently out of tune to irritate, like the buzz of an insect, were doubtless heard by him as the sweetest of tones. Alleria remembered what the naaru sounded like . . . before. But she would never again truly hear them as her husband and son did.

If Turalyon regarded the crystalline being with nigh rapture, her son seemed to view it with more respect than reverence. Like his father, he acknowledged it, but with a nod rather than obeisance. *A soldier, rather than a priest,* she thought, reminding herself again that Turalyon had been with the church his entire life before taking up arms for the Light.

"Does A'dal consider you a friend, too?" she asked her son.

"I'd like to think so. It's seen me often enough. I expect that it thinks of me as one of those friends whom you like but who also annoys you to no end."

"I don't suppose it told you where we could find Lyana," she said to Turalyon as he returned his attention to them.

"No," Turalyon replied, a little irritated. "That's our task."

"That tracks," Arator said. "It never passed along much information in my experience."

Turalyon, still deeply moved by his encounter with the naaru, frowned at his son. "A Knight of the Silver Hand should be ever humble in the presence of a naaru, son."

"Arator, since you have been here more recently," Alleria said quickly, "I'd think you would have an idea of where we might find her."

"I do, but it's a big place," her son reminded her. "And Illidari are not an uncommon sight here."

"Arator!" a voice called. The three turned to see a draenei in mage robes waving at him. "Welcome back!"

"It would seem *you're* not an uncommon sight here, either," Turalyon said to his son, looking bemused.

"Oh, that's Iorioa," Arator said. "An old friend. Let me go talk to her. She's one of the mages who provides portals for travelers. She might have seen Lyana. You two talk to the flight masters. I'll find you there."

Alleria watched as he strode toward the smiling draenei, breaking into a trot as Iorioa extended her arms for a hug. Beside her, Turalyon sighed deeply and shook his head.

"You're still bothered by the Illidari," Alleria said quietly. It wasn't a question.

Turalyon nodded. "I love Arator," he said to Alleria. "I'm proud of him. There are days when I even *learn something* from him. But more often than not, our son completely confounds me."

"You never knew your parents, but *I* confounded my mother to the point of breaking several millennia of tradition. By comparison, this is nothing."

"At the very least, it's unexpected."

"You never expected to see a paladin enjoying the company of people who have demons inside them?"

"No," he replied, mildly irritated, "and neither did you."

"I was a bit surprised," Alleria admitted, "but he seems to be thriving in said company. He has friends and allies everywhere."

"In high and low places," Turalyon grumbled. "And I thought the *tattoos* were bad."

She gave a chuckle at that. "I'm certain that other knights have them."

"Some do. It's not that he *has* them, it's . . . his choice of subject matter."

"I saw," Alleria replied, understanding what he meant. "The light, and the dark."

He was silent for a moment, then nodded. "Yes. A Knight of the Silver Hand pledges to serve the Light. If I am being honest . . . I wonder if that pair of dragons might have counted against him in his evaluation for promotion."

"It's simply a piece of body art," Alleria replied, growing exasperated.

"It is not, and we all know it," came Turalyon's reply. "He's no impetuous, rebellious youth. He's a man grown. The symbols he chose have meaning for him, and they do for others as well."

Turalyon was sincerely troubled. Alleria knew, as Arator didn't, that at the heart of her love's complaint was an honest concern for their son's future. She loved both men deeply and despised their squabbling.

"Remember when we hated orcs?" she said.

"Of course. *You* in particular."

She nodded, knowing it was the truth. "I held every one I saw responsible for the deaths of my family. I enjoyed hunting them, as if they were animals. I killed the orcs I saw because I could not kill the ones who took my brother from me. And I was not alone. The Alliance as an entity hated the entire race."

Turalyon looked somber. "I later learned the order exiled Tirion for aiding Eitrigg."

"And you fought beside him in the depths. Now we count Eitrigg as a cherished friend, equal among the Sons of Lothar. Tirion befriended Thrall, too. The most revered member of the Silver Hand and the orcs' warchief. Today it is not uncommon to see the Horde and Alliance working together and sometimes becoming friends. Perhaps you are too close to see it, but I have watched as the order has changed and grown, my love."

Alleria stepped in front of him and placed her hand on his chest. "It has opened its mind and heart, as you do."

He covered her hand with his own, gently.

"I do not think a bit of ink on our son's skin, even if it *isn't* just for decoration, will harm his chances with the Silver Hand. He is a good man."

Turalyon looked away for a moment, back to where his son stood waiting as Iorioa opened a portal for a pair of orcs, then looked down at her again.

"Alleria?"

"Yes, love?"

"Have I become a cranky old stick in the mud?"

"Yes, love," she said solemnly. "But you are *my* cranky old stick in the mud."

His eyes crinkled in the warm smile she knew so well. "Well. Thank goodness for that, then."

Their connection, old, almost more familiar than their own heartbeats, was still there. It was always there, though sometimes, in moments of anger, or pain, or guilt, Alleria thought it gone. But it was too powerful a thing and seemed to weather every challenge, a deeply comforting constant in a universe fraught with chaos and war and grief. And she was glad of it.

But they had a task ahead of them. Alleria stepped back, still smiling. "Let's go find the flight masters."

The Terrace of Light was a pleasant place, bustling just enough to be lively. The structure was circular, the center area, capped with an open dome high above their heads, vast and airy. Several wide, curved entrances, large enough to permit even a dragon to wander inside should they choose, opened to other terraces on the exterior.

Side by side, still in that sweet place with each other, they passed through one of the large entrances. Instead of a glittering naaru and stone walls, they saw gold-hued levels that felt in harmony with their environment. The rich, deep green of a forest stretched out below, and small lights glinted from its depths.

"There was beauty in this world once," she said to Turalyon.

"Some yet remains. The draenei told me about this place. This is what's left of the Terokkar Forest."

"It's lovely," Alleria said. "It reminds me a little of Eversong. The olemba in particular." She indicated the dark green trees dotted with light in the landscape below.

"The draenei say the olemba's glowing seeds are the forest's way of reminding them that no matter the darkness, the Light is always there."

And no matter the Light, the darkness is always there, too, Alleria thought.

And there it was. No matter how gentle and quiet her world became, Alleria could never dwell there long. Almost as if it was a physical thing, Alleria felt the itch to move, to act, to do something. There was no time for beauty. Xal'atath was still out there, regaining strength, plotting her next move, as was a demon who might or might not be paving the way for another Legion invasion. Her home, her world, was facing multiple dangers while she tarried here in another.

"Alleria? What's wrong?"

A distinctive *caw* and flap of wings reminded them of their purpose. "Nothing," she lied, her gaze following the gryphon to see where it alighted. She strode toward it, and Turalyon followed.

By the time they reached him, the flight master was engrossed in soothing an agitated gryphon, which, along with a wyvern, appeared to have taken a disliking to a would-be passenger.

"I am so sorry," the flight master was saying to a vulpera. "He has never had a bad attitude toward passengers. He's sweet, like a cute kitty cat and a little birdie put together, truly!"

The gryphon at this moment, still restless and angry, did not look sweet, cute, or kitten-like. The wyvern, for its part, was hissing, its enormous fangs bared and its hackles raised.

"Please," said the flight master. "I'll calm them down. A free flight for you!"

"Not to worry, friend," the vulpera said, nonetheless keeping her distance. "I get that a lot." She laughed. "I'll use the portal!" Her bright eyes landed on Alleria and Turalyon. "And I shouldn't keep you from paying customers."

"We were actually after information, too," Alleria said. "Have either of you seen a kaldorei Illidari come through here in the last few days?"

"A few, yes, but not so many as there once were," said the flight master. "What do they look like?"

"Average height, blue hair, green runes," Turalyon said. "She has a veil covering her face, carries glaives."

The vulpera, who had started off, paused and turned. "Did she, perchance, happen to be carrying a *really* big tooth? Like—bigger than the wyvern's?"

The wyvern in question snarled again, demonstrating its fangs.

"One that glowed?" the vulpera said, with a slightly crafty smile.

"Indeed, that's her," Turalyon said.

The vulpera chuckled. "Kind of sticks in your memory."

"I imagine it would," Turalyon prompted. "Do you know where she was going?"

"She was looking at desert gear. I had a lot of suggestions for her, because, well, *desert,* but she was kinda standoffish." The vulpera wrinkled her muzzle in annoyance. "She put that big old fang away right quick, too." She pointed south. "Headed off in that direction."

"Auchindoun, probably," Arator said, striding up. "We should ask around Allerian Stronghold."

Allerian Stronghold. The stronghold might have their answers, but it would also give confirmation of those who'd been lost since Alleria had been gone, and questions from old acquaintances she'd rather not answer. Attention she didn't want.

Her son glanced at her and half shrugged in a *sorry* gesture. To the vulpera, he said, "Thank you, you've been a great help."

"When you folks get back, look me up at the World's End Tavern! I'll buy you a round of Sargeras Sangria. I have *got* to know the story behind that tooth!" She waved and ambled away.

Arator shuddered. "Don't take her up on it," he told his parents. "It turns you into an imp. Don't ask how I know." When that did not get a smile out of them, he said, "I'm sorry. I know you don't want to go."

"It's fine," Alleria said, and took a gryphon's reins.

■ ■ ■

The flight, at least, was beautiful. The gryphons flew close to the ground at times, as if enjoying dipping beneath the olemba treetops and their radiant seeds. There were several streams and small lakes in the forest and a clean, fresh scent throughout—something that Alleria would never have associated with Outland.

Alleria knew, of course, that she had a stronghold named after her. Her lieutenant and friend Talthressar had suggested building the structure in this place that had clearly reminded him, too, of the Eversong Woods they had forever left behind. He'd named it for her.

She should have come to see it. To see him and the others.

Was he still here? She realized she had no idea who had returned home from Outland and who had chosen to stay behind. When Arator had suggested traveling to the stronghold, she had wanted to refuse, but she realized the more she protested, the more awkward he and Turalyon would feel. Fortunately, they were here on a mission, and Talthressar and the other Farstriders would certainly understand there would be no time to socialize.

As if wanting to make sure Alleria made an entrance, the gryphons angled upward, clearing the forest canopy, and the first thing she saw was a glint of white and gold. Her breath caught as she glimpsed the quel'dorei tower, slim as a needle. The graceful structure was a twin to those she had grown up with.

Then, a flash of blue—how often had she seen these kinds of roofs in Stormwind, when flying above the city? Her ears found a rhythmic, soothing splash: a waterwheel. And now she beheld it fully. The towers marked it as a stronghold, but more than one of them bore the scars of previous attacks. No, it was more of a small, cozy city, truly a place that welcomed all races of the Alliance, all who had braved the Dark Portal and its former sentence of exile.

Tears stung her eyes for a moment, but Alleria blinked them back hard, and by the time the gryphons landed in their aerie beside the waterwheel, Alleria had regained her composure.

The paladins' armor attracted some curiosity from the pair of dwarven flight masters, but no one seemed to recognize them. Yet.

She took control of the situation before either Turalyon or Arator could speak. "We wish to speak with Lieutenant Talthressar, if he is still in charge here."

The dwarves exchanged glances. Alleria's heart sank. The female wore an expression Alleria had grown to hate: that kind, sad look that ever and always meant only one thing.

"Mother?"

Alleria turned and saw her son looking at her with a similar expression.

"I thought you knew. I'm so sorry. He fell in the last war with the Legion."

Alleria simply nodded. She could not look at Turalyon. One more sympathetic face would be too much. Talthressar had been her friend since childhood, as had a handful of others who had joined her when she left Quel'Thalas to assist the Alliance. She had not seen any of them for a thousand years, and people died in wars. Yet her heart was heavy. It was one more link to the past, gone. "Then please take us to whomever is in charge."

The news cast a pall over her appreciation of the stronghold. Alleria paid little attention as they crossed over a small bridge and strode past the very tower that had so moved her upon their approach. More eyes turned their way, and Alleria ducked her head.

She knew it wouldn't really help, not while walking beside the gleaming paladin who most of the Alliance knew belonged to her.

They continued on, following the street, and were approaching a fountain watched over by a statue—of whom Alleria did not know—when she heard her name being called. She stopped dead in her tracks, as did everyone within earshot, turning their attention to her and her family.

"Alleria!" the voice cried again, and, reluctantly, Alleria turned to see a high elf ranger, still clutching her bow, racing toward her. The other woman caught the expression of confusion on Alleria's face and said quickly, "I'm sure you don't remember me, but I was present the day you left to join the Alliance. I was very young, but—I gave you flowers."

A pang went through Alleria. The night before her departure, the Windrunner family had gathered for what turned out to be the last time. When next Alleria returned to Quel'Thalas, her parents were dead, and she had not found time to see her brother. *The next time,* she had told herself. *I will see Lirath next time.*

She would not see her homeland for hundreds of years.

And she would never see her brother again.

The Farstriders had gathered near the border of the kingdom, cheering her on as she and the few who had chosen to join her departed. She remembered now—the girl, so small, her dirty hands clasping the messy little nosegay of drooping flowers.

I'm going to be a Farstrider one day, and I'll come fight with you when I'm older!

Alleria had forgotten the moment until just now. There was so much she had forgotten . . . more than she wished.

What would have happened if I hadn't gone? Would I ever have met Turalyon? Could I have been able to defeat Arthas, had I been ranger general? Would more or fewer have died over these last years?

The questions were all moot. She had made those choices and had to live with them.

"I see you kept your promise to become a Farstrider," Alleria said. The woman broke into an enormous smile. "I remember a little girl and flowers . . . but I do not know her name."

"A thousand years of fighting demons has not dulled your memory one bit. I am Taela Everstride. I'm so glad to see you again, especially here, in this place named for you."

"*At last,*" Arator said. Confused, Alleria turned to him.

Arator was grinning at Taela, who had suddenly turned bright red. "When we met after I arrived in Outland the first time, she told me that story. And she told it again. And *again,* every time I came through here."

"I did not!"

"I'm sorry, but you must admit, Taela, it's kind of funny. And hey . . ." He put his hand on her shoulder. "I'm glad I got to be here to see you meet her. Truly." To Alleria, he said, "She thinks the world of you, Mother."

Alleria suddenly felt like a fraud. This young woman had based her life choices on nothing more than hero worship. She had put Alleria on a pedestal, but Alleria well knew her own deep flaws, her weaknesses. Her moments of unkindness, of failure.

Turalyon handled such moments better than she. When faced with this sort of adulation, he was slightly embarrassed and humbled, but he was able to give a blessing and some kind words about everyone being equal in the Light. What was she to say, to do?

"I am . . . glad," she said. "To hear that you've so honorably served both the quel'dorei and the Alliance."

Fortunately for her, Taela suddenly realized that there was a fourth person present and inclined her head.

"High Exarch. I did not mean to be rude. You are welcome here, too, of course."

"No offense, Father, but as you may have figured out, you're more respected here for winning Mother's heart than anything else," Arator said.

"I approve of the stronghold's priorities," Turalyon said.

Alleria knew it was true. She appreciated both him and Arator for lightening the tone, even if for only a moment.

"How long will you be here?" Taela asked.

"Not long," Alleria replied. "We need to speak with the current leader on an urgent matter."

"I'll take them to the captain, Furnan," Taela said to the dwarf, who nodded, bowed deeply to Alleria and Turalyon, and trundled back toward the aerie.

The three followed their new guide, who set a brisk pace toward a building with a clock tower. It looked like a town hall of some sort, and as they started up the steps, someone called Arator's name. He paused to wave and call back, "Aeman! Theine! Good to see you!"

"Oh!" said Taela. "That reminds me—we're rather famous for our Brightsong Wine. It's quite good—and quite powerful. I'm sure I can persuade Aeman to open a keg for such distinguished visitors."

"Thank you, but no," Alleria said, "we're here on business."

"Well," Taela said as they followed her into an entry room and then into an antechamber, "at least you will be conducting business with an old friend."

They stepped into the main hall. At the far end, past piles of books, tables, and benches, an elf with long, fair hair sat working. Books and parchment surrounded him, but he glanced their way and sat up straight as an arrow, disbelieving.

"Alleria," he said. "You—you're *here*!"

Alleria stared for a moment, then, as Auric Sunchaser stepped lightly down from the raised area, she hastened toward him and they embraced.

As with Talthressar, Alleria had known Auric her entire life. He had been one of her mother's favorites among the Farstriders. He had surprised Lireesa by choosing to accompany Alleria, to serve the Alliance.

"I just learned about Talthressar," she whispered. He hugged her tighter for a moment and released her.

"A Farstrider to the end," Auric said. He seemed lost in a memory for a moment, then smiled. He turned to greet Turalyon. "General," he said warmly. "Or rather, High Exarch. It's good to see you again as well."

"Turalyon is fine, my friend," the paladin demurred. "An unexpected pleasure."

"Very unexpected," Arator said. "You told me you were going back to Silvermoon the last time we talked."

"I did," Auric said. "Yet I discovered I missed this place. After spending so many years here, friends became family. This stronghold now feels more like home than my actual homeland. But . . . I don't suppose you've come all this way to catch up."

Alleria took a deep breath. "I'm afraid not."

"We're hunting a demon," Arator said. "But we're hunting a demon *hunter* first."

"I see," Auric said. "I hope to be helpful on both fronts."

Alleria had only just started to describe Lyana when Auric nodded. "Lyana is not a stranger to us. She stays here and gets supplies when she is working with the Auchenai."

"I'm . . . I'm sorry, did you say she works with the *Auchenai*?"

Turalyon was trying and failing to conceal his shock. Auchenai were draenei priests with the sacred charge of tending to the dead interred in Auchindoun. Given the mausoleum's tragic history, restless, sometimes violent spirits roamed its subterranean halls. Auchenai were loving and fierce custodians of the ancestral spirits and known to be mistrustful, at least initially, of even the most well intentioned.

Alleria placed a hand on Turalyon's arm supportively. *My poor love,* she thought, with equal parts true kindness, sympathy, and gentle wry humor.

Even Arator looked surprised. "That's not a pairing I would have anticipated."

"I don't think anyone would," Auric agreed. "But over the last few years, the draenei have been rediscovering their heritage. Work is being done by many kind hands to help the spirits find peace, one by one, and to restore their resting place to its former glory. The increased activity in the center discourages the more common type of crimes. But Auchindoun is an enormous place, and the fringes, neglected more than ever for the time being, can be a welcome hiding place for more dangerous activity."

"She's pest control," Arator said. "It's . . . kind of brilliant, actually."

"I don't know the details of the arrangement, but she notifies them when she's coming, and, of course, they're happy to let her." Auric hesitated. "Prior to Lyana's arrival, Nemuraan sent word that there might be such unwelcome guests in the outer crypts. I dispatched two scouts to investigate and report back. They're overdue."

"Of course we will look for them," Alleria said.

Auric inclined his head in gratitude. "We are happy to equip you with anything you need. I would offer to accompany you, but given who your family is, I do not think you need the aid of a humble captain."

"Not this time," Alleria said. "But I'm sure we've not fought our last battle together."

The days of their youth were long gone, and Auric's smile turned wistful as he read that truth in her eyes. "Good hunting" was all he said, and it was enough.

CHAPTER SEVEN

Auchindoun

TEROKKAR FOREST, OUTLAND

Arator knew that visiting Allerian Stronghold for the first time would be hard on his mother, but he thought that she found some comfort there, too. Certainly a genuine welcome. He berated himself for not telling her about Talthressar. His parents moved in more elite and important circles than he, and he realized he'd fallen into the trap of assuming they knew about everything important.

The opposite appeared to be true, actually, when it came to the more common, everyday things, and their reactions were sometimes amusing. He smiled a little, thinking about how stunned his father had been at the thought of an Illidari trusted by draenei. The three had not spent much time together, and this—mission? Adventure? Working family reunion?—was revealing a lot about all of them.

Arator did wish his father didn't feel the need to constantly test him. He'd told his mother that, just once, he'd like to go fishing with Turalyon rather than train with him. Or cook a meal together, or trade amusing tales from their youth.

It's hard to remember that your father may be very experienced in some areas, but he never had any idea how to be part of a family, Alleria had once reminded her son. *He never knew his parents. He thought he wouldn't travel far from the confines of the church for his entire life. Then one day, he's told he's going to be a paladin. Fighting, confronting moral decisions every minute, being responsible for so many lives . . .*

Falling in love, Arator added.

For a moment, his mother's gaze had grown distant, her face softening. *Neither of us expected that,* she said, smiling, as if she knew a beautiful secret. *It was terrible timing, of course.*

Would you do it again?

He'd been surprised when she took a moment. But then she said, firmly, *Yes. I would. After all, we wouldn't have had* you.

Arator thought about that moment a lot.

Like any son, he supposed, he wanted his parents to be happy together. Over the years, he had seen them be very close at times, and then distant. But maybe that's what centuries together did to a couple.

He'd watched them earlier, coming back from his chat with Iorioa. He couldn't hear what they said, but he'd watched them walking together, talking. They'd laughed, and smiled, though they did not touch, and their strides were easy and in sync. Alleria's posture was relaxed, and his father's brow was unfurrowed. The connection between them was palpable—not the fiery sparks of new romance, but the long-burning warmth of a fire that kept the cold night away.

And then, Arator had watched it change right before his eyes. Something shifted in his mother, and, as if a door had been closed, she was all business again.

He often wished they'd just figure it out.

Arator turned his attention to the landscape unfolding beneath them as they approached the Bone Wastes. Once, the entire area was populated by beautiful olemba trees. That ended when the draenei survivors of the orc's initial assault had fled into the depths of Auchindoun, thinking to defend their most sacred site from the Horde. The orcs, in an attempt to slay them all, had summoned a fearsome entity who blasted the sacred mausoleum and the surrounding area.

Even if Draenor had not become Outland, it would have taken time unknowable for the forest to reclaim the Wastes. Arator was not sure anything could grow here again. But even in this bleak expanse, there was hope and healing. Auchindoun could be, and was being, repaired. Arator could glimpse it now: curving, fractured stone fragments jutting up from the sand like rib bones themselves. The center always felt exposed to him, although the tombs were below the surface.

The area below buzzed with activity not from tomb robbers, which had long plagued the site, but from the draenei. Slowly, slowly, debris was being cleared, and what still stood strong and solid was being cleaned and reinforced.

Above it all soared D'ore. Healed and whole, the naaru radiated a quiet joy. It had suffered long, but it had been tended with care and love, and now it gave its blessing to all who came with kindness in their hearts.

The newness of its restoration gave its energy a different feel from the naaru in Shattrath or other places where Arator had encountered them. He glanced at his father and saw that Turalyon was sensing it, too. It seemed to confuse him a little, and the older man's smile was tentative as he breathed deeply, letting D'ore's Light calm and strengthen him.

Their eyes met, and Turalyon's smile widened as the armor of both paladins became limned in the Light.

Something softened in Arator. They might clash from time to time, but there was love there. And a shared bond in the Light. Suddenly he wanted to do something for his father, something they would both enjoy.

"Come, Father!" he beckoned, and urged his gryphon to a swifter speed. The beast, enjoying herself, soared toward the shining figure and began to fly in a circle around it. The naaru's chiming voice became lighter, a friendly, playful staccato, and Arator was giddy for a moment with the gryphon's speed and the purity of the naaru's joy and his own. This . . . *this* was the Light he loved. After a full circuit, he veered off with its blessing singing in his veins.

Flushed and smiling, he looked around for his father, but Turalyon and Alleria were nowhere to be seen. The pleasure of the moment dimmed as he spied their gryphons on the ground. With a sigh, he brought his own mount down to join them in the Ring of Observance.

Turalyon and Alleria were already deep in conversation with Nemuraan, one of the tenders of the dead, as he approached. Nemuraan paused and turned a smiling mien toward him. "Arator!" he said. "It is a pleasure to see you all together at last. I was just explaining to the high exarch about our association with the demon hunter Lyana. She came here a little while ago, just ahead of you."

"We were waiting for you to land after your . . . whatever that was with D'ore," Turalyon said. "I hope we haven't missed the Illidari."

Arator flushed. "I was just saying hello, and D'ore gave me its blessing." Out of the corner of his eye, he saw Nemuraan look concerned and start to move toward Arator and his father. Alleria put a hand on the draenei's arm and shook her head.

"One bows to the naaru out of respect," Turalyon said. "That's how you greet them, not . . . flying rings around them."

For the life of him, Arator had no idea why Turalyon seemed upset about this of all things. "Father . . . I know and love the power of the Light, but I don't have to whisper and walk softly every minute when I'm actively trying to *serve* it."

"That's not what I'm saying." Turalyon's voice dropped lower, and his armor started to glow with a faint nimbus of gold. "Just . . . a little more respect is warranted, particularly in a place like this."

Arator sighed. "*Respect?* I told you: I have been here before. I know these tombs almost as well as an Auchenai. You didn't even bother to learn that D'ore was healed!"

"Your mother and I have been rather preoccupied over the last thousand or so years. And it has little to do with what we're discussing. What exactly brought you to this place while we were gone, anyway? How did running around Shattrath, or—or drinking wine in the stronghold, or playing explorer in draenei tombs help the order you vowed to represent?"

Something inside Arator snapped. "What do you *think* I was doing?" Arator exclaimed, his color high, his voice rough with both anger and pain. "I was *looking* for *you*!"

Shock and comprehension flooded his father's face. *Did he really not know?* Arator thought wildly.

"Oh . . ." Turalyon murmured. He closed his eyes, wincing. The Light around him faded, and when he spoke, there was no anger in his voice, only regret. "Arator," Turalyon began, reaching out a hand, but Arator was having none of it.

He stepped back and shook his head. His father had irritated or angered him before, but his ignorance of Arator's search for him was different. This moment, being here with them both when he'd spent so long in this very place, chasing any scrap of information about them—it should have felt like a beautiful symmetry, the healing after a dark time. Instead, this whole thing just . . . *hurt.*

"Turalyon! Arator!"

Father and son both turned. Neither had noticed that both Alleria and Nemuraan had left during the argument. Alleria strode toward them now in the company of a tall, striking woman whose face was completely covered by a dark veil. Her arms and midriff were bare. Runes crisscrossed her dark purple skin, and fel emanated from her pauldrons, undulating eerily inside the green gem of her helm. One massive glaive was strapped to her back, and she grasped a second with easy familiarity.

In her other hand, she held a large canid incisor. Runes scrawled in Eredun glowed green against the yellow-white color of the tooth.

"Alleria tells me you've been looking for this," said Lyana Darksorrow. "You may have it, but not just yet. I require your assistance first."

▪ ▪ ▪

Alleria didn't know what Arator and Turalyon had been quarreling about this time, but the chance to break up their squabble was one of many reasons she was grateful to have spotted the Illidari. It did not escape her notice that the two men looked relieved at the interruption.

"Kayn Sunfury informed you correctly," Lyana said, getting right to the point. "My quarry is indeed a demon that once had been assigned to Felsoul Hold, Varaskar the Flayer. I assure you, it is an apt name. We all know that most demons enjoy torture. Varaskar, though . . . she craves it to a degree that is disturbing even to the Illidari. That can be helpful as, of course, her enthusiasm makes her careless from time to time. I almost had her a year ago because she kept the victim alive for so long that—"

"We do not need details," Turalyon cut in.

Lyana nodded. "Yes, of course. Alleria told me you thought perhaps this demon may be able to provide you with information about your quarry."

"That would be ideal," Arator said. "But even if not, we would be honored to assist you."

Lyana nodded. "Good. Do you know how to use the fang?"

"Sunfury explained how it operates," Turalyon said. "The runes are active, so I assume it is tracking your demon."

"Picking up the scent, as any good hound would," Arator said, trying to lighten the mood.

Lyana turned her head to him. "It was never a dog. It was a demon. And even in life, it did not use a demon's scent to track it."

None of them could see her expression, of course, as her entire face was hidden. But Lyana's voice had not varied, even when a little humor might have been warranted. Alleria respected that. This Illidari was utterly focused. She had done away completely with introductory courtesies, and Alleria suspected that she would never have conceived of the kinds of pranks Kayn played. Lyana Darksorrow would have considered that a waste of time.

"Observe," Lyana continued. She demonstrated, turning in a circle so that the tooth pointed in all directions. The three noticed that the glow was weakest in the east and strongest when it was pointed west. "You see? Simple. The closer you are to your prey, the more intense the glow."

"How do you reset it, for want of a better word?" Turalyon asked.

"Once it gets close enough, the runes will flare and then become inert until it is exposed to another demon's essence," Lyana explained.

"And if the demon escapes, I guess you have to start over again," Arator said.

To all their surprise, Lyana chuckled. It was less an expression of mirth than of bitterness. "Oh no," she said. "It will never track that demon again."

"What?" It took Alleria an instant to realize that she was the one who had almost shouted the word. "I . . . are you telling us that we have only *one* chance to kill the demon?"

"Of course not. If you survive, you always have another chance. But you cannot use the Fang of Haa'zuun again."

"So, you would truly have to start all over again," Turalyon said heavily.

"Now you understand my pleasure at encountering you. Our odds of destroying the Flayer are much better. It would be"—Lyana's grip tightened on the hilts of her glaives—"*extremely* frustrating to fail."

Alleria certainly understood that feeling. She knew better than anyone how slippery prey could be on a hunt—particularly when it came to certain demons who could change their form at will.

As soon as the thought came, she tried to banish it. But Alleria couldn't help but remember Eradication. Even though she had slain him twice—the second time, for good—he never quite left her thoughts when her loved ones were close. The demon had been unique in her experience, terrifyingly good at eluding her. So good that she and Turalyon hadn't even realized he'd been following her that first time, when she had drawn a knife through the throat of the being who looked so much like—no, was identical to, *indistinguishable* from—Turalyon. There had been no telltale whiff of fel about the demonic doppelgänger, only Turalyon's scent, warm and earthy and uniquely *him.* No flaw in the replication of his strong features and bright hair. No indication in the timbre of a voice that made Alleria's heart beat faster when he spoke her name.

Yet Eradication had not been the only enemy who had wielded her love against her. Xal'atath had done the same, had forced her to fight an illusion of Turalyon in an effort to unbalance her . . . and that was a fight Alleria couldn't overcome on her own. Something for which her mentor had given her no end of chastisement.

"Mother?"

Alleria snapped out of her reverie. She had been foolish to think their present problem so easily solved. Their focus now needed to be on a different enemy, one who also enjoyed inflicting torment. Although Alleria chafed at the time being wasted, they had to satisfy Lyana's hunger for victory and then tend to their own. At least Thalyssra and the Duskwatch could—she hoped—take care of the soul engine in their absence.

"I'm fine," Alleria said, her voice calm, her face trained to reveal nothing she did not choose to. Turalyon, of course, almost certainly knew what she had been thinking about. Perhaps to help her recenter, he indicated the fang.

"Does this provide information about how many demons we may be looking to encounter?" Turalyon asked.

"It is an excellent tool for tracking a single demon, but we must rely on our own skills to determine how many we face. I anticipate we will encounter many. Azoran thought highly of Varaskar. It was sheer good fortune that, when I and others entered Felsoul Hold, she was not present, or I doubt I would be speaking with you now. She is one of a handful left with something of a reputation. I anticipate that, like those others, she is pointlessly trying to gather more unto herself to become some sort of warlord leader of this broken world."

There was no longer detachment in Lyana's voice, but neither was it heated. Rage and anger were hot, Alleria knew, and as well, she knew that hatred was cold. The ranger did not know Lyana's history, but in a way, she didn't need to. Something terrible had happened, perhaps long ago, perhaps in recent memory. Was the hatred targeted at only the Flayer? Would killing Varaskar give the Illidari a measure of peace? Or would this hatred that turned her so icy stubbornly persist, a hunger that would need to see the last demon in existence die by her own hand?

"You may not be specifically hunting Varaskar," Lyana continued, "but the one who is feeding the soul engine may well be one of her lieutenants, thinking to fill the position that Azoran left behind. Who knows, Alleria? We may both taste satisfaction today."

Alleria knew that the Illidari could not see her face. Not as others saw it, at least. And the elven ranger wondered if, somehow, the fel sight Lyana had bought by gouging out her own eyes allowed her to see how much—*too* much—Alleria was like her.

"Then lead on," Alleria said, "and we shall see what awaits us."

■ ■ ■

What awaited them, it turned out, was hot, sandy, physical labor.

Mounted once more on their gryphons, Arator, Turalyon, and Alleria followed Lyana's bat as it flew close to the rocky earth of the Bone Wastes, the felhound fang glowing ever more brightly. Arator flew alongside her for a while, trying to engage the Illidari in conversation, but she was disinterested, replying in monosyllables, so he ceased his efforts. After what felt like an eternity of awkwardness, the demon hunter motioned for them to land. There was no tomb entrance, no marker, nothing but the vastness of the Wastes and the bleached bones of the dead.

"She is here," Lyana stated.

Arator looked around. "I . . . don't see any entrance."

"This tomb had never been pillaged by scavengers before Varaskar claimed it," Lyana said. "The demons made their own way in. And," she added, "closed the way behind them."

"Of course," Arator said heavily, "now that they've occupied it, they can come and go through portals and conceal the entrance."

"I had intended to acquire excavation materials from either the Auchenai or the stronghold," Lyana said. "But we four can manage without them."

Alleria, who was examining the rocks, now shot Lyana a look. "Excavation tools would have helped."

Most of the rocks were large, easily placeable with demonic strength but more challenging to mere mortals. "I assumed paladins would not need them. I apologize for overestimating their strength," Lyana said.

Before his father could rebuke her for the barb, Arator said cheerfully, "Oh, we're not half bad if we put our shoulders into it."

"We're not the first to try," Alleria said. "Look at this." They went to join her. It took Arator a minute to see what had caught his mother's attention, but when she pointed, he saw it. Someone had moved several of the smaller stones. "Look at the sand, too," she said, rising.

"They mixed the darker soil in with the sun-bleached," Arator said. "Otherwise, they did a good job. A very good job." Mother and son looked at each other. "The missing stronghold scouts, perhaps?"

Alleria nodded. "And I'm willing to bet they did most of our excavating work for us. We'll thank them when we find them."

"I would not count on them being alive to appreciate your gratitude," Lyana said.

"They are quel'dorei rangers," Turalyon said sharply before either Alleria or their son could speak. "Do not dismiss them so quickly, demon hunter."

Lyana shrugged. "Hope if you wish, but I am here for demons. Let us set to work."

Despite Lyana's quip, it did not take terribly long for the two paladins to move the stones. While they worked, Lyana and Alleria carefully widened the entrance to admit the bulky armor worn by Turalyon and Arator. They paused at the opening to check their packs and weapons before descending. When they were ready, Turalyon closed his eyes.

"May the Light be with us this day," he said quietly. Golden radiance suffused him, gently, affectionately, and he lifted his hand. There was a burst of bright light, and Arator felt the familiar sensation of warmth and comfort and an assurance of well-being.

"Are you all done?" Lyana asked.

"Hey, you're the one with the tooth," Arator said. "Lead the way."

As they entered, Arator inhaled the familiar scent of cool, stale air lightly tinged with incense. He was instantly transported to the first time he had stepped inside Auchindoun, in search of answers about what had happened to his parents. Back then, he always felt that his mother would be less of an enigma. Arator had been raised with her sister Vereesa, had lived in Silvermoon City when he was younger. And, most significantly, he had felt her reach out to him once, when he had been gazing up at her statue in the Valley of Heroes. They had connected in more ways than one, even if he could not be with his mother physically.

But the famous paladin, the mighty Turalyon, one of the first of the Order of the Knights of the Silver Hand . . . he was an intimidating figure to a young half-elven boy. A yearning to know his father was the main reason why Arator had followed the path of the paladin. The stories. The Silver Hand. Auchindoun. When he'd first learned these things, he had been a young man trying to find his family . . . or, if he couldn't find them, at least *know* them. Now, years later, in the dimness of a tomb that few had seen in centuries, Arator felt he was no closer to his father than he had been when Turalyon was little more than a statue and other people's memories.

Arator puffed out a breath of the stale air, returning to the moment. Lyana took point, her feet finding steady purchase amid pieces of rubble and chunks of earth. Arator and Turalyon followed, with Alleria bringing up the rear.

Arator listened closely for movement, voices, any sounds of violence. And his gaze roved the stone beneath, beside, and above them for any signs that might indicate the missing scouts. Among the vast subterranean stretches of Auchindoun he had traversed, the other draenei tombs he had entered bore almost no indications of the original occupants. Their physical remains were long gone from the carefully carved niches, ground to dust under uncaring feet or hauled into the light of day to be tossed into the ivory-hued piles that gave the Wastes their chilling name.

But here in this chamber, the bodies had not been violated by either necromancy or the greed of tomb robbers. The armor had not rusted, though dust and spiderwebs had left a thin film over the once-polished metal. Cloth and leather had fared less well with the passing of time, and Arator could glimpse holes that smaller creatures had chewed. Though there was no sunlight to leach the bright colors from their robes, the hues had faded. Flesh had abandoned bones, which stalwartly held threadbare cloth and dull armor in the shape of what had once been draenei.

And then, there they were.

The hair on the back of Arator's neck lifted. He felt a prickle at the edge of his consciousness, like a barely heard whisper, or the last lingering traces of a scent.

"Ah, you sense the spirits now, too," Turalyon said. "They've been roused from their slumber."

"Hopefully they don't think we're responsible for their rude awakening," Arator said. As paladins, both he and his father could sense the presence of the undead. But because Turalyon had initially trained as a priest, he could do more.

"I don't believe they mean us harm," Turalyon said. "There are only a few, and they're more confused than malicious." A thought seemed to occur to him, one that caused him to smile a little. Turning to Alleria, he said, "Sounds like someone else I know when she's been awakened without a good reason."

Alleria was still focused, but her lips twitched. "That was *one* time."

"Oh, it was enough."

Arator cringed inwardly. One minute, it seemed as though his parents were distant from each other, parallel forces that shared a mission yet never met. The next, they were like this, smiling with secret little jokes built on centuries of companionship. He'd seen them go from one to the other so fast it gave him whiplash.

A thought he did not like but that had occurred to him more than once did so now, like a bitter spirit: *It might have been best for all of us if they had not returned.*

Arator stuffed the thought into the back of his mind just as Lyana came to a halt. Slowly, she placed the fang into her pack and drew the second glaive from her back.

"Demons," she said. "A pack of them. Small."

Faint sounds reached Arator's ears but rapidly grew louder. Even so, by the time a pack of felhounds leaped upon them, the group was more than ready. Arrows flew from Alleria's bow like a steady rain. Arator caught his father's eye and Turalyon nodded. They charged forward, each to one side as they had done before against the felbats. Arator called down the Light, then released it in an explosion that sent the felhounds flying, yelping in torment as they slammed into the walls. Most lay where they had fallen. A few staggered to their feet, stumbling almost drunkenly toward him. Arator swung his two-handed sword like a pendulum, twisting and leaping as it sliced rhythmically through the beasts.

Turalyon, meanwhile, stood and let the first wave of slavering, fel-addled creatures come almost within a hand's length. Then he lifted his sword, and Light crashed down into the stone beneath their feet. The earth shivered, and for a moment, it appeared as if golden lava was swirling upon the rocky surface. It might as well have been, for the beasts yowled when the Light burned their feet and fur. A second prayer brought holy energy down into them directly until all that remained were piles of canid corpses.

Before the second wave could reach him, the high exarch ran to meet it. He swung his Light-blessed sword with controlled, practiced skill, cutting a swath through the beasts first one way, then the other. Holy energy exploded from it, and more demons fell.

Lyana had not been idle, but neither did she waste energy. These creatures were, as she said, small, and she simply put her glaives to work. The style of combat utilized by the Illidari was unique in Arator's experience, and he never ceased to marvel at its combination of grace, power, and pure violence. Now she leaped over and almost danced away from the frustrated felhounds, who growled and snapped with a vengeance, but their gnashing fangs landed only on air or, in a few cases, one another.

The first two waves were eliminated in almost as many minutes, but the third had a little surprise. There were more felhounds, but this time, imps sat, stood, or capered astride the animals' backs. Some launched from one beast to another, springing off backs and heads, cackling hysterically as they fired volleys of fel fire.

"Ugh," groaned Lyana, "what a nuisance. Varaskar cannot truly believe this rabble is enough to stop much of anything."

Annoying though the fel imps might be, there were a *lot* of them. And they had a nasty habit of darting in and out of the Nether, disappearing from one area in a fight and materializing in another, usually behind their intended victim's back.

Arator swung around and caught a gleeful imp just as the portal behind it closed. It leered at him, its mouth full of jagged teeth contorting into a comical *O* of shock as the paladin's blade cut it neatly in half. Arator realized Lyana's style would be well suited to this moment, so he sprang from place to place, as unpredictable as the imps themselves and twice as deadly.

A wave of Light surged forward, dropping the remaining felhounds and stunning their riders. They were not the sharpest swords in the demonic armory, but they knew enough to scurry back to the Nether through a couple of abruptly opening portals. A second blast of Light came from Turalyon, incinerating them on the spot. The hall, which had been filled with the cacophony of creatures shrieking first in defiance and then in pain, fell silent save for the occasional whimper of a dying felhound followed by the hum of Alleria's arrow. None of the four had even broken a sweat.

Alleria approached to stand beside Turalyon while Arator stepped over the bodies to join them. Lyana, a few yards away, had taken out their tooth compass and appeared to be studying it.

"Everyone all right?" Turalyon asked. Arator realized that his father had automatically stepped into the role of commander. He supposed he should not be surprised. It was one thing to embark on a simple reconnaissance mission with family, as they had set out to do initially. It was another to be fighting a pack of demons alongside a stranger.

All said, this mission was actually Lyana's, and if she didn't have a problem with Turalyon's behavior, Arator wouldn't, either. Besides, even if it often chafed, the truth was that Turalyon, High Exarch of the Grand Army of the Light, had led countless campaigns, every one of them likely infinitely more dangerous than what they were presently doing, and with infinitely more at stake.

Everyone nodded.

"Good," Turalyon said. "Lyana, what's in store for us next?"

She shook her head. "I sense no demons nearby."

"I'm not surprised. There's a good chance they don't even know we're here. The hounds and the imps are likely a constant fixture here in case anyone stumbles across the entrance. How far away is our target?"

The Illidari did not answer at once, and she sighed. They exchanged glances and went to her. She showed them the fang.

Its runes no longer glowed.

"What happened?" Alleria asked, her voice sharp.

"I regret to inform you that felhound-tooth dowsing is not an exact science," Lyana said, an edge creeping into her own voice.

"I wonder if something is masking the signal." Arator glanced at the tooth. "Arkonite is fashioned into the mausoleum's structures . . . placed with the bodies when they are laid to rest. The draenei use the crystals to power various technological objects and magic. They might well have confused Haa'zuun when he was alive, just like too many scents and false trails can cause a dog to lose the scent."

Alleria shook her head and turned away, glancing at the walls and floors.

"That makes sense," Turalyon said, "but I don't think it changes anything. We came here to cleanse this holy place of demons. We'll do just that. If Varaskar is still here—and she should be, if Lyana is correct and we've not alerted her to our presence—then we kill her. If she's not, we will resume the hunt when the tomb is purged."

"We came here for Varaskar," Lyana said tightly. "She is the priority. We should not squander our time ridding the entire place of every imp that takes a nap."

Turalyon's armor began to glow, faintly. He took a step toward the demon hunter, straightening to his full height. Lyana was a night elf, and Arator knew she was the taller. But as the high exarch approached her, she somehow did not seem to be.

"You have invited a pair of paladins to assist you, Lyana," Turalyon said. His voice resonated with every word. "We have a sacred duty here, and we *will* perform it."

"You've invited an elven ranger, too," Alleria said. "And I have my duty."

Arator turned. His mother stood facing the wall, freshly painted with imp and felhound gore. But that interested her not at all. She was regarding another, smaller splotch on the wall. It, too, was blood, but dried, and dark red.

Carefully she extended a hand and plucked a single thread of golden hair from the red splotch.

"They have the scouts," she said.

CHAPTER EIGHT

Auchindoun

TEROKKAR FOREST, OUTLAND

"Now we must look for hostages, too?" Lyana exclaimed. "Let us at least eliminate Varaskar first!"

"No," everyone said, almost at the same time.

"Look," Arator interjected, stepping forward. "Lyana, I understand your frustration. The scouts may have valuable information about Varaskar and her forces. And if we make sure no demon survives to report back, our chances of surprising Varaskar are much higher."

Her head turned toward each family member and then she sighed. "Very well." To Turalyon, she snapped, "You must have annoyed Lord Illidan to no end."

"The feeling was mutual," Turalyon replied.

They continued deeper into the tomb. Alleria had been keeping an eye out for any signs of the missing scouts the entire time, and she knew Arator had as well. This was the first sign, and it was both heartening and alarming. Lyana's dark prediction that they would not find the scouts alive had been Alleria's as well, though she did not say so, and she loved Turalyon for speaking up for them. Finding blood on the wall indicated that the demons were carrying the scouts, and demons had no reason to carry corpses. But if Varaskar was the one reviving the soul engine, she could be preserving the scouts as sacrifices.

Alleria reminded herself that where there was life, there was a chance to save it. Arator and Turalyon were also in better spirits with the discovery, and they fell into a rhythm as they made their way through the tomb. Fighting demons was one thing on which they could all agree, all excel, and it was satisfying to be in harmony. Back-to-back they fought, the reek of fel around them, the cacophony of so many different demonic noises battering their ears. In their souls resided a calm surety that *this* was where they were meant to be, what they were meant to do.

But Alleria found herself glancing at Lyana, noting a strange resemblance between herself and the Illidari.

Lyana seemed to have nothing in her life but the hunt. In the hours since dispatching the felhounds, she had spoken of nothing but tactics. Nothing but her goal; nothing but the Flayer. At this moment, she had the opportunity to speak with two people who had spent countless years pursuing the same end. They had learned much the Illidari could have benefited from, yet she asked them no questions. She knew they would perform well, and that was all she needed to know. Lyana was not cool, but cold; not focused, but obsessed.

It was a mindset with which Alleria was all too familiar. After the destruction of Dalaran, and even the year before, she had given free rein to her extreme focus on the Dark Heart and Xal'atath. As she permitted neither her son nor her lover to accompany her, she could speak to the cost of so singular a purpose. She heard again the words of Locus-Walker, her ethereal tutor in the ways of the Void: *Your greatest fear is endangering your family. But you must let go of that fear.*

In Locus-Walker's mind, the only way to accomplish this would be to let go of *them.*

There had been moments—many of them—when she came close to taking that advice. When she thought to trade her own happiness for their safety. For now, though, she chose to wear the love of Turalyon, Arator, Vereesa, and her friends as a strength. Where the Void had once whispered to her of fears and futures that might befall them, she had grounded herself in the challenges before her and the power she held to face them. The Void was part of her now, and she had learned to integrate its powers without assuming its form or constantly hearing its maddening influence. And she had done it by holding on to those connections.

Did Lyana have such friends or family to comfort her? People she sought to protect?

Was Lyana what Alleria would have become, had she made that difficult choice?

"Alleria?"

Turalyon's touch on her shoulder caused her to jump. His gold-brown eyes were troubled.

"Sorry," she said. "Just . . . lost in thought."

"We will get to the bottom of all this, don't worry," he reassured her. He smiled that smile she loved, the one that made her believe, just for a moment, that everything really might be all right in the end.

But Mauvara and her child would not celebrate. They would mourn. And there would always be another threat, and another. They would never really be safe.

Between her rumination and the fast pace with which they moved through the tomb, Alleria was off her stride the next time they charged into a room full of the enemy. Instead of focusing on her own targets, as she had done previously, the ranger found her attention drifting to Arator, then flitting back to the battle. She would pepper the demons with arrows, locate her son, then return to the next cluster to fall beneath her missiles.

Arator was good. He did not need her watchful eye. Alleria knew it, and yet she found herself distracted again and again, growing angrier with herself each time.

Alleria knew Turalyon's fighting style down to the last detail and would recognize him on any battlefield, no matter what armor he wore or weapon he wielded. He charged into the fray, drawing the enemy toward him, and then utilized his blade and his prayers to make all fall beneath him. Sometimes he would appear to go down under overwhelming numbers, but it never lasted. Sooner or later, he would rise, plant his feet, and those who sought his death would perish.

While his father had shared some sword skills with him, and Arator did make use of them when they were to his benefit, their son was far lighter on his feet. Alleria noticed that despite his armor, he sometimes even employed *her* moves, leaping toward an enemy but from the side, and every now and then he'd employ the deeply familiar Farstrider techniques, no doubt imparted to him by Lor'themar. At one point, Alleria caught him darting through a group of demons with nary a blow falling upon him, and she realized that her son had adopted the Illidari techniques, dancing lightly through the battlefield. This unsettled her, and she did not understand why. If it worked for him, why should he not take this tactic for his own?

Even as she thought this, she saw a demon fall at every zig and zag. Arator whirled to slice the head off an imp, ducked the dive of a felbat, and thrust forward with his blade at a felhound who seized his arm and pulled him off his feet. Alleria glimpsed another felbat diving toward him.

"*Arator!*" Alleria nocked an arrow and let it fly. It hit the creature in the eye, even as Arator brought his sword up to slice himself free of its grasp. Slain at once, the felbat tumbled in freefall, Arator caught up in its erratic plunge toward the stone floor.

Alleria watched in helpless horror. Arator had been pulled off-balance by trying to deal one blow too many. He likely would have freed himself cleanly, and called upon the Light to protect himself from falling, but her son and the demon were now entangled and he could not do so.

Turalyon's voice, backed by the Light, cut through the chaos like a powerful, pure chord of music. Light swirled around Arator, seeming to weave a protective net about him, and when the felbat's body crashed into its fellow demons, Arator landed on his feet and proceeded to attack. He was completely unharmed.

"*Look out!*" came Lyana's voice.

Alleria did, springing up and turning around to see Lyana. Her glaives moved so swiftly they blurred in Alleria's vision and looked like nothing so much as the propellers on a gnomish flying machine.

The felbat that had targeted Alleria dropped in multiple chunks, and Alleria realized that the Illidari had saved her life. A life that Alleria herself had put at risk out of fear for Arator. She'd jeopardized all of them. Alleria grumbled softly, but there was no time to rebuke herself about it. She had to fight.

It was all over soon afterward. They caught their breath, and Alleria braced herself for blame. It did not come. Alleria noticed Turalyon's face was drawn. So did Arator, who said a soft prayer of his own and bathed his fellow paladin and father in warm golden light. The color came back into the older man's face, but he sat down and reached for water.

Turalyon drank deeply, then looked up at his son. "You overextended on your lunge and left yourself completely open," he said. There was no heat in the words; Turalyon seemed to not want to waste energy on anger. Alleria slipped down beside him. It was the first time he had paused to rest. The others had, but he had remained standing and alert. He must have endured a grave wound, and she had not even noticed it happening.

Arator, too, was subdued. "You're right. I did. It won't happen again."

"Your mother and I might not be there the next time."

"I know." Arator looked away and blew out a breath. "I'm going to take a look around while we're on a break."

As he strode off, Turalyon said softly, "You were distracted, too, my love." His voice was not chiding but concerned. He reached to brush the lock of hair that had fallen over her forehead, then stopped, realizing his glove was covered in ichor. He lowered it.

"Yes," she said. "I am on edge about the scouts." It wasn't a lie. But it wasn't the reason she had been distracted.

"I meant what I said. We will not count them out."

"I must say *again,* clearing every area is a waste of our energy." Lyana stood over them, her head moving as she met Turalyon's gaze with sightless eyes.

So, she, too, had noticed Turalyon's injury. Alleria was not worried. Turalyon had survived far worse and been able to heal himself. It tired him, of course, but he had recovered. This was little more than a scratch, but Lyana was not so familiar with the paladin's stance and fighting cadence as Alleria.

"If we continue to rouse demons we could simply bypass, one of them is sure to escape and warn her. Our opportunity will vanish."

Ah, so that was it. It was not concern for Turalyon that troubled the Illidari, but the hunt. Always, only, the hunt. Alleria wished she did not understand the other woman quite so well. Out of the corner of her eye, she saw Arator approach, a finger to his lips. Soundlessly, Alleria got to her feet. Turalyon rose as well, slowly and carefully to be as quiet as possible. Lyana stepped forward to join them.

"If this structure has the same design as others," Arator said softly, "there should be a larger open area up ahead. I expect it to be empty, as the last rush of demons came from in front of us, not behind us. Still, we should be cautious, just in case. After that, there should be another pair of chambers, one on either side. I think the left, but I can't swear to it."

He beckoned them to follow him down the wide corridor. After about fifty feet, he paused and pointed.

There had been a scuffle of some sort up ahead. There was more blood, three long smears on the wall and two puddles on the floor. Both were small. Alleria noticed that while the edges had dried, the center of one was still slightly wet.

Best of all, the second had been disturbed.

Bloody prints from a small foot with long, clawed toes smeared the stone of the corridor, continuing for some distance before the blood had all been wiped off, or else the maker of the prints had disappeared.

"Thank the Light," Turalyon said.

"Yes," Arator agreed. "But we should temper our expectations. The imp may not have accompanied the demons and the scouts for long."

"In what world would an imp not torment an injured prisoner as long as possible?" Lyana said drily.

Alleria's heart lifted. This scout had been alive hours ago. They had been alert enough to drag bloody fingers along the wall, indicating the direction. And fate had intervened in the unexpected but welcome form of a sadistic imp. She looked at Turalyon, who smiled at her expression.

"No world that we know of, and we've seen a few," Turalyon said.

Alleria felt the start of a smile of her own. "Then let's find this little fellow and show him our appreciation."

They pressed on with renewed energy and soon discovered Arator had been correct. The corridor opened into an enormous chamber whose original inhabitants provided a gory obstacle course as the four made their quiet way forward. These tombs had been built later than the ones in the heart of the mausoleum. While demons did not have much use for the sort of treasure mortals coveted, they did appreciate magical artifacts. This center area appeared to have been of interest, as several of the niches had been ransacked.

"I can sense some spirits, up ahead," Turalyon said, keeping his voice soft.

"There are about seven demons ahead of us, too, fairly evenly distributed among the chambers. Arator, you said you thought your scouts could be in one of them," the Illidari continued. "Can you or Alleria determine if that's correct and, if so, which one?"

"Not from this distance," Alleria said, gazing down the corridor. "I don't see anything from here. If we could get closer, we might find something to confirm it."

"Or you might not," Lyana said. "And you'd have alerted them to our presence and both rooms would come at us."

"Which would be fine under other circumstances," Arator said. "We could handle them. But they might kill the scouts first."

"I think it's worth the risk," Alleria said. "There's no way to know if we don't check."

"Yes, there is," Turalyon said. His head was still turned as if he were gazing down the hall, but his eyes were closed, and his face had softened. He was limned with a faint light.

Arator understood at once. "Which corridor?"

"The spirits are in the left one," Turalyon said, opening his eyes. "It's a good bet they'd be where the scouts are."

He shone in that moment in a way Alleria hadn't seen in a long time. Not with righteous wrath or implacable justice, but with a peaceful calm, strong but gentle. Their eyes met, and she saw the wonder and joy in his, the resolve to do something *good,* and the gratitude that he could do it.

My love, she thought.

The deliberate clanking of paladin armor had alerted the demons, who charged to meet them. Even as the enemy raced at them from both sides, Arator darted through them, searching for the scouts while his father distracted the demons with both the Light and his sword. Alleria stood back several yards, firing her arrows even as Turalyon and Lyana fought. Most of the demons went down quickly, but two felguards had been stationed among them and the hulking creatures initially seemed more irritated than injured. This was the first time the group had clashed with a major threat as opposed to an army of smaller ones, and they were down one, as Arator's attention was focused on the captives.

But even so, the combination of ranger, Illidari, and paladin quickly disabused the demons of an easy victory. Turalyon, Light-blessed and focused, held the full attention of one felguard. It started bellowing at him in Eredun as it was slammed again and again with the Light while Turalyon slashed its unprotected side. The felguard toppled over, and Turalyon delivered a finishing blow. Lyana's glaives sliced ribbon after ribbon of cuts in the other while Alleria fired. At one point, it swatted at the rain of arrows, turning to glare at her—which did nothing save give her the opportunity to sink arrows into its tiny eyes. It keened, an echoey, deep sound, and swayed. The nimble Illidari sprang upward with a cry of her own and slashed its throat. It tumbled, dead before it hit the stone floor.

A cry of relief came from one of the rooms, and the combatants turned to see Arator . . . and the two scouts, both on their feet. The bloodstains and cuts in their clothes were testament to at least some of what they had endured at demonic hands, but Arator had healed their wounds. And it would seem watching Arator's parents bring down the demons had helped mend their spirits as well.

One of them swayed slightly. Turalyon caught him and eased him down gently. "Don't push too hard," he cautioned, handing him his own waterskin. "Drink and eat something first."

"Thank you, High Exarch," the scout said, accepting gratefully.

"All of you," the second scout said as Turalyon handed her some rations. "We were as good as dead."

Turalyon looked at Arator. "You took good care of them quickly, son. Well done."

"Thanks," Arator said, and Alleria could see he was genuinely pleased by the compliment.

As they ate, the scouts gave their report. Their four rescuers already knew the first part: why they had been sent. What they wanted to know was why the scouts had been spared.

"We have been wondering that ourselves, although we are grateful," said the woman, Endriss. "They knocked us unconscious, and when we awoke, we were gagged, bound with fel chains, and being carried by a felguard."

"We struggled, both of us," Tiramin said. "I fear I struck my head on the wall and only succeeded in rendering myself unconscious again."

"You did more than that," Arator told him kindly. "We saw the blood and strands of gold hair."

"Then the lump was worth it," Tiramin said, rubbing the back of his skull.

"What did they say?" pressed Lyana.

"Not much," Endriss said. "They said only a little that we understood, and I'm certain that was done to frighten us. I cannot vouch for any of its veracity. They spoke about someone called the Flayer. I think she's the one in charge here. One of them seemed to enjoy telling us in detail what she would do to us."

"Varaskar the Flayer," Lyana said. "Whatever this demon told you about her methods of torture is likely true. Go on."

"I think they were saving us for something special," Tiramin said darkly. "An imp latched onto my arm at one point and tried to bite it off, but the felguard killed it at once."

Alleria glanced over at Turalyon. "Couldn't risk him bleeding to death," she said, and he nodded.

"Did the demons mention any other names, or reveal any plans? Refer to soul engines, perhaps, or Felsoul Hold?"

Both scouts shook their heads.

Lyana sighed. "Imps will chat about anything at any point if you let them talk long enough. A pity the felguard cowed them all."

"I'm not familiar with Felsoul Hold," Endriss said. "Why would they mention that? What's going on there?"

Before Alleria or Turalyon could say anything, Arator spoke. "It's a place in Suramar, occupied by demons during the last Legion war. There used to be a soul engine there. It was destroyed years ago, but now it's up and running again. You might have been spared death here in order to feed it."

Alleria bit her lip as she watched Turalyon's face, so open a short while ago, shutter, and he was very still.

"Inform Auric upon your return," Arator instructed the now

wide-eyed scouts. "Tell him if anyone comes through Allerian Stronghold with any news about similar activity, he's to report it to First Arcanist Thalyssra in Suramar."

"Of course," Endriss responded, getting to her feet. Tiramin did likewise.

They both embraced Arator. "It's just like you to randomly wander in when we needed you most," Endriss said.

"Next time, we'll buy you as much Brightsong Wine as you can hold." Tiramin turned to the other three. "We owe you everything. Thank you."

"What, no Brightsong Wine for us?" said Alleria, hoping to lighten Turalyon's mood.

"Of course! All of you," Tiramin exclaimed.

"You're pretty free with Aeman's wine," Arator said. "We'll hold you to that."

"You should be able to get out the way you entered," Turalyon said. "You won't be bothered by any demons. Light be with you." He lifted a hand and blessed them; they stood straighter, and Alleria knew that any lingering weariness would be gone. The two inclined their heads in thanks once more and set off, running at an easy pace.

"You should not have told them anything about the soul engine, Arator." Turalyon's voice was calm. "It's a serious breach of protocol. We report to Thalyssra."

Arator stared at him for a moment. "What about Kayn? And Lyana?"

"Kayn is a leader of the Illidari, and someone you know and trust," Turalyon replied. "Lyana is in possession of something we need. Both are deeply involved with demon hunting and used to keeping information confidential. Those two are *scouts.*"

"You championed them well enough before."

"Of course I did! But we do not know what we are getting into yet. If we inform the wrong people—"

"So now people who served with you—people who live in *Allerian Stronghold,* for Light's sake—are the wrong people?"

"They quarrel a great deal," Lyana observed.

Alleria did not reply. She strode forward. "You both have good points. And next time we sit down over dinner somewhere with plenty of wine, we will discuss it in detail, but *now is not that time.* Or shall Lyana and I go on without you while you hash it out?"

Arator blew out a breath. "What do you say, Father? Shall we go a few more rounds?" He was still angry, but there was a hint of a smile on his face.

"No," Turalyon said, with no humor at all. "I apologize, my love." He turned to look at Arator as he said, "We will talk later. Let's go."

Lyana was waiting with her arms folded across her chest. "Now that you've done your good deed for the day and had it out, can we go kill Varaskar?"

Arator chuckled ruefully. "Yes, Lyana. We can."

■ ■ ■

Down another level they went, then one after that, eliminating whatever demons they chanced upon. "We have to be getting close," Arator said as they paused for a moment and took swigs from the waterskins.

"We are," Lyana said, and she could not suppress a tremor of excitement in her voice. "The next area marks the end of the tomb, and I can sense several demons clustered together up ahead. If Varaskar is still here . . . she will certainly be with them. Do not be careless. All shivarra are powerful, and she is particularly ruthless."

"Then I won't hold back," Alleria said. "I'll do whatever I must."

It was out there now. The family had, deliberately or not, avoided discussing Alleria's connection with the Void ever since she'd returned from Khaz Algar . . . for the moment, at least. Arator had brought it up once or twice but had never had a candid conversation about it—how she controlled it, what it meant now when she used it—and that suited Alleria. As she spoke, she glanced over at the man she loved.

For centuries, Alleria had embraced the Void as Turalyon grew ever more dedicated to the Light. It remained odd and awkward, that two as close as they were connected to powers that inherently repelled each other. Alleria had made peace with it, but she knew the Void, reasonably enough, still concerned Turalyon. It was well integrated into her now, and she rarely needed to call on the true extent of her power. But she needed to know that she could.

Turalyon understood. "I trust you, your judgment, and your strength."

"Father and I are in agreement on this," Arator said.

"Do what you will, just bring her down," Lyana said. "Are we ready?"

Something shifted in Alleria. The wariness in her did not disappear, not yet, but she saw no wariness in Turalyon. Heartened, she nodded.

"Let's go."

They hastened toward the turn, paused, listened, then started down the wide hallway. But as they approached the final chamber, they realized that the next room was barred. Not by swarms of demonic defenders, but by a huge door. Draenei runes, intended to protect this, the innermost sanctum, had been defaced, covered by demonic glyphs and insults. Fel radiated from it, and it towered over them as if mocking them for having come this far, only to be thwarted.

"They are on the other side," growled Lyana. "But I recognize those runes. They make for powerful wards."

"And draenei built these walls to withstand exactly such an attack," Turalyon said.

"And yet, Varaskar breached them . . ." Arator began, trailing off. "Something's not right."

"Indeed," Turalyon said. "I see the wards, but I'm not sensing them."

"Neither am I," Arator said. "Could something of the draenei's power still be resisting them? Diminishing their strength, somehow?"

"I have studied with many who are strong with the Light, including the draenei," his father said. "I have learned their history. I've never heard of anything like this."

"I'll go investigate it," Alleria said. "The demons may have a surprise or two for those who would simply put their shoulders to it."

"They likely know we're here," said Lyana. Her body was taut, and she gripped her glaives tightly.

Alleria understood how she felt, but when confronted with something completely outside the knowledge of four experienced fighters, caution was the only way to proceed. She examined the area with her eyes first. The dust had been disturbed, verifying that someone had recently entered. The scent of fel was strong, although unlike their Illidari ally, she could not sense the power of that cruel energy.

Alleria approached the chamber, lightly and indirectly, ready to leap out of the way in an instant should a trap close about her.

She knelt at the foot of the gargantuan door, wondering how tightly shut it was and if anything could slip in—or out. The draenei gave the dwarves a run for their money when it came to carving stone, at least when protecting their honored dead. The bottom of the door seemingly created a seal with the ground, perfectly level.

Alleria frowned.

Perfectly level. There was no sign of burrowing creatures, of chips or flakes. She thought about the scent of fel. So strong . . .

She reached out carefully to touch the door.

Her hand went *through.*

"Look out!" Alleria cried, leaping back as four heavily armed felguards and dozens of felhounds ran through the still-active illusion. Part of her brain was still working it out, wondering how none of them had noticed a single sound from the small army waiting with the patience of eons to ambush them. The other part was commanding her body to twist in midair, retract her bow, and fire.

Her warning saved their lives. All had been as tense as she, and equally ready to respond. The ground beneath the demons began to glow with Holy Light, and most of the felhounds either died on the spot or collapsed, shrieking.

The felguards, though, were made of sterner stuff and kept coming. Turalyon met one head-on, swinging his blade and shouting prayers, the image of a mighty golden hammer slamming down upon the enemy with the Light's power behind it. Arator and Lyana darted around the larger, more lethal demons. Glowing green fel that passed for blood spattered everywhere as demons dropped before sword, glaive, and arrow. As usual, Alleria stayed back far enough to kill from a distance, finishing off badly wounded demons so the other three could keep up the speed of their attacks.

"Press forward!" cried Turalyon from his position at the front.

"I have the rear!" Alleria called back. The other three surged, stepping over bodies, some still writhing. As she had promised, Alleria followed, making sure that those still trying to fight went down for the last time.

Lyana, Arator, and Turalyon had sprung past the pile of corpses by the time Alleria had finished her task, and as she raced after them, she saw their quarry and three of her lieutenants.

Varaskar the Flayer was, like most shivarra, both beautiful and terrifying. She held back, smiling cruelly, as more felguards surged forward to take on the intruders. Alleria realized that while the door had been only an illusion, the chamber was indeed grander than any she'd seen before. The Flayer was perched atop a structure that doubtless housed the remains of many noble draenei, one leg dangling languidly while her six hands busied themselves prepping for her own fight, should her lieutenants fail her. Two hands grasped blades, while a third held a whetstone as large as a boulder, alternating between honing one black sword then the other. The long, sharp nails of a fourth hand drummed against the crypt's roof. Her remaining pair of hands held a whip crowded with spikes and a long, thin fillet knife. Varaskar's tongue snaked out to lick her lips in anticipation as she surveyed the slaughter before her.

"Clever," she called. "Most intruders attempt to break it down and run right in. Yet you still fell into my trap."

The demon's voice was lyrical, and Alleria sensed its mesmeric power but was utterly unmoved by it. Compared to the years she had held the Void at bay, this distracted her as little as a leaf falling against her cheek. Alleria hoped the enemy could sense her utter indifference, perhaps even mild amusement.

"I know who you are," Varaskar continued to taunt. "It's an honor, truly. The high exarch himself. So bright and shiny! I will rip that metal skin off you with a single finger . . . and remove the softer one beneath it with more delicacy."

Her words did not rattle Turalyon, either, of course, and Alleria seldom feared for her lover. But she had not spent enough time with Arator to know what, if any, his experiences with shivarra had been thus far. She knew his heart was strong, if sometimes impulsive, and his nature as kind as his father's. But still—

"And my, *Arator*, how nice to meet you at last!"

Alleria froze for an instant, forgetting to breathe. Then logic returned. Of course the shivarra would know her son. Alleria had little doubt that Arator had made his own impression on the demons of the Legion.

Even so, neither of his parents liked hearing their son's name coming from fel lips. It was a constant reminder that despite their centuries scouring the Great Dark Beyond, they had somehow still failed to fully protect him.

Arator uttered a heartfelt prayer, and Light buffeted a felguard. Alleria could see it oozing green liquid from dozens of wounds. It bellowed and drew into itself, trying to hide from the Light that would not permit it to escape.

Alleria fired arrow after arrow, aiming for the wounds themselves so the arrowheads would pierce even deeper. As she did, Lyana, Arator, and Turalyon closed in, each from one side.

With a defeated groan, the felguard stumbled, swayed, brought down his weapon erratically, and then toppled.

Varaskar was down to a single defender.

The shivarra had sat back thus far, toying with her weapons and shouting distractions at the interlopers. Alleria wondered if the demon would continue to do so, wanting to have the undivided attention of her esteemed guests. Instead, the Flayer rose with effortless grace and hurled the enormous whetstone at Turalyon, who deflected it with a protective shield of Light. The final felguard descended upon him, and Arator rushed to his father to help him repel the fiend.

Lyana Darksorrow did not.

Varaskar held blades in her middle right and left hands. Her lower hands held her skinning knife and the whip, which she now cracked with enthusiasm. Her upper hands drew symbols in the air, whorls and dots of shadowy energy, almost hypnotic.

Lyana stood before her, raising her glaives, staring up at the face of the demon she had hunted so diligently. Varaskar chuckled softly, walking slowly toward the much smaller figure.

"Little Illidari," the demon purred. "Have we . . . met before? I don't recall your name, but you look so familiar. Do you think you can defeat me all by yourself?"

"She doesn't have to," Alleria shouted. She fired at the demon, and all at once, Varaskar's movements became swifter than the eye could follow, dodging the arrows, moving in a blur.

Nonetheless, the arrows were distracting and disorienting her, and now, done with their target, both paladins raced toward the object of the hunt. Turalyon sprang forward, wreathed in Light, bringing his sword down with all the strength of his body and faith behind the blow. The blade sliced cleanly through all three arms on Varaskar's right side, but Turalyon was not quick enough to evade the lightning-fast strike of her spike-studded whip. Varaskar, too, had swung with all her might. The whip snaked around him, the spikes finding the weak points in his armor with hundreds of little daggers, then the demon snapped the whip and released the paladin, hurling him several yards away to slam into the wall.

A Void arrow embedded itself into the demoness's lovely, hate-filled face. Furious, Varaskar clapped a hand to the wound and turned the full force of her anger upon Alleria, gathering fel energy around her free hand. Turalyon stirred, recovering as the Light rushed to heal him. He ran back toward the fray.

But Lyana was not about to share her kill.

A cloud of fel energy whirled around the Illidari as she arched her back, screaming wordlessly. Varaskar's head whipped around, her lips curling in annoyance. Lyana leaped upward on feet transforming into hooves, howling her fury as her body grew larger and larger, her purple skin darkened, and the fel runes glowed and pulsed. Wings all but exploded from her back, and she hovered in the air as they beat, roaring as she fixed her magical gaze upon her enemy. Fel shot out from where her eyes had once been, and Varaskar staggered back a pace, gasping in pain and surprise.

Alleria understood that the Illidari housed a demon within them, and she knew something of what that was like. That the Illidari sometimes manifested a demonic form to access that demon's powers, she also knew, and had glimpsed from a distance on the battlefield. But witnessing the metamorphosis in someone a few steps away from her was still a shock.

"*Lyana!*" came Turalyon's horrified voice.

Alleria couldn't blame him for his fear. Before them now was a being who was one reckless step away from becoming a true monster, and for an awful moment Turalyon seemed uncertain as to who he should kill first.

But Varaskar made the choice clear when she extended a long arm, grasped Arator with one hand, and brought him close to her face. Her lips formed words that could not be heard over the fray. Turalyon threw himself into attacking with all his power and skill. Green fel and golden Light flashed, directed with ferocity toward the same demonic target. Alleria, her own fear and fury near boiling, took aim at the demon's eye and fired repeatedly.

Varaskar threw Arator down, one hand going to her injured eye. Lyana sprang upon her with a gleeful cry, unleashing every reservoir of power she had in this form to beat her adversary to her knees.

With three arms severed, the shivarra was off-balance and fell, and the floor trembled. Turalyon placed the tip of his sword on Varaskar's throat.

Lyana slammed a cloven hoof down into the demon's abdomen and lifted her glaives. "You'll remember me now," the Illidari cried, her voice much deeper and echoing.

Arator had rolled as he fell, springing up at once. Now he raced toward the fallen demon. "Lyana, no! Father, keep Varaskar down!" he cried.

Turalyon gestured. Light flared, forming yellow-white shackles that clamped around the shivarra's ankles and remaining arms. She thrashed in agony as Arator rushed up.

"Tell them what you told me!" Arator shouted, his face flushed and his voice raw with outrage.

Varaskar chuckled, then coughed, spewing fel. "You all think you're such heroes. So strong."

"We have you bound, wretch," Turalyon shot back.

"And how many others are left to take my place?" Varaskar kept her eyes locked with the paladin's.

"It is immaterial," Lyana growled, still in her demonic form. "If I alone remain in this world, I will hunt you down one by one."

"The Legion is broken," Alleria said.

Lyana stamped again, and this time Varaskar couldn't mask the pain. Still, she forced a smile.

"The Legion may have lost its leaders," she agreed, "but the Grand Army of the Light has lost its *purpose.* While the Lightforged lick their wounds on your pitiful planet, a hundred thousand Legion worlds rally our forces! Did you really think you could hide here forever? You've led us right to—"

Her words ended in liquid rasps as Lyana, snarling in impatience, shredded her throat. A river of liquid fel gushed forth. Arator and the demon hunter both leaped clear of its path, Arator springing to the side and Lyana flying upward. She hovered for a moment, then landed a few feet away. Heaving a sigh, she leaned slightly on her glaive, exhausted. Turalyon marched up to her, seized her arm, and spun her around to face him.

"What did you do, demon?" he shouted. "She was going to—"

"Do nothing but buy time and get under our skin." Lyana yanked her arm free from Turalyon's grip as her cloven hooves and wings vanished, and she regained her smaller form. "You of all people should know *that*, High Exarch! Deceit is as intrinsic to them as fel! There was no need to listen to her poison. They've been saying the same thing since we crushed their forces years ago. Trust me, I know."

Alleria bit her tongue. Likely, the Illidari *did* know more about the remaining demons than her family. Still, whatever Varaskar had said to Arator had unsettled him.

Lyana went to her backpack and brought out the wrapped fang. "Here," she said stiffly to Alleria as she handed it to the other woman. "I kept my word." She paused, then said more calmly, "Thank you for your aid. Varaskar was the last of the demons that I know operated in Felsoul Hold."

Alleria started to ask how she knew, then realized it was because the Illidari had already killed all the others. She accepted the fang wordlessly.

"Where will you go next?"

Lyana shrugged. "Wherever there are demons." She nodded politely to Arator but ignored Turalyon, walking toward the corpse of her fallen enemy, her glaives still dripping fel. Then, she gracefully sat on the cold stone floor, simply staring at the demon's slack face. Alleria could not even guess what was going through the Illidari's mind, and she was glad of it.

"Let's go," she said quietly. The three turned and left Lyana alone with her thoughts and the dead demon.

Once they were out of earshot, Turalyon said, "I am still furious with her for killing Varaskar so quickly. What did she tell you, Arator?"

"Nothing I didn't know, really, but I had hoped she'd keep talking. She said the demons know all about me, and I'm a dead man, and you're both dead, too, and they'll keep hunting me till the ends of time just to torture you, and so on." He grinned a little. "Lyana was right. The usual."

Alleria's heart felt as though someone had squeezed it, and her eyes sought Turalyon's. Her pain was mirrored in them. The reason they had fought for so long, so hard, and given so much of themselves had been to keep their world, and their child who lived in it, safe. In her son, she saw a young Turalyon, innocent and full of hope. Turalyon had been forced to move past his innate nature by war. Alleria had as well, but it had been easier for her.

She had hoped so fervently that Arator would not choose a path that would place him in harm's way, but in their absence, he had done exactly that. She supposed that was inevitable; their blood ran in his veins, after all. And now she and Turalyon were forced to accept that their efforts to spare him the worst, in the Nether and since their return, had little changed his course.

They continued without speaking, quietly stepping over the bodies littering the stone floor. At last, Arator broke the awkward silence. "We should call the gryphons back and return them to Shattrath City," he said. "After that, I think we've earned some rest before continuing."

"We should return to Felsoul Hold and attune the fang," Alleria said.

"Wise," said Turalyon.

Arator scoffed impatiently. "You two never stop, do you? I mean . . . look what we did here today." He gestured at the trail of bodies surrounding them. "At least we could stop *somewhere* for a drink and a bath. I stink of fel, and frankly, so do you."

To her surprise, Alleria found herself chuckling a little.

Arator seized on it. "Besides, you've never returned to Hellfire Peninsula. To see it, to see old friends."

"I . . . don't need to," said Alleria. "You and Turalyon can—"

The older man sighed. "Love, I think our son is right."

"We have already been to the . . . stronghold." Alleria still couldn't bring herself to say the name.

"Yes, and I'm glad, and I hope you are, too," Turalyon said. "But Arator came to Hellfire as soon as the Dark Portal reopened." He was speaking to Alleria, but he turned to look at his son. "He came looking for us." Arator acknowledged his father's effort with a slight nod. "We all know people there. We should stay, at least one night while we rest and recover our strength."

"The soul engine . . ." Alleria began, but already she knew she had lost the fight.

"We will return first thing in the morning. Besides, Thalyssra was sending a Duskwatch contingent to keep an eye on it in our absence," Arator reminded her. "Even if they've done nothing more than establish a perimeter, we'd be stronger for resting a few hours before resuming the hunt. We've been up for . . . what, two days straight? Three? Traveling to other worlds skews my time sense."

Alleria knew that the soul engine wasn't the true reason she wanted to hurry back to Azeroth. It was, she suspected, at least in part, her desire to resume another hunt . . . for the frustratingly elusive Xal'atath. She did not *want* to see old friends. The emotions stirred up by Auric and Taela had been difficult enough, and she'd had the excuse of finding the demon to keep those interactions as brief as possible. How to explain to those at Honor Hold what she and Turalyon had been through without seeming arrogant, or neglectful? And how to justify the fact that, once the Legion had been defeated . . . they had not returned?

But even though she did not like Turalyon's decision, she was glad he had supported their son. And she could see on Arator's face that he was, too.

"I suppose we owe it to them," she said. And they did, even if it meant they might be received with resentment.

"And," she added, "we all need a good scrubbing."

"It's settled, then," said Arator, but Alleria noticed that Turalyon had a contemplative look on his face.

"Before we go," he said, "there is one more place that your mother and I should visit."

"Take your time," Arator said. "We'll meet at the inn."

CHAPTER NINE

The Dark Portal

HELLFIRE PENINSULA, OUTLAND

Alleria and Turalyon stood before it, silent, staring, each alone with their thoughts.

The Dark Portal.

The orcish Horde, manipulated by Gul'dan and the Shadow Council, all puppets for the Legion, had flooded through, intent upon claiming fertile, vibrant Azeroth for their own, and the courage of that world's people closed it.

Without speaking, without moving, each sought the other's hand and clasped it firmly, entwining fingers as if they would never let go again.

Alleria and Turalyon had landed their gryphons at the base of the second level of the Stair of Destiny, unwilling to set foot on the vilely named Path of Glory, which led to the Dark Portal. From gryphonback, one could not discern the skeletons that had been trampled into the sunbaked soil by countless orcish and demonic feet. The path had been paved with the bones of fallen draenei; it was long and wide, and Turalyon could not bear to think of the uncountable number who had been slain during its creation. Everything about this monument to hubris, fel rage, and brutality was outsized. It had been designed for an army of orcs to climb and pass through, countless in number, shoulder to shoulder, fueled by cursed blood and lies. To inspire terror and obedience from those who could see it from miles away.

Massive demon horns lined this final set of stairs climbing up to the portal itself. Alleria looked at the two hooded figures guarding either side of the aperture. Two orbs of fel whirled inside each of the empty cowls, giving the appearance of glowing green eyes. Perched atop the structure lurked a dragon, only its gargantuan stone head and foreclaws visible.

The harshness of the dying world had worked its grimness upon the stone. Chips and cracks dotted the figures and the dragon. Some of the damage had been caused by the cruelty of fel and time; some seemed to have been made by mortals and their weapons of war.

"It looks . . . small," Turalyon finally said. "Frail, almost."

"It is still tall," Alleria said.

"You know what I mean." His voice was soft. He squeezed her hand, and she squeezed back. "It's stone now. No flood of enemies, no battle sounds. It's merely stone that's been worn by the elements. As if it was nothing of import, or threat."

"As if lives, generations, had never been sacrificed for it," Alleria said, her voice equally soft. "But we were there. Many now living weren't, or were too young to remember, like our son. For them, this is what they know of it. Stories, and this."

"I wonder if it will ever be forgotten," mused Turalyon. "Or if it should be. I wonder if they will keep telling the stories, long after Outland itself crumbles into stardust."

"I do not know," Alleria said. "High elves have always lived long lives. Things must be ancient indeed to become tales others must tell us."

He chuckled softly. "Remember when we went to Stormwind and saw the statues they'd erected in the Valley of Heroes?"

Alleria winced. "It was . . . awkward to see statues memorializing our deaths."

He shook his head. "I am still surprised that Faol thought I could even be a paladin, for Light's sake. The people I led were more worthy. They followed without question or knowledge of how the choices had been reached most of the time. They fought, and they died trusting us."

Now it was Alleria's turn to squeeze his hand. "Yes. Many did. But many more, so many more, *lived,* my love. Because of your wise head, and your kind heart."

He was blushing now, something Alleria enjoyed immensely. "The same is true of you," he countered. "Your tactics, your courage, your unstoppable desire to save your people."

She laughed softly. "I do not think my heart would be described as *kind,* though."

"It is to those who know and love you," Turalyon replied. "And even those who do not would still say your heart is strong and fierce. Every day of this strangely long life I have lived since I met you, I am grateful that somehow, that heart found room for me."

The words, spoken at this place, at this time, moved Alleria more than she thought he would ever understand. This was no flirtatious conversation, no comfortable, relaxed moment at a gathering of loved ones. They were here, at a place that represented the end of so very much. And yet, these were his words, his thoughts, uncalculated and simple and pure.

"Found *room*?" she said. "Save for my family, my heart was hollow before I met you. It knew no joy, no life, only duty, death, and struggle. You filled it, Turalyon, in a way I never thought to experience. And that heart grew even fuller when Arator entered it."

"As did mine," Turalyon replied. He lifted their joined hands and kissed her fingers. "I never knew my family, but you gave me one to belong to. I am more fortunate than I ever deserved, I think."

"Perhaps," Alleria said playfully.

He laughed out loud at that.

Alleria wondered if the Dark Portal had ever witnessed laughter before. Real, true laughter, of joy and warmth, not the scathing cackling of demons or the battle-crazed. In a way, it was another act of defiance. She looked again at the stone monument to hatred, to lust for power, greed, and ruination. Those behind its creation—the demons and then the deluded orcs—had failed. Those they sought to subjugate remained free. The Legion was scattered, leaderless, and the orcs had rejected their erstwhile masters, liberated themselves, and recovered their lost honor, becoming a proud and great people as they once were.

Impulsively, she squeezed and released Turalyon's hand, knelt, and grasped a stone. She weighed it in her palm, studying the statues, searching for a weakness. Then she took aim and hurled it with all her strength. It turned over in the air as it flew but landed exactly where she wanted it. A crack rippled through the stone muzzle, then the very tip of the dragon's nose—small to the statue, fairly large to the mortals beneath it—crashed to the stone platform.

Turalyon tried to stifle his laugh by covering his mouth with his hand, but a grinning Alleria would have none of it and tugged his hand back into hers. Of one accord, as they so often were, they turned around and began to walk back to their gryphons.

"Do you think . . ." he said, and paused.

"What is it, my sweet?"

"Could you do that to my statue in Stormwind? I've always hated the nose."

■ ■ ■

The flight from the Dark Portal took Turalyon and Alleria over red, rocky land. Nothing grew here, thanks to the destructive power of fel. Turalyon remembered the first time the Sons of Lothar had made their approach to what would become Honor Hold: the dust, the strange sky, the lack of life. It was sickly familiar, as that same force had claimed portions of Azeroth. They had seen this in the Blasted Lands of their own world, but it was devastating to behold here. Turalyon had used the bleakness to rally his troops. *This is the fight we were made for!* he had cried. *More than ever before, we fight for our world now!* And, he mused, for him and for Alleria, it truly had been the fight to which they had dedicated their long lives. The Sons of Lothar had erected Honor Hold in defiance of the land called Hellfire Peninsula. Alleria had been very reluctant to return, and he had been unsure himself, but now he was glad.

The beasts settled down smoothly, and as he handed the reins to the flight master, Turalyon took a quick look to see if he recognized her. No. The dwarf looked to be younger than his son. He did not know her, but he wondered if he had known her parents.

She seemed to know them, though. "I'm guessin' ye're Arator's ma and da," she said.

Turalyon blinked and turned to Alleria. For a moment, they gazed at each other, dumbfounded, and then he cleared his throat. "Yes," he said, "we are indeed."

"Och, lovely tae meet ye!" she exclaimed. "He's a fine lad, ye ought to be right proud of him."

"We are," Alleria said, in a slightly strangled voice.

Turalyon could feel his own laughter trying to escape.

"He left this tae give ye," the flight master continued. "An' welcome back . . . High General. And Ranger Captain." The dwarf's pleasant smile widened into a mischievous one, and she winked as she handed them a small pouch and a rolled-up scroll.

Alleria took them from her. Turalyon didn't dare speak. They walked some distance away until finally Turalyon leaned against the side of a stone building and started shaking with laughter, trying his best to muffle it. Alleria joined him, her hand over her mouth, her face flushed with a similar effort. After a few moments, they caught their breath.

"This will teach me humility," the paladin said at last. "Priest, paladin, high general, high exarch. And now . . . Arator's father."

"Arator's *da,*" Alleria corrected, and hilarity briefly overtook them again. When they had recovered, they opened the scroll to read their son's note.

Sorry I'm not here to meet you as we planned. I hope your visit to the portal was a meaningful one and you're ready to spend time with people who'll be very glad to see you. Because I love you, but mostly because I wish to keep the good reputation I have here, I've arranged for your rooms so you can clean up before you see those people. The keys are in the pouch. I'll see you at dinner, and you'll get to meet some of my friends.

—A

"You know, we could have stayed at the inn at the stronghold," Turalyon mused.

"No," Alleria said flatly.

"I imagine the soap there smells like a forest," Turalyon continued, as if he hadn't heard her. She gave him a mock glare and started striding toward the inn. "Water's precious here, remember," he added as he followed her. "We *may* have to scrub ourselves with sand."

"Not. Another. Word." But Alleria was trying not to smile.

Turalyon was enjoying the banter. For so long, they had been stiff around each other, only occasionally slipping into a softer way of being. But during the trip, bit by bit, they had behaved more like the people they had been before. Before the Light and the Void had changed them.

It was cool inside, a refuge from the unnatural heat. Even here, it seemed, an inn was an inn. Dim lights, raised voices, a stickiness to the floor that felt the same from Stormwind to Suramar. There was presently no large, cheery fire in the hearth, but Turalyon had memories of cold nights when the fire burned bright and warm.

They glanced around. Most of the patrons were weary adventurers, coming in for a meal or a drink. They looked weary and travel-worn, their clothes stained and torn. Turalyon noticed a dwarf so covered with sand that it sifted downward every time she lifted her tankard, and he nudged Alleria.

"See?" he said. "Sand."

Before she could deliver a glorious retort, they heard a familiar voice.

"Turalyon and Alleria! About time you showed up!"

Several heads turned at the names, but Turalyon paid them no mind. Sid Limbardi had been one of the finest cooks in the army. He'd willingly continued to prepare meals for them at the hold, and after all this time . . . he was still here.

Turalyon strode forward to meet his old friend's outstretched arms, then paused, mindful of his spattered armor. Sid read his expression and laughed, and the two men clasped arms. His voice was slightly higher, and raspy, but it was still recognizable.

"I didn't really believe Arator until I saw you both with my own eyes," Sid exclaimed. "Your armor's much nicer than it used to be—when you haven't gotten it all filthy. I'll have it sent over to the blacksmith and get it cleaned."

"It's good to see you, Sid," Alleria said warmly. "I thought you said that when the war was over, you were going to take your pension and open a little inn just outside of Redridge!"

"Bah," the innkeeper said, "I already have an inn. And the ridges are certainly red around here."

Turalyon had once told Sid his long auburn braids made him look like a dwarf. Sid had taken it as a compliment. The braids were still there, but they were graying. He looked smaller now, too, and the smiling face had deep lines etched in it. Turalyon thought of his own face, weatherworn and scarred, and wondered what Sid thought of him. Alleria, of course, had barely changed at all.

"It'll be wonderful to see the three of you together at my inn tonight. What brings you all here?"

"Demon hunting," said Alleria.

Sid laughed. "Of course, why did I even bother asking? Well, I've got a bottle of the good stuff out here I've been saving for a special occasion, and if this doesn't qualify, I don't know what would. It'll be waiting for you."

By the time Turalyon was dressed in clean, if wrinkled, clothes, he felt as if the hot bath had washed away more than sweat, dirt, and demon blood. The lighter mood that had been building between himself and Alleria had been buoyed by seeing Sid and having a moment to relax. He left his room feeling more like himself than he had in some time.

Alleria was at a table already and looked up with a welcoming smile as he approached. Turalyon felt his heart skip a beat. They had both wondered how they would feel upon returning to Hellfire Peninsula, but it seemed they need not have worried. He was grateful that they both seemed to be recalling earlier times, when their love was new and joyous and they faced both perils and wonders together.

"Greetings, startlingly clean stranger," she said. "Come join me for a drink."

"It would be my pleasure, gracious lady."

"There you are," Sid scolded as he hurried to the table carrying a dusty bottle and three glasses. "Thought you'd never come out."

"I was enjoying the sand," Turalyon said, looking perfectly sincere. Sid looked askance at him, and Alleria rolled her eyes. Sid, being a very wise innkeeper and bartender, caught the energy between them and said nothing more, allowing himself a little smile.

The bottle he uncorked was a thing of beauty: old and rare, the spirit within a rich amber hue. Sid poured a small amount into each glass and then set the bottle down. He raised his own glass.

"To old friends," he said simply. Turalyon found himself deeply moved and lifted his glass, clinked it against Alleria's and Sid's, and inhaled the rich, smoky scent before taking a sip. The liquor was fiery and invigorating, but the years had smoothed out its harshness.

"Sid . . . thank you. This is something special," he said.

"Well, so are the two of you. And this one, too!" Sid said, turning to the entrance of the inn. "Looks like we'll need more glasses."

Arator was there, as he had promised, and he smiled at all of them. Beside him was a man clad in priestly raiment. Turalyon didn't recognize him at first. He was elderly, his pate bare save for a few wisps of white hair that clung to it stubbornly. But he was hale and fit, and he radiated joy as he gazed at Turalyon and Alleria.

Then it clicked.

"Father Malgor!" Turalyon exclaimed. He sprang up to embrace the man who had been one of the finest healers in the entire army. Old enough to be Turalyon's father, Father Malgor Devidicus had doted on the paladin as if Turalyon were indeed a son.

Arator's face was soft, shining the same way Devidicus's was. "Father Malgor was one of the first people I met when I came through the Dark Portal," he said.

"It was the strangest thing," Malgor said. "When I first laid eyes on him, I was so confused. I think he got the best of both of you, and that's saying something. I missed you two so much. No one knew what had happened, and I . . . I kind of lost myself there for a while. Made some bad choices." For a moment, he looked haunted, and suddenly older.

Arator's eyes flickered to a tankard someone was raising, back to Malgor, then to his father. Turalyon understood at once, and empathy flooded him.

"But your son helped me find my way back. And you two found *your* way back, too. I thank the Light I lived to see this day."

"I see the father found you," Sid said as he approached with two glasses and a jug of water. He plunked them down, saying to Malgor, "Happy now, you old coot?"

Sid's voice was kind; it was clear this was nothing but affectionate banter between the two men. "Yes, Sid," said Malgor. "I am. Very happy indeed!"

Sid pulled up two extra chairs, and Arator peered at the bottle. "Sid," he said slowly, "is this . . ."

"The good stuff? Indeed it is."

Arator mock-glared at his parents. "I should have brought you here sooner." He poured a little for himself and filled the priest's glass with water. "So," he continued, seeming to choose his words carefully, "your visit . . . how was it?"

He meant the Dark Portal. Turalyon and Alleria exchanged a glance. There was so much to say, but now was not the place or time.

"Profound," Alleria said at last.

Arator nodded. "Good. Now, Sid, are you still serving your famous clefthoof ribs?"

Turalyon's stomach growled at the mention of the dish. Everyone laughed. "Well, the general's placed *his* order, I think," said Sid with a laugh. "Any other takers?"

Alleria and Malgor requested the same. Arator declined, saying his friends were due to arrive any minute. When Sid left, Turalyon said to Arator, "When Sid was an army cook, he always managed to figure out how to make good food with limited, sometimes questionable, ingredients. I don't know how he does it, but I still remember my first bite of clefthoof. *So* good."

"Is it strange, having so many memories?" asked Malgor. "I imagine elves are used to it, but humans don't usually live as long as you have, son." It was a term that the priest had used often with him, so many years ago, but as the paladin regarded Devidicus, healthy but stooped and lined with wrinkles, the word struck Turalyon poignantly.

"I've never thought about it like that," he said. "I'm certain I've forgotten many of them. I think no matter how long you live, the important ones stay with you. Good . . . and bad."

"There are a few I wouldn't mind forgetting," Malgor said, and Turalyon nodded.

There came the sound of people talking over one another and laughing, and a small group poured through the door. They were a lively crew: dwarves, gnomes, draenei, humans, even a few night elves. The customers seemed to know most of them, and the cluster moved of its own accord, like it was a single unit made up of many parts.

Arator sighed. "Alysandria, I told you to just find a *couple* of people."

The kaldorei, her skin a light lavender and her braided hair forest green, shrugged, embarrassed. "You know how word gets around, Arator."

"Ara-*TOR*!" one of the gnomes bellowed.

"Gilfroy," hissed the blood elf, nudging the gnome. "Cut it out. His parents are here!"

"Excuse me while I slip under the table and dissolve into mortified goo," Arator muttered, placing his head in his hands.

Turalyon was delighted. He was going to enjoy this. "Hey, kids," he said, waving at them. "It's nice to meet you all." He noticed a youth standing a bit outside the group, his eyes wide with wonder. He held a cap in his hands and had all but tied it in knots.

"It's all right," Turalyon said kindly, waving the boy forward. "What's your name, son?"

"I, uh, Eadred, sir," he said.

Arator's head snapped up. "Oh, no," he whispered. "Eadred, we talked about this . . ."

"I'm just . . ." Eadred struggled to speak, his face red but his eyes bright. "You're the *high exarch*!"

"That's what they tell me."

"And Lady Alleria! I mean, Windrunner, I mean—"

"Breathe," Alleria said, a little amused.

Eadred gulped air and then said, "You're a legend, and you're so . . . so . . ."

Beautiful, Turalyon mentally filled in. So did Alleria, because she said, "So good an archer?"

"Hey, watch it!" Gilfroy exclaimed. "That's Arator's mother!"

Poor Eadred looked like he'd expire on the spot, but the draenei stepped in, gently pulling his starstruck friend back, unobtrusively shielding him with his body. *He's a born paladin,* Turalyon thought.

"Our apologies, Lady Alleria, High Exarch," he said. "Your son is much loved by those who remained in Outland."

There was a round of nods and murmurs.

"I am Vardaas. My father is one of the Auchenai," the draenei continued. "I met Arator through him, when he first came through the portal. He is a bright spirit, always so kind to my father and our people. My father told him stories about both of you, while you were long away."

The rambunctious crowd was quiet now. "Way to kill the mood, Vardaas," someone in the back muttered.

"Thank you for your kindness to our son when we could not be with him," Turalyon said.

"We of all people certainly understand missing Arator," Alleria said. "We're glad to be here with him."

"Go on," Turalyon said quietly, leaning toward his son. "You needn't stay with us. Have fun with your friends."

"I'm so sorry about Eadred. And Gilfroy. Actually, I'm sorry about every one of them," Arator said.

"Don't be," Alleria said warmly.

Arator rose, clapped Malgor on the shoulder, then started to leave. The priest caught his sleeve, and Arator looked at him inquiringly.

"I . . . thank you, son," Malgor said. "For what you've done for me, all these years."

Arator smiled, warmly, sweetly. "I'm just glad things had a happy ending."

The Light is good, Turalyon thought, and he felt it nestle warmly in his heart while the excellent whiskey warmed his belly.

Arator stopped to say goodbye to Sid and said something to him Turalyon didn't catch. Sid grinned and nodded, and Arator strode off to join his friends.

"I can't take you *anywhere,*" he scolded them, but Turalyon could hear the smile in his voice.

They moved out as one happy throng, their youthful laughter fading, followed by a last, faint "Ara-*TOR*!" from Gilfroy.

Then, Turalyon heard something else, something he knew by

heart but had not heard in far, far too long, and he realized what instructions his son had given Sid as the whole inn lifted their voices:

Oh, rise up, ye Sons of Lothar,
And aye, ye Daughters, too,
Rise up and face the foe, my friends,
We know what we must do!
We're answering the call, and so,
To battle go we all!
Rise up and fight the battles right,
Prove your mettle, show your might,
We'll show the demons such a sight—
Rise up, rise up, rise up!

The song ended with applause, whoops, the clinks of tankards, and cries for another round to wet dry throats. Turalyon's eyes filled with quick tears, and for a moment, he was young again, riding beside Alleria and Khadgar discussing strategy while this marching song had risen around them.

"Sounds like you gave it new lyrics, Sid!" he called to his friend, who was dutifully refilling the empty mugs.

"Oh, that's right . . . there's been a lot of verses added since you two left!"

Things, it seemed, had now swung into high gear. For the next hour or so, as word got around, more people came to either reunite with the famous pair or meet them for the first time. The evening culminated with a rousing group performance of all the verses of "Rise, Sons of Lothar" that those present could remember, then Sid called it a night. He pressed the bottle and a pair of glasses into Turalyon's hands. "Take it to your lady," he said. "She slipped out around verse fourteen, I think."

Alleria was perched on a rock not far from the inn, looking up at the strange sky. Turalyon regarded her for a moment. Her beauty was captivating, of course. Her skill with a bow, exceptional. But others were beautiful, or skilled, or of noble blood. Only Alleria was Alleria. She alone had won and kept his heart. He had witnessed her great deeds, her weakest moments. Felt the weight she had borne when no others would rise to the occasion. There was no one like Alleria Windrunner in all the Great Dark Beyond, and no one knew that better than the man who loved her.

He made his way to the rock's flat surface and sat beside her, silently pouring a small splash into a glass and handing it to her. "Is my hammer still up there?"

When they had first arrived, Khadgar had studied the skies, making up names for constellations as he went along. Turalyon wondered if any of them could still be seen, given what had happened to Draenor.

She took the glass with one hand and pointed with the other. "Mm-hmm. Just barely. Turalyon's Hammer." She did not drink but kept her gaze to the sky.

Turalyon looked down into his own glass, though he knew there would be no wisdom there. "My love?" he said quietly. "Do you ever wonder what would have happened had we not been pulled into the rift?"

He saw her hand tighten on the glass. "I wonder about many such things. But they do not change the present."

Or the future? he wanted to ask, but he refrained.

"I do as well. We would still have been parted from Arator . . . but we would be more as we had been when we left him. We would have had friends. Community."

"Perhaps, but you would never have become Lightforged. I would never have found the powers of the Void. How would we have answered the Legion when it came for Azeroth once more? Or Xal'atath?"

Turalyon hesitated, then stretched out his hand, palm open. Alleria, too, took a moment, then placed hers in his. *So much smaller than mine,* Turalyon thought, as he always did, closing his fingers over hers. *But no less scarred, or strong.*

"Before the Nether, you were more a warrior than I was," he said, running his thumb over her calluses as he spoke. "You were born into it. I was a priest and had to learn weaponry as an adult. I've always been a little in awe of you."

She chuckled, a bit sadly. "I know. I knew from the first. Are you still?"

"I told you I always would be, at least a little, and time has made no liar out of me. But I love you even more."

"Flatterer."

"You know it's true."

Emotions flitted across her face, usually so schooled, but they were fleeting and varied and he could not read them. "I know that, too" was what she said.

Silence. Turalyon searched his memory for something to shift the somberness of the moment back to the playfulness they had found a few hours earlier. "Do you remember the little picnic guest?"

She thought for a moment, then started to smile, covering it with her hand. "I can't believe it, but I had forgotten about that until just now. You were so pleased to have gotten a basket of delicacies shipped to the front."

"I agonized over what to get," he said. "What's her favorite cheese? Wine? Does she like berries? And I had to pay extra for them to pack the pastries carefully or else they'd fall apart." He was so joyful to see her light up as she remembered.

"A wine and cheese pairing, *a pause in the horrors of war,*" Alleria said, mirth in her voice. "You even brought a blanket. You told me we were going to discuss strategy, but for some strange reason, we needed to be *alone under the stars* to do so."

Turalyon felt himself blushing. "That obvious, huh?"

"Part of your charm," she said. She lay back on the flat rock, arms beneath her head, looking up at the unique sky, at other worlds, at stars that looked so close one might touch them but that were somewhere in the Great Dark Beyond.

"And here I thought I was sophisticated. I so badly wanted to impress you."

"Oh, you made an impression," she said. "It *lingered* long afterward."

He grimaced, even now feeling the heat in his cheeks. "I was utterly mortified. I couldn't face you. I almost never wanted to see you again."

Alleria was laughing now, and Turalyon was giddy to see it. "You'd been trying so hard," she said, and then, dropping her voice low, quoted, "'Alleria, I know you are accustomed to beautiful things and rare delicacies'—"

"I did *not* sound like that!" he protested.

"—'and there has not been a pause in the horrors of this war for me to show you such luxuries. But I assure you'—"

"'You're going to love this!'" they said at the same time.

"You poured the wine."

"And spilled it. *And* dropped the goblet."

"Which rolled down the hill, and you sprang after it and then you let out this terrible . . . howl? Shout? I thought something awful had happened."

"Well, you weren't wrong."

Alleria put her hand over her face, trying to smother her mirth. "Who knew that a tiny little skunk could make such a big stench!"

"Oh, Light," he groaned. "So bad. So very, *very* bad."

"Right in that handsome face of yours!"

"And you did nothing," he accused, still smiling, "just laughed, like you're doing now."

"In my defense, your reaction was hilarious," she said, giggling. "And then you started shouting, 'Pickles! P-Pickles!' And I still don't know why."

He stared at her, open-mouthed. "You . . . *what*?"

"I don't know why you wanted pickles so badly right then."

"All this time . . . !" He buried his face in his hand, shaking with silent mirth. "Alleria, my darling, my life, pickles are made with *vinegar.* And vinegar can get the skunk smell out—or so I was told."

"Oh!"

"The only vinegar we had at camp was pickle juice," he said. Then he added with genuine regret, "To this day I can't eat them."

For reasons unknown to Turalyon, this somehow struck Alleria as the funniest thing yet. Laughter burbled up inside her, a font unable to be dammed, escaping her lips although now she had both hands on her mouth. Her shoulders shook, and Turalyon laughed, too, booming and deep and carefree.

"Oh, oh," Alleria said, catching her breath and wiping tears from her face, "no one would come near you for days!" She rolled over onto her side and propped herself up on one elbow, smiling down at him.

"Least of all *you,*" Turalyon replied, tapping her nose gently with a finger. "I thought you had decided you'd had enough of us humans and gone back to Quel'Thalas."

"You were much more entertaining than *anyone* in Quel'Thalas," Alleria said. "And . . . endearing. And genuine."

"Handsome?"

"I already said you had a handsome face." Amusement still tinged her voice, though the peals of laughter had faded. Her face was flushed, and the smile was still in place. A real one, born of delight, not the one Turalyon had seen all too often recently. The one that seemed genuine to others but not to him, who knew her so well. "How could I leave after that?"

"After I got sprayed by a skunk and shouted about pickles like a madman?"

"Of course! I had to stick around and find out what would happen next!"

Their gazes met and held. "And so you have, for more days than I can count," Turalyon said, his voice soft and warm. "Thank you."

Her smile faded a little, and for a moment, Turalyon wondered if he had just made a misstep. Then she touched his face, and he leaned into her hand.

"We have spoken of regrets tonight," she said. "But staying with you . . . has never been one of mine."

She lay down, her head resting against his shoulder, his arm around her, and they searched for the stars in a broken sky.

CHAPTER TEN

Felsoul Hold Ruins, Suramar

BROKEN ISLES

It was with hope and confidence that the three returned to Suramar and Felsoul Hold. All had believed that in their absence, the fel fire of the forge would have waned, or at least remained as they had left it. Especially under the watchful eye of the Duskwatch.

They had been terribly, tragically wrong.

When Felsoul Hold came into view, Alleria could see that the surrounding area had started to take on a horrifyingly familiar shade of green.

The soul engine was growing stronger.

This is my fault, Alleria thought instantly. Rage and shame rose within her as she gestured to the other two to follow her down. Thalyssra had indeed set up a perimeter. The Duskwatch who were stationed in small groups all around it snapped to attention as they spotted the three approaching. Arator took the lead and directed his gryphon to fly lower. Alleria couldn't hear what was said, but her son appeared to have gotten clearance, and they followed him to a landing area. The officers watched them carefully but offered no interference or engagement.

"They won't tell me what's happened," Arator said, "but they've been instructed to let us enter the hold to do whatever we need to, no questions asked. So . . . let's do it. Before they change their minds."

Alleria could not agree more. They had landed close to the soul engine, released their mounts, and swiftly descended into the depths of the hold. The quiet was tense, heavy, with none of the pleasant chatter they had enjoyed on their first visit here a lifetime ago, now. They prepared for battle with few words and a sense of urgency.

They moved quickly but quietly, and the sickly glow of fel grew brighter and stronger with every step. At last, they paused where they had the previous time, near the soul engine. The family looked at one another and nodded. They did not need the advantage of surprise. They just needed to annihilate the enemy.

Turalyon charged forward, consecrating the ground he and his son ran upon. Alleria hung back, her eyes flitting, alert for any movement, any change, that would permit her to aim, fire, and kill. As before, the area was empty of demons, but something else was different.

This time, the victims had not been tucked away in a room. There were twelve of them this time, all nightborne, all killed in the same tidy and efficient manner. All appeared to be civilians.

"It's onto us," Arator said. "The demon wants us to see what it's done."

Alleria rushed to examine the area, her elven sight scanning every inch of the gruesome scene. Her guilt increased when she realized that Thalyssra's own had paid the price for her false certainty. In the same area where Arator had discovered the woman and the youth with the rune on his hand, six Duskwatch guards lay, slaughtered.

As before, Alleria scouted the way, so she would be the first to see those who had paid the price for her false certainty.

They had been killed quickly, efficiently. As if these half-dozen battle-hardened warriors were little more than insects—an annoyance, a momentary interruption crushed for simply being in the way, their souls the only thing of use to their murderers.

Son and lover both joined her and regarded the corpses. For a moment, no one spoke.

"That's Niandar," Arator said. "The guard who took care of Mauvara." He swore and turned to head up the stairs.

Her own voice, cold and commanding, stopped him. "No."

"Why not? If there's someone else here who might—"

"There is no *someone else*!" Her words cracked like a whip, startling Arator, who fell silent.

Turalyon, too, said nothing.

At last Alleria spoke. "We reported no traces of active demonic activity to Thalyssra other than the state of the soul engine and the attacks on the citizenry. A few felbats."

I should have been here.

"Alleria," Turalyon said quietly, stepping toward her. "We followed up on what we saw here, reported what we knew, and Thalyssra made her own determination as to the next steps. We, and she, expected the Duskwatch would be able to hold their own."

"What's important now is that we find the demon, right?" Arator said. "Let's do it, then. Let's do what we came to do. We can attune the fang to it and hunt it down."

Realistically, it was the only thing they *could* do. Alleria could not change what had happened. But if she had been wrong to underestimate this demon, perhaps she had also been wrong to dismiss what Varaskar had said before they dispatched her.

While the Lightforged lick their wounds on your pitiful planet, a hundred thousand Legion worlds rally our forces! Did you really think you could hide here forever?

Something snapped inside Alleria.

"This needs to stop. *Now,*" Alleria said. "*All* of it. Varaskar hinted at something that sounded a great deal like an invasion plan. Maybe Lyana was wrong, maybe those words weren't bluster."

"Mother, I know you've greater experience overall, but Lyana is much more familiar with the current level of demonic activity than you and Father are. And we all know demons do love to lie."

"It's a warning we need to heed. And by we"—Alleria paused, drawing a deep breath—"I mean . . . me and your father."

"Alleria?" Turalyon looked at her questioningly.

"I . . . what are you saying, Mother?"

"I am *saying* this mission has escalated to the point where it demands complete focus."

Her voice was cold. She could hear it, could see it in the reactions of Arator and Turalyon. But she was burning inside, hot with anger and guilt, and so she pressed on.

"You and your father needed rest, yes. I could have continued on. Been here. This is my fault."

Arator shook his head. "Don't say that. We couldn't have known they were—"

"But I *did* know!" she cried, her voice cracking. "I did know, and I broke my focus, and now these people are dead and our enemy is stronger."

Turalyon was there, calm and solid, his voice gentle. "We are here, love. We are focused now, alert to the severity of the threat. And there will be no further diversions, nothing to shake us from our goal. Right, Arator?"

Arator nodded. "This was my mistake. I'm the one who pushed you to stay longer. You shouldn't have to bear the brunt of it. Let me help you find the demon, Mother. Destroy it. Three are better than two . . . even if the two are you and Father."

Her anger ebbed at his sincerity. Alleria took a deep breath. She still blamed herself, but who was or wasn't at fault didn't matter. However many innocents this demon had killed to feed the soul engine, those people were gone. No amount of remorse or anger would bring them back. Her task—and Turalyon's, and, yes, Arator's too—was to make sure no one else joined them.

"It's just the one demon," she said, rising. "A single set of marks. Hopefully, it will be easy for the Fang of Haa'zuun to identify it."

She pulled out the artifact and then paused, making a decision. "Here," she said to her son, extending it to him. "Attune the fang to it." It was not an honor but an order.

Arator accepted the relic, looking at it for a long moment. It was a simple thing now, just the large tooth of a long-dead creature. But in a few moments, it would be so much more. Arator stepped forward, trying to determine where best to place the fang so that it would, as Lyana had explained it, pick up the "scent." At last, he brought it close to one of the bodies. As he held it over the chest of a young male, his form long-limbed and awkward from youth, the inert object suddenly flashed bright green along its entire length, momentarily blinding them, and then the glow subsided until it was concentrated in the runes, just as it had been when Lyana had tracked the ṣhivarra.

Arator looked at his family in cold triumph.

"The demon's ours now."

■ ■ ■

Arator was troubled by his mother's shame. He understood it—he was angry with himself, too. It had pained him to see Niandar among the dead. It hurt him also to watch his mother shift from the open joy he had seen in Honor Hold to the icy focus of a ranger. He had been happy to see a warmth and connection bloom within the family in Outland, an ease, as if they each had left some of their hardness, their burdens, behind. Arator wanted his mother and his father in his life. He had hoped that they'd begin to figure out how to start living in this present, instead of in the past. It seemed, though, that the moment had passed.

For now, the only thing he could do—for her, for his father, for Niandar and all the fallen—was to destroy this demon.

They were swift but silent and somber as they retraced their steps, climbed out, and told the guards what they'd seen.

They nodded somberly. "We weren't able to get them all out," one of them said. "Not yet."

Arator's spirits dropped even lower.

Like the demon hound from which it had come, the fang could not track its target from the air. Arator cursed silently when he discovered this and brought the gryphons down to the ground. They knew their quarry enjoyed hunting locally. It didn't make sense; even mortal predators did not like to hunt too close to their homes, lest they be too easily followed. Either this demon was less dangerous than they had given it credit for, or it was so arrogant—so powerful—that it just didn't care.

Arator might not have had a thousand years of practice killing demons, like his parents did, but he had eliminated his share of the fel creatures. He had learned much from those who understood demons in ways he never would, like Kayn and the Illidari, plus some warlocks he had encountered. He'd fought demons solo and as part of an army. He knew how to use the quirks of different demons against them and where each was most vulnerable.

In the face of his mother's obvious distress, he'd put on an air of calm, precise confidence. It wasn't entirely feigned; the three of them together were by anyone's measure a force to be reckoned with. But he didn't know what they were about to face and how it scaled to the fel threats they'd encountered in Outland.

But whatever, whoever, this demon was, it didn't know about the fang. It didn't know that this time, the three were *tracking* it, not simply following its trail of carnage. And that gave Arator hope.

The fang was an interesting artifact. There was a peculiar sense of life to it when it was activated, on the hunt. Was the creature's soul bound to it somehow? Did it live, in a sense, when it was chasing prey? Arator was not at all certain he wished to know. Some things, he was beginning to realize, were best not meddled with.

They were lucky that the demon had not opened a portal in the time they had been following it. Lyana had assured them that even if the trail went "cold" due to a portal or a flight, the fang would continue tracking, but the glow would dim depending on the distance. It was glowing ever more brightly in his hand as they continued on.

"Hold!" The command came from his mother, and Arator pulled his gryphon to a halt. She rode up beside him and pointed. "Another settlement. Our quarry is probably there."

Arator squinted, but night was falling, and her eyesight was better than his. If she saw it, it was there. "The fang agrees with you. Our friend is straight ahead."

"Gathering more captives while we sit here," Alleria muttered. "Put it away. We can't risk it getting lost—or taken. Let's go."

A few days ago, he and his parents had arrived at a similar scene, but this time was different. This encampment was not empty of people. This settlement stood a chance. But there wasn't much time.

With the quarry in sight—at least, in the ranger's sight—there was no need to stay on the ground. Their mounts leaped skyward, delighted to be airborne once more, and they soared high to get an aerial view.

It was chaos.

The expected felbats were there, of course, swooping and circling, although the nightborne below were firing arrows and arcane spells with fierce determination. Arator saw one of the felbats fluttering erratically, and a blast of fire finished it off.

Arator brought his gryphon swooping down, his attention focused on a felguard wreaking havoc on a handful of warriors. Arator leaped off his mount, who banked, then soared skyward as her rider landed smoothly in the center of the group. He looked up directly into the face of the felguard towering above him, then whirled, grasping his sword tightly in both hands as it glowed with the Light and slicing it deeply across the demon's broad gray chest. The blow was not lethal, though, and it bellowed as it drew back its enormous axe.

A shadow passed over Arator, and he glanced upward, but it was only his mother, wheeling her gryphon about and firing arrow after arrow into the felguard's face. He returned his attention to the felguard, lifting his hand and sending a blade of Light to impale it from below. They would be done here any minute . . .

But then Arator heard a terrible screeching sound. He knew instantly it was one of the gryphons. He again looked up into the darkening sky to see Alleria hurtling downward. Two felbats had seized her shrieking gryphon, each grasping a wing in an effort to rip them off.

Arator dropped his sword and reached for the Light with both hands. It swirled around Alleria, protecting her from injury as she hit the ground, and the same power struck both felbats to deadly effect. They, and the mortally wounded gryphon, tumbled to the earth.

In his haste to protect his mother, Arator had taken his attention off the felguard. Now it reminded him of its presence, a glimmer of motion out of the corner of his eye, caught barely in time to evade the full power of the sword strike. The blow was glancing but painful. Arator grimaced as he summoned and hurled a hammer of Light into the demon, sending it crashing down. Arator seized his sword and plunged it into its unprotected chest, and with a feeble roar that was more of a groan, the demon was dead.

Catching his breath, Arator looked around to assess the state of the battle. Alleria had taken upon herself the task of dropping as many felbats as possible, if the number of those dead on the ground was any indication. A flash of Light told him that his father was busy healing the nightborne who had been injured, and he heard Turalyon's commanding voice ordering them to flee the battlefield and get to safety.

He agreed with that decision. It was easier to fight without worrying about civilians. There appeared to be only one other felguard standing, and Arator was confident that Turalyon could bring it down quickly. It was grim work, but Arator turned his attention to finishing off any demons that Alleria had only wounded. There were not that many, and even as it was growing dark, he could easily see that there were far fewer shadows flying across the star-studded sky.

A flash of light, brighter in the twilight, signaled the last demon erupting in righteous flame. Was the one who had been operating the soul engine among the dead? Even the felguards were usually foot soldiers, not commanders, but it was possible he had just killed the very demon they sought. Arator started to reach for his backpack to check.

At that moment, he heard a sound he knew all too well: that of a portal opening.

It was right behind him.

Arator leaped forward, propelled by the Light, wrapped in an aura of safety. His only thought was to put distance between himself and the demons surging forward so he stood at least a chance of fighting them. The ground beneath him turned golden, turning demonic cries of excitement into howls of pain, and Light in the form of hammers struck down several creatures where they stood.

He landed and whirled to see not just a handful of demons but a small flood of them emerging through the portal: imps, felhunters, felguards, and—he inhaled swiftly—a dark crimson monstrosity with horns, hooves, and a mouth crammed full of needle-sharp teeth. Massive leathery bat-wings jutted from its outsized shoulders.

A doomguard. It snarled and cracked its whip. This, then, must be the master of the pack of lesser demons. Arator narrowed his eyes, tightening his grip on his sword. He was more than ready, eager to fight more fiercely than he ever had before. His mother had lost faith in him and had blamed herself. Arator would succeed for them both.

He ran straight toward them, utilizing a move that Kayn had taught him: Never be in one place for long.

Strike: Three imps went down, all cleaved in half.

Strike: The head of a felhound, neatly severed, bounced on the earth as its body stood, then fell.

Strike: Entrails spilled from a felguard as Arator sliced him open and—

Arator gasped as his own sword was knocked from his hand by a felhound, and he heard a *clank* as something struck his armor. He glanced down to see chains crafted of fel energy wrapped around him, dragging him *toward* the portal. The doomguard grinned horribly.

Even as Arator started to call on the Light to blast the links, Turalyon was there. Arator had never seen him like this before. Limned with gold, the paladin's face was set in a mask of righteous fury as he turned his full attention on the new threat.

Arator blasted the chains encircling him while Turalyon severed them at the source, first slicing through them and then turning on the wielder.

But the doomguard was already teleporting, laughing at the paladins' inability to stop him. The portal began to close as well, and the demons, apparently deciding that retreat was preferable to facing the high exarch defending his son, turned and raced through it. Turalyon bellowed in fury, the Light whirling around him in a terrible storm, and several demons died instantly. Those that didn't screamed as the ground beneath them sent Light coursing through their bodies, dropping between one stride and the next.

Then, as quickly as it had opened, the portal closed.

Arator took a deep, gulping breath and exhaled. Then he started to laugh softly. "That was invigorating."

His parents, however, did not seem in a celebratory mood, even though it had been a clear victory. Arator noticed them exchanging one of those meaningful looks that frustrated him. Then, almost as one, they turned to him. In their eyes, he saw love and sorrow.

"All right," he said slowly, "now I'm worried. What's going on?"

They looked at each other again, but just as Turalyon opened his mouth to speak, they all heard a faint cry. Turalyon looked at Alleria and tilted his head quickly in Arator's direction before hastening to help the wounded. Arator started to go after him, but his mother's hand on his arm made him pause and look at her inquiringly.

"What is it, Mother?"

Now that she had his full attention, she suddenly didn't seem to want to speak. Then she took a deep breath.

"Your father and I both believe that you may be in danger."

"Did you not notice that *I* saved *you,* Mother?"

"Arator." Her voice held a certain tone, and his irritation faded. "I do not think you saw it, but we both did. They separated us."

"A good tactic," he said, ready to listen but wondering where she was going with this.

"Yes. And if that was all, we would not be having this conversation. But the portal opened right behind *you.* Not me or your father. And they tried to *take* you. Not kill you."

The hairs on the back of his neck lifted.

"Alleria," Turalyon called. It was almost fully dark now. Arator could see his father's form clearly, much better than a full-blooded human would have been able to, but not the details on his face. His mother clearly could, however, and as he beckoned, she went to him. Arator followed.

As they had been instructed to do, those whom Turalyon had been able to heal during the fight had fled to safety. All that were left were bodies, and a single survivor. His robe was torn, and he was bleeding slightly from claw marks across his chest, but the nightborne had only been grazed. He'd been extremely lucky.

Turalyon knelt beside him, his face grim. "Tell them what you told me."

"They—they came right before you did," the survivor said, gulping the water Turalyon had given him to drink. "First just two of the bigger ones. They had axes and wore armor on only the right side, I think . . . they had horns, or a helmet with a horn, I'm not sure . . . then the others came, the flying ones."

"Felguards, then felbats," Arator said. "Did they take people away?"

The nightborne nodded. "Maybe ten, twelve . . . I don't know. But that didn't happen until after . . ."

"After what?" Alleria prompted.

"They asked questions. They were *looking* for someone. They said they'd let us go if we turned him over to them. Someone named Aramor, or Arator." He glanced up at Turalyon. "Do you know him? You seemed to recognize the name."

For the second time, Arator's skin prickled. Alleria's eyes had narrowed, but otherwise she was calm. She placed a hand on his arm. "Sweetheart, why don't you check your pack? We may have something for this fellow to eat."

The pack. The fang.

The demon. Had it left through the portal, with the others? Was it hiding in the woods, waiting to ambush them?

"Of course," Arator said, as calm as his mother, and reached for the pack.

▪ ▪ ▪

Alleria watched her son intently. Hoping she was wrong, but also that she was right. Because if she was, it would all be over shortly. Arator's fingers were steady as he untied the string that held the pack closed, and she loved him even more in that moment for his courage.

Arator pulled open the pack. There was a blinding flash of green fel.

"It's past time we met formally," said the nightborne.

Time seemed to slow to a crawl. One of Alleria's hands moved to her side, grasped the blade tucked there, as if she were moving through mud. The other reached toward Arator, to push him away. She turned to the nightborne—no, the demon, who had just played them, who had *been* playing them, like a puppeteer.

The disguise he had worn vanished, as if it had never been there, revealing the enemy's true face: a *man'ari,* a perversion and twisting of the decency that was the draenei race known as eredar, a face that was not a shade of blue or gray, but red, red as anger, as hate, as blood.

Alleria had lifted the knife in this sludgy, nightmarish moment and brought it down at a glacial pace toward one of the demon's gleaming green eyes.

One massive, red-clawed hand shot up, shattering the illusion of dreamlike slowness, clutching her entire head in his palm, lifting her and hurling her away. Alleria hit the ground hard. Turalyon had sprung to his feet, and his sword, glowing fiercely and scattering the darkness, descended upon the eredar.

Except—the demon wasn't there.

He was beside Alleria, who had risen halfway. Void swirled around her hands. She unleashed it in a blast, but the demon had already appeared behind Turalyon, who also swung—and missed. Now the creature was nowhere to be seen.

Arator was at his father's side, his body taut and alert, his eyes searching the darkness for a thing he would never be able to see if it did not wish to be seen.

"Arator!" Alleria cried, racing toward him. "The fang!"

He understood immediately, reaching into the bag and bringing it out.

The radiance was gone. He held only an ordinary, if large, felhound fang.

It will never track that demon again.

"No!" Alleria screamed as fear and fury struggled for control.

Arator, her boy, her anchor, her heart, had been beside her until the demon hurled her away. Now his body shot up in midair and hovered there, first choked by the invisible adversary and then thrown yards away, as his mother had been.

The demon materialized beside Arator before the paladin could even start to rise, again lifting him up into the air with his fingers around his throat.

Alleria reached for her bow while Turalyon raced toward their son. Chains, fel-forged and powerful, abruptly wrapped around them, forcing each to the ground and enveloping them almost entirely. Alleria gasped for breath.

"It is truly a pleasure." The demon's voice was smooth. Cultured. Contemptuous. "The high exarch. The fallen ranger. And . . . their pride and joy?"

Through a link in the fel chain, Alleria could see Arator resisting with all he had in him. Her son's left hand pried at the slowly closing fingers around his throat, and the sword in his right hand struck the eredar's arm. It seemed to have no effect, glancing off it again and again, and Alleria writhed against the chains futilely.

"Lady Alleria, please, stop squirming. It's undignified. Now that I have your full attention . . . to business." The eredar strode casually toward her and Turalyon, ignoring her son's struggles. "I arranged this meeting to introduce myself. I am Sarothar."

"Never heard of you," snapped Turalyon.

"No." Most demons had such a sense of their own importance that they would be outraged if their name did not cause terror. This one, though, smiled a little, as if at a private joke. "But *your* names are well known to *me*." He came to a halt, gazed down upon them, and continued in an almost conversational tone. "You are entertaining, but you are disruptive, and that must stop."

"Which, the entertainment or the disruption?" Arator rasped. Sarothar paused, flicked an unnaturally long index finger, and Arator bit back a scream.

"The latter, as I have just indicated. Playtime is *over*. You've won some grudging respect among more sophisticated demons such as myself, and, as I am very busy and prefer not to waste any more time on you, I offer you the chance to turn away from your present course of action. It is a simple proposal. Do not interfere with me, and I will not interfere with you."

"Why?" demanded Alleria. "Why not just kill us now?"

"It serves all our interests to have you toothless, rather than headless. It is also the easiest solution, and I value efficiency. You may trust my word. You may also trust that I shall not hesitate to toss all of you into the soul engine if you continue to trouble me. And I will start . . ."

Sarothar abruptly dropped Arator, who sprawled, gasping for breath as he glared up at the demon.

The eredar bent, almost like a very tall man about to pat a very small kitten. He tapped Arator's forehead with one long, scarlet claw.

". . . with *you*."

Sarothar straightened and gestured, and a portal whirled open. "This has been a treat. But I hope, for your sakes, that I never see you again."

The Void can free you. The Void can defeat him.

They still came on occasion, the voices that had once been her constant companion. Rarely, and Alleria was always able to ignore their temptations. But this time, she knew they were right. The Void *could* free her. Arator was no longer in immediate danger. She could destroy Sarothar and end it all.

In that instant between one heartbeat and the next, between consideration and decision, the Light that so loved Turalyon exploded all around them as the high exarch shouted a prayer that sounded more like a curse. She heard a series of loud cracks and then hissing as the fel chains that bound them shattered and dissolved beneath the power of the Light. Through slitted eyes, Alleria beheld Turalyon's form wreathed in the Light's power of righteous fury and closed her eyes against the brightness. In that darkness, she saw the afterimage, bright and distorted, then it faded.

It took but an instant, and when she opened her eyes, Alleria realized that Turalyon, too, had been too late.

Sarothar had eluded them once again.

Alleria hurried to her son. Turalyon stood for a heartbeat, staring at where the portal had been, then joined them. Alleria could not help herself. She touched Arator's face, needing to reassure herself that he was still there, that there was still time, that she could stop what Sarothar had so smugly promised.

He endured it briefly, then gently brought her hand down.

"What do you two make of this?" Arator asked. He did not joke or shrug off what happened, and that was how his mother knew that the encounter had rattled him. "I mean . . . *he* set this up?" He uttered a bark of harsh, disbelieving laughter. "*We* were hunting *him*! And trying to bargain? He's nobody!"

"True, none of us recognized his name," Turalyon said, "but that is irrelevant. All we need to know is that this is the demon who came back to Azeroth, rebuilt the soul engine, and has been murdering innocents to get it up and running."

"He's behaving more like a dreadlord than an eredar," Arator said thoughtfully. "This isn't a lark, or a killing spree for entertainment."

"And that is why killing us outright now would have tipped his hand before he was ready," Turalyon said. "Rallied the Horde and Alliance to urgent action. He's already drawn more attention than he expected. I think Varaskar was telling the truth. Something very big is happening."

"I will say it." Alleria's voice was cold. Flat. She was always the one to make the call, say the words, that no one else wanted to. This time was no different. "He's orchestrating an invasion."

The three were quiet for a long moment. Alleria suspected each needed a little time to find their own way to accept the fact, painful though it was. She had certainly found hers.

"Still," Arator said, "if he knows us as well as he claims to, he *must* know that all of us would accept death in an instant rather than let our world fall to the Legion. He may have had others crumble and accept the deal in the past, but if he really believes this family can be swayed—then he doesn't know us as well as he thinks he does."

"There are things that make death feel like a relief," Alleria said, "and I suspect Sarothar is familiar with most of them. But most likely, there's something more to this. Or he's simply doing what demons always do. Lie."

"Whether we have actually met a sincere demon who keeps his word, which would be a first, or he's just trying to manipulate us, one thing is certain," Turalyon said. "Demons always do what is best for them, and for the Legion. If killing us now would have served Sarothar's purpose best, we would be dead." He put a hand on his son's shoulder. "We will learn what it is eventually. I think it's highly possible he believes your mother and I will agree, if it means keeping you alive."

Arator looked at them both. "We can't do that," he said quietly. "And *that* gives us an advantage."

He straightened, and Alleria saw him resume the mantle of a Knight of the Silver Hand. He fished out the fang from his pack and regarded it. "Well," he said, "Lyana did warn us. We found the quarry, and this fang won't give us a second chance."

A shadow fell over his face. "We know where to find him now, anyway. I wonder if Sarothar teleported to Felsoul Hold directly, and if the sacrifices have already been made."

"If that's so, then we would have been too late even if we had flown back the second that portal closed," Turalyon reminded him. "And keep in mind, son, that *he* knew how to find *us,* too. I cannot imagine a demon making an offer without keeping an eye on us afterward. We should proceed accordingly. Sarothar will doubtless expect us to return to Thalyssra and Lor'themar, hoping we'll give them false information."

Arator nodded, returning the fang to his pouch. "We may *want* to discourage the nightborne from mounting a major attack at this point, honestly."

Turalyon followed his train of thought perfectly. "If Suramar sends an army now, Sarothar would simply use every death to fuel the soul engine. And they have the advantage in the hold."

Arator nodded, thinking. "We need to stop him quickly, but not there. Maybe we can get him to come to us. Trap him, somehow."

"Agreed. Alleria?"

Alleria had remained silent during this exchange, listening, thinking. Feeling. She did not have many dreams left to her, and most of those that remained revolved around her son. Now she herself was about to destroy one of those dreams, because it was time she knew something. *Or, really, to simply acknowledge what I've always known.*

Arator frowned in confusion as he looked at his mother's face. *Because my son does not know what I do.*

Alleria looked at them both in turn: The scarred, strong, gentle man at her side, priest and warrior both, who had been the first and only she had ever loved. And the man before her, conceived in love, carried, birthed, and surrendered with love—a man she was only beginning to know. Neither was naive. But they both bore something innocent, something simple and true, unsullied by the vagaries of life, the cruel dispassion of the world, even the violence that came with the path they had chosen. Alleria had watched that part of Turalyon slowly retreat over time, eroded by choices they'd had to make, and duties thrust upon them. It was not entirely gone, but she did not see that side of him often now.

She had wanted so deeply to protect her son from the path that had chipped away at his father's inherent kindness. *Every parent wants their child safe,* she told herself. *But every parent must let them go, if they are to realize their true selves.*

The blood of adventurers ran in his veins, binding them all together, but also binding Arator to his own unique destiny.

She had tried to keep him safe, keep that rare and sincere viridity unmarred, but such was not and would never be his nature. Confining him was like keeping a falcon on a creance. Sarothar had made it clear that this was Arator's battle, too, even more so than theirs, and their son had done so much already to guide their journey.

It was time for the falcon to soar.

Alleria stepped forward and again gently touched Arator's face. He looked at her, uncertain, but did not try to shrug it off, sensing the power of the moment. Turalyon, too, regarded her intently, with a hint of apprehension, as if he knew what she was about to do. *Of course you do,* she thought. *You know me too well.*

She took a deep breath.

"I agree that Sarothar almost certainly knows where we are, and what we will attempt to do. We should not attack, not now. As you say, that will waste lives and give us no chance to find another solution. And since we all agree on this, we must do everything we can to gain the upper hand. Arator, Turalyon . . . you return to Suramar. Get the first arcanist on board with your plan. I will go in search of such solutions myself."

"What?" Arator exclaimed. "No, Mother, you can't do that!"

"It will divide his attention," Alleria said. "His threat is not the death of one of us. It's that we would be forced to witness the horror of that death. *That* is his power."

And Sarothar knows it well.

"I can protect myself. And you two will be with each other."

"No," Arator kept saying. "No. I don't understand this. We are all strongest *together.* You agreed that we should do what Sarothar would expect us to, right? Would he *really* believe you'd leave at this point?"

He looked to his father for support, for protestation, but found none. Turalyon knew, as she did, as Arator did not, that leaving was precisely what she would do at such a moment. Alleria's heart hurt to see them both before her now: her great love, his face showing weary resignation but unable to hide the pain, and her fierce love, his face open and raw and hurting, and, worst of all, uncomprehending.

There were no words to soothe the ache of her lover's heart, and Alleria could find none to ease the shock of her son's.

So she simply stepped forward, kissed her son on his brow, to offer what comfort she could, and her love on his lips, a reminder of all that had been, and left them in silence.

CHAPTER ELEVEN

Suramar

BROKEN ISLES

Arator stood for a moment, frozen, then started after his mother. Turalyon caught him by the arm, but Arator yanked free.

"You're just going to let her go?"

Turalyon gave a humorless little laugh. "No one 'lets' Alleria Windrunner do anything."

The shock was starting to fade. "No," Arator said, more calmly, "I suppose not. I just . . . didn't expect it. But you *did,* didn't you?"

Turalyon sighed. "It's a part of who she is." He removed one of his gloves, brought his thumb and forefinger to his mouth, and emitted a sharp, loud whistle that startled Arator. There were answering caws in the distance as the gryphons approached. Arator recalled the one that didn't make it, who had been killed by the felbats. He turned abruptly, looking around, trying to find where it had fallen, seeking the body of a noble creature amid the litter of fallen demons.

Its white head and throat gleamed in the moonslight, as if the Blue Child and the White Lady themselves wanted Arator to find it. He knelt and removed his glove, running his hand along the noble creature's head, the feathers soft and smooth and cool. And he was, perhaps selfishly, grateful the night hid how cruelly it had been tormented.

"I'm so sorry," he whispered. "Thank you."

He rose with a sigh and saw that his father was standing nearby, giving his son privacy. Arator walked over to him, and together, they made their way to an open area.

"I feel like I've failed everyone today," Arator said quietly, not looking at his father.

"I wouldn't say that," Turalyon said, his eyes on the sky.

The words were unexpected, and Arator was surprised at how much he welcomed them.

"I've gotten used to it," his father continued, "your mother leaving. Over centuries, we have parted, reunited, and parted again. Sometimes she doesn't even say anything. And sometimes . . ." Turalyon was quiet for a moment before resuming. "Sometimes, she's gone for a long time."

Now Arator looked at his father's strong profile. His parents' constant shifting from warm to cool, close to distant, irritated him to no end. It made more sense now. He'd always wanted to think of his mother as warm and nurturing. He felt closer to her, as if he understood her better. Part of that, he felt certain, was being raised with his elven aunt and half-elf cousins, and being trained by Lor'themar in the Farstrider tradition early on. His father felt colder, though it was clear—sometimes painfully so—that he loved his son; he just had no idea how to express it outside their shared profession.

Arator wanted to say *I'm sorry,* but that felt presumptuous, at least here and now, with Alleria's departure only minutes old.

"Ah," Turalyon said briskly in his normal voice, as if everything was just fine and Alleria had not just . . . left. "There they are."

The gryphons were small, dark silhouettes, drawing closer. As they landed gracefully, Arator suddenly knew what to say. He swung himself into the saddle and turned to his father.

"That whistle," he said. "Can you teach me how to do it?"

Turalyon turned to him in mild surprise, then smiled. "Sure," he said. "I'd love to."

■ ■ ■

Things felt very different from the first time Arator had arrived in the Nighthold, ready to make his case to take over a simple scouting mission. The mood was somber, and he noted the increased presence of the Duskwatch. People moved with more purpose and with serious looks on their faces. As soon as they dismounted, they were greeted politely but with no pleasantries, and were shown into not a study or a dining hall but a war room.

Thalyssra and Lor'themar looked haggard, as if they had not slept in some time. Thalyssra stood speaking with a Duskwatch patrol captain, briskly asking questions in a low voice, then listening intently. Lor'themar was at a desk covered with scrolls, scribbling correspondence. Both looked up as Turalyon and Arator entered. Thalyssra nodded but continued her conversation.

Lor'themar eyed their armor. "I see you found more demons."

"We know the Duskwatch did as well," said Turalyon. "You have our deepest sympathies."

Arator waited for Lor'themar to explain what had happened; the guard had been vague. Instead, Lor'themar merely nodded.

"Thank you. Where is Alleria?"

"She's investigating on her own for the moment," Turalyon said.

Arator did not miss the quick flicker of comprehension on the regent lord's aquiline face as he nodded.

Thalyssra dismissed the captain and went to join her husband. She gave them a weary smile. "It's good to see you, even under these circumstances. Was Sunfury of help?"

"He was, to us and also to you," Arator said. "The Illidari stand ready to aid Suramar, should you need them. He loaned us this," he continued, producing the fang and briefly explaining it. "It led us right to our demon. He's a man'ari eredar."

Their eyes widened.

Thalyssra took a deep breath. "Anyone you know?"

"His name is Sarothar, but none of us had heard of him before," Turalyon said. "Does that name mean anything to you?"

Thalyssra shook her head while Lor'themar jotted the name on a piece of parchment and handed it to an assistant.

"Our archives might turn up something," said Thalyssra.

At that moment, a guard stepped up to the regent lord and whispered something in his ear. "Yes, do," he said, and the guard hastened off.

Thalyssra smiled at the paladins. "Will you pause for a moment?" she asked, indicating a sideboard with easy-to-eat fare. "Our hospitality is a bit spare at the moment, but we have some victuals, juice, and water, if you wish."

The two paladins exchanged glances. Something was going on. They accepted some water but nothing else, and a few moments later, a familiar figure strode into the chamber and stood at attention.

Arator's heart sank. "Lady Liadrin," he said, nodding to his friend. "I . . . didn't know you would be here."

"Sir Arator," Liadrin said, formally. "High Exarch. I understand Lady Alleria won't be joining us, but I hope she is able to bring back some information that will assist us. In the meantime, I understand that you have something to report."

Us?

"I was just about to brief the first arcanist and regent lord," Arator said, matching her formal tone. "We encountered the demon we believe to be responsible for rebuilding the soul engine and for the deaths of Duskwatch guards and dozens of civilians. A man'ari eredar, Sarothar."

Liadrin inhaled swiftly but was otherwise admirably calm at the revelation. Once the two paladins were finished, their audience simply sat for a moment, digesting it all.

Thalyssra was the first to speak. "You're certain about this?"

"Based on what we know and what he has said, yes," Arator replied.

"Obviously, this changes everything."

Turalyon nodded. "For many reasons. While the nathrezim are most well-known for disguises, Alleria and I have run across at least two eredar who had mastered it as well. Sarothar changed his form before our eyes when we encountered him. We should tightly control who has access to information."

"Liadrin," Arator said, "what did you bring me on the day you told me about this mission?"

"A jar of honey from the twins," she replied at once.

"Which one?" Arator said.

Her eyes narrowed slightly. "You didn't ask."

"If Sarothar wishes to infiltrate and see things for himself, he likely wouldn't pose as anyone so high-profile as Liadrin," Turalyon noted. "There may well be spies already in place. Lor'themar, Thalyssra . . . my recommendation would be for you to be seen often with Liadrin. Make a bit of a show about training warriors, let yourselves be overheard planning an assault. Get some rumors going."

An uneasy silence fell. Then Liadrin said quietly, "There will be no need for rumors. Lor'themar invited me here to discuss strategy on that very topic. My Blood Knights will be arriving soon."

"I apologize," Turalyon said. "Did I not make the situation at Felsoul Hold sufficiently clear?" He was calm, almost casual, but Arator knew him well enough to see the first hints of anger. "You will be sending your troops to their deaths, *strengthening* our enemy. Supplying him with the very ingredient he must have for the soul engine to become fully operational."

He rose abruptly and went to the map. "Look at this. Your troops must enter from above and descend into the hold—a perfect chokepoint. Sarothar doesn't have sizeable numbers, not yet, but he will be waiting with more dangerous demons than imps or felhounds, siphoning souls all the while. You will run out of soldiers long before he runs out of demons."

"What do you suggest, then?" Thalyssra snapped, her own temper rising. "This began with a handful of sightings that *you* were tasked to investigate and report back on. Instead, you did your own reconnaissance and, in so doing, revealed yourselves to him."

Arator abruptly felt even worse. Reporting back and awaiting further orders was exactly what his father had wanted to do, but Arator and Alleria had convinced him otherwise.

"Had we reported back, likely the same chain of events would have happened," Arator found himself saying. All eyes turned to him. He sat up straighter in his chair. "We'd have offered to follow up on the trail. You'd have accepted that offer. Except by that point, the people we were able to save would have died, like Mauvara and her child, the thirty or so survivors we just sent your way—"

"*Arator,*" Turalyon said, his voice a gentle warning.

"I told you we found a way to track him," Arator barreled on. "And yes, because of who we are, we're always going to be targets. But it got him to reveal himself. Now we can get him to come to us. You have to let us try!"

"Arator," Liadrin said, compassion in her voice, "it's gone beyond that now. This is the spearhead of an *invasion.* I know you and your parents know that, too. We must stop it here, now, before other clusters of demons start to emerge."

"We will have to notify other Horde leaders before too much more time passes, as well," Thalyssra said. "This cannot be allowed to get out of hand." To Turalyon, she said, "If we must sacrifice a hundred, even a thousand now—you, better than any of us, understand that number is *nothing* compared to what we risk losing if we delay too long."

"We will wait for him to return, and we will kill him, and that is the end of it," Lor'themar said, then, softening, "Thalyssra and I are grateful for the lives of those you and your family's warning have saved. And now that we know we're facing an eredar, we can be better prepared. But you have been relieved of duty—all of you."

"*Please,*" Arator said. "Give us just a few more days. I believe this plan will work or I would not ask it of you."

"Arator," said Thalyssra, more sternly than he had ever heard her before. "The decision is made. The reconnaissance and investigation phase of this military operation is over, and your services are no longer needed. As the regent lord said, we are grateful for your service and the information you've brought. You are dismissed."

Arator felt his face flush with anger and shame. He took a breath and inclined his head, afraid to speak lest he say the wrong thing. He didn't dare look at Liadrin, who had been the one to set him an easy path to commendation—one he had fumbled.

"Then we will take our leave," Turalyon said. The high exarch turned on his heel with perfect military precision and strode from the chamber.

Arator hesitated, then followed. He waited, braced for the recriminations that were certain to come. He could practically hear his father's voice, always deep, even lower with disapproval or anger. *I told you we should just come back. You should have let the Blood Knights handle it from the first.*

Turalyon remained silent as they walked through the Nighthold. At last, Arator couldn't take it anymore. He was feeling the weight of all that had happened both today and over the last several days. Thalyssra's dismissal was the final dagger in his heart.

"I made a huge mess of everything, didn't I?" Arator said quietly, not looking at his father.

"What makes you say that?" asked Turalyon.

Arator scoffed. "For starters, I shouldn't have asked to take this on."

"I agree," came the expected response. "But Liadrin knew better than to approach you without clearing it with your superiors. She put you in a difficult position. Once you were in charge, generally, you made the right calls."

"But . . . you said we should report back after we found the soul engine, and so did Thalyssra."

"We should have," Turalyon said. "But your insistence we do otherwise revealed Sarothar's plan to attack encampments. Places where the demons could easily take everyone, and no one would remain to alert Suramar about those missing. We don't know how many lives were saved because of that."

"I fell right into Sarothar's trap."

"We *all* did. Alleria and I should have been much more careful. We put you in harm's way needlessly."

Alleria. *Mother.*

Softly, Arator said, "I drove Mother away."

Turalyon stopped and turned to face his son, placing a hand on his shoulder. "Son . . . I told you. This isn't the first time your mother felt the need to leave. I'm confident it won't be the last. She's been doing it her whole life. She didn't leave because of you, Arator. *Never* think that. She loves you more than the world."

Arator didn't realize how much he needed to hear this. Not just the words, but his father saying them, speaking them with a voice full of emotion. He felt something inside him settle, ever so slightly.

He took a breath and let go of his self-pity. "So," he asked his father, "what do we do now?"

His father smiled a little, without humor, and began walking again. "The only option left to us: Return to Light's Hope and report this to the Silver Hand. They'll take it from there. I'll return to Stormwind and send a formal offer of assistance. Which, given what just happened, will likely be formally refused."

Arator stopped in his tracks. He knew that his nature to go against protocol had often damned him—had complicated this mission, was the crux of the many disagreements he'd had with his father. But . . . he could not accept this. He wouldn't let his father retreat to his world of rules and protocol, not after Turalyon said what he did. Not after his mother—

"Father, this mission is *ours.* We found the soul engine operating, we found out about the encampments, we tracked down Sarothar. We've risked our lives how many times in the past few days? We can't just walk away."

"Yes," Turalyon said firmly. "We can. Trust me, I was as shocked as you, and the words *relieved of duty* and *dismissed* are never pleasant to hear. But you must respect the decisions of your superiors and follow their orders, or chaos will ensue."

Arator racked his brains to think of something, *anything* to sway the stubborn high exarch. "Father. They are lining up people to walk into a trap!"

A thought popped into his head. "Sarothar told us to stay out of it, didn't he? Well, you're choosing to do exactly what he wants."

That got Turalyon's attention. His father's implacable footfalls ceased. He was listening.

"He couldn't have asked for a better solution. You, Thalyssra, Lor'themar—you're all playing right into his hands. But we don't have to."

Turalyon rubbed his temple with his hand. "Arator," he began.

"We no longer report to Thalyssra on this. They have their plan. Their operation. Well . . . why can't we have ours? How many times have you been in a situation like this? Seven, eight thousand?"

Despite himself, Turalyon had to suppress a smile. "Add a couple of zeroes," he said. "But we're not talking about *my* operation, are we?"

Arator had already said he had an idea, and he did. It was a good one. It would work, he knew it would. But he also knew that his path to success was one his father would balk at.

"No," he confessed. "Just . . . come with me. I'll need your help. If you're with me, no one will question you because, well, you're *you,* and in this case, that's a good thing."

Now his father was actually smiling. "In this case? Now you've done it. I'll have to report you for insubordination."

"I'll add it to the list for Lord Tyrosus. In all seriousness . . . I feel I must at least attempt my plan, whether you come with me or not."

Turalyon looked at him, really looked at him, as if trying to assess a stranger. Arator stayed silent. He'd said everything he could, made every argument for his case, and now Turalyon would make his decision.

"If I let you go off by yourself knowing Sarothar is out there, your mother would kill me, then you."

The tension Arator hadn't realized he'd been holding melted away. "I doubt that," he said, grinning. "She loves me too much."

"That she does."

"She loves you, too."

His father smiled. "I know."

▪ ▪ ▪

"All right, we're here," Turalyon said. "Ready to tell me your plan yet?"

Arator looked a bit sheepish and scratched his chin, not looking at him. He'd staved off his father's questions over the last several hours as they made their way here, with pauses to swap the gryphons for various other methods of flight, hiring mages, and stopping off in Stormwind to grab a quick bite to eat and a very large cloak in an attempt to cover Turalyon's armor. It worked.

Mostly.

They were now in Eversong Woods, near the Shepherd's Gate entrance to Silvermoon City, and Arator had run out of time to stall. "I don't think you will respond more positively to this suggestion than you did to the Illidari, but I will remind you *that* worked out well."

"This does not instill confidence in me," Turalyon said.

"Really, it would be best if you just stayed here, out of sight. That tree over there is nice. Oh, look, there's one of the dragonhawk hatchlings!"

Turalyon folded his arms and looked at his son flatly.

Arator sighed deeply. "All right. Just . . . follow my lead, be quiet and try not to draw attention."

"I'm a human paladin in shining, demon blood–spattered armor in the middle of Quel'Thalas."

"*That's* why we got the cloak. Just try not to clank too loudly."

Turalyon did indeed draw a few interested looks, but Arator would smile and wave, and that seemed to be enough for most people. His father was quiet, for which he was grateful, but when his son's path took them out of the main areas and down a road that was narrow and dark, Turalyon spoke up.

"Do you have some disreputable friends hiding in the shadows, ready to rob me at knifepoint? I'm sure this old armor might be worth a copper or two."

Arator smothered a smile. "Give me some credit," he said. "I'd get you drunk first."

"Ha!" Turalyon said, smiling himself. "Where are you taking your old father, anyway?"

"Well, there's hardly a sign, but this place is known as Murder Row."

"So I was right. You *are* trying to hock my armor."

"Too shiny. You put people's eyesight at risk when you stand in the sunlight."

"Nonsense."

Arator was enjoying the lighthearted moment while he could, because he could predict what would happen when he told his father about his "friend."

Up ahead there was some light from the Silvermoon City Inn. "Are we meeting your contact at the inn?"

Arator coughed. "No, and I think it's best if you just . . . wait outside." He came to a stop before a building that had several doors, each draped with gauzy violet fabric. It did not hint at what went on inside, but neither did it project virtue and piety.

Turalyon took it in for a moment, then turned to his son. "Explain. *Now.*"

Arator sighed. "There is an organization that was formed during the Legion invasion called the, ah . . . Council of the Black Harvest."

Now Turalyon, too, was alert. "That does not sound very prepossessing."

"It's an organization of warlocks."

"*Arator,*" Turalyon said sharply. All playfulness was gone from his tone, and his face was hard as stone. "This is unbecoming of a Knight of the Silver Hand. You could be seriously reprimanded. These are dangerous and erratic people."

Arator sighed again. "See, this is exactly why I didn't want to tell you till we arrived here."

"It's not too late for me to get us both arrested for brawling in public," Turalyon said, his voice simmering with anger.

Arator lifted his hands in a gesture to placate him. "I promise you, this isn't the Shadow Council, and *nobody* in the Black Harvest ever liked Gul'dan. Things . . . have changed. *Evolved.*"

"Not *that* much," Turalyon said.

"Yes, *that* much," Arator said, not backing down. "Our order was founded not just on justice and retribution, Father, but also on compassion. Those are the three tenets, aren't they? You've known the Light all your life. You were a priest, and you accepted and befriended Lothraxion, a *nathrezim,* as a true paladin. I would think you well know how none are beyond the reach of the Light, nor past the possibility to be called into its service."

Father and son glared at each other, then Turalyon took a deep breath.

"Do you have a *friend* in this organization? Someone you trust, like Kayn?"

"No, but I do have a friend *here,*" he said, and he gestured to one of the curtain-draped doors. "She knows someone in the Black Harvest and might be able to get us an audience with them."

His father looked unconvinced. "You're asking me to trust a friend of a friend of my son. About warlocks. You must know how ridiculous this is starting to sound."

"Listen," Arator said, slowing down. "You and Mother have both been gone a long time—even by our way of measuring it. For years now, those who have chosen to work with demons have tried hard to prove their trustworthiness. Their loyalty to the cause of Azeroth, complete command of their demons. The Black Harvest is made up of people who are not our enemies but our *allies.* It's led by six of the most powerful warlocks in the world—"

"If you're trying to persuade me, try harder," Turalyon said.

Arator snorted. "If you would stop interrupting me, I might have a chance!"

At his father's silence, Arator continued. "They were well aware how much they would be mistrusted when the Legion arrived, so they did what most everyone else did. They focused on growing stronger, more powerful, to defend Azeroth. They did serious damage against the Legion, and they're sharing information and technologies they've discovered from the demons they've destroyed. I've fought in battle beside some warlocks. I've watched them save lives—including those of my comrades."

Turalyon's face had not softened. "Fighting alongside properly trained allies in a military conflict is one thing. Courting individuals and asking their assistance at a confidential mission's critical juncture is another. You, a paladin, should not be personally involved with people who cultivate demons and constantly expose themselves to fel energies."

Arator cut him off. "Fel is terrifying and dangerous, yes—"

"And *highly* addictive," his father plowed on. "The stronger the addiction, the stronger the power, and it doesn't end until that same power, the demons, or *someone else* destroys them!"

"You're not listening." The words came through clenched teeth. Arator's face was hot, but he was trying to control himself. "No one denies that, least of all the warlocks themselves. And yes, many have been lost to it. Good people, strong people."

"Then they should serve as a warning!"

"They do! But not the way you think! Arthas was a paladin, and he did far worse things than any warlock of Azeroth has. It's who you are, and how you walk your path, that matters. The warlocks of our world have studied, *learned.* It's like Mother and the Void. She's able to control it and taught many others how to do so as well. In the end, it's all energy. How is fel any different from the arcane, the Void . . . or the Light?"

"The Light is *nothing* like fel!" his father snapped. This was the harshest he had ever been with Arator. "It—it heals, it comforts, it *inspires*! You're a *paladin,* Arator! Light, you're supposed to know this!" His voice cracked on the last sentence with more anguish than anger.

"I do, Father. I do. I love the Light, and I can feel its love. You and I both know how much Thalyssra and even Lor'themar are underestimating Sarothar. The Council of the Black Harvest are the only people I know who are both powerful and trustworthy enough to trap him."

Turalyon looked away, and Arator could see the struggle within. "Father . . . this may be our last chance to stop this invasion."

His father sighed, adjusting his stance. "I will go with you," he said at last. "We will speak with your . . . contact."

"Oh, no, no, that would *not* be well received."

"Then we're done here."

Arator's patience abruptly ran out. "Is that an order, High Exarch?"

Turalyon twitched. The retort had stung. Recklessly, Arator continued. "You know what? Maybe I'm thinking about this all wrong. Maybe Mother was right to leave. Perhaps we should *all* split up. I'll go by myself to get the warlocks' help with Sarothar, and you can tell her why."

His father flushed bright red, then paled. Instantly, Arator regretted the words. His parents hadn't chosen to be taken to the Nether for a thousand years. And he'd seen his father's reaction when his mother had left. Arator had taken that vulnerability, that pain, and wielded it as a weapon, and he was ashamed.

"Your mother wanted us to stick together," Turalyon said quietly. He swallowed. "I will not disappoint her."

All the fight went out of Arator. "I understand that after all you've witnessed and done, this feels very wrong. Just . . . trust me, Father. *Please.*"

Turalyon closed his eyes. Arator waited, watching the faint, healing hue of the Light envelop his father for a moment. Turalyon's fists unclenched, and his body relaxed.

"Help me to understand. How exactly do warlocks get their demons?"

His father was listening, and that was all he could ask. "Warlocks know how to summon demons," Arator said. "That's how they get their minions. They pull them through a portal, get control of them, and the demons then obey them. That's much more difficult than trying to simply kill them, which is all we need. The Black Harvest are the best of the best. They have access to more knowledge than any other warlocks, and they're the most powerful Azeroth has. They killed the pit lord who ruled the Dreadscar Rift. And the demons the pit lord had tormented were so grateful, they pledged to serve the council."

To his consternation, Turalyon's frown deepened. "So, they ally with demons rather than force them to obey?"

"The Dreadscar demons have no loyalty to a Legion who abused them, Father. And you know better than anyone that even demons can change."

Turalyon could not argue that. He counted Lothraxion, a Lightforged nathrezim, among his closest comrades. Arator pressed his advantage. "Speaking of nathrezim, did I mention the council helped kill one? So they won't just help us trap Sarothar, they'll help us fight him, too. Though I wish we had Mother with us for that."

"I do as well," Turalyon said. He took a deep breath and shook his head. "I cannot believe I'm saying this, but . . . this is a solid plan. We will give it a try."

"Thank you," Arator said, sincerely. "So . . . are you going to stay here, let me get through this quickly, and make this easier on all of us? Or do you, High Exarch of the Grand Army of the Light, want to march, unannounced, in full golden armor, into a room full of warlocks and demons to ask a favor?"

Turalyon paused. "Go on," he said at last. "I'll wait out here, avoiding disreputable people with knives."

Arator exhaled in relief. "Thank you. I shouldn't be long." He lifted one of the curtains, then paused. "You know . . . warlocks really aren't all that bad. My friend even gives her demons pet names."

"That," Turalyon said bluntly, "is a bridge too far."

■ ■ ■

Arator lifted the curtain and slipped inside, pleased that he had remembered not to mention the name of the place. It might be a bit too much to ask his father to be fine with the idea that a warlock den was called the Sanctum.

The trainers were all busy with their students. At first glance, Arator thought it could almost be a scene from Dalaran, with students practicing and succeeding to various degrees. Except that instead of turning someone into a sheep, these students were trying to force an imp to follow their instructions—which was arguably more difficult and certainly more dangerous. It was an amusing but also a somber thought. He had spent many years in Dalaran with Vereesa and his cousins; it was the second home he had now lost, after Silvermoon.

He shook off the memories; there was no time for that now. His friend Thalonia was focused on working with a young woman whose felhound, for the moment, appeared to be under the student's control. As Arator descended the stairs, an airborne object suddenly zoomed toward him.

The thing was hideous: a fel orb in the shape of a large yellow-green eye, with banked fire for its slit pupil. Arator smiled at it. "Haven't *seen* you in a while."

A few yards away, on the floor of the Sanctum, Thalonia laughed, and the eye disappeared.

Thalonia, strikingly beautiful even for a blood elf, with a long fall of fire-hued hair, smiled as Arator approached. She was of an age with him, and they'd met as teenagers. She was someone he always made sure to see when he was in Silvermoon.

"Melnarra, take a little break and try that command with your puppy. We'll try the voidwalker next," she told her student. "Arator, how nice to see you. Are you in town for long?"

"Unfortunately no," he said. "I'm here on a mission, and . . . I need to ask a favor."

"You have but to name it."

"You know one of the warlocks in the Black Harvest. Do you think you could arrange an introduction? I greatly need their help with a demon."

"Oh, yes! Delightful woman. Not too keen on Light wielders, of course, but I think she'd make an exception for you. I can't guarantee she'd be willing to help, though."

Now was the hard part. "It's . . . not just me she'd need to make an exception for. And I wouldn't ask if it wasn't absolutely necessary."

Her eyes widened. "Please tell me it's not your father."

". . . It's my father."

"*Arator!*" She stared at him, aghast. "This is one of your pranks, isn't it?"

"Unfortunately, I'm serious, but for what it's worth, I believe the demon we're after may be of particular interest to the council . . ." Arator thought of his earlier mistake, disclosing unnecessary context to the quel'dorei scouts in Outland. The need for secrecy was now doubly important with an eredar in the mix.

Luckily, Thalonia had known him for a long time. She softened and brushed a lock of scarlet hair out of her eye.

"Arator . . . I'm not sure you appreciate what you're asking me to do. These are the most powerful warlocks on Azeroth, and requests to see them come at a cost. The suggestion she meet with the high exarch . . . even saying his name could get me in trouble," she muttered. "But if you say it's important, I will. For you. But you're going to help me repay this debt."

He sagged in relief. "Of course. Anything. Thank you so much." Arator watched as she shook herself a little, squared her shoulders, and strode into another room as if into battle. He wondered what *delightful woman* really meant, when one warlock was talking about another.

Melnarra's felhound sat at her feet. Arator had never seen one so obedient before and, frankly, didn't know such training was possible. It was obvious that felhounds had not been twisted from anything natural but were purely created fel beings. The beast looked terribly awkward seated there, as its hindquarters were much smaller than its massive chest and head. It sported two enormous, bony horns that jutted from its powerful shoulders, and a mane of spines that ran along its body, which, when raised, gave it the appearance of extra height and bulk. Two of the spines were really more like leathery tentacles, and opened like mouths to drain magic from their spell-caster victims. It felt odd, being so close to one and not having it try to kill him.

"You're doing well," Arator said. "Its spines are relaxed."

"Thank you," she said. "We get along pretty well."

"What's its name?"

"Flora."

Arator blinked. "Why did you name it that?"

Melnarra pointed to the little mouths, undulating like separate living things. "They look like flowers, don't they?"

They did not, but Arator agreed they did, and brought out the fang to show her. They were deep in discussion about it when Thalonia emerged. She had a surprised look on her face.

"Well," she said slowly, "not what I expected. She's quite interested in meeting your father. But you both have to be on your best behavior. If he steps out of line, there will be consequences, for both of you . . . and for me, too."

"I'll make sure he understands that."

"Make very sure, Arator. Very."

■ ■ ■

"Good news and not so good news," Arator told Turalyon as he emerged from the Sanctum. "We should be expecting a summons at any moment. Someone named Bulzan will meet us. My friend asked me to say hello."

"Well, that is good news. And the rest?"

"She's willing to meet us and hear what we have to say. That's all. Whether the council chooses to help or not is up to them."

"Why wouldn't they?" Turalyon looked irritated.

"For one thing, given their expertise, they're probably dealing with so many different things they have little time or resources to spare. And for another, I'd think it would be pretty hard to be helpful and obliging when you're used to people despising you."

"I'm fairly certain even if I were to spit at their feet, they'd want to stop another Legion invasion."

Before Arator could reply, he was interrupted by a whirring sound as a portal, its opening defined by greenish swirling fel energy, appeared as promised. Turalyon looked at it with suspicion.

"What happens now?" Turalyon asked.

"It's a portal," Arator said. "You walk through it."

"You know what I mean."

"It's not a trap!" Arator explained, exasperated. "Before we step through, you need to know that if you cause any trouble, all of us are going to be held responsible. They're making a huge gesture. We should be properly grateful."

"So, no killing minions. Got it."

"Father, I mean it."

"I do, too."

They stepped through together. For a brief instant, all was green, painful to look at, and uncomfortable to sense. A heartbeat later, their feet trod upon hard stone, not paved as the streets of Silvermoon City were, but uneven rock.

The rock trembled as two massive, clawed feet slammed down. The creature's body, partially obscured by tendrils of fel mist, was purple, save where blade-adorned armor covered it. Its broad chest was defiantly bare, daring them to attack, and its near-featureless head—glowing green eyes and a slit of a mouth—was crowned by a helm of arching horns and spikes.

"*Welcome, pathetic mortals!*" rumbled the wrathguard.

CHAPTER TWELVE

Dreadscar Rift

THE TWISTING NETHER

"Bulzan, cut that out!"

A Forsaken warlock ambled over to the imposing demon and craned her neck, scowling up at him. The terrifying creature began to laugh, looking, if possible, even more terrifying, and the Forsaken sighed, turning to the visitors with a shrug.

"Our apologies. If ever you require an enthusiastic audience, get yourself some demons. When they like your joke, they'll laugh at it *every* time."

"Presumably if they do not like it, they kill you," Turalyon said. He was clearly not amused.

"You are correct," Bulzan said. "We will then carve the offending being into extremely small pieces."

Arator snorted.

Bulzan folded his arms and glared.

Arator's smile faded as he realized that the demon had likely not been joking.

"Let's try this again," said the Forsaken with a sigh. "High Exarch Turalyon, Sir Arator—welcome to Dreadscar Rift. This fellow is Bulzan, the leader of the Dreadscar demons. Our present leader defeated the demon who used to run this place, and Bulzan pledged that he and his people would henceforth ally with the Black Harvest. The Dreadscar are superior bodyguards, but I doubt you two will be needing their services. And I am Jubeka Shadowbreaker, the one who summoned you."

The three visitors inclined their heads, and Bulzan bowed.

Arator looked at Bulzan speculatively. "Thalonia sends her regards."

Bulzan grunted, but he looked pleased.

Arator turned to Jubeka. "We appreciate you receiving us."

"Heard you have a problem we might help with. Demon hunting does make for strange bedfellows, eh?" She chuckled. "Please, follow me. The council awaits us in the archives."

Arator glanced back quickly at his father. Turalyon was on high alert, but he nodded to Arator and followed. Arator could feel Bulzan's fel gaze on him, but he paid it no heed, falling into easy step beside Jubeka as they walked.

The rift was open to the air, such as it was; rocky and barren, a string of landmasses floating about. It was unmistakably inhabited by warlocks. Demons seemed to be around every corner, some presumably scurrying about on errands, others chained and being interrogated. They passed an area that was, effectively, a felhound kennel, and Arator smiled a bit, thinking of the fang in his pouch. Torches and braziers of fel fire provided green illumination, and above, the dark sky was crowded with rocks and ribbons of green.

"I know it was an unusual request," Arator said. "Please know we're very grateful for any help or information you might have."

"Oh, my young friend," the warlock said, "you may not be quite so grateful as you think. But it's good of you to say so." She looked over her shoulder at Turalyon. "Who raised your son with such good manners while you and Alleria were in the Nether?"

From almost anyone else, it would have been an awkward comment, bordering on rude. But Jubeka had a rare combination of pragmatism, pleasantness, and humor that put Arator at ease.

Turalyon answered politely. "Arator's aunt Vereesa, and her husband, the late Archmage Rhonin," he told the warlock. "No one could have done a finer job. Alleria and I are very proud of him."

The words surprised Arator, and he smiled slightly.

"And a paladin, too," Jubeka continued as if she had not noticed Arator's expression, but he was certain she had. "Like father, like son, it would seem."

It was Turalyon's turn to look slightly uncomfortable. "Arator chose his own path, but I am glad we walk the same one. I would venture to guess that you do not see many paladins. I want to assure you, we will respect your ways."

That caused Jubeka to turn and laugh. "You think I don't know any paladins? I've saved many in battle, High Exarch." Had she still been human, Arator thought her eyes would have been bright with humor. "It's always a delight to see their faces when one of my demons cuts down their attacker. But you're quite right. Few of your calling find their way here."

"I told my father about the Black Harvest's accomplishments during the last Legion invasion," Arator said quickly. "He was impressed."

"Kind of you to notice," Jubeka said. "We're rather proud of them, too. Liberating Dreadscar Rift, helping to end a pit lord. If you're so inclined, you might remind your own order about our contributions."

"We'll keep that in mind, won't we?" Arator said pointedly to his father.

Turalyon grunted a reluctant affirmative, unable to stop scanning the area for possible threats.

"The world hasn't been without its troubles, even since the Legion was defeated," Arator continued. "Have your members been kept busy?"

"Despite the prejudice they face, I'm proud to say that most of our warlocks still work to defend Azeroth," Jubeka said. "The council continues to focus on demonic activity, as that's where we can be most effective. In recent weeks, we've been kept hopping, curiously enough."

Arator glanced at his father, who was paying close attention. Maybe now his father was starting to understand his son's reasoning.

"Many of us are therefore unfortunately elsewhere at the moment—the Netherlord, for example," Jubeka continued. "I imagine you may have met them at one time or another. They'll be sorry to have missed you. Ah, here we are."

The archives came into view as they ascended a gentle incline. The pit lord who dominated the rift had left his successors with a trove of knowledge. Enormous tomes, sized appropriately for the demons who would be consulting them, emanated wisps of fel as they hovered in the air. Shelves were piled high with more books, scrolls, and assorted items that Arator didn't recognize and honestly didn't want to.

He sensed movement nearby and turned, staring into a large green eye. It belonged to, but was not attached to, an inquisitor demon. It and several of its fellows, like the inquisitor itself, hovered in the air. Arator thought about Thalonia and the floating eye she commanded, but her "eye" wasn't *literally* her eye. There was no kind of demon that Arator liked, but the inquisitors were particularly disturbing. Curving horns emerged from the hood of a flowing cloak, and it was hard to glimpse its featureless face.

An impressive variety of demon skulls were impaled on spikes, and scattered here and there were other bones that might not have been demonic. Turalyon stared at them, his mouth a tight, thin line of disapproval.

Jubeka saw it, too. "Oh, that. The pit lord left those behind. We should get around to cleaning it up one of these days."

As they reached the top, four other warlocks turned from their various tasks to regard their guests. Arator knew something of what to expect, but it was still sobering to be in the presence of five unquestioned masters of demonic power.

The group before him was composed of a human, a Forsaken, an orc, and a blood elf. Arator had often found that unless the members of such organizations were generally good, true people with firm rules as well as steady souls, such power tended to cause them to turn on one another. Even as he had the thought, though, Arator realized that his observation wasn't limited to groups of those with darker inclinations. As he'd said to Turalyon, power of all kinds, even for good, had turned hearts to dark deeds.

He could all but sense his father's desire to call on the Light and prayed quietly that Turalyon would remember the conditions of the visit.

Jubeka continued. "Although our numbers aren't complete, you'll find those here have amassed a great deal of experience among us. Our founder, Kanrethad Ebonlocke, for example," she said, indicating a tall male human, "was present at Illidan's defeat at the Black Temple and was able to enlighten us on how that fellow had transformed himself from kaldorei to demon and still managed to live."

Kanrethad inclined his head. He bore himself with dignity and composure, and though still handsome, his face was lined. It bore a hint of sorrow, as if at one point, he had stepped too far, done or seen too much.

"It's an unexpected honor to receive the both of you," he said in a rich, pleasant voice. "After the shattering of our world and the fall of Deathwing, I realized that if the most powerful warlocks in our world unified to study and target our common enemies, we could be uniquely effective. Our name refers to that harvesting of . . . darker knowledge, so to speak."

"There's an old saying, keep your friends close and your enemies closer," Jubeka said. "Such a thing becomes much easier when, over time, they're more or less the same thing."

"Not all of us are friends here," a human woman interjected. She was glaring, not at either of the paladins, but at someone else.

Arator followed the woman's gaze to see who had so vexed her. Despite himself, his eyes widened.

The orc's face was wreathed in green flame that appeared not to consume his flesh . . . well, not any more than it already had. This warlock had been so badly burned that his features were little more than a mass of scar tissue, but he managed to laugh at the woman who openly disparaged him. The flames danced a little brighter and continued to burn.

"Kira speaks the truth," he said. "And yet the council, under our present leader, works well indeed."

"Kira Iresoul and Ritssyn Flamescowl," Jubeka said quietly to the paladins. "Don't mind them. It's an old grudge. Master, apprentice, you know the story. Shinfel Blightsworn has some grudges, too." She indicated a blood elf who had remained seated. Her garments were black, and for a moment, in the less-than-perfect green glow of the place, Arator assumed she was fully clothed from head to toe. Then he realized that the woman's arms were nearly covered in thick black scars.

"Corruption," Arator murmured.

Jubeka nodded. "Shinfel was imprisoned in her own mind by one of the world's most evil ogre mages, then abducted by the pit lord who used to rule here. Without the help of the Netherlord—"

"And Calydus!" came a raspy, eager voice. A squat demon about the size of a dwarf capered up to them. "Calydus help everyone!" The demon was known as a wyrmtongue, Arator knew, although he hadn't encountered very many of them. They were some of the lowest in the demonic hierarchy, little more than laborers or servants who were used and discarded, devoured, decapitated, or otherwise disposed of on a whim.

This one had a hideous face, with squinting green eyes and an enormous mouth that seemed crammed with far too many teeth. He bore a pack that was almost as large as he was and carried candles, books, spell ingredients—anything and everything a high-ranking warlock might need. He looked up at Arator eagerly and moved his mouth in what was meant to be an ingratiating smile.

"Ah, your timing is perfect as always," Jubeka said, and the little crimson demon wriggled with pleasure at the praise.

"Whose minion is he?" Arator asked. "Yours?"

"No, no, he doesn't belong to anybody anymore. He's an ally, like

Bulzan. More like a friend, if we're being honest. Essentially, what he said was true—he *was,* and is, of enormous help to us."

"We were told you wished to speak with us," Kanrethad said, waving to Jubeka to sit. "Please. You have our full attention."

Even though this had been his idea, now that it was unfolding and the eyes of several master warlocks and assorted demons were upon him, Arator was nervous.

He had to convince the council to help. These warlocks, who alongside others had crushed Illidan; who bore the mark of a Firelord's living flame; who had withstood the twisting of their own minds. And it wasn't just them. There were two audiences here: the Council of the Black Harvest, and his father. If there was any chance to stop Sarothar, everyone in this room had to be completely on the same side.

Arator didn't think of himself as particularly persuasive or inspiring. It was his father who possessed those qualities. Alleria had once told him, smiling in remembrance, that the speeches Turalyon gave to his troops were the most rousing words she had ever heard. Arator had asked what was so special about what his father had said. His mother had replied, *He cared about his people, and he spoke from his heart.*

That, though, was a different man, in a different situation . . . in a different life. Speeches weren't Arator's strength, but he, too, could speak from his heart. He'd just have to do it his own way.

"Thank you for agreeing to meet with us. There are some folk, even in my order, who would rather forget how Azeroth defeated the Burning Legion . . . but I remember. We triumphed because we turned our differences into a source of strength, combined our knowledge and power in pursuit of victory. My father, me, priests, warriors." Arator shook his head. "We got accolades, parades, promotions back home when the war was over. The Black Harvest's contributions went unsung, unremarked upon. And that was wrong."

"We did not expect such a frivolous thing as approval," Ritssyn growled.

"I hope you did not come to waste our time with flattery," Kira said, frowning at Arator.

Wonderful. I've barely said anything, and I've already got two people who dislike each other united against me.

Arator thought about the conversation he'd just had with his father. Turalyon didn't trust anyone here, be they demon or warlock. And as the high exarch, Turalyon represented a real, and rare, threat to the council. They had to work together before it was too late. They had to trust one another—two sides that had every reason not to.

He took a breath and began again. *All, or nothing.*

"What you say is true, and no, I did not come here for that. You do what you do because it must be done, whether the world appreciates it or not. I'm not here to waste your time, so I'll get right to the point and tell you everything we know. We have encountered a demon believed to be heading up a new Legion invasion."

Turalyon made a startled sound of surprise, and the warlocks looked pleasantly surprised.

"His name?" asked Kanrethad.

"Sarothar," Arator said, adding, "a man'ari eredar."

They all regarded him blankly. Not a soul in this group, who might be expected to be familiar with even less-significant demons, recognized the name. He felt despair tugging at his soul, but he deliberately pushed it back.

"Calydus, see what you can find out about this Sarothar while Arator continues," the former leader of the council said. The wyrmtongue scurried to one of the books, reached up to pull it down to his level, and began to leaf through it.

"So," Kanrethad continued, "Lady Alleria, she who coexists with the Void, the High Exarch of the Grand Army of the Light, and Sir Arator the Redeemer—all are convinced of this?"

Arator glanced at his father, who nodded. "My mother is not with us only because she is using her abilities to hunt the demon in ways we cannot," he said. "And we are here because we can't stop him alone."

"Please—continue."

"A few days ago, my party and I went on a scouting mission to Felsoul Hold to investigate reports of fel activity. I believed it was just a prank, right up until the moment we found a functioning soul engine—and several nightborne corpses."

The energy in the room shifted instantly. Looks of annoyance, boredom, or politeness became intense interest.

"That wasn't all," Arator continued. "The demon has been abducting folk from small communities and has attacked at least two encampments. We arrived too late to prevent attack on one; felbats had absconded with all but two nightborne. We asked for help from the Illidari, who offered us the Fang of Haa'zuun. In life, Haa'zuun was a loyal felhound trained to scent the essence of a specific demon; the artifact could help us track our quarry."

Kira Iresoul, the black-haired human who nursed a hatred for the aptly named Flamescowl, sat up straight in her chair. "Do you still have this relic?"

"I do," he said, and excitement rippled through the group.

"May we see it?" asked Kira, trying and failing to look detached. Arator reached into his pouch, holding it up for them to see.

Kira extended her hand. Without hesitation, Arator walked to where she sat and carefully placed it in her palm.

Trust.

"Unfortunately for us," Arator continued, "the fang was being used by the demon hunter Lyana Darksorrow. We joined her in Outland and aided her in bringing down a shivarra, Varaskar the Flayer."

The Flayer at least was known to the council, and they murmured approvingly. Jubeka, who had risen to assist Calydus in leafing through the books, looked up.

"Glad she's gone," she said. "Nasty piece of work, that one. Liked to take off skins." She paused. "Slowly."

"She was masterful at it," came an elegant, almost wistful voice. It was the first time Shinfel Blightsworn had spoken. "A loss, really."

Arator didn't need to see his father to know he'd react to the disturbing comment, and he pressed on.

"Of course," he said quickly, "she had a few choice words for us when we defeated her: 'The Legion may have lost its leaders, but the Grand Army of the Light has lost its purpose. While the Lightforged lick their wounds on your pitiful planet, a hundred thousand Legion worlds rally our forces. Did you really think you could hide here forever? You've led us right to—' "

He paused. They were listening. Truly listening. Light be praised, he was getting through to them.

"And then Lyana killed her."

Some of the council members groaned in frustration, but a few shrugged.

"It sounds like every demon when they realize they're about to die," Ritssyn said.

"Liars, all of them," said Kira.

"Oh, they'll tell the truth right enough, if they think it'll save them," Jubeka said. "The trick is to know which is which."

"There was no way for us to know, but her words *did* reinforce what we were beginning to suspect. Lyana gave us the fang, but we needed to return to Felsoul Hold to attune it to our target." Arator glanced over at Kira. She seemed particularly interested in anything concerning the fang, which she now held almost possessively.

"We discovered more corpses upon our return, and the soul engine was more powerful than it had been. The fang worked very well, and we followed where it led—to another encampment. This time, we arrived in the middle of an attack, and we were able to save several lives. The scale of the strike was different. A portal was open, and in addition to the felbats we'd seen before, there were felhounds, imps, felguards, even a doomguard."

"Quite the escalation," Kanrethad said, almost distantly. He wasn't looking at anyone, but more inward, turning everything over in his mind.

"We defeated most of them, and the rest fled back to the portal and closed it behind them. My father and I started healing the wounded. I couldn't check the fang in the heat of battle, and afterward, when I did . . ." Arator took a deep breath. "Sarothar was posing as one of the survivors of his own army's attack."

"That sounds more like a nathrezim trick than an eredar, but it's certainly not unheard of," said Ritssyn. "Kil'jaeden was known to employ that tactic, among others."

Jubeka looked up sharply from one of the books, then said something to Calydus. He nodded, excited, wiggled out from under his pack, and began enthusiastically rooting through it. A moment later, he handed a small book to Jubeka.

"We thought that as well," Arator said. "Throughout, Sarothar behaved much more like a dreadlord than an eredar. He toyed with us for a time, then made us an offer. We were told to stop interfering with him, or we would all die." Arator looked over at his father. "He said we could trust his word."

Ritssyn scoffed.

"I know how it sounds. But . . . we believed he actually would have honored the bargain," Arator said, knowing that this might make him and his parents look foolish in the eyes of the council. "He was very . . . practical. Regardless, we seek to stop him, and would ask for your aid."

He went to Kira and extended his hand for the fang. For a moment, she gazed at him speculatively. Arator really hoped that the aid of the council wouldn't rest on whether they kept the fang. Kayn would not appreciate it. At all.

With a sigh, she plunked it into his palm, kind enough not to do so with the point down. "Haa'zuun's fang cannot be used to track the same demon twice. And so . . . now you know. We've come to you for help. We cannot *do* what you do. I do not think that anyone but this council has the strength and skill to compel Sarothar to come when called, and to help us eliminate him when he does. And I would hope that, should the Black Harvest choose to aid us, they may find gratitude from not just my family, but Suramar, Silvermoon, and the Order of the Silver Hand."

"Are you done, Arator?" Jubeka asked.

Arator was taken aback for an instant until he realized it was simply a genuine question.

"Ah . . . yes, I am."

"Good. As you know, none of us recognized the name of Sarothar. Granted, we don't know the names of every single demon, but we should have heard about someone with his, ah, credentials before. There are three possibilities. One: We're not as knowledgeable as we think we are. Two: It's a false name. Or three: He didn't want to be known at all."

Jubeka held up a small tome no bigger than her hand. "It would take a very long time to read all the books and scrolls in our archives, of course, but Calydus is a most efficient researcher, and enjoys some light reading of his own from time to time. Thankfully, he was reading this."

Calydus nodded confirmation, squirming with delight. The little wyrmtongue's "light reading" appeared ancient, and there were stains on the cover that looked like dried blood.

"This little book is the journal of a priest, Osgyth the Mad, written while he and a few others were interrogating a sayaad who broke under torture. Listen to this," Jubeka said, and began to read.

"Xylyss. Day 354. Today, the succubus spun us a tale so mad, so foolish, G. grew angry and slew her when she finished. Xylyss claims there is a demon named Sarothar. There exist no tales of suffering and woe at his hands, yet all suffering and woe bear his touch. He is the first of any demon to set foot upon a free world, unseen, unheard, unknown. None can boldly state, 'Pray you, look upon this horror, for Sarothar has wrought it.' But where he goes, the Legion follows, and it has seldom claimed a world where he has not first stepped.

"Xylyss would have us believe that Sarothar does not come to conquer, for his black heart cares not for such things. He comes but to observe. To plant seeds. To listen, to say, 'This world is vulnerable here, and strong there,' so that Kil'jaeden and Archimonde shall know best how to destroy it.

"This one, she asserts, deals not in lies, for he has no need of them. Sarothar breaks no bargains, for he is too wise in their wording. So unnoticed, as he slips through a world, that he has never once tasted death. Many faces does he wear, and many ears have harkened to his whispered words. Kings have reigned because of him, and fallen, too. He knows what coin suits which mortal—power, riches, knowledge—and pays them generously in their currencies.

"Quiet is he, truly unseen, and so gently does he betray a world to the Legion that his dispassion appears as benevolence.

"When a world is ripe for the harvest, he takes his leave and travels to the next, while others claim and kill and reign. But if he speaks his name to you, then make your peace as you would with the lengthening shadows of the coming night, for your own darkness approaches, and as like as not, a new dawn shall not follow.

"G. did not believe Xylyss, and I, a coward, did not stay my fellow priest's hand as he slew the succubus. But I have her words in my head now, and, pray as I may, I cannot unhear them, and I believe the frightened creature died for speaking truth."

The silence was absolute. Arator was reeling. This couldn't be true, yet all the pieces came together.

"Demons of the Burning Legion are arrogant and power-hungry," he murmured. "We know that, we've seen it. But they would have needed someone like this, someone who'd leave no stone unturned, someone patient, slow to anger, to scout their targets."

Turalyon had stepped beside him. "The eredar who behaves like a dreadlord. Because he studied them, just like he studied the worlds he prepared for them. I pity Osgyth. No wonder he was called the Mad. And no wonder no one's ever heard of Sarothar."

Jubeka closed the little book and placed it in her lap. "Seems like you've gotten yourselves into a bit of a pickle," she said. "This isn't some run-of-the-mill demon. Summoning him is certain to be dangerous. I have but one question for you."

Arator swallowed. "Yes?"

"When do we start?"

CHAPTER THIRTEEN

Dreadscar Rift

THE TWISTING NETHER

Kanrethad gave her an irritated but affectionate look. "Jubeka, you know we must discuss this between ourselves before we extend an offer of aid."

"You do, but I don't." She turned to Arator. "Whatever they decide, I'll come."

"Then you can sit downstairs with them," snapped Ritssyn, and Arator's heart, which had just given a great leap, suddenly sank. He desperately hoped that in her enthusiasm Jubeka had not alienated the rest of the group.

"Very well. Come along, I'll take you to the arena."

"The *what*?" asked Turalyon.

"Whatever you decide, we are grateful that you listened," Arator said. "We're happy to wait but have no wish to pull Jubeka away from the council if you need—"

"She doesn't matter," said Shinfel.

"What Shinfel means is, if Jubeka wants to go, she can," said Kanrethad. "We are not slaves to unanimity."

Arator noticed that Kira's eyes were not on him nor on his father, but on his satchel and the fang within it. He smothered a smile. He suspected that Kira, too, would be joining them, if only to learn more about the artifact. The others, Arator couldn't read.

"We will let you know what we have decided. In the meantime, you may wander where you will." His eyes danced with a hint of humor. "I think we can trust you not to aggravate the demons of Dreadscar."

"Or kill them," Ritssyn muttered. "We *can* trust you not to do that, yes?"

"Of course," Arator said quickly. "My friend Thalonia is a friend of Bulzan's."

That seemed to impress Ritssyn. Or maybe it annoyed him. He inclined his head respectfully as Jubeka rose and motioned for them to follow.

They were all silent for a while, then Jubeka said, "That went very well."

Arator exhaled in relief. "I honestly couldn't tell."

"Really? You've certainly gotten Kira interested, and I don't think Ritssyn has ever heard of anyone being a 'friend' of Bulzan's."

"Thank you for speaking for us so quickly, Jubeka," Arator said.

"Think nothing of it," the warlock said. "It's quite the story. I'm *really* looking forward to ending this fellow. Although I do have so many questions for him, too."

As they talked, Jubeka led them down a sloping path, which eventually turned into a tunnel that continued ever deeper into the rift. Strange little creatures that were perched on the wall, looking like a nightmarish hybrid of bats and insects, began to chitter loudly. They radiated an eerie fel glow as the party approached, illuminating the path before them while they walked it.

"So, what is the arena for?" Turalyon asked.

"What you think . . . and also *not* what you think." The little creatures scolded them, blinking off and on, and Arator saw that they were coming to a dead end. He tensed.

"It's a trap," Jubeka said casually, pressing her palm to the earthen wall, then added, "for demons."

There was a scraping sound, and then a thin line of fel raced up in a vertical line from the floor, made a sharp turn, then sped downward. A doorway appeared, leading into darkness, and Jubeka walked through.

They followed their guide.

Glowing green light and an angry hum shattered the darkness and the silence. They stood in an enormous natural cavern that had been cleverly carved to indeed resemble a fighting arena, but writ small. A circle was outlined in the center, with various runes and inscriptions carved into the stone.

"It's a pen," Arator murmured, craning his neck to look up at the various tiers. There were at least two dozen of them, each divided into open compartments that were similar but different: platforms, some open, some with barriers for partial concealment.

"An accurate word," Jubeka said, "but much less evocative."

"You summon them here, contain them in the circle, and then fight them in a place where you have every advantage," Turalyon said approvingly.

"They're a bit like hunting stands. Some demons, one needs no help with. Others, well, the more, the merrier. We've got plenty of wards in place as well. We're always trying to come up with the best way to summon and control particular demons," Jubeka said. "We've got all kinds of designs. There's the main summoning area, of course, very traditional. When we had to deal with the eredar twins, Ritssyn suggested we do so on the outskirts of the rift, on one of the smaller islands."

Arator halted. "Wait, what? Eredar . . . twins?"

"Yes, Alythess and Sacrolash. It was a good idea, too, as they were hard to bind and did make quite a mess. They serve the Netherlord now."

"So, you've literally done this before. Bound an eredar," Turalyon said, visibly impressed. Arator resisted the urge to say *told you so.*

"Two, at the same time, no less!" Jubeka was, justifiably, quite proud. "Won't be as easy this time, though. There aren't as many warlocks available, and we don't have the bloodstone to bind your demon with—the Netherlord has it at the moment. We'll have to do this the old-fashioned way. Chains.

"But enough chit-chat. Let's start gathering some soul shards while we wait on the others."

Turalyon looked at Jubeka sharply. "You can't mean . . . you want us to help you harvest souls?"

"If you want to summon your demon, yes, of course." Jubeka chuckled. "How else do you think we control them? Ask nicely?"

Arator opened his mouth, hoping to explain what Jubeka meant before his father reacted badly, but he was too late. Paladin though he was, even he squinted a little at the brilliant glow of his father's Light.

"I will *never* take the soul of an innocent!" Turalyon roared, his voice reverberating and augmented by the Light. "And whether you aid us or not, I will stop you, no matter the cost, if you attempt to do so in my presence!"

Arator was momentarily transfixed. Turalyon was generally cool, in control, and acted from duty not anger.

Jubeka, other than turning her head and reflexively throwing up a bony hand to block the Light as well as she could, seemed amused.

"You paladins are so predictable. Please, calm down, I've no intention of hurting so much as a rabbit today. My word, you're almost worse than Grayson."

At the name, Arator was jolted out of his momentary disorientation. So, it seemed, was his father, or else he believed Jubeka's assurances, for his radiance dimmed and his expression changed to surprise rather than anger.

"Grayson?" Turalyon repeated. "Grayson . . . *Shadowbreaker*?"

"Yes," Jubeka said. "He's my brother. Or . . . *was,* I suppose I should say. And I've had quite enough paladin indignation from him, thank you very much. We don't need to harvest the souls of innocents. We can get everything we need to take down your demon *from* demons themselves. Two birds with one stone, as it were."

Arator turned to Turalyon. "Father, I know I bend the rules sometimes, and this whole detour has run us far afield of the Silver Hand's protocols, but . . . I hope you know I would never associate with people who would harvest innocent souls."

Emotions flitted over Turalyon's face, then he settled himself. "Please accept my apology, both of you. It was wrong of me to assume the worst of you, Jubeka, especially after you have been so cordial to us."

Now it was the Forsaken's turn to look surprised. "Huh. You're a rare one. Paladins are generally a stiff-necked lot. Never seen one express kindness to a Forsaken. Sentiments accepted, High Exarch."

Arator was less focused on his father's apology than on the shocking news she had so casually revealed. "I had no idea Lord Grayson had a sister. He's never mentioned you."

Jubeka cackled bitterly. "I'm not surprised. I'm both an undead horror *and* a fel-cursed warlock, after all. Bad form for a paladin to have a relative who's both. In the haze of reanimation . . . somehow I didn't think it would matter to him.

"Honestly, when I was raised to undeath, I was glad of it. I felt I'd been given a second chance at life, of a sort, and I wanted my brother in it. Traveled all the way from Lordaeron to Stormwind City, and I assure you that is one hard journey for someone like me. We met outside, in Elwynn Forest. I was looking forward to our reunion, but when he saw"—she indicated her form: withered, gray, eyes shining a dull yellow—"well, he was repulsed, *mortified* that I existed like this, that I didn't have the decency to just die. I represented everything he stood against. I had to set a few wolves after him to escape, and even then I barely made it."

Arator winced. To his surprise, Turalyon did, too, and his father looked away for a moment.

Then Turalyon said quietly, "I . . . used to believe the same. I didn't understand until I met Archbishop Faol again, eight years ago. I admit, I was ready to kill him on the spot. Only the order of my king to listen to him stayed my hand. And then I realized . . . he was *changed,* yes, but in many important ways, he was still the same, moral, compassionate priest who founded the Silver Hand. Who made me a paladin. Free will meant that he could choose how he would act. What he would do. Even if many other things had been denied him because of his state. It is still hard for me to extend that thinking to warlocks . . . but I am trying."

Arator was stunned. His father had never mentioned this incident. Now that he thought about it, he had never heard Turalyon speak ill of the Forsaken in general. He was surprised, but pleased, and proud of his father. In many ways, though, it reinforced Arator's notion that paladins, in general, had a long way to go. And Jubeka's tale about her brother was hard to hear.

"I squired under Lord Grayson when I started with the Silver Hand. I admired him very much," Arator said. "It's terrible to hear that he treated you so. I would have thought better of him."

Jubeka shrugged. "It was a long time ago. I've grown used to that kind of attitude in general, especially from paladins. Oh, they love to talk about justice and compassion, but when it comes down to it, they've a very narrow definition of who is *deserving* of those virtues. Present company excepted, clearly, but they lack the creativity to live what they yap about where it matters most. I've managed very well without him. Over the years and our misadventures, Kanrethad has made a fine substitute for my living friends and family, and on the council, my knowledge and insight have value. It's a good undeath. But enough about me. Let's be about gathering some soul shards."

"And . . . exactly how do we do that?" Turalyon asked.

"While the Legion has been defeated as a functioning entity, there are still a lot of worlds crammed full of their kind. I'll simply open a few portals, we kill as many of the pests as have the guts to come through, and I'll siphon their souls into shards. A word to the wise—try to stay on this side of the portal, but make sure they *die* on the other side. If you don't, we'll end up with far too many demon bodies to dispose of, and honestly, we've run out of places to put the bones."

"Ah . . . good idea," Arator said.

"Now. Everyone ready?"

Turalyon glanced at Arator. "Son?"

"Just try to keep up," Arator said, grinning.

Jubeka actually rubbed her hands together gleefully. "Let's start small, with a little warm-up," she said, and opened the first portal.

▪ ▪ ▪

Arator had no idea which worlds they glimpsed over the next half hour or so. He was kept too busy to observe much, and most worlds claimed by the Legion ended up looking the same anyway, no matter what beauty or uniqueness they may have possessed before invasion came to them.

The warlock herself initially performed only two tasks: opening the portals and siphoning the souls. Arator found it oddly compelling to watch Jubeka extend her gray hands and pull out the souls, each one a thin stream of green and purple that eventually turned white, then disappeared as the demon slumped over, now harmless.

The "warm-up" consisted mainly of smaller demons, like imps or lesser felhounds. Arator realized Jubeka was testing them when she opened two portals at once—one directly above them, and one right at Arator's feet. And this time, their opponents were not small, chittering creatures but felguards, shadowy voidwalkers, and a doomguard from above. Jubeka shifted into an active combat role now, summoning and shaping various energies in her hands with surprising delicacy, then unleashing crackling bolts of fire, fel, and shadow upon the enemy.

"Jubeka!" called a new voice, having just entered the pen. "Did you tell them to make sure the demons fall on—"

"Yes, yes, Kira," shouted Jubeka over the din of roaring, dying demons. "You and Ritssyn come help us harvest the rest of the shards!"

The pace accelerated quickly as they were joined by Kira and Ritssyn. Arator barely had time to choose a target and kill it himself before it dropped beneath the onslaught of his father and the three master warlocks. Within the span of a few minutes, Jubeka shouted for them to stop killing and start shoving bodies back into the portal. The scene had shifted quickly from intense to embarrassingly easy to downright amusing as Turalyon and Arator tossed or dragged corpses into the other side of the portal while the warlocks picked off any demons that still had fight left in them.

"And . . . now come back!" The two men leaped through the portal, and an instant later, it was gone.

"While we're all here," Kira suggested, "let's pull another major demon in after we capture the first."

"I admire your ambition, Kira, but let's cross that bridge when we come to it," Arator said.

"From what we've learned about Sarothar," Turalyon said, "he's planning a full-scale invasion. We would like to engage him in further conversation."

"Which means," Ritssyn said, "that we three must stay focused."

Turalyon nodded. "Indeed. Much as I would dearly love to strike a killing blow myself, he must remain alive until we can ascertain the full extent of his plans."

"We'll do our best," Jubeka said, amused.

"If he is half as impressive as your book said he is, he should be orchestrating the entire plan," Arator said. "We just need to get the details out of him."

"And *then* we can kill him?" Kira asked hopefully.

"Yes, dear. The moment our guests are done with him," Jubeka said. "Though I might want a go at him, too, if we're feeling up to hanging on to him a little longer. He's fascinating."

We can do this, Arator thought as he looked at the warlocks and his father. *We can stop an invasion in its tracks.* He lamented that his mother was parted from them, wishing again that she had stayed. But he had to trust that their combined power would be enough.

"What's the next step, Jubeka?" he asked.

"We prepare. Reagents, potions close at hand, and so on." She waved a hand in Turalyon's direction. "Blessing . . . things."

Arator wondered what would happen if he petitioned the order to start calling their prayers *Blessing Things* from now on. The paladins would probably explode on the spot.

"Then, we activate the portal." Jubeka fixed her glowing eyes on Arator. "And I'm afraid, my young friend, you're going to have to be the bait." She held out a dagger, glowing faintly with fel. At Turalyon's expression, she added quickly, "We just need a few drops of blood as part of the ritual."

"Take mine," Turalyon said immediately.

"While it would be fun to claim I spilled the blood of the high exarch, I'm afraid yours won't do. You're Lightforged, and any demon would pick up on *that* energy right away."

Arator laughed. "You're more demon *repellent,* Father."

"I'll do it if you don't want to," Kira said.

"That's kind of you," Arator said, though he wondered if she was only being kind to get at the Fang of Haa'zuun. "It's fine, Father. The blood is the bait, not me."

"It's much less dramatic than you're expecting," Jubeka said.

He removed his glove and went to the center of the circle, where Jubeka met him.

"I'll make a cut in your palm," she said. "We need at least one drop per rune. More is better. That'll wake up the wards. Then I'll cast the spell and call him by name." She chuckled. "That'll shake him up a bit, since he doesn't share it often."

"How long will it take?" Turalyon asked.

"Little ones come right away. The big ones are another story. Some are eager, and others hold out for a bit, so we should be prepared for that. Once he's here, we'll all have at him until he's weak enough that I can bind him."

Everyone nodded.

"We're ready for the Blessing Things, Father," Arator said.

Turalyon wasn't amused. He murmured a prayer, and the room was filled with a golden radiance that, for a moment, eclipsed the fel.

Arator wordlessly held out his hand. The warlock made a quick cut, and a thin trickle of blood dripped onto the floor. Jubeka waved for Arator to follow her as she returned to her place just outside the circle, picking up a small book she had placed there. Arator extended his hand, and the crimson fluid dripped onto the rune at her feet. It flashed green, sizzling as it consumed Arator's offering, then the glow subsided to a rhythmic pulse. He could smell his scalded blood.

Jubeka began to recite the summoning spell.

Arator didn't understand the words, but something inside him did and compelled him to continue walking around the circle, dripping blood on each rune until all had been activated.

A small flare of Light materialized in the paladin's hand, turning the red gash golden and healing it completely. Arator replaced his glove and stepped out of the circle.

Jubeka continued to chant.

Hurry up, Arator thought. *We're ready for you.*

More ugly-sounding words Arator did not know, and then, finally, one he did.

Sarothar.

Jubeka was still holding the book when a sudden green flash enveloped the room, followed by a sharp crack like thunder. A portal burst into being, and Arator realized with shock that Jubeka had not been the one to cast it.

CHAPTER FOURTEEN

Dreadscar Rift

THE TWISTING NETHER

Felguards, imps, felbats, and a doomguard swarmed out of the portal in the handful of seconds it took Jubeka to close it. In that sliver of time, the warlocks had blasted six imps and a felhound, but the felbats took advantage of the high ceiling and attacked from above. It caught them off-guard, as they were only anticipating one demon who couldn't fly. The air quickly became a battlefield, with the felbats swooping down on Kira.

Turalyon had curbed his first instinct to attack and instead concentrated on healing the youngest of the warlocks. She had summoned a felguard to aid her, and it hurled its axe at the felbats, keeping them busy. Even so, she'd been wounded. Turalyon sent the Light in her direction, glanced up, and saw Arator neatly put his sword through the last felbat's throat.

Then he heard his son shout, and the earth beneath them surged with Light. The demons howled and chittered in pain, and then several ignited before his eyes. It was not the Light's fire, though, not this time, but that of Ritssyn, who laughed and continued the bombardment. He was surrounded by some of the largest, ugliest imps

Turalyon had ever seen, who appeared to take as much delight as their orcish master in destroying demons.

Jubeka, like the other two, had called her own companion, a wrathguard. Unlike her fellows, she was not attacking but continuing the summoning ritual.

Arator stood over the bodies of two felhounds, flushed and angry. "Sarothar!" he cried. "You want me? *Come and get me!*"

The unmistakable sound of the whirling portal pierced through the chaos. Turalyon didn't know if it was Jubeka's or Sarothar's, but it didn't matter.

The eredar stepped through, as casually as if he were inspecting his own domain.

"This is not the outcome I desired," he said, sounding genuinely disappointed. "Nor did I anticipate meeting your friends. It's a pity you chose to involve them." The voice was deep. Turalyon could feel it reverberating in his bones. He sent the Light to his son for strength, the first time he'd done so since the fight began. He needed it now.

"You claim to know us and yet you didn't expect this?" Arator shouted at the eredar.

Sarothar drew his hand back, then swung it out in an arc, as if backhanding an impudent minion. All three of the warlocks went flying, landing hard but getting up. Turalyon realized that Sarothar was using him as a distraction. As a paladin, Turalyon needed to take care of everyone in his charge, not just those most dear to him, and Sarothar knew it.

Turalyon spared a few precious seconds to reach for the Light, to ask for its aid, and it came to him. Clarity, glass-clear and calming, descended. Jubeka needed focus; she winced as the Light granted it. Arator needed special protection; the Light bestowed it. The warlocks would need repeated and regular healing, and protection every step of the way. He could keep them all in the fight, but he could not fight with them.

Light, please . . . help us prevent this creature from yet again setting the Legion upon us.

Arator pointed his sword at the eredar. Light crashed down on Sarothar and, to Turalyon's surprise, knocked him slightly off-balance. He stumbled and righted himself.

"Not bad, young paladin. Such a good bloodline, yet I must end it. But first, where is . . . ah."

Sarothar extended his clawed hand, palm outward, and shadow began to wreathe Jubeka as he chanted in Eredun. A tendril darted down her throat, filling her mouth so that she couldn't keep chanting the spell. "You think to bind me as you did the sisters, Jubeka Shadowbreaker? Oh yes, I know *all* of you. Let's turn the tables."

The tendrils became tentacles of shadow, wrapping around Jubeka like a python made of smoke as Sarothar continued to chant.

"Foul creature, the Light will steal your words!" Turalyon shouted with all his might.

The horrible chanting ceased. Sarothar looked completely taken off-guard. He clutched his throat, his mouth still working, but nothing was coming out. Neither could he use his magic.

And in that silence, Turalyon heard the mocking laughter of his son. "What, no insults? No taunts?"

Turalyon had never been more afraid in his entire life.

Jubeka was only now recovered enough to continue the binding spell, and there was no indication that it had started to work . . . or if it would work at all. This was a dangerous moment. Sarothar had been embarrassed, thwarted, quite possibly for the first time in his very long existence. This demon had walked untouched on countless worlds, dispassionately evaluating them for the Legion. He had doled out riches and power to mortals like a parent giving candy to children. Laughter would have been a tool to use against him once they had subdued him, but now—

Arator raced toward Sarothar, sword raised, starting to descend—

As if he had anticipated that very strike, the demon—silenced, his spells useless, but extraordinarily strong—eluded it, reaching to seize Arator in the same motion.

"Arator!"

Nothing existed for Turalyon now other than Arator. Arator, his only blood, so bright, loved by the Light, loved by Alleria, loved by *him*—

Arator, and the unholy thing that had snatched him right before his father's horrified gaze. Tears poured down his face, and his heart was gripped with fear.

But not for long.

Screaming rose around him, the sounds of a fight still going, of anguished cries. Turalyon did not heed them. He roared his fury, uttered words that were raw and powerful, calling on the Light's justice and power to annihilate this wretched, terrible being of fel, of darkness, of cruelty. To use him, however it saw fit, to accomplish this task.

Turalyon felt the Light answer at once, racing through him, its radiance, its heat, building, enveloping him, ready to be unleashed.

He called for justice.

Fury.

Wrath.

The world went white.

■ ■ ■

The Void.

It had been part of Alleria for so long, and yet it was only somewhat recently that she had been able to integrate it fully into her being. The Void was her, same as a scar or a new battle stance, separate from her only when pointed out, or when it interfered with what she wanted.

She was here for the hunt, and she hunted best alone. In leaving her men, Alleria knew she had hurt the two people she loved more than she could articulate. She saw in her mind's eye the familiar pain in Turalyon's face as, yet again, their paths diverged. The fresh confusion and hurt in her son's eyes, the first time he had experienced such behavior from her. Alleria was troubled by how curt she had been, but it had been necessary to strike out on her own, to be certain her lover and son stayed safe in Suramar. With Thalyssra's resources at their disposal, which hopefully included a way to get past the runes of protection, she was confident Arator and Turalyon could do what they did best: rally troops, strategize, and prepare to hit the soul engine with a commanding force.

She would do what she did best: hunt down Sarothar's forces, thin his numbers, and compel any survivors to talk. While the Duskwatch worked to defend another encampment in the wilds around Suramar, Alleria Windrunner had followed her prey here, to the Broken Shore.

She hunted in the very shadow of the Tomb of Sargeras.

Millennia ago, it was the Temple of Elune, dedicated to the night elf goddess of the moon. But that was a distant memory of some of the longest lived of Azeroth's children. It had housed evil, and most recently had served as the Burning Legion's reentrance into the world. Dark clouds had swirled around it. Fel rivers once flowed, and it had swarmed with demons. All that was left of them now were their bones and discarded, rusting weapons.

And, of course, the imp.

It had led her on a merry chase, she'd give it that. Blending in with the landscape, the occasional flicker of fire all that betrayed it, the creature had shaken her pursuit for a few moments, but she now heard a scrabbling sound from above. Alleria looked up to see it climbing one of the tall, jutting rocks. Where it thought it was going, she had no idea.

Alleria lifted her bow and opened her other hand, extending it to the Void. It wrapped itself around her fingers like an affectionate snake, bending to her will and forming an arrow as it had so many times before. She grasped the shadowy missile, brought it down to nock—

It exploded in searing violet light.

Alleria cried out and staggered back, her entire body alert, shivering painfully, uncontrollably, as if struck by a bolt of lightning. Her heart slammed against her chest, and she struggled to breathe.

For the first time in a long while, she heard the voices.

They were *afraid.*

And then.

"Turalyon!"

Alleria gathered shadows and focus, homing in on the one who had so aggrieved the very essence of the Void. She tore open a rift in reality, hoping with all that was in her that their connection and the Void's urgency would be enough to avert the danger of traveling utterly blind. Without hesitation, she hurled herself into the rift, imagining a thousand horrifying scenarios on the other side.

If she made it to the other side.

When she emerged, her senses were instantly assaulted: Light blazed, blinding her. Voices demonic, thundering, chanting; cracking of flame and spell. The reek of burned flesh and spilled blood and fear and fel. The Void, hammering on her mind, rushing to shield her eyes with shadow so she could see.

A male figure, tall and powerfully built, wrapped in gleaming, harsh white-gold light that obscured his features, but flooded every part of the rocky space.

It was, as she knew and feared it would be, her beloved.

And yet it was not.

Alleria had seen Turalyon call upon the avenging aspect of the Light many times before. But it had never done *this* to him. As the sun lit the land, as a naaru shimmered and gleamed, thus was Turalyon. His white hair was the hue of a shaft of sunlight, his skin glowed gold, and brilliance poured from him almost like a waterfall of Light.

And his *face* . . .

His handsome features were contorted in sheer, perfect rage. The scars on his face burned white, and his eyes were now twin suns. He was shouting, his melodic voice ringing out yet still his, still beautiful; church bells not calling the faithful to fellowship, but sounding the warning of a conflagration. The words were filled with hate, fury, and righteousness, but Alleria could not understand them, only feel their power.

Sarothar, as calm as Turalyon was raging, his skin bright red in the Light, towered over the paladin, over others whose presence Alleria only now glimpsed, but she spared no thought for them.

Because the eredar clutched her son.

All of this registered in an instant.

Turalyon's eerie voice reached a pounding crescendo, and then, where the man'ari stood gloating, there was now only Turalyon's Light, summoned in outrage and unleashed in annihilation. It blossomed, intolerably, impossibly bright, and Alleria cried out, her eyes snapping shut in instinctive protection as she clapped her hands to her ears at the resulting bone-shaking explosion.

Silence.

Slowly, almost surprised that she was unharmed, Alleria realized she'd been knocked off her feet by the power of the explosion. She opened her eyes, slitting them immediately against the Light that had dimmed only slightly from its blinding apex.

. . . Arator!

Where Sarothar had stood an instant before, there was now an enormous crater. And in its center, covered with fine dust, some of it still settling, was her son, easing himself into a sitting position. Relief shot through her, but hard on its heels was the sickening realization that although the eredar was more than destroyed, the Light that had obliterated him had not withdrawn from its wielder.

Turalyon stood almost in the same position as he had been a moment earlier. The Light still enveloped him, and his expression had not eased. He seemed not to have noticed that his son had survived and made no acknowledgment of Alleria's abrupt arrival.

It does not linger with him like this. The Light—it aids him, then it is over. How . . .

Slowly, Alleria got to her feet, her mind racing as she tried to process what was transpiring. Her gaze fell upon a strange tableau: demons, their weapons in hand but not raised, standing beside an orc and a human, wounded and shivering. The two had closed ranks around a Forsaken woman, doing their best to spare her the Light's judgment upon her undead state.

Almost immediately, Alleria understood that the demons weren't guarding prisoners, but defending their masters. Arator's idea had been to enlist the aid of warlocks to summon and destroy Sarothar.

It had worked. The fight was over . . . but the group was not out of danger.

As if to confirm her worst fears, Turalyon spoke. "*The Light has destroyed a dreadful enemy today. And so shall it be ever thus, that* all *forces of darkness,* all *foes of the Light, shall know oblivion!*"

The resonance yet permeated his voice, elevated it, honed it to melodic purity, but Alleria did not find it beautiful. It chilled her to the bone.

Stop him! STOP HIM! the Void urged.

"*The shadows shall be banished, the demonic contagion wiped clean. Those who ally with evil, who dare walk outside of the Light's blessings—*"

"Turalyon!" Alleria cried, surging forward. Her voice sounded small in her own ears, fragile and faint after hearing his Light-augmented one.

The radiant being turned his head. His eyes were pools of white-hot light, and his expression did not change.

Turalyon, beloved, what have you done?

"Turalyon," she called again. "It's me. Alleria."

There was no response. *See me,* she thought. *See me, my love.*

"*. . . Alleria?*"

The voice was still not truly his own, but its clamoring had faded, ever so slightly.

"Yes, love, I'm here." Slowly, she stepped toward him, but paused as the white brows drew together again.

"You left," Turalyon rumbled. There was anger there, but it was threaded through pain. It cut Alleria sharply. How many times had she turned away from him? She had lost count. Most were for good, necessary purposes, but some were not. And he had never rebuked her. Never shamed or attempted to dissuade her. It had taken time, but he had come to accept her and her choices.

Or so she thought.

"I shouldn't have," she said, her voice thick. "But I'm here now."

Suddenly the thought of never again being able to gently brush his arm, to steal a quick kiss, to melt into the solid, warm strength of him was unbearable. For years, Void and Light had kept them apart. But they were stubborn, she and Turalyon, and never walked away from the possibility that one day, they could again share what was so common, so everyday to others, and so precious and hard-won for them.

Alleria could not, *would* not allow the Light to take that from them.

Despite the Void roaring in her ears, she closed the distance between them, bare hand extended.

The Light faded from Turalyon. He swayed, then dropped to his knees. He looked up at her as she knelt beside him, and his eyes were his normal, beautiful shade of gold-brown.

"I told you, I would never leave you behind," he said. And he reached out his hand.

A sharp pang pierced her. He had, so long ago, when she had refused to let him go to battle without her. When their love was new. *I will never leave you behind,* he had said.

And she had replied, *And I will never leave you.*

Their fingers first brushed, then entwined tightly. "I'm not going anywhere," Alleria said. "Not without you."

"He needed you. *I* needed you. The demon nearly had us."

The vulnerability of his words almost undid Alleria—but they also gave her hope. "I'm here, now. It's over, beloved. You saved our son."

She sought her son's eyes and could see the tears in them, but also the wariness in his body. She beckoned to him, but he didn't yet move.

"Arator," said Turalyon. "My son."

Arator had heard it, as Alleria had: his father's voice. His real voice, stronger now, emerging from beneath the din of the Light's bell tones. Alleria extended her other hand to him. Now, slowly, eyes still on his father, Arator stepped beside Alleria. He removed his glove and grasped her hand. This simple contact, of unspoken connection and comfort, struck her powerfully. The knot of apprehension in Alleria's chest began to loosen, and she gripped her son's hand hard, grounding herself in the reality of the moment.

"It's over, beloved," Alleria whispered. "We're safe. We're together."

Turalyon pulled her, and their son, into his arms, and they clung to one another as if they were the only solid things in a sea of chaos.

■ ■ ■

The warlocks, wisely, had left the arena while Arator and Alleria had focused on Turalyon. The family emerged from the corridor to see Bulzan awaiting them. He looked as he had when they had first arrived, but this time, there was no lightening of his countenance.

"You will follow me," he said.

Wordlessly, they did. Arator had no idea what to expect. He'd made a promise to Thalonia that Turalyon would conduct himself with respect toward the warlocks. Given how this had turned into near disaster—albeit after his father had done . . . something, Arator wasn't entirely sure *what,* to Sarothar—he couldn't know what would come next.

Bulzan led them to the same place where Arator had spoken to them from his heart, trying to gain their trust. How optimistic he had been then. And how badly things had gone wrong.

"Jubeka," Kanrethad said, "these are your guests. And your responsibility."

The Forsaken nodded. "Before I get to the good part," she said,

"Lady Alleria. I'm sorry you did not arrive under different circumstances. But allow me to convey our appreciation that *you* did arrive."

Alleria inclined her head respectfully. "I'm grateful to have been here during . . . to have been here. And if I may—"

"You may not," Jubeka said. "First things first. Arator, did Thalonia pass along my message?"

He nodded. "Yes, she did."

"And what, pray, was that message?"

Arator closed his eyes briefly. "That my father needed to be on his best behavior. If he caused trouble, all of us would be deemed responsible and there would be consequences."

"And would you say that your father held up his end of the bargain?"

Before Arator could speak, Turalyon interjected, "No. I did not. We came under a flag of truce to ask a favor from you. I violated that solemn agreement, destroyed your property, and excessively used a powerful force that could have harmed you. I submit myself to your judgment. My only request is you allow Alleria and Arator to depart."

"You are in no position to ask anything," Jubeka replied.

Arator started to speak, but she silenced him with a glance. She rose and started to walk around them, sizing them up.

"Paladins," she said, with a hint of disgust. "Always more trouble than you're worth. Passing judgment on folks trying to help you. Making craters in their arenas. Scaring their demons. What would you have done, had not your son and lady come to remind you who you were?"

Turalyon looked her directly in her yellow eyes. "I don't know," he said simply. "What happened was something I've never experienced before—not on that level, with that . . ." his voice trailed off. "I don't know what happened."

"That's what I thought," Jubeka said. She sighed, shook her head, and said, more kindly, "But I do."

Arator was completely confused by now, but he held his tongue. Jubeka spoke without rancor. "Your whole world is about saving people. From their enemies, from corruption and falling to darkness. From themselves. And you're so tightly wound by all that judging that if you get too much winding, you'll break just like an old clock. So when you show up for help with an eredar who has already beaten you once, find out he's much worse than you thought, and he goes after your boy—"

She mimed turning a key. "*Snap.*"

Arator glanced at his father. Turalyon was looking at the floor, trying to remain composed, but a muscle twitched near his eye.

"Alleria, your only part in this was to help, so you're free to go. Arator," she said, "I've a question for you. Did you ever have any real concern your father would attempt to cause us harm?"

"Real harm? No. Not unless he saw or was asked to do something that would harm innocent people."

"The soul shard confusion," Jubeka said, nodding.

"But," and he glanced at his father, hoping Turalyon would understand, "I *did* worry he might say something in a heated moment he couldn't walk back. His beliefs are very important to him."

It was all true. Jubeka appeared satisfied. "Your assessment is similar to mine. The council and I have been talking. Alleria, of course, did nothing but assist. You, Arator . . ." She gave him a smile. "You showed us respect. You fought courageously. And let's not forget you saved our lives at great risk to your own. These are acts we do not take lightly. You also brought a fascinating demon to our attention, and your father . . . well, whatever else he did, Sarothar is most certainly dead. You are all free to go. But there is one thing Turalyon must pay for."

Arator took a quick breath and looked at his father. Turalyon gave him a reassuring nod. "It will be all right, son."

"Turalyon, Lord of the Silver Hand, High Exarch of the Grand Army of the Light . . ." Jubeka placed herself directly in front of him, craning her neck. "You must pay . . . whatever expenses we incur repairing our arena."

She laughed at Arator's visible relief.

Turalyon looked uncertain. "Of course. Is there . . . nothing else I can do, to make reparations?"

"Think twice before judging folks," Jubeka said. "And take good care of your family. Those who stick by you are rarer than you think."

"And now, if you will excuse us, we have work to do," said Kanrethad.

"Of course," Alleria said. "Thank you, Jubeka. Thank you all for your aid, and your graciousness in the matter." To her family, she said, "We should return and let Thalyssra know what has transpired."

"Agreed," Arator said. "And . . . Kira? I can't give you the fang. It's not mine to give. But when I return it to Kayn, I will tell him of your interest—"

"And knowledge," Kira said quickly. "I'm extremely familiar with these kinds of felhounds."

"—and your knowledge," Arator amended. "He might be willing to meet with you and discuss it."

Kira's face dissolved into a delighted smile. "That would be so exciting. Thank you!"

"*Whaaaat?* You got Kira excited about something?" exclaimed Jubeka in pretend shock. "Pffft, that's a bigger victory than destroying Sarothar! A final piece of advice, if I may?"

"We would welcome it," Turalyon said.

Jubeka turned her glowing eyes to Arator. "Find that soul engine. Remember what I told you about it. Make sure it's completely destroyed, not just disabled. Sarothar is gone, and there will be some disarray, but as long as that engine's active, his forces can make a whole lot of mischief with it."

Arator smiled warmly at her. He'd known her for only a brief time, but she had made an indelible and positive impression. "I'll remember. Thank you, Jubeka. You stood with us from the start to the end, and we won't forget that. The next time I see Lord Grayson, I'm going to tell him what happened here. To remind him of his oath, if nothing else. And . . . maybe to make him feel just a *little* bit ashamed."

Jubeka's undead face twitched in a smile.

CHAPTER FIFTEEN

The Nighthold, Suramar City

BROKEN ISLES

Previously, all three would have relished the aftermath of their victory. But this time, unspoken matters hung heavy in the air, and Arator, usually the one initiating the difficult conversations, found himself exhausted. He'd been fully healed, and the travel back to Suramar City hadn't been difficult, but he needed a quiet moment by himself to think. He felt off-balance, unsettled, and also anxious as to how they would be received by Thalyssra and Lor'themar.

It became apparent very soon. As they landed their loaned gryphons, several Duskwatch guards approached. Arator started to dismount, but one of the guards motioned for him to hold. "Sir Arator, please remain seated and state your business in Suramar."

The guard looked uncomfortable, though it was hard to tell through her helm. Arator didn't mind. She had her orders, and a military operation was in progress. "Of course. Please tell the first arcanist that my party wishes to speak with her immediately. We have important information regarding Felsoul Hold."

"I'm sorry, sir, we were informed that you are no longer involved in the current military operation."

Alleria gave the paladins a surprised look.

"We have news," Arator said, deliberately not looking at his mother. "News the first arcanist needs to know."

The guard looked uncomfortable. Another noticed the conversation and stepped forward. "We can take a message if you wish," he said.

Arator started to say something, then closed his mouth. Sarothar might be gone, but the threat was not over. He recalled grilling Liadrin about the honey she had delivered. If there were any other shapeshifters in Sarothar's army, posing as a guard ferrying messages would be an ideal disguise.

"Only this," he said. "We're not leaving until we have delivered our news to her in person and in private."

The Duskwatch guard's expression hardened. "You may be waiting a long time. Or perhaps I should arrest you, and you can deliver your news from a prison cell."

"If that's what it takes," Arator said readily, "arrest me now. It might speed things up."

Arator was surprised that neither of his parents interrupted. He imagined they would if the Duskwatch guard followed through with his threat, but he wasn't sure. It was also possible they might all soon be sharing a cell.

The guard looked at each of them in turn, swore under his breath, and, sighing, said, "Tell the first arcanist who's here. And let her know his . . . terms."

It did not take long. The guard brought her manasaber back at a brisk pace and cleared them to land at the Nighthold. She started to give them directions, but Arator smiled and said, "Thank you, we know the way." As the gryphons leaped into the air, Arator glanced back at the second guard, who was still scowling.

A short flight later, they were admitted to the war room. Thalyssra was at her desk, reading what looked to be dispatches, while Liadrin and Lor'themar spoke quietly. All activity abruptly ceased as the three entered.

"Arator," she said. "You were relieved of duty. Yet here you are." She folded her arms. "Speak."

"We hunted down Sarothar. In the process, we learned a great deal about who he is, what he's done, and how he thinks. We found him, we killed him, and we're here to tell you everything we know." He paused. "You didn't give orders for us *not* to follow any leads," he said, "but . . . I know it was implied. You should know that my father was against this idea, my mother was unaware, and I take full responsibility."

She stared at him for a moment, then looked to Alleria and Turalyon. "Is . . . this true?" she asked. "Is he really dead?"

They nodded.

She and Lor'themar exchanged glances, then Thalyssra indicated three chairs. "Tell me everything you know. And I will decide how to proceed from there."

Everything you know. That was exactly how he had phrased it, wasn't it? Very well.

"You remember I mentioned bringing Sarothar to us. The only way to do that was through a summoning, which would require a warlock."

"You know I have a great mistrust of warlocks," the first arcanist said. "A *justified* mistrust."

"I know this. But I wanted to make sure that, if we attempted this, it would work. I would need warlocks who were both powerful and trustworthy. So I approached the Council of the Black Harvest."

"I know of this council."

"Then you must know that they have acquired knowledge and artifacts that have helped the world turn back the Legion. My father and I journeyed to Dreadscar Rift, where the council granted us an audience. First Arcanist Thalyssra, we gave you the demon's name. Did you research it?"

The sudden change of topic caught her off-guard. "Of course we did," she said, though the recollection seemed to irritate her. "We found nothing, not in any archive. Demons lie, so I am certain this eredar lied about his name. It was a waste of time."

Arator smiled a little. "The council had the same luck. No information. Until they located a single source: a journal from a priest, interrogating another demon."

He told her then about Sarothar's role. How more infamous demons relied upon his thorough investigations of worlds, how he quietly scouted a world to prepare it for invasion. All the strange and frightening things he could recall, read to him from a tiny, battered journal by a Forsaken warlock.

Thalyssra listened, first skeptically, then curiously, and finally, intensely. So did Alleria. This was her first time hearing this new information, but Arator noticed she looked more thoughtful than surprised.

"Sarothar was far more dangerous than we knew. The council understood they were taking a terrible risk, and yet they gave their help willingly. Without their aid, we would be in the same position we left you in. Sarothar was successfully summoned and dispatched."

He did not tell them of the moment when Sarothar had seized him. When his father had all but become the Light, and the demon had been ground to dust. The moment was too powerful, too personal, and it was his father's story to share or keep close.

"The council charged no coin, asked no favors, pushed no bargains. I promised them I would not let their efforts go unrecognized."

Arator hoped his father was listening, too. He wanted them to understand that people were not always who one expected them to be, for good or ill, and that no one should condemn an entire group without asking themselves as to why they would wish to do so.

Thalyssra was quiet for a long time. At last, she spoke.

"Your friends and allies are fortunate to have you as their champion," Thalyssra said. "I appreciate that their efforts contributed to the defeat of this enemy. I shall consider their service to this kingdom going forward. Though," she added, with the first hint of a smile he had seen since they arrived, "it is a rare paladin indeed who discards orders."

"Why did you support him?" The question came not from Thalyssra, but from Lor'themar. He regarded Turalyon with narrowed eyes, arms folded across his chest. "None of this sounds like you, Turalyon, if I may be so bold as to say so."

The high exarch seemed to consider for a moment. "It is indeed unlike me to disregard the will of any leader, Horde or Alliance. It is neither respectful nor does it promote good relations. I assure you I did not do so lightly. I also am disinclined to work side by side with warlocks and am not overfond of the Illidari. I fully trust neither of these groups. I would not have sought them out on my own. What I do trust is my son's integrity and his ability to see things that more traditional ways of thinking can overlook.

"Arator is a man of courage and compassion, and a loyal friend, and he inspires these qualities in others. Both instances, those in whom he put his faith, and sometimes his life, were sincere and willing to help. Both instances, that help was necessary to move forward, and his plans were based on grounded assessments. That is why I agreed to stay with him."

He continued to speak but looked at Arator now. "He relied on chance, luck, and the goodwill of others far more than I would like. These are unpredictable and fragile pillars."

Turalyon returned his attention to Lor'themar and Thalyssra. "But, Sarothar had a long history in ensuring things work out the way he wanted them to. I have no doubt that we would still be playing guessing games with him at the minimum and inadvertently furthering our own demise at the worst if it had not been for Arator's . . . unconventional methods and unlikely friendships."

Arator stared at his father. He wasn't sure what he was expecting Turalyon to say, but it wasn't this. These were not the kind words of a father; they were the sincere assessments of a military leader. Turalyon loved him, and Arator knew that. But he also knew that the high exarch, when asked why he disobeyed orders, would not have said a word of praise he thought was undeserved. Tears stung his eyes and he blinked them back.

"I imagine it was hard to hold your tongue at moments," said Thalyssra, clearly thinking of the warlocks.

"There were several times that I didn't."

"And you, Alleria?" asked Lor'themar. "You struck off on your own for a while. Was your search fruitful?"

"I was determined to thin Sarothar's numbers and interrogate any subordinate I could find. Knowing what I know now, though, I'm not sure I would do the same. Arator had the wiser plan, and the superior result."

"The important thing is that Sarothar is dead," Arator said, trying to bring the conversation back to the present moment. "There you have it."

Thalyssra sank back in her chair and closed her eyes briefly, allowing herself the first moment of relaxation Arator had seen from her since they'd walked into the room. "This news could not be more welcome," Thalyssra said. "We have been dealing with our own battlefront. Shortly after you left, demons stepped up their attacks and struck four new communities. The Duskwatch were able to fight them off, but not without casualties."

"The Blood Knights coordinated their assault of Felsoul Hold with the Duskwatch, attacking on two fronts," said Liadrin. "The area was successfully cleared, and the nightborne they had captured are now safe and with their families. I cannot say the same for many of my knights, though."

It had been Liadrin who had sent Arator on this adventure, thinking to spare her Blood Knights boredom. In the end, she spared them nothing. He felt a pang.

"I let you down, Liadrin," Arator said quietly. "If you would allow me, it would be an honor to fight alongside you and your knights to make up for it."

"There's nothing to make up for," she said. "The Blood Knights would have made the same choices you did. At this point, it's just clearing out some stragglers here and there. But . . . thank you." She gave him a tired but genuine smile.

"And . . . the soul engine?" Turalyon asked.

"Utterly destroyed," Thalyssra said, with satisfaction. "Once the area was cleared, I sent an expert in Eredun to decipher the runes, and a hand-picked team of Duskwatch to ensure it was completely dismantled. Since Sarothar is defeated, there's no one left to rebuild it. A better outcome than I had dared hope . . . and one that we almost didn't have. Arator, Alleria, Turalyon, please accept my apologies. I should not have removed you from the investigation."

"We were all trying to do what we thought was best for our people and the future of our world," Alleria said.

"Alleria speaks for us all," Turalyon said.

"A gracious response," said Lor'themar. "Correct me if I am wrong, but . . . it sounds as if this mission's success hinged on decisions and suggestions made by you, Arator."

"Oh, oh no," Arator said immediately, flushing with embarrassment. "Regent Lord, I disagree with that assessment, and if you came to that conclusion, you could not be more—"

"Correct," said Alleria.

Turalyon nodded.

Lor'themar rose. "I will pen formal letters both to you, Lady Liadrin, commending your decision to send Arator our way, and to the Highlord of the Silver Hand. Arator, the five of us are veterans and much older than you. We are hard to impress. Somehow, you've managed." A smile touched his lips. "You've come a long way since the first time you practiced with a sword. If I recall correctly, you tripped over it more often than you struck the training dummy."

"In my defense, it was a very long sword and a very intimidating dummy," Arator said with a smile.

Liadrin rose. "I should give the troops the good news."

"Liadrin, thank you," Thalyssra said. "Your help was invaluable. I and my people are grateful."

"I will pass that along to them."

Arator rose with her. "The offer still stands," he said. "I'll come with you if you like."

"No need, but I thank you. Go get some sleep." She squeezed his arm affectionately. "Well done, my friend," she said, and left.

"I'll follow Liadrin's lead and usher *all* of you off to baths and some rest," Thalyssra said. "I shall add my commendations to those of my husband. Your superiors should know of your deeds, Arator. They are not only impressive, but they were motivated by a desire to unify and to work to the benefit of all involved. You have the grateful thanks of Suramar, Quel'Thalas, and I expect many more nations, once word reaches them. Will you not stay for a few days? We never did finish that dinner, and my chef would be disappointed twice if you refuse."

"Well, we can't have that, can we?" Arator said.

"Never disappoint the chefs," Turalyon said with mock solemnity. "Doesn't end well for one."

Alleria sighed. "Oh, you two definitely need some sleep."

■ ■ ■

Alleria indulged in a long, hot bath. Two, actually: one to scrub away sweat, grime, blood, and fel from hair and skin, and the second to simply soak, relaxing into the warm water to ease deeper aches in her body and release knots tied for too long. Minerals infused with fragrant night-blooming flowers and healing herbs turned the hot water into a treatment all its own, urging her to relax and let go.

Alleria wished she could.

The comforting words she had said to Thalyssra were true. Yet she was unable to accept the very advice she gave the other woman. After Sarothar's ambush, leaving to use her own methods to locate him had truly felt like the right course of action. It was what she had done before, for so long.

Hunt the prey alone. Draw it to you, not to those you love.

But Alleria saw now that what she thought was a selfless act had put her greatest loves in harm's way.

Wincing, she sank beneath the perfumed water for a moment, holding her breath. She should have been there, fighting beside them, lending not only her skills and unique abilities, but her *presence.* Without anyone he fully trusted to aid him when their son was in danger, Turalyon had done something reckless and extremely dangerous.

His face . . . so cruel, something Turalyon *never* was. His features, blurred by the Light.

Her head broke the water and, panting, she gulped air. *If I hadn't been there . . .*

But she had been there in time. She had reached out with her whole heart, and Turalyon, *her* Turalyon, had reached back. The demon was dead, the soul engine destroyed, the invasion thwarted, her family together and on good terms with Thalyssra and Lor'themar.

It was, as Thalyssra had pointed out, a better outcome than any of them had the right to expect.

The water had grown cold. Alleria sighed and stepped out, shivering, and reached for a warm, soft robe.

Several unexpected things awaited her. The first was a cheerful, crackling fire, very welcome after the bath. The second was a woven basket placed on the bed. In it were all the clothes from her journey, mended, washed, and neatly folded. Beside it was draped a lovely gown of shimmery green fabric, the hem beautifully embroidered, and a selection of slippers. A note was tucked into the basket:

> Dearest Alleria,
>
> I hope you do not mind that I took the liberty of having your travel clothing repaired and cleaned. I've also had a gown of mine altered. My tailor is excellent, but please do let me know if it doesn't fit. I offer a pair of slippers that should suit you as well. Please wear whatever you wish.
>
> I would have liked to have had our master armorer do as our tailor did, but my Lor'themar told me you always insisted on cleaning and repairing your own, so I have merely provided any necessary items you might need for that task.
>
> We are so grateful to you all, and we will be pleased to, at long last, finish our dinner for you tomorrow evening.
>
> —*Thalyssra*

Alleria sank down on the bed beside the gown and reached out to touch it, finding it as silky as it appeared. She plucked a tunic from the basket and found it spotless and fragrant. The gown and clean clothing were lovely, but it was the first arcanist's consideration about the armor that affected Alleria the most. She *had* always been insistent about her armor. Alleria allowed herself to be pleased that after all this time, Lor'themar still remembered.

All the fighting they had seen when they were younger. All the decades, centuries, spent stabbing, smiting, and otherwise destroying their enemies.

She had been the ranger captain, the huntress, a member of the Grand Army of the Light, a practitioner of the Void . . . titles, terms, identities that she had donned like clothing on first the girl and then the woman who was simply Alleria Windrunner. She recalled the formal occasions the family had to dress for, and how they all despised such events. Now, though, to her surprise, Alleria welcomed the offer to shed her armor and titles and simply appreciate elegance and beauty, at least for an evening. Yet . . . the reminder of her armor dispelled the little languor the bath had imparted.

They had prevented an eredar from launching a fresh invasion. But Azeroth was not yet safe. It would *never* be safe, not when Xal'atath was out there. Alleria knew that on the morrow following the dinner she would awaken, breakfast with her kind hosts, and leave. Again.

But she would remain one day. She owed it to her family, and to her hosts.

■ ■ ■

Alleria did not drink alcohol often, and when she did she sipped sparingly. Tonight, though, she was on her second goblet of arcwine and her mood was lifting. She suspected, however, that the heady wine had little to do with that.

The mission had begun here, over a meal in the company of the regent lord and the first arcanist. Yet again intuiting what her guests would most appreciate, Thalyssra had prepared not a lavish seven-course meal, as before . . . but a picnic with simple fare.

It was not entirely rustic, however. The blankets on the grass had been furnished with soft, supportive cushions made of the finest material. A lone performer plucked the strings of an instrument that was certainly rare and ancient, which doubtless had a name and an intriguing history. Beautifully carved stone lanterns provided a soft warm glow in the lavender evening.

What the food lacked in formality it made up for with flavor. Bread, cheeses in a variety of color and texture, imported fruit—"One of the unexpected pleasures after opening to the outside world," Thalyssra quipped—and meat, fowl, and fish dishes.

It had amused their hostess to note that all her guests had opted for the formal clothing to attend what had turned out to be informal dining. "Did you plan it this way?" Turalyon had asked, gazing at the area with a bemused expression, looking slightly uncomfortable in a shirt, coat, and trousers.

"I simply left it up to my guests to choose what gave them pleasure." Thalyssra swirled the arcwine in her glass, gazing thoughtfully into its dark purple depths. "I have lived both sides. I was Highborne and grew up with all the luxuries such birth provided me. I have also known the horrors of mindless despair. Of exile and starvation. Clinging to life by the thinnest of threads in places of utter squalor. I led rebels against the very world in which I'd grown up. Now, *all* my people have nourishment. Arcane sustenance. Safe places to live."

She lifted her eyes to his and smiled. "But life is more than simply existing, Turalyon. From time to time, everyone needs something they don't *need.* Beauty. Music. The perfect confection. But . . . sometimes, I just want bread, cheese, and friends to share them with. Would you prefer something more formal?"

"Oh no," said Arator. "I love the mix."

And he would, Alleria realized at that moment. Her son, who was a mixture of high elf and human, noble grace and necessary violence on the battlefield, friend to paladin and warlock alike. "The Redeemer," he had been named. It was a little mystery, what he would redeem and how. Of course, prophecies and predictions were notoriously open to interpretation. If not precisely "redeem" in a literal sense, Arator did seem to summon forth the best in people. He encouraged them to fight harder, become less judgmental. To be willing to join with others for a worthy cause. Perhaps her son had already lived up to his name not by some grand gesture, but simply by being himself.

He somehow managed to look right at home anywhere he was, even now, in a full formal robe with magically glowing embroidery, the sleeves rolled up, away from the messy, hand-eaten food.

He had a smudge of sauce on his face. Before she realized what she was doing, Alleria had leaned over and wiped it off.

Half laughing, half indignant, Arator sputtered a protest, ducking away from her and raising his hand, still holding a leg of meat, as if to block her.

Everyone laughed at the simple motherly gesture, and Arator rolled his eyes in mock exasperation. Alleria shrugged, a little abashed, but the laughter was warm and genuine. She looked at Turalyon, sprawled out next to her, and gave him a look of chagrin.

"I suppose a mother has to mortify her son sometime," she said.

"It's not the most embarrassing thing you've seen at a picnic," he reminded her, and Alleria started laughing again.

"Now, now, share the joke, you two," Arator said. "If I get laughed at, *you're* going to get laughed at."

Alleria saw he was still a little pink.

"Oh, just . . . nothing. It's between Alleria and myself," Turalyon said, but the gauntlet had been thrown down, and both his child and their hosts were clamoring for the story.

It was perfect. Alleria listened with laughter and love in her heart as Turalyon warmed to the task, sparing not his own excruciating embarrassment nor Alleria's not-at-all-disguised avoidance of him.

Throughout, Lor'themar had remained slightly apart from the joviality. He chuckled at the stories, replied courteously when appropriate, and was at his warmest when interacting with his wife. Alleria understood, and expected nothing more. Despite Thalyssra's genuine warmth, there were still things that divided Alleria and her family from Thalyssra and hers. But Lor'themar had obviously been proud of Arator, and she was glad that her son seemed to bring out the kindest in the regent lord.

Then, to her surprise, after the tale of the skunk had been shared, he helped himself to another glass of arcwine and said, "Alleria, do you remember Lirath's kitten?"

"I do," she said, touched and surprised.

"Lirath was the most imaginative Windrunner," Lor'themar said to the others. "Lireesa and her daughters were much more practical."

Everyone, including Alleria, laughed.

"He was always making up things, even as a small child. Lots of friends and creatures we couldn't see, and they'd all have their own story."

Alleria leaned against Turalyon's shoulder and he put his arm around her, warmed by the tone of Lor'themar's voice as he told the table about Lirath's imaginary kitten and its misadventures. "He said that the kitten—oh, what was its name, Alleria?"

"Rew," she said.

"Ah ah, say it right." He was enjoying himself, and she was, too.

She protested vigorously, but her family clamored for it.

"Traitors," Alleria said, then cleared her throat and emitted a high-pitched mew. It was several minutes before everyone had stopped laughing long enough for Lor'themar to continue. "As I was saying," he said, and took another sip of arcwine, "Lirath told us that Rew loved the sound of his pipe and if he was around when he played, it would come out and purr and play with him."

"Of course, Rew was somehow never within earshot when Lirath tried to prove this story," Alleria said.

"Naturally," Turalyon said, his eyes dancing.

"So, one day, I was chatting outside with Alleria and her sisters, and we heard Lirath playing his pipe. It was time for supper, so we went to get him." Lor'themar paused for effect, then put down his glass and spread his arms out, his hands more than a yard apart from one another.

"Rew was *this big,* he was a *lynx,* and damned if he wasn't purring!"

The table erupted with laughter, along with calls for more wine and tales of the Windrunners from their younger days.

"Lireesa loved her family," Lor'themar continued, "but she was far more comfortable commanding units than mothering children."

"And it certainly showed," Alleria cut in. "She would have loved to run the house like the Farstrider barracks. It would have been cleaner, certainly. We brought in half of Eversong every time we came back inside."

"Ah, but it was a happy home," said her old friend. His hand reached for his wife's, and she stroked his hair, smiling lovingly down at him. "Shrieks of laughter when you all were young. Sylvanas's interminable pranks. Your father humming lullabies in the evening after a meal or reading aloud to you. Lirath's playing."

"Stepping on *everything,*" Alleria said. "No toys or weapons ever got put away."

"That, too! And we could always tell when you and she had a fight over whether you'd become ranger general," Lor'themar continued. "She would put us through extra drills."

Alleria looked mortified. "Did she really?"

"Oh yes," he said, and Alleria covered her face and laughed. "No one got under her skin like you did. Not even the Amani. You were such a rebel."

Alleria brushed her son's tattoos. "Rebellion runs in the family."

"Oh good," Arator quipped. "Then I will surely never get in trouble for it."

"Don't push your luck, son," Turalyon said, but he was smiling.

"I would like to propose a toast to our gracious hosts—Thalyssra and Lor'themar," Arator said. He rose. "Thank you for entrusting this mission to the three of us, and for all the kindness you've shown us since our return to Suramar."

"Hear, hear," said Alleria, clinking her glass against Turalyon's and drinking.

"And to our honored guests," Lor'themar said, lifting his own glass. "Not just for their courage and heroism on behalf of others, for which we are most grateful, but for themselves. I always laughed so freely when I was with the Windrunner family. And I am glad to be doing so with two of them again. To the Windrunners, past, present, and future."

"To the Windrunners!" Alleria raised her glass and sipped again, glad to be with her son, missing her brother and sisters. The dead, the living . . . and the one in between.

"I wish to toast the gentlemen present," Thalyssra said. "You are all, truly, gems among men. First, dearest husband, having you by my side during these past years has been the great joy of my life. I value your support and kindness, your keen mind and great heart, more than you may ever know."

"And I yours, my darling. To many, many more years of facing the world side by side, hand in hand."

Thalyssra gave her spouse a light kiss and a smile that shone like the stars while Alleria teased, "What was it? Your secret to happiness? Portaling, poetry, and prioritizing?"

"Indeed! I heartily recommend all three."

"I do not think Father would make a great poet," Arator said, grinning.

"Oh, I don't know about that. You didn't know him when we were younger."

She blamed the wine this time for her frankness. Turalyon then gave her one of the shy, boyish smiles that usually only she ever saw.

"Oho!" Thalyssra said, pouncing on the opportunity. "You are full of surprises, Turalyon. Pray, give us an example of a line so lovely as to win the heart of the fair Alleria Windrunner."

Without batting an eye, his face serious, Turalyon said in his rich, warm baritone: "There once was a fellow from Goldshire—"

The entire group dissolved into whoops of laughter as Turalyon, looking as innocent as the priest he had once been, said repeatedly, "What? What's so funny?"

Arator shook his head. "You two," he said, sounding for all the world like an adult admonishing two teenagers. "You should really just get married and be done with it. Never understood why you didn't."

It was unexpected . . . but, finally, it was out.

The ebullience of the party abruptly shifted into awkward silence.

"Does it bother you, my son?" Alleria asked, hoping to salvage all the evening's closeness.

He shook his head. "No," he said, "it just seems odd. A thousand years is a very long time to drag your feet."

Soft, cautious chuckles emerged. Alleria leaned into it. "Well, when you put it *that* way . . ." More laughter, and she continued. "The years may have been long, but I think we all know how fast moments can fly by when one is constantly in battle or training for one. Every morning was a victory, every day a gamble, and every night we fell asleep with exhaustion and gratitude to have survived. There was no time to even think of the future, except in terms of the next few hours. I promise you, anyone under those circumstances would be hard-pressed to think about guest lists, venues . . . *cake*," she finished, directing it gently at her hosts.

Even as Lor'themar and Thalyssra smiled at her words, Alleria was acutely aware of what was on everyone's mind: *The war is over. What's stopping them now?*

"Well, in terms of the next few hours, I do hope no one chokes on the wine," quipped Lor'themar drily. "It would be a pity if an excellent vintage accomplished what all those demons failed to do."

Arator had been taking a sip and actually did start to choke, laughing and coughing but clearly in no danger of anything except staining his beautiful robe. The little cloud had passed, and Alleria exhaled. Turalyon, reclining close beside her, was a steady, quiet comfort, doing nothing, saying nothing, and the conversation moved on to other things.

Wine bottles and witticisms accumulated, and the pile of dessert fruit, pastries, and cheeses diminished. Lor'themar discovered that Thalyssra had never heard the story of the Battle of Five Arrows and turned to Alleria expectantly.

"Lireesa was your mother," he said with respect. "Would you care to tell the tale?"

Alleria glanced at her son. He lay on his back, hands clasped behind his head, gazing up at the night sky with a half-smile on his face. With no demons to hunt, no arguments to interrupt, no battles to fight, he was fully present in this moment, in this pause before the next chase, or argument, or battle. *I would have taught you how to count by using stars,* she thought. *I would have told you all the stories, kissed you good night, and tucked you in.* Arator was a grown man, not a boy, but beneath the candle- and starlight, in the innocent awe inspired by something vast and beautiful, she caught a glimpse of the child he had been.

With the wistfulness came a trace of melancholy, and Alleria's thoughts turned from the laughter and warmth of the gathering to the cold light of dawn, not so far away. They would be leaving shortly thereafter, to pick up their weapons, and the hunt, once more.

"I think I will retire," she said. "Recent events are catching up with me. Thank you so much, both of you, for everything. It's been a lovely and memorable night."

"Of course," Lor'themar said. "We will see you in the morning."

Turalyon sat up and started to rise as well, but she touched his shoulder gently. "No, love, stay. It's a good story, and I don't think I ever told you about it."

"Even after a thousand years?" he asked quietly. "Rest well, love." He settled back in to listen, and Alleria walked the short distance back and climbed the stairs to her room, opening the door.

She stopped dead in her tracks. "Alleria, you are a fool," she said aloud, looking at her stained, chipped, and dented armor. It sat there accusingly, reminding her she had promised herself to clean it before she slept. The bed's posts were wrapped in flowers now, though, and the covers had been turned down, revealing pale sheets that looked silky and inviting.

I'm a soldier, Alleria told herself, *and soldiers always make sure our armor is ready to throw on at a moment's notice.* Even here, where she was highly unlikely to need it and so ready for sleep, she found she could not break the habit, so she pulled up a small bench and set to work.

The work was so familiar as to be a meditation. She focused on the weapons, envisioning their use, and her armor, remembering the blows of various battles. Her mind went to the hunt, to Varaskar and Sarothar, and then to Xal'atath. Tonight was lovely, but it would be good to be on the hunt again tomorrow.

She was polishing the bow when there came a knock on the door, so faint as to have not awakened her had she been asleep. "Come in," she called absently.

Turalyon sighed as he entered. "Of course you're cleaning your armor," he said, the words critical but his tone amused. Alleria smiled up at him through the fringe of fair hair that had fallen over her face.

"Come lend me a hand," she said, and patted the space on the bench beside her.

"I'm surprised you forgot. Usually you remind *me.*"

"I think you forget deliberately so I'll help you."

"That's quite possible. I'm delighted to return the favor."

He reached for her spaulder and a soft cloth and set to work. The activity was as natural to them as breathing, and in a way just as necessary. Each knew exactly how to mend and clean not only their own armor, but each other's as well. They settled into a comfortable silence, partners in all things.

"I can't say as I've ever seen a repair shop so fancy as this," he quipped when they finished.

"It even comes with complimentary wine, although you will have to serve yourself."

"I'll pass, thanks. I've indulged enough for tonight." He placed the spaulder with the other tools, then resumed his seat.

"So," Alleria said. "I do not imagine that you knocked on my door at this hour just to help me fix my armor."

"I confess, I did not, although I was glad to." He stared at the pile of armor, but she knew he wasn't seeing it.

Alleria placed her things on the floor and turned toward him.

"I came to apologize."

"For what?" She tried to think of anything he might have said or done, but nothing came to mind. His face—better known to her now than her own—appeared open but concerned.

"About what happened with Sarothar. And . . . afterward."

". . . Oh."

Alleria realized that, after her brooding earlier, she'd been trying to forget it, to tuck it away and not speak of it again. Because, really, what was the point? They had made their choices, difficult, painful ones on this mission, and it had been good to not have to think about them.

"I saw that creature about to abscond with Arator. I felt so helpless. I'd tried to guide him, to help him, and when he was in real, true danger, he had only me to protect him. And I was *failing.*"

Turalyon's voice broke, and he looked down at his hands. Alleria knew he was not intending to hurt her. She didn't think he even knew how his words would sound. He was blaming himself for not being enough, but in those words, Alleria felt that *she* was the one who had failed.

"So I begged the Light to take me. I gave it all my fear, my wrath, my very life, if it would only let me save our boy."

If I had not left, Arator would have had both his parents to protect him. You would not have needed to offer yourself as sacrifice.

"It—I . . . killed Sarothar on the spot, and after that I stayed there, in the Light. I can't remember everything, but I do know that all our worries and problems . . . the answers seemed so simple. And then, suddenly . . . there you were." He turned to look at her now, and his eyes were bright with tears, even as he smiled. "You came back to me."

My sweet love, my gentle Turalyon . . . had he suffered so every time she left? He never protested; he let her go, time and again, with no reproach.

She reached out and took his hand, closing her slim fingers over his.

"I said I would never leave you," Alleria whispered, and this time, it was her voice that broke.

"Alleria . . . no, no, that's what I came to apologize for!" He took both of her hands in his and pressed them to his heart. She could feel it pounding. "I didn't mean to—to shame you for leaving. I never have. I love you, I *trust* you, and I know when you go it's because you must."

He had said he didn't remember everything clearly from the Dreadscar Rift, and Alleria believed him. But she remembered.

He needed you. I *needed you.*

The memory shamed her, not Turalyon's words. Somehow, she had never really thought of Turalyon—steadfast, warm, unshakable—as having moments of bleakness, losing hope.

"I do miss when we were together in the Light. I cannot deny that."

Alleria tensed, and she could see he felt it.

"But that doesn't matter anymore. We understand it. Light, Void . . . we've each made sacrifices for these powers and will continue to do so. But that will not dictate who we are."

"How do you know?" Alleria asked brokenly.

"Because you came back to me. And you brought *me* back . . . to you."

Alleria recalled staring at him in horror, the Light having claimed him. *Taken* him from her.

Beneath the warm cover of Turalyon's hands, she opened her own, pressing them onto his chest, feeling his heart beat. They did now have parts of themselves the other could never know. But they also had a connection that stubbornly persisted as strong as ever, despite coming under constant attack. The Light might work through

Turalyon. It might give him power, and it had surely made him more than human. But this man before her was solid, was real and warm, constant and true. And the Light had *nothing* to do with that.

Alleria lifted her gaze to his, falling into the golden-brown eyes that had never looked upon her with anger or resentment, when many another man's might. She felt her heart, so often guarded, even against him at times, almost physically soften, open to him in a way she had not done before.

"I should not have gone," Alleria said. "I left you both vulnerable, and for that, and all the ways that I have hurt you, forgive me. You and Arator are the last people I would *ever* want to wound."

He lifted her chin with a finger to meet her eyes. "Then . . . stay, my love," Turalyon said. "Stay with us. Not for a night, not for a mission. We have tomorrow, and the tomorrow after that one. There is a future for us, all of us, together. *Think* about that. We had more time than anyone and yet could never simply *be.* When have we ever truly had a chance to dream about tomorrow?"

"We didn't dare," she said, so quietly.

"But we can now. It's been so long since I allowed myself to remember how it was in the beginning. But in this time we've spent together, we've had to remember the past. Some of it was . . ." He couldn't even find the words. "But we were together for it, even when we were physically apart. And some of it . . ." Turalyon took a deep breath. "Some of it was so beautiful, so powerful and *true,* it sustained me even in my darkest and most despairing hours."

We have been apart so often, for so long. I did not know . . . forgive me.

"I will *never* leave you behind. If there is danger, or fear, or sorrow—we will go through it together. When you face Xal'atath, Arator and I will be at your side. I want to meet the future *with you,* Alleria, because for me, there is no future without you."

Alleria realized she was trembling, and suddenly that night, so very long ago now, flooded her mind. The first night she'd gone to Turalyon, but now, in this moment, she was not seeking refuge from the cold, nor from tragedy.

She had been broken then. From hope shattered, from gut-wrenching loss, and an alien sense of not knowing what to *do,* how to handle it. The only thing that swam into her grieving consciousness was this face now before her, this man's kindness and gentleness even in a place of war and battle and death, a beacon in the darkest night of all. Alleria had gone to him, utterly shattered in spirit, seeking escape, and instead had been gifted with unquestioning refuge and healing. She had been icy—nay, cruel—to him afterward but received no censure.

We had more time than anyone and yet could never simply be.

And now it was Turalyon who was being vulnerable with her. Who had, perhaps, *always* been vulnerable with her. He was trembling, too, perhaps also remembering that night, and others afterward, when she had no longer shuttered her heart and pretended not to love for fear of loss.

For so long, they could not touch at all. Light and Void separated them. With time, they had overcome that. But something had still lingered that kept them from the connection, the intimacy in all areas that had been present before the Dark Portal, when their small world had been turned upside down.

Love and fear cannot coexist, she thought, and the knowledge freed her.

Turalyon placed one hand on either side of her face, so gently. "The only blocks in our path have been the ones we've put there. Arator was right. So . . ."

He took a deep breath.

"Marry me, my love. Marry me, and there will be no war so brutal, no duty so severe, that it will ever divide us."

She reached to touch his face, in no hurry, her fingers exploring the short bristles of his white beard, tracing the length of the scars that spoke undeniably of what they had undergone together yet in no way damaged his beauty in her eyes. Alleria slipped a hand around the back of his neck, lifting her face to his.

"Yes," she whispered.

CHAPTER SIXTEEN

The Nighthold, Suramar City

BROKEN ISLES

Arator and his hosts had just finished a light fruit salad when his parents arrived. "There you are," Thalyssra said. "I gather you slept well."

"We must thank you again for such a lovely evening," Alleria said, seating herself. "Everything was perfect."

There was an unusual softness in his mother's voice. Arator was instantly alert.

Turalyon poured her a glass of juice as he spoke.

"The best hosts provide more than delicious food and pleasant company," he said. "They create a space where their guests can truly feel comfortable. Last night, you did that for the two of us."

And his father. There was something easy and relaxed about how he spoke, *moved* . . .

They looked at each other, and something secret passed between them. Turalyon extended his hand, and Alleria placed hers in it. "Turalyon and I spent a long time talking last night. About the past, present . . . and future. We remembered what the two of you said was your formula for making your marriage work."

"And I decided that another element needed to be added," said Turalyon.

His parents were . . . *happy,* Arator realized. *Nervous. Excited.* Could . . . Did . . . ?

"Proposal," Alleria said.

Later, Arator would marvel at it. Here were gathered four leaders of countless people. They had lived long lives, seen so much, fought against staggering odds. They had negotiated treaties, led covert resistances, slain many foes in battle. They would be talked about for as long as there was an Azeroth. And yet the one thing that seemed to matter most to all of them was, well, *love.*

Thalyssra sprang to her feet, and hastened to Alleria to embrace her. Arator's private, reserved mother hugged the other woman earnestly in return. Turalyon and Lor'themar were more restrained, although the paladin did rise to shake the regent lord's hand. And Lor'themar, who had always kept his distance around Turalyon, actually clapped the "lucky fellow" on his shoulder.

And then Turalyon turned and quite literally swept his future wife off her feet and into his arms, kissing her fiercely and tenderly. She kissed him back with just as much fire. Arator watched it all, wondering why his face hurt, then realized it was because he could not stop smiling.

His parents parted, flushed and joyous, and turned to their son. Before Arator realized quite what was happening, the three of them were holding one another close, their hearts racing with emotions, breathless with laughter and surprise.

Arator closed his eyes, relishing the moment.

Since their return from the Twisting Nether, he'd wanted them to figure it out, and he'd told himself he'd be all right with whatever they decided. But he needed to see this mending between them. Arator had been so frustrated with them because he knew, on some level, that their commitment would shift everything, for all of them. There was a completeness here, a solidity.

A *family.*

■ ■ ■

Thalyssra's joy for them all was sincere and pure. Lor'themar, of course, was more naturally reserved to begin with, and while she and Turalyon were not precisely enemies, Lor'themar still kept them at arm's length. She had seen him softening last night, and had hoped it wasn't just the wine or the connection they shared in her son. But he'd shaken her future husband's hand with what looked like genuine goodwill, and while he did not embrace her as he might have done in times past, his voice as he congratulated her was tinged with affection.

"We're hoping to have a quick ceremony soon," Alleria said as they resumed their seats after a few moments. "Small, simple."

"The sooner the better," Turalyon said. "We've waited at *least* nine hundred years too long already."

Thalyssra put down her knife and fork and fixed them with a disapproving gaze. "This will not do," she informed them. "The beginning of what will doubtless be an extraordinarily happy marriage must have a celebration worthy of such a lengthy prelude. Please let us take care of everything."

"As we were at least partially responsible for it, I agree," Lor'themar said. "If things go wrong, then you can blame us and our bad luck with cakes . . . and guests."

Thalyssra threw him a withering glance.

"Do not listen to him," she said. "It will be glorious."

Alleria and Turalyon exchanged glances.

"I'm sure it will be," Alleria said. "But that would take too much of your time. We'd like to formalize it quickly and—"

"It will be glorious *and* fast," Thalyssra said.

Lor'themar smiled at her and said to the couple, "There's no arguing with her when she gets like this. Best agree quickly."

Alleria smiled and nodded, telling herself it would be nice to have someone else take care of things for her. She certainly wasn't an expert in arranging large formal functions. But as Thalyssra started discussing specifics, the glow of the initial moment dimmed. Alleria had wanted the breakfast to continue the camaraderie of the night before, but instead, it felt like she and Turalyon were gearing up for another mission.

She could feel herself retreating, her mind scurrying away to find other things to focus on. Things she really didn't want to focus on. Like Xal'atath, who, if she knew Alleria was whiling away her time discussing cake flavors, would no doubt laugh in anticipation of triumph.

But there was something else, too.

Alleria had witnessed Turalyon's terrible anger, and the explosion of Light that came to his aid; the image of her Arator, covered with dust that had once been an eredar lord, sitting up in that deep crater. She could not imagine anything surviving the Light's wrath as granted to a paladin protecting the life of his son. Even the Black Harvest was certain the eredar had been destroyed. It was both ridiculous and arrogant of her to believe that somehow this demon had survived all of this just to spite her.

But Alleria knew from bitter experience that demons had an inconvenient way of not staying dead.

Under the table, clearly observing her distance, Turalyon reached for her hand. Their fingers intertwined, and Alleria recalled standing with him at the Dark Portal, their joy a defiance; but then also the Void roaring in her ears as she stepped toward him, steeped in the Light's wrath. And oh, the relief, the gratitude, when his simple, human hand touched hers, to know he was still here, still her Turalyon.

The familiar touch settled and strengthened her a little. So did Arator's question to Thalyssra: "Would it be helpful for me to be a go-between? I'd be happy to help where I can."

"If you're certain—" Thalyssra began, but Alleria interrupted.

"I . . . I've never been one for formal occasions, especially one thrown for me."

"That's why I want to help," Arator said.

Alleria could have stood against anyone but him. There was so little of family traditions, of rituals, that they had shared with him, and his face was so bright with pleasure she could not bear to take this away from him, too. And so she forced a smile, for her son.

"Alleria, love," Turalyon said quietly, "all that matters is that by the end, I am able to call you my wife." He leaned over and whispered softly, for her ears alone, "And I confess . . . I can't wait."

Alleria swallowed her words. *And* I *wonder if . . . maybe we should.*

■ ■ ■

Arator lay on the grass, gazing up at the sky, the pouch of scrolls and ink beside him. He sat up as his parents approached.

"Are you so efficient that all we need to do is enjoy the day?" Alleria asked, hands on her hips as she peered down at him.

"I am efficient enough to realize, after a few moments of reading the master list, that anything I did at this stage would be a waste of time. It's all things *you* need to decide."

"Sadly, that probably was the right course," Alleria said.

Turalyon extended a hand to help Arator to his feet. As they retreated to a table and cushions, Arator drew out ink, quills, and a couple of scrolls.

"I honestly don't know how Thalyssra can possibly get everything done by tomorrow evening," Alleria said.

"Think she's using a spell to copy herself?" Turalyon asked.

"That would certainly explain it," Arator muttered.

"We all have a lot scheduled for today, so we can try to work around that. I'm hoping to have most of this decided by lunch."

"That seems like more than enough time," Turalyon said.

"I think you're both optimists," Alleria said.

"According to Thalyssra's master list," Arator said, unrolling the very long scroll, "you two are responsible for selecting the guests, deciding on which, if any, official ceremony you wish to follow and who will officiate, selecting the flowers for the bouquets, choosing the menu, and . . . you know what, I think your first call should be to ignore the back half of this list."

"Brilliant," Turalyon said. "I agree."

"Dear son," Alleria said. "Why were you not negotiating peace in Azeroth at the age of fourteen?"

"I was too busy loudly blaming Giramar for breaking Galadin's scale model of Quel'Thalas." There was a pause. "It was an accident. Let's move on. Guest list. Thoughts?"

"We can't invite every inhabitant of Azeroth," Alleria said to her fiancé.

"But we know so many of them. Not just acquaintances, either. People we've fought and bled for. Your friends from Quel'Thalas, mine from the order and the Grand Army of the Light."

"And Arator's friends," Alleria said.

"What?" Arator stammered. "Oh, no, this is *your* wedding, not mine. And your lists are likely to be long enough."

"I do not think we need to copy our hosts in every respect with regard to the wedding," Turalyon said. "But perhaps we can use their list as a starting point."

At his mother's nod, Arator continued. "Now, as to the formal part of the ceremony, I know there is an old tradition in the Church of the Holy Light regarding marriage, but I'm certain the quel'dorei have rituals as well."

"Many of those who would remember them were lost to the Scourge," Alleria said. "Turalyon . . . let us write our own. We know what we wish to commit to and what is between us."

For a few heartbeats, Arator wished he were not present. Not because he felt embarrassed, but because his mother was so deeply right that even a look between the two of them spoke more than any formal wedding vows could represent.

"That sounds perfect," Turalyon said.

"No poetry, though," Arator said. "Father has already proved he can't be trusted."

Turalyon emitted a short bark of laughter at that.

"Any thoughts on who you would like to officiate?" Arator asked. He had a suggestion to make, but he wanted to see if his parents had someone they particularly wanted for the task. It was, as he had said, *their* wedding, after all.

Silence fell. Arator had known this one would be . . . difficult. Turalyon was a paladin, literally raised in the church. He was Lightforged. He might be amenable to not being married in the cathedral, but Arator knew his father would desire someone of the Light to officiate. But Alleria was decidedly not of the Light, and the last thing anyone wanted was for her to be lectured at her own wedding.

"I . . . could do it," he said softly.

"Sorry, I didn't quite catch that," Turalyon said.

But Alleria had. Her eyes grew wide, and she smiled, her lips trembling slightly.

"I know it's unconventional," Arator continued, "but . . ."

Then Turalyon understood, too, and his strong-featured face softened. "But we are an unconventional family," he replied, his voice shaking, just a little.

"Arator . . ." Alleria put a hand to her mouth. "My sweet boy. It couldn't be more perfect."

"Father?" Arator was still worried, but Turalyon nodded.

"You have always been a blessing to us. To receive *your* blessing . . . it would be an honor, my son."

Arator didn't know what to say. He was used to having his guard up around them—due both to his mother's long absences and to his well-meaning but often overbearing father's constant corrections. He wasn't prepared to see the two of them like this. So, as he often did, he deflected with humor.

"I think we should take a break so I can check in with Thalyssra, and you two can determine a guest list in my absence. This gives you a chance to privately marvel at the brilliant solution that I have provided."

"One that would have impressed even your grandfather," Alleria said. "I wish you had been able to know him. Verath Windrunner was a great statesman. Advisor to a king, a listener from the heart, a finder of solutions. He managed to be both kind and wise. I see so much of him in you, Arator, and I know he'd be as proud of you as I am."

Arator swallowed hard. He thought of a thousand jokes, quips, or deferrals, but he chose none of them.

"Thank you, Mother."

■ ■ ■

Arator had been right. The tasks that Alleria had dreaded became bearable when it was the three of them making the decisions. They opted to work through lunch to accomplish as much as possible. It was decided to surrender the menu and bouquet choices entirely to Thalyssra, and by midafternoon they had created a guest list, paring Thalyssra's down severely by limiting it only to people they knew personally and well. They were interrupted by Thalyssra, who was pleasantly surprised by their accomplishments. "I'm glad you set the guest list," she said. "Everything else can be arranged last minute if need be, but guests need time to make preparations." She glanced at the list. "This is . . . quite short."

"We know and trust everyone on that list with our lives," Turalyon said. "You won't need so much security."

Thalyssra chuckled. "How considerate! It's as you wish. Any thoughts on the menu or the flowers?"

"We, ah, were thinking that you would be better suited to perform those duties," Arator said. "You're familiar with Suramar fare and its flora. You'd know what food is in season and what flowers are in bloom."

"Wise of you, Sir Arator," Thalyssra replied. "Now . . . you've all worked so hard, you may have lost track of time."

Alleria abruptly realized what she meant. She sprang from her seat as Thalyssra turned around, beckoning. The twins rushed out from the door first, pelting across the walkway and utterly disregarding the few steps down into the courtyard, shouldering each other out of the way good-naturedly to be the first to tackle their cousin. Giramar and Galadin shouted Arator's name loudly, as though he were across a field, even though they were already thumping his back and laughing.

Vereesa wasn't far behind her boys, and she and Alleria rushed toward each other and held on tightly.

"I'm so sorry! I can't believe I—"

"*I* can, and it's fine; we were a bit early anyway," Alleria's sister said. Vereesa glanced over at Turalyon, who stood back a little bit, watching the happy reunions.

"Turalyon!" she called merrily. "It's about time!"

"I know, I know," he said, smiling sheepishly as he approached them. Vereesa gave him a brief hug, turning to Arator as he disentangled himself from his cousins and enveloped her in a bear hug.

"You're not in armor!" Vereesa said jokingly. "It makes it easier to do this." She gave him an extra squeeze, kissed his cheek, and patted his head. He laughed, feigning embarrassment, but even that was comfortable. It was the least awkward of things, Alleria noticed; a familiar ritual known only to them, likely begun the first day Vereesa had held him.

Alleria suddenly felt a phantom ache in her arms, recalling how Arator fit snugly in them, once; and how empty her arms had felt handing him over to her sister's care. They were together, now, but that handful of years, a pittance of time compared to that she and Turalyon had known in the Nether and serving in the Grand Army of the Light, were gone, their unique and ephemeral joys remaining unknown to her forever. Tears stung her eyes for a moment.

"I hate to interrupt this," Thalyssra said, "but the leyweavers are waiting," adding, "for all of you."

"Wait," Arator said, "I thought that was tomorrow."

Thalyssra sighed. "The *wedding* is tom— Perhaps I should remind you of the schedule." She ticked off her fingers as she spoke.

"Wedding party members arrive this afternoon and all will be fitted before the rehearsal. After, you will dine on sample dishes from the menu, including a tasting cake."

"Maybe this isn't so bad," Giramar said to Galadin.

"Tomorrow morning," Thalyssra continued, ignoring the interruption, "you will all have final fittings, approve the bouquets, and address any last-minute items. And in the afternoon . . ." She beamed at them. "You will embark upon your journey as husband and wife."

Alleria felt exhausted already. "Well," she said, with the best smile she could muster, "let's be about it."

Turalyon reached for her hand and pressed it to his lips, and she saw understanding in his gold-brown eyes. Soon all the nonsense would be over, and they could get on with, as Thalyssra said, their new journey together. Her hand was still warm from his kiss as she and Vereesa stepped through the portal Thalyssra had opened to Leyweaver's Hall in the Grand Promenade.

Four leyweavers awaited them, smiling. One stepped forward and bowed.

"Allow me to introduce myself. I am Azayna, and I lead the Leyweavers Guild. I've asked Jorjana and Inondra to assist me."

The women inclined their heads. "This is a tremendous pleasure and honor," Azayna continued. "Such distinguished guests for so momentous an occasion!" She waved them over to follow her into the back room, and even Alleria, who did not much care for such things, was stunned by the beauty of the fabric bolts. Hues of every color imaginable, it seemed, were on display. Soft silk, warm wool, cool linens, all were here. And Alleria was supposed to decide all of this?

"Traditionally," Azayna was saying, "wedding garments have been made of silkweave, but if you prefer—"

"Silkweave is fine," Alleria replied quickly. "Whatever you think is best."

Azayna brightened, pleased at the leeway she was being given. "Excellent. Do you have a style in mind? I have a design book to spark your imagination."

"Thank you," Vereesa said. "We'd love to take some time to go through the book."

"Of course," Azayna said. "I'll send in some refreshments and give you some privacy. I will be outside if you have questions."

When the leyweaver had departed, Alleria said to her sister, "I'm so glad you're here. I know it was short notice."

"A few hours was indeed short notice, yes," Vereesa said, grinning.

"I couldn't have anyone other than you by my side tomorrow," Alleria said. "Thank you."

"I wouldn't miss it," Vereesa said, as she moved to sit at a small, round table. "How are you, Lady Sun . . . really?"

For a moment, Alleria thought about telling her everything. How happy part of her truly was, to make this commitment to her family. How she'd caught glimpses of what it would be like in the banter and jokes that flew so easily between Turalyon, Arator, and her, when they were together.

How safe Turalyon could make her feel . . . and how alarmed he had made her feel, when the Light had gripped him so tightly she could barely call him from it. How free she had felt hunting for the demon on her own, and how she longed to return to the hunt for Xal'atath . . . without either of them. How she couldn't shake the feeling that maybe Sarothar, or at least his influence, was still out there machinating, despite every piece of evidence to the contrary.

She knew what her sister, her Little Moon, would do. Vereesa would demand that she, Alleria, and their sons leave. Immediately. She would call for renewed investigation into Felsoul Hold, likely accusing Thalyssra of negligence, and forbid Turalyon from seeing his lover or their child until he could answer for his wrathful moment. And this would only be to start. Vereesa was not above creating a diplomatic incident if she thought her family was in danger.

None of this was what Alleria wanted. She *did* love Turalyon. She *did* want to be with him, and their son. And if she had been present, instead of turning her back on them, Alleria knew that Turalyon would never have offered himself so completely to the Light. So, she told a partial truth.

"Choosing fabrics, fittings, hair styling, trying to integrate paladins and high elves and write vows . . . it's all starting to be too much."

"You could elope," Vereesa said so matter-of-factly that Alleria laughed.

"Thalyssra would never forgive me. And ceremonies, rituals—they are important. At least it'll be over soon."

"Well . . . let me take care of your hair." Vereesa smiled. "Just like I used to."

In Quel'Thalas high society, it was expected that female family members would style the bride's hair. That worked fine with most families, as beauty and fashion sense was the norm, although it was usually servants who dressed the women day-to-day. It did not work in the Windrunner family, where all the women were rangers and had little interest in "fancy" things. Vereesa was the only one who displayed any interest—or aptitude—so, often those tasks fell to her.

"I can do it," Alleria said.

"Let me," Vereesa insisted. "I know you can. But . . ." Vereesa's smile turned a little sad. "I didn't have a mother or sister to do mine when Rhonin and I married, and I want to do yours."

Alleria reached for her sister's hand. "I hadn't thought about that. I'm sorry."

How different would we all have been, she thought, *had we had our family complete at all the important moments of our lives.*

Azayna swept into the room in a swirl of robes and the scent of dusk lily, holding an enormous book, followed by an apprentice bearing a tray with a bottle of arcwine and two delicate glasses. Alleria was grateful for the distraction.

"Here you are," the leyweaver said. "Take some time and leaf through it. I'm sure you'll find something to your liking."

Once the leyweaver was gone, Vereesa poured them each a glass.

"A toast," Vereesa said. "To my big sister, my Lady Sun, and her betrothed. May they have a very happy marriage." They clinked glasses, but before they drank, Vereesa took her sister's hand and looked deep into her eyes. "Alleria . . . you are marrying a very good man."

"I know," Alleria said. "I know."

■ ■ ■

Turalyon had asked Khadgar to be his best man, and Danath Trollbane and Kurdran Wildhammer to finish out the rest of his wedding party. Arator had warned his father that the dwarf would be harder to locate so quickly, but Turalyon had wanted to make the attempt. As expected, the first two arrived together late in the afternoon. Arator watched, smiling as three of the Sons of Lothar greeted one another with much love and laughter. Khadgar caught sight of him and moved his arcane wheelchair over to the knight.

"Arator," he said fondly. "Hello again, young sir."

"If you say 'My, how you've grown,' I cannot be held accountable for my actions," Arator said, hugging him. For all his brilliance, his place in history, and power, Arator thought Khadgar one of the warmest souls he had ever known.

Khadgar laughed heartily. "Very well then, I won't. It's so very good to be here for this."

"Is that little Arator?" cried Danath, striding over. "By the Light, you've grown!"

Arator threw Khadgar a pained look and Khadgar tried to stifle his laughter.

"Never have I seen anyone with more assurance than you, that day you came through the Dark Portal," Danath continued, jovial but with a catch in his voice. Danath was one of the first people Arator had encountered in Outland.

"Well, we did find them in the end, didn't we?" Arator replied, and smiled.

"That you did," Turalyon said heartily.

Danath shook himself a little and said cheerily, "Where's Kurdran? Don't tell me he'd miss an opportunity to celebrate!"

"We've not been able to locate him to deliver an invitation," Alleria said.

"Some things never change," Khadgar said wryly.

"I'm still hoping he'll show up. But he'll miss out on a wedding outfit," Turalyon said.

"Which *you* four are about to do," Alleria said. "You'd best hurry. Trust me, you *do* not want to irritate Thalyssra."

▪ ▪ ▪

The wedding would be held at the Lunastre Estate, the same site as that of the first arcanist and the regent lord's. The rehearsal went flawlessly. Thalyssra insisted they repeat it, just to make certain.

Dinner, too, was a rehearsal. The table, open to the air, was laid as it would be tomorrow: a beautiful tablecloth, porcelain dishes, flowers, and candles in protective globes. As everyone located their seat, Arator noticed that there was an empty chair at the end. A place for Kurdran, should he somehow manage to make it. *Good. There should always be room at the table for old friends.*

There was an empty seat beside Alleria, too, for Halduron Brightwing, Ranger General of Silvermoon, the only person requested by Alleria other than her sister to stand with her tomorrow. He had warned he might not be able to make it, but just as the main entree plates were being cleared, he hastened to join them.

"Do not sit down if you did not get fitted for your outfit," Thalyssra warned.

He laughed. "Your tailor was waiting for me when I arrived. I've done my duty, First Arcanist."

"Your timing is perfect," Alleria said, as he slipped into the chair beside her. "As always." Halduron followed her gaze and his own eyes widened.

Everyone turned now, their chatter falling silent as the cart with the noble task of bearing the wedding cake arrived at the table. There were murmurs of approval and excitement, and the twins actually applauded. Arator couldn't blame them.

It was a work of art. A collection of pastry castles, stunningly frosted and topped with delicate spires of spun sugar, stood united in a forest tableau of candy trees. Flanking the castles were lakes of various sweet sauces. It smelled of spices and sugar. Arator had thought he had more than eaten his fill, but his mouth watered.

"Your baker is astonishing," Turalyon said.

"It's almost too beautiful to eat," Vereesa murmured.

"Almost," said Lor'themar.

"This," Giramar said, as the servers began to cut and pass around slices, "is my *favorite* wedding tradition."

"Really? And how many others do you know?" Vereesa challenged him.

"It doesn't matter. Nothing could beat this."

"Wise man," said Lor'themar. Turalyon nodded his agreement.

"I actually know about many wedding traditions," Arator said between bites. "Our hostess offered me some reading on them while we were planning, and I would just like to say it's a shame we couldn't incorporate some of the more unusual ones."

"Please, my son, simple is best," Alleria said.

"But Mother," he said. "Wouldn't you have enjoyed shooting Father with arrows?"

"What?" exclaimed Turalyon, rising. The twins burst out laughing, and several other guests followed suit. Including Halduron, who thought it hilarious.

"Without the points, of course," Arator continued, unruffled. "Mother would fire arrow shafts at you, then you'd collect them and break them together as part of the ceremony. Thus ensuring your love lasts forever."

"I have arrows," Halduron offered.

"No, thank you," Turalyon said, resuming his seat and putting his arm around Alleria. "A love that's already lasted centuries doesn't need broken arrows to help it endure."

"What else did you learn, Arator?" Khadgar asked, his eyes sparking with amusement.

Arator considered. "The night is young," he said, "and there's plenty of time for Father to serenade Mother beneath her window tonight."

"That's quite romantic," Thalyssra said. "Dearest, would *you* serenade me tonight, standing in the moonslight beneath my window?"

Lor'themar smiled. "Perhaps not tonight . . . but yes, I would and shall if you wish."

Thalyssra leaned on his shoulder, sighing happily. "Alleria, I am sorry, but I fear you must be content with being the *second* happiest woman in Azeroth."

"I shall try to accept my fate," Alleria replied.

"What else, Arator?" Danath pressed. "Anything we all could participate in?"

Arator was pleased. He knew his parents had worried about the composition of tonight's gathering. Former enemies, old friends—sometimes one and the same. It was a potential powder keg, but thus far everything seemed calm and companionable. Arator pretended to ponder the question.

"There's one from Draenor involving a talbuk, Mother rides in and Father—"

"You're making these up," Vereesa challenged.

"All right, *some*."

"I knew it," Galadin said, elbowing Giramar. "Pay up!"

The conversation turned to battles, and weapons and armor. It didn't escape Arator's notice that no one mentioned any battles that involved the Horde fighting the Alliance. As his mother once said, he truly had friends everywhere, as he had recently demonstrated to her and his father.

We change and grow, he thought. *Hopefully, we change in good ways, and grow kinder, not crueler.*

There came a lull in the conversation, the only sounds the scraping of plates to catch the last bits of frosting. *Not an awkward silence,* he thought. *The opposite. Comfortable.* After a while, an elven voice, male, began singing softly in Thalassian. On the final verse, Vereesa joined Lor'themar, singing in Common, so that all could understand.

> The years have passed, and find us hand in hand,
> Upon the edge of timelessness we stand;
> And all our yesterdays have slipped away,
> Eternity awaits us as I say,
> "I loved you then,
> I love you now,
> I love you always."

Again, silence, but this time, the hush was profound. Arator glanced at his mother and was surprised to see her wiping at her eyes. Vereesa slipped her arm through hers and placed her head on her sister's shoulder. All the Silvermoon elves were looking at Alleria and one another with soft expressions, and suddenly Arator understood.

"Was that . . . one of Lirath's songs?"

"Yes," Vereesa said quietly. "It's called *Then, Now, Always.*"

Alleria took a deep breath and pushed her chair back. Turalyon rose beside her. "It's been a long day," she said, "and a big one tomorrow. It means so much to us that you are all here for it."

"Alleria speaks for us both," Turalyon said. "We are all here, after so much, and we are blessed to be. Good night."

■ ■ ■

Alleria and Turalyon walked back to their quarters, wandering hand in hand along the winding lanes beside plants and fountains and statues. Alleria was quiet and seemed lost in thought. After a while, he squeezed her hand gently.

She looked up. "Hmm?"

"Are you all right, love?"

Alleria gave him a nod and a tired smile. "It was so strange, being in the same place as their wedding. And then the song . . . It was beautiful, and I loved it, but I'm rather drained."

"Alleria . . . ?" They had reached their quarters. Turalyon stopped and looked at her searchingly. He didn't want to ask, but he had to be sure. Had to give *her* the opportunity to be sure, as well.

"Do you still want to get married tomorrow?"

She looked at him slyly. "Getting cold feet?"

He laughed at the absurdity of the question. If it were up to him, Turalyon would find Arator right this minute and get him to marry them on the spot. "Never. I just want to make sure you have no regrets the day after tomorrow."

"I won't. I love you, and I love Arator, and I want us *all* to be together."

Turalyon exhaled, more relieved than he cared to admit. And . . . more nervous. As nervous as the young general who'd tried to impress this astonishing woman with a starlit picnic, so long ago.

"I am *so* glad to hear that." Alleria cocked her head to the side in curiosity, a lock of hair falling across her eyes. Turalyon opened the door to their quarters and motioned her inside, closing the door after them.

He reached for her hand, and he knew she could feel him trembling.

The ring was deceptively simple, considering how challenging it had been to acquire. He'd called in a favor from Magni's craftsmen to get the ring made in time, trusting in their experience to meet all his criteria. They had outdone themselves. A large center stone, black and gleaming, was ringed by a circle of smaller, clear ones. They had been set with care, so that when Alleria wore her gauntlets, neither the gems nor her aim would be damaged.

"The center stone is a black spinel, and the surrounding stones are diamonds."

"Bright and shiny, like you," Alleria said lightly, not looking at him. Then she added, "And strong. And beautiful."

"Not with these scars, my dear."

"Oh yes, with these scars. I know where you got every one." She looked up at him now, his Alleria, and added softly, "And what they cost you."

He couldn't read her reaction, so he kept talking. "A diamond . . . well, everyone knows what *that* is. Pretty ordinary. This stone, though, the black spinel, was very hard to find. It symbolizes endurance, protection, and strength in hard times. And even though it's dark, it still shines."

He wanted her to see it, to understand what he was telling her. *Darkness in the center, protected by the Light. Forever in harmony upon her hand.*

At last, when Alleria still didn't speak, he said, "If you don't like it, I'll—"

"You're wrong about the diamond," she said abruptly.

"I—I am?"

"Yes. It's not ordinary at all."

She kissed him then, long and sweet, and whispered, "Thank you. It's perfect."

And yet. Turalyon stepped back, gazing down at her. "What troubles you, my love?" he asked. "I can tell something does."

She sighed. "I didn't want to worry you, and it's probably nothing, but . . . Turalyon, I'm waiting for something to go *wrong*. I'm not used to things going smoothly, and I do not trust it when they do."

Turalyon chuckled softly. He squeezed her hands gently.

"Light, do I understand *that*," he said. "It's to be expected, given our lives. We've been on high alert for centuries. It's almost impossible to imagine that anything we're involved in could be ordinary and uneventful."

She nodded.

"Tell you what," he said. "I can sleep in my old quarters if you'd like the whole place to yourself tonight. After all, we're much more used to sleeping apart than not, so this way you could get a good night's sleep. You've more than earned it." He stroked her face with the back of his hand.

"Are you sure *you're* not the one having second thoughts?"

"I will be there, on time, in my gorgeous doublet, wearing whatever flower Thalyssra wants me to, ready to kiss my wife. I promise."

"You'd better be," she said, "because I *will* hunt you down."

"I would certainly hope so." He lifted her chin and kissed her gently. "Sleep well, dearest."

"You too, love," she said. Turalyon stepped into the night, closed the door, and took a deep breath. He wasn't tired at all, and the palace grounds were beautiful and suited to solitary wandering. Tomorrow, everything would change. It was a change the paladin deeply wanted, but he was less certain of everything than he had been a few days ago. And Turalyon did not like uncertainty.

There were some things in his long life that went without questioning. That he loved Alleria Windrunner and their son, and they loved him. That he loved the Light. That he would gladly sacrifice his life to save an innocent.

He had no memory of his parents, only the church, the smell of incense, the Light. When Archbishop Faol had called him from its shelter to go into the world with a hammer, he went. These things were simple, clear.

But his heart had led him to a woman who was assuredly *not* simple, and who had made a choice that he still didn't entirely understand. Nonetheless, he had tried, and in the end, he loved and trusted Alleria completely, and that was enough.

Nor was Arator simple, running around with Illidari and warlocks and . . .

Turalyon winced from the memory of the Light, flashing in his mind's eye. He sat on a bench near a fountain, breathing deeply, focusing on the sound. He'd told Alleria that he couldn't remember much of that moment.

Couldn't . . . or wouldn't.

He did remember ceding control of himself at a level he had never experienced before. The deep peace of utter certainty, of everything abruptly made perfect, in the Light's divine sense. Dwelling in absolute purity—and all-consuming, white-hot wrath for all that was not. And out of that impossible melding, an unyielding desire to enact righteous punishment.

In that instant, Turalyon had seen only the warlocks' alliance with evil—not their efforts to destroy it. He had seen only his son's "mistake" in defending them, not the courage it took for Arator to face him and protect their allies with his life. He had seen only the Void in Alleria for a brief, awful flash, but then had seen *her*.

She was bound to the Void, as he was to the Light. It had prevented them from even touching each other at first, but they had stubbornly refused to accept that. Years, it took, and pain, to train these changed physical forms. But they did it.

Whatever facet of the Light had made use of him . . . this would not come between them, either. His beloved, his Alleria, had brought him back from that place. In that moment, Turalyon's simple, human self had chosen the brush of his lover's hand over anything the Light had offered.

He was shaken, not just from the experience, but from understanding that there was something else that he could not remember, that he should. Alleria had mentioned that she did not trust it when things went smoothly. Turalyon did not either, but he had attempted to soothe her even as he, too, wondered. What had happened in that moment he could not recall? The soul engine was destroyed, but . . . was it the only one? Sarothar did not seem like the type to gamble on one single option. Was there someone else waiting to take over from the eredar, whom they didn't even know about? A force he had already summoned from the Nether?

Was all this wondering simply his way of coping with the fact that Alleria had left him many, many times, and might well do so again tomorrow?

Strangely enough, that fear grounded him. Because it was familiar, and it had been faced countless times over the last thousand years, and Turalyon knew Alleria's leaving always led to her return.

Turalyon knew sleep would not come for him tonight, but perhaps rest, and a little peace, could. He lifted his face to the sky, thinking of their night together on Outland, gazing at the stars. He closed his eyes, and asked for the Light's blessing, on him, on his family, on everyone who might be struggling this night. Turalyon felt the familiar warmth settle upon him, and thought no more about demons or fear or wrath, and meditated upon the Light's peace.

CHAPTER SEVENTEEN

The Nighthold, Suramar City

BROKEN ISLES

Although the wedding was but a few hours away, Arator still couldn't quite believe it was really happening. Thalyssra had suggested a final breakfast for the five of them and Vereesa, a moment of calm before things started becoming hectic. He heard happy chatter as he approached and smiled to himself. He would miss all of this, but like his parents, he was eager to be off doing things other than wedding planning.

He was the last to arrive, and he discovered his hosts standing on either side of his mother, their backs turned to him as they looked at something. Vereesa stood watching, smiling even as tears poured down her face. Turalyon was half turned around in his seat, facing his future wife, and glanced up, smiling, as Arator approached.

"What's going on?" Arator asked. "Did the chef leave eggshell in the omelette?"

Thalyssra and Lor'themar stepped back as Alleria turned to her son and extended her hand. Arator took it, puzzled for just an instant, and then he saw the ring.

He was no gem master, but he understood the significance of the stones at once. He regarded it a moment longer, then kissed her hand. Straightening, he said to his father, "Nice rocks," and everyone laughed. But he held Turalyon's gaze and nodded, ever so slightly, and his father's face softened into a smile.

"And I thought you'd forgotten," Vereesa told Turalyon, wiping at her eyes.

"No. Like the proposal, it just took a while," he responded, and again there was laughter.

Arator realized it wasn't the jokes, which were amusing but not that funny. People were simply full of joy. He certainly was.

As he sat beside Turalyon, though, he glanced over at his mother. She was staring down into her plate but not really seeing it. Her attention was elsewhere, and whatever was in her thoughts, it troubled her. An instant later, though, the mask was back on, and she smiled at something Vereesa had said, and the moment was gone.

"Oh, yes, do bring it in!" Thalyssra's voice was full of pleasure as she responded to the servant who had clearly posed a question. The woman smiled and waved to someone out of Arator's view.

Thalyssra turned to Alleria. "I thought you might like to get your bouquet a little early. You can have it in the dressing room with you when you begin preparing."

Arator was not overly interested in flowers or their arrangements, but he was determined to show enthusiasm. Yet, as the florist entered with the bouquet, he found himself deeply moved and grateful to Thalyssra for undertaking the task with such care.

Alleria would never be mistaken for a young woman. Her features were beautiful and unlined, but there was something about her that spoke to all she had undergone. At this moment, though, Arator saw her unguarded. His father, too, although his face was weatherworn and scarred, appeared genuinely affected. Alleria had once confided to her son that she thought Turalyon had an innocence that no amount of hardship could touch. Arator could see that now.

"I'm not sure how much botanical expertise either of you has, but almost all of these flowers have been gathered from Quel'Thalas," Lor'themar said quietly.

Alleria seemed unable to speak. Vereesa cleared her throat. “We . . . we recognize them all,” she said.

“We put in a few from Suramar as well, including the dusk lily,” Thalyssra said. “So you will know today, when you walk to join your great love, that those in Suramar wish you nothing but happiness.”

“This . . . this is . . . Thank you. I—I think I’ll start getting ready.” Alleria all but bolted to her feet, taking care to turn her face away as she strode off. Vereesa rose and accompanied her.

Thalyssra was confused and concerned. “Did . . . did I do something wrong?”

“No, my dear,” Lor’themar said. “Alleria has always valued self-control. She’s not upset.”

“You touched her heart,” Turalyon said quietly. “And, sometimes, she doesn’t know how to respond when that happens. But she always comes back.”

Arator was silent, watching his mother’s quick strides. He thought about his father’s words, how Alleria often left, sometimes with no word or warning. He hoped that one day soon, his mother would not feel the need to leave so often.

Even if she did always come back.

■ ■ ■

“Alleria, wait!” Vereesa called.

Her sister didn’t slow, and she heard Vereesa break into a trot to catch up with her.

“If you really want to start getting ready early,” Vereesa said, “then you’ll need me to help, and if you’re planning to make a run for it, I’ll pack for you.”

Alleria uttered a half-laugh, half-sob and turned to embrace her. They clung wordlessly to each other, then parted. Vereesa searched her eyes. “What’s wrong?”

“It’s just so much. You know me. For her to have gone to all that trouble just for *flowers* . . .”

“I know. The first thing I thought of was the wreaths we used to make as children. This is stirring up a lot for you. For me, too. For all of us."

Alleria nodded mutely and took a breath, then began walking toward the dressing room.

"I was joking, but not really, about packing for you," Vereesa said quietly.

"It isn't about Turalyon," Alleria said. "And honestly, if I were having second thoughts, I'd simply tell him, and we'd see how we felt in another century or so." It was a light comment, meant to reassure her sister, but both things were true.

"It will all be over soon enough," Vereesa said, opening the door to the dressing room. "We should try to enjoy it. You'll certainly look beautiful enough to deserve all the compliments."

"I'm sorry I missed your wedding," Alleria blurted out abruptly.

Vereesa took her hands. "You were there in my heart. You, Mother, Father, Lirath . . . even Sylvanas. You'll feel them as you walk toward the man you love, I promise."

"Not helping," Alleria grumbled, blinking back fresh tears.

"Sit down," Vereesa said, "and let me do your hair."

They were quiet for a while as Vereesa brushed Alleria's silky hair, letting it flow freely with a single small braid. Alleria felt herself settle and began to ask her sister about the twins. She thought of the silly but charming stories that had been told over the picnic dinner and smiled, listening and also remembering.

Alleria did not care for makeup, but accepted color on her eyes, lips, and cheeks. And then—it was time for the dress.

"Oh, it fits perfectly," Vereesa murmured. "Look, the lacings are on the side."

"Oh thank goodness," Alleria said. "I hate not being able to get out of a gown by myself."

"Well I'm sure Turalyon would be more than happy to help," Vereesa said, smirking.

Alleria, utterly caught by surprise, gaped at her and actually blushed. For a brief, sunshine-bright moment, the two women laughed like girls, as if playful innuendos and beautiful gowns were the only things that mattered in the world.

The giggles subsided at the knock on the door. "Bride inside," Vereesa called, still smiling.

"Arcanist outside," came the response, and Alleria invited her to come in.

Thalyssra was carrying the bouquet. As soon as she caught sight of Alleria, her eyes widened and she gasped softly. She placed the bouquet on a small table. "Please . . . please stand up, let me see."

With unaccustomed shyness, Alleria rose and impulsively twirled, surprised and content at how comfortable and easily she could move in the gown.

"Oh, Alleria," the first arcanist said, "every bride is the most beautiful . . . but you may outshine the sun itself."

"I think anyone would look lovely in this dress," she said, sincerely. Azayna's design was exquisite.

"And I think any dress would look lovely on *you,*" Thalyssra said.

"Thank you for bringing the bouquet." Alleria felt calmer now, in a better place to appreciate and receive the gift of the thoughtful arrangement. "Vereesa, pick a flower and put it in my braid," she said, impulsively, and was glad to see Thalyssra smile. "I'm sorry I left so abruptly."

"Nonsense," Thalyssra said. "You're about to get married. Jitters are perfectly normal."

"Thalyssra . . . you and Lor'themar," Alleria began, "you've done so much for us. Been true friends. We will be forever grateful."

"Your family is a joy to us," Thalyssra said. "And I do truly hope you enjoy today." She looked at Vereesa. "We are women who have all been through war and loss and hardship. We have led our people through some of our world's most terrible times. It can be hard to stop being a leader, a symbol, and just be us. That is why we have these rituals. To breathe, to laugh, to connect with ourselves and those we love. Just for today, Alleria, lay your armor aside."

She smiled gently. "Let yourself be happy."

"I will try," Alleria said.

■ ■ ■

"You know," Danath said, "if you decide you don't want to go through with this, Khadgar and I will help you beat a swift retreat."

"Count me out of that plan, please," Khadgar said with a chuckle, holding his hands up in protest. "I wouldn't risk Alleria's wrath for anything."

"A wise man," Turalyon said. "No need, Danath, I've no intention of running. Would be a waste of this fine doublet."

Thalyssra hadn't told him much about the designs, but she did let him know the colors: green and gold. They were Farstrider colors, but Turalyon liked them well enough, and if she wanted those hues, she would have them. He, Danath, Arator, and Halduron now all wore perfectly fitting doublets, black trousers, and shiny black boots. The colors also suited them well, and each outfit was painstakingly embroidered with gold thread.

Khadgar preferred robes. The leyweavers preferred robes, too, and it showed; the modest archmage almost outshone the groom.

When they all arrived in the outfits, they congratulated one another on how surprisingly good they looked. "How does the same style manage to flatter each of us?" Arator wondered aloud.

"That's the imbuing part of imbued silkweave," Turalyon replied.

The twins were nearby, looking uncomfortable in their formal garb. They had no desire to partake in the good-natured ribbing, preferring instead to keep their eyes on the portal and take quiet bets as to who would arrive first. Turalyon didn't blame them. They were adults now but not their uncle's age, nor even their cousin's. "Old man talk"—as Turalyon had heard Giramar referring to it when he thought he was out of earshot—held no interest for them.

Several mages would be opening portals as needed. Today's wedding was not a state occasion—as the union of two significant world leaders had been—and he and his future wife had felt comfortable simply inviting friends. But they had friends in high places, and in far-flung places, so it would be a lively and diverse gathering.

Turalyon heard the slight change in sound indicating one of the portals and turned expectantly, wondering who the first guests would be. It was the Ironforge portal, and Turalyon smiled as Magni Bronzebeard, Moira Thaurissan, her son, Dagran II, and—

"Kurdran!" Turalyon exclaimed as he and the others strode over to greet them. "I wanted you in the wedding party, but—"

"Dinnae worry lad, I know, I'm hard tae find," Kurdran said. "But I'm here when it counts, eh?" He shook Turalyon's outstretched hand enthusiastically.

"Arator!" Dagran scurried as fast as a dwarf could toward his friend. Arator grinned from ear to ear as Dagran hugged him about the waist.

"Dagran, it's good to see you again!" Arator said. "I hear you've decided to stay in Khaz Algar. I hope they're treating you like the hero you are."

The young emperor's gray cheeks turned positively charcoal as he blushed at the praise.

"Please follow us," said Galadin. "There are refreshments available."

The portals continued to hum. Three royals arrived together: Queen Tess Greymane and her mother, Queen Mia, and King Anduin Wrynn. Accompanying them was Prophet Velen, who chatted briefly with Turalyon and gave the wedding party his blessing. Turalyon was glad to see Anduin here and knew Alleria would be even more pleased, the two having been through much on their journey through the depths. Liadrin and Eitrigg arrived together, greeted Turalyon and the others, then left, most of them grumbling about having to leave their weapons on a table outside the venue.

"My dear boy," came a well-known and well-loved voice. Smiling, Turalyon turned to see Archbishop Alonsus Faol.

Beside Faol was the person who had caused the most friction of the entire wedding process: Jubeka Shadowbreaker. Arator had suggested they invite her, and his parents had agreed. Thalyssra had initially flat-out refused, but the family united in their defense of the warlock. They argued, truthfully, that Jubeka and the council were vital to the eventual defeat of Sarothar, and that Suramar would have been the first place to be invaded. Eventually the first arcanist relented, but with great reluctance.

"What a momentous day this is!" Faol exclaimed. "I'm so pleased to be here."

"I am, too, my old friend," Turalyon said. "It wouldn't be the same without you."

"Hello again," Jubeka said. "Traveled a bit with your friend here. He had some very nice things to say about you."

Turalyon glanced at Faol. "That was kind of him. I . . . wasn't sure you'd be here, Jubeka."

"Had to think about it pretty hard."

"I imagine you did." He paused, then said, quietly, "I'm glad you accepted."

Jubeka peered at him, then gave a little grunt. "I figured it's been some time since I attended anything fancy. At least they don't have to pay for my dinner."

"Archbishop! Jubeka!" Arator approached them, smiling. "No Rouzoch this time?"

The warlock grinned. "I hear I have you to thank for the invite. It was good of the first arcanist to bend her rules just a bit."

"Jubeka told me about Sarothar," Faol said. "I would like to hear more about that . . . from both of you." He gave them a kind smile. "Sacramental seal in place, of course. Congratulations again, Turalyon, and may all joys be yours. Light's blessing be on you all."

Quietly, Arator said, "I think that's a good idea, Father. To talk with him."

Before Turalyon could respond, Lor'themar approached. "It's almost time. Start making your way to the back of the crowd. The musicians will begin playing shortly. It's all just as we practiced."

Turalyon's heart suddenly sped up. How was it possible that after so very long of being with Alleria, he felt giddy, nervous, as if they had just met?

"Are you all right?" It was Khadgar peering at him questioningly. "Cold feet?"

"No. Butterflies," Turalyon answered.

Khadgar smiled. "I remember thinking you two would never figure it out. Then you go and wait a thousand years."

"Everything in its time, old friend," Turalyon said. And that time . . . was now.

"I'm more than ready—wait. Khadgar . . . do you have the rings?"

"Oh, for Light's sake, Father—"

Khadgar chuckled. "Right here," he said, patting an embroidered pouch at his side. "Breathe." But there was affection in the word.

The music shifted. Arator began to walk toward the dais. Turalyon waited, then followed. Khadgar floated after them in his wheelchair, followed by Danath.

The music changed again, and now Vereesa and Halduron were making their way up.

There was a pause. And then, there she was.

Every doubt that had plagued Turalyon fled, like the shadows of a dark night before a brilliant dawn.

My love.

She wore an exquisite dress with a fitted bodice that flowed into a shimmering, loose skirt. Fastened about her slender neck and shoulders was a lattice of delicately wrought chains and gemstones, woven together into a stunning pattern that extended into epaulets on either shoulder. Golden chains draped down her arms and across her back, where a translucent cape was gathered like wings, mostly white but dyed faintly green at the ends. Her hair was free, pale gold silk floating behind her, except for a single braid that had flowers woven into it.

Turalyon moved, almost hypnotized, to join her in front of Arator.

"Alleria, Turalyon . . . please join hands."

So often, they were in armor, their hands covered in protective gloves of metal or leather. But now her smaller, paler hands slipped easily into his as they stood smiling, paying no attention to the words their son was saying to the audience, eyes only for each other, and Turalyon thought himself the luckiest man in the world.

▪ ▪ ▪

It had been a long time since Alleria Windrunner had been nervous about anything, but as she walked, straight and tall, holding the bouquet, a blending of her and her beloved, of past, present, and future, her hands were trembling and slightly slicked with sweat.

She wanted to run.

At the end of the aisle waited her two good, kind men, with great hearts and courageous spirits. At the end of the aisle, she would experience for the first time in so very long a family not only bound by blood, but bonded by love and solemn commitment. Yet every fiber of her being urged her away from them, from this place and these people, to be alone and on the hunt once more.

Where her enemy was, what scheme Xal'atath was plotting, Alleria did not know, but she did know that this creature she hunted was not waiting idle.

This was the weaving of her life, to be torn between one thing and the next. Between duty and yearning, between home and the world. Between Turalyon and her solitude, between Light and the Void. Some of these tug-of-wars had been rendered moot. Some, she had found the balance. In all, she had made a choice.

And I choose them *today. I choose* us *today.*

So she walked, alone, to the strings of Lirath's music, her gaze first on Turalyon, his deeply familiar face alight with the purity of his love and wonder, then upon Arator, their gift, their unexpected blessing. Time had been lost to them all, but now, that didn't matter. All three were saying *Yes, we want to be a family, and here is the love that will endure all, together.*

Alleria no longer trembled as she reached out her hands to Turalyon. How often had their hands touched so, but how new it felt now, how sensitive her skin was to the warmth of his. How wonderful, after so much familiarity, to still feel her pulse quicken at his touch.

"Welcome, everyone," said Arator. "Family. Old friends and new. I know that many of you, including myself, have wondered if this day would *ever* come."

Good-natured laughter ran through the crowd, and Alleria grinned and shook her head, her gaze locked with Turalyon's. He smiled, too, the wrinkles at his eyes creasing, and Alleria loved every line.

"Two souls, so very different, stand before you. A human paladin, raised in the church. A high elven ranger of a legendary bloodline. They say opposites attract, but when all is said and done, they share a great deal. Respect for each other. The desire to protect those who cannot protect themselves. A love that has been challenged by so very much, over so very long. And, of course . . . *me.*"

More affectionate laughter, with love behind it, and a son whose words filled Alleria's heart. *Sometimes,* she thought, *this life is kind.*

"Because of their devotion to the safety of this world and all who dwell upon it, I didn't get to meet them until a few years ago. But I heard all the stories. About great battles fought, and grim horrors endured, and profoundly heroic deeds performed. I know their love story will be as remembered through the ages as their battle tales."

Alleria squeezed Turalyon's hands and whispered, "Maybe not the details, though." And she delighted in the blush she knew she would cause.

■ ■ ■

Arator paused for a moment, looking out at the happy, familiar faces, and he was pleased to see Lor'themar and Thalyssra standing in the back with their arms around each other and a look of accomplishment as well as pleasure on their faces. Before continuing, out of force of habit, he also double-checked where people were seated and where security was, noting that, as planned, several Duskwatch guards were spaced out on either side, with three in the back as well. They stood at attention, holding their maces parallel to the ground.

As he regarded them, though, the one in the middle lowered his mace. Arator frowned, wondering why. The others standing beside him appeared not to notice.

Then, moving casually, the guard removed his helm, shook out his long black hair, and locked eyes with Arator.

Arator's heart seemed to explode in his chest.

Niandar.

Time stopped.

Niandar.

He's dead, he can't be—

The guard gave the paladin a small, almost apologetic smile. And then, it was not Niandar but Mauvara, who had conveniently survived . . .

The nightborne youth with the rune carved on his hand.

The vulpera in Shattrath.

Arator's own friend, Eadred, from Honor Hold.

And then Sarothar, who had been with them nearly every step of the way, lifted a hand.

CHAPTER EIGHTEEN

Lunastre Estate, Suramar City

BROKEN ISLES

The exchange lasted a century, it lasted no time at all, and Arator lifted his own hand, calling the Light to it, praying as he had never prayed before: *Light, Light, help me stop him before it's too late.*

But Sarothar twitched two fingers of his right hand, as if batting away an insect.

And it was too late.

The awful, familiar sounds of fel portals and the bellows of demons drowned out the shocked and angry cries of the wedding guests. The spells disguising the Duskwatch flanking Sarothar vanished, revealing two felguards who rushed the crowd on either side. A scream of warning, fear, and fury cut through it all, and only the rawness in his throat made Arator realize the cry was his.

A blazing, golden hammer of Light flew toward the eredar, but he was simply not there. Arator leaped from the dais, the Light propelling him forward into the swarm of demons the portal vomited forth. Another prayer, and the instant his foot touched the ground, the earth before him glowed with the holy blessing and cleared the way. A third, and Arator was enveloped in the Light's shield, and he slipped through, over, and under the demons who charged at him as he raced toward the weapons table.

He heard the sound of portals as he reached the table and seized his sword, but as he whirled he saw this portal was not emitting the ugly green of fel, but a swirl of blue. Others had the same idea, and he was heartened to see Anduin reaching for Shalamayne, and Eitrigg grabbing his axe. More portals opened, and Arator was grateful that so many mages were on hand.

Arator plunged back into the battle. His gleaming sword cut a path through a pack of felhounds and their imp riders, then he spun, gritting his teeth, keeping the blade moving, a scythe harvesting the heads of demons. He leaped and landed, consecrating the earth, and the howls and bellows and shrieks turned from cries of gleeful savagery to those of agony.

A voice carried through the din, reverberant and sepulchral. "Arator!"

Arator glanced around, searching for Jubeka. She and a wrathguard were focused on the pair of sayaad guarding one of the portals, the wrathguard hacking away at one and Jubeka draining the life out of the other. A felguard was halfway through the portal. Arator smashed it with a radiant hammer of Light, then ran it through and as it fell, the portal closed.

Jubeka whirled on Arator. "This is exactly what we were afraid of! As long as that soul engine is functional, these portals will open faster than we can close them. We *told* you to destroy it!"

"It *was* destroyed!" Arator protested.

The Forsaken gesticulated furiously around her. "Sure doesn't look like it to me!"

It didn't to him, either. But Thalyssra had assured them that only the best of the Duskwatch had—

And just that quickly, all the pieces came together.

▪ ▪ ▪

Alleria had glanced up at her son to see him staring, transfixed with horror, at something to the rear of the assemblage, then he raised his hand to call the Light.

He leaped off the dais, crying out with rage, just as the sound of a portal filled the area, followed instantly by the familiar sounds of creatures from the darkest place she had ever been.

Turalyon's hands had tightened painfully on hers, commanding her attention. They locked eyes. They knew what they had to do.

Somehow, the soul engine had not been destroyed after all. Their quarry was undefeated, the invasion begun.

They didn't want to let go.

Tighter their hands clung to each other's, for one more beat, and then they turned away, each calling upon the powers that were part of them but that also pushed them apart. *The Light and the Shadow* cannot *exist together.*

Alleria heard Turalyon's prayer as he called on the Light, only a little unpleasant, as Turalyon summoned its aid, and she opened herself up to the shadow. It was easier, now that she had finally found the balance. It was like grasping a weapon perfectly made for her but that would cut her fiercely if she did not wield it with the same perfection.

"I need my axe!" cried Eitrigg.

"We'll be cut down before we—"

"Over here!" It was Khadgar, acting swiftly, opening a portal. "Go, quickly! Grab your weapons from the table near the portals!" Some were already going through, and Eitrigg, Danath, Halduron, and Vereesa all rushed to join them.

Where is Arator? Even in those few heartbeats of time, the area had grown thick with demons. Coldly, Alleria stood on the dais, aiming tendrils of Void energy with the same precision as she did her arrows, but with much more dramatic effect even as she scanned the battlefield for her son.

A golden flash drew her eye. There he was, swinging his bright blade and cutting down demons before they could go three steps. He was heading toward Jubeka Shadowbreaker, who was attacking the demons who guarded a portal. Of course Arator would be there, right in the thick of it. Not even the Void flowing through her veins altered the purity of the love that swept through her.

A chittering sound brought her attention to a blanket of imps swarming the dais. Alleria reduced them to chunks of fel goo. Another cluster of imps had gone for Turalyon, peppering him with ineffectual bolts of fel fire. He smote them quickly, and moved on to the next enemy.

Over to Alleria's right, a mage had erected an arcane bulwark. Behind it, non-combatants and the wounded huddled, moving as quickly as they could through a portal to safety. Mia Greymane kept the line moving quickly. A squat felhound feasted on the arcane energy, attempting to weaken it. Alleria scowled, and it burst apart. She glanced to see who was holding the portal open, and stiffened.

Thalyssra.

The Void stoked her anger, dark and rich as Alleria slashed open a Void rift.

You trusted her. Why did she lie to you about the soul engine?

Alleria pushed aside the intrusive thoughts as she stepped through, instantly appearing beside the first arcanist.

"The soul engine!" she cried. "Why isn't it destroyed?"

Thalyssra was startled at Alleria's abrupt appearance but recovered quickly, maintaining the portal. "It was!" she said, shouting to be heard. "The patrol captain led a team, they took care of it."

"Then they failed! *What happened?*" It would be so easy to compel her to speak, but Alleria would not do that.

Not unless she had to.

The patrol captain—

No.

NO!

■ ■ ■

Arator made an angry noise, parrying an attack from a felbat by cutting it in half. A quick prayer of healing, giving him a chance to assess the situation.

It was bad. Very bad.

How? How did he survive? Arator had little time to ponder the question.

The wedding of two legendary individuals had been a stroke of luck for Sarothar. Arator and his parents had, in a sickly ironic twist, given him an enormous gift—the opportunity to take out some of the world's most famous heads of state and great heroes all in a single, easily containable space. *Including us.*

Anduin, Lor'themar, Thalyssra, Velen, Khadgar, his parents—even the loss of one of these figures would be a serious blow to any resistance. But as he looked around him, Arator took satisfaction in knowing that in Azeroth, at least, there were few leaders who could not handle themselves in a fight. Sarothar was a careful demon, and his entire purpose was to evaluate and execute the proper, perfect preparation of worlds for invasion and subjugation.

He would have calculated this attack with precision and determined this was the best way to proceed. Arator knew the demon was probably right and now possessed every advantage.

Except two.

Sarothar hadn't predicted the wedding. No one had. The speed of the planning had forced the eredar to adjust his plans quickly, so he might not be as prepared for every eventuality as he believed. And, unless Sarothar was different from every other demon Arator had encountered, there was a good chance he wasn't fully prepared for the illogical, irrational heroism, compassion, and cooperation that was on full display before him.

Eitrigg and Danath fought side by side, the two former enemies now both Sons of Lothar. Behind them, Alonsus Faol kept them on their feet. Arrows whizzed overhead, targeting demons already wounded to bring them down swiftly. Arator spotted his parents, one limned in golden light, surrounded by the scorched, slashed bodies of demons, the other with swirls of purple energy writhing about her.

Golden flashes of rejuvenescent Light flashed throughout; with so many priests and paladins on the field, including extremely powerful and experienced ones like Velen, Faol, Anduin, and his father, few except the demons appeared to be severely injured.

The humming sound of another sort of portal made him whirl, to see Rouzoch rushing through to preempt the next wave. Three imps darted through his legs, and Jubeka showered the little demons with a rain of fire.

Right now, they were battling lesser demons, and Arator could see that others, like Rouzoch and Jubeka, had been able to close some portals. But for every one they closed, another opened. Jubeka was right. There was only one solution.

Where are you, Sarothar . . . or rather, who *are you?* Even an Illidari would have trouble spotting him in this chaos, if he had opted not to be seen.

He looked around for aid and spied Liadrin's red armor. Arator shouted her name, gesturing. She headed in his direction, slashing a patch through the imps in her path.

"I'll go to the soul engine," he told Jubeka. "Liadrin will protect you."

"What? Arator—" Liadrin started to protest.

"These portals will keep opening unless the soul engine is shut down. I know where it is and what to do."

"That eredar is probably waiting for you!"

"I'm counting on it." He gave his old friend a lopsided grin. "Someone told me once I had to walk every step of my path. That sometimes, it might take me places I didn't want to go."

Her eyes filled with tears. "Damn it, Arator—"

"Protect Jubeka and the others. Promise me!" He raised his voice, needing her vow.

Despairingly, Liadrin nodded. She whispered a prayer, and the Light heard it. Strength and clarity of purpose flowed through him.

"Tell my folks I love them," Arator said, tightened his grip on his sword, and stepped through.

■ ■ ■

Shock and anger vibrated through Alleria's body as she turned to Thalyssra. The Void relished it. *She has earned death for her foolishness. She has doomed your world. Punish her!*

"We found Niandar's body in Felsoul Hold days ago," Alleria said, forcing herself to speak calmly. "Whoever you've seen since then is *Sarothar,* and now he could be *anybody.*"

Alleria's vision was not so clouded by the Void that she could not see how stricken the first arcanist was, but Thalyssra recovered quickly. She clenched a fist.

"That creature will *not* succeed. Not in my city!"

Alleria nodded. "I must tell my—" But the words died in her throat.

Jubeka was still beside a fel portal, attacking its guardians. Liadrin fought beside her now. There was no sign of Arator.

Alleria opened a rift.

Turalyon had paused in his fighting to heal his fellow combatants. He turned as Alleria appeared beside him. She spoke quickly, coldly, cleanly.

"Sarothar killed Niandar and assumed his identity. Arator's gone—he must have left for the Hold to destroy the soul engine."

Turalyon was radiant with the Light, but his face was still his own, and she saw horror on it. Horror . . . and anger.

"Get to Jubeka." Without another word he began to hack his way through the enemy, cutting them down easily.

Alleria used the Void rift to reach Jubeka.

"Any sign of Sarothar?" Jubeka asked.

"I was going to ask you the same question," Alleria answered. She sensed Turalyon approaching and moved to the other side of the warlock. Turalyon joined them.

"Where's Arator?"

Jubeka paused.

"No," breathed Turalyon.

"I'm sorry," came a voice. Liadrin stood beside them. She was spattered with ichor and fel blood. Her face was bleak, but stoic. "He was determined to go."

"More portals keep opening, and if the soul engine isn't—" Jubeka started.

The nimbus around Turalyon suddenly blazed. With a bellow of commingled pain and rage, he grabbed Liadrin's shoulder, shaking her. *"Did you even try to stop him!"*

"Turalyon!" Alleria cried. "Focus on Arator!"

He stared at her, then the Light surrounding him faded to its more familiar hue. He nodded, panting, and looked down at Liadrin. "I'm—I'm sorry." He shook his head as if to clear it.

Alleria said his name again, urgently. Calling him back to her, to what mattered.

He looked at her, as full of pain as she was.

"Let's go save our son," Alleria said.

Turalyon rushed through the fel portal first, consecrating the stone ground of Felsoul Hold, sending out bolts of Light from both hands. Like a flash of lightning, the radiance starkly revealed a mighty flood of creatures, struggling to push through into the wedding. Alleria wove the shadows, tendrils of darkness that twined and choked and smothered, blades that pierced. There was no finesse in how they killed, only purpose and the drive to find the one person who was everything to them both.

"Alleria!" Turalyon shouted. "The bodies are piling up!"

Twining purple energy thickened, became less tendrils than tentacles that seized the demons, alive or dead, and hurled them out of the way. Turalyon's aura of golden light seemed to never dim, so constant was his attack. They pushed on, sometimes climbing over the corpses, bare hands squelching in fel goo.

Alleria opened a Void rift and emerged several yards away. Jumping atop one of the Legion's abandoned war machines, she looked with her own keen vision.

Nothing looked familiar. She had anticipated that the portals would open near the soul engine, but Sarothar was far too clever to permit that vulnerability in his plan.

Her hands curled into fists, and purple writhed about them. Then she leaped down and fought her way back to Turalyon. At her words, he nodded grimly.

"I'll keep looking for something familiar," she said, "and when I find it, I'll come get you." She hesitated for a moment, her gaze falling to his once-elegant doublet, so carefully embroidered, woven of finest silkweave, now spattered with fel blood and demon gore.

"Yes . . . armor would have been nice," Turalyon said, following her gaze. He gave her a quick smile.

My gown must be a ruin. Why did I let myself—

Alleria opened a rift. She would waste no more time.

She had no idea how long she spent in the Void, stepping through portal after portal in Felsoul Hold, trying to locate Arator, Sarothar, or simply recognize a part of this deeply loathed place. Had it been a moment, it would have been too long.

The Void itself was little help, tapping on her mind with panicked urgency or dire images of a tortured Arator or an Azeroth wreathed in fel. Alleria knew it for what it was: a distraction, one the Void would capitalize on. But she and her dark power would soon be in alignment, once Arator was found and the three of them faced Sarothar. At last, she emerged in a place that felt familiar. Yes . . . this was where she and Turalyon had stopped to remark on how strange it felt, to be in a place recovering from the ravages of demonic occupation. When they had begun to cautiously be playful again—not walking on eggshells, afraid to tease or touch. Or trust.

An age ago, an eon, yet only a handful of days.

She needed to make a decision: to keep looking for Arator, with no idea where he was, or return to Turalyon, and the two of them would make their way to the soul engine. Her heart cried for one thing, her brain and all her experience demanded another.

Alleria made a decision, hoped it was the right one, and opened a rift.

■ ■ ■

Turalyon had made good progress while Alleria had been gone. The crush of demons thinned out as he traveled farther from the portal. It was clear the demons had their orders, and even though a paladin without armor, like a crab without a shell, must have been an appetizing sight, each of the Nether-creatures headed without hesitation to the portal.

He sighed with relief when the purple-black, starless rift appeared and Alleria stepped out. "I did not find our son," she said, answering the question she knew was foremost in his mind. "Nor have I encountered any signs of Sarothar. But I can get us back on track to the soul engine. Follow me."

He did. There was no need for her to scout ahead. No demon would be surprised to see them. They just needed to stay alert and be prepared to fight.

"I don't think Sarothar is sending them after us, at least not this moment," Turalyon said. "I noticed earlier they went directly to the portal."

"That does not comfort me," Alleria said.

They turned a corner. Turalyon paused and pointed.

At first, she didn't understand the significance of what she saw. The demons were still coming, but now they were leaping over the corpses of their fallen.

And then she understood. The fallen demons were not their kills.

"Arator's alive!" she cried. She hastened forward, stooping, analyzing. Turalyon watched her and saw that there was a trail of demons that went, not directly to the soul engine, but a different way. Alleria stood, her back to him, then opened a rift with a quick gesture and stepped through.

"Alleria!"

Turalyon surged forward, trying to stop her. His fingers closed on empty air.

Alleria had rushed through the portal after their son without a word, seemingly without caring this trail of bodies was more than likely a carefully laid trap. Arator was everything to them, but he was only bait to Sarothar. Together, the three of them were powerful. Separately, each was more vulnerable.

And wielding each against the others made them weaker still.

"She *knows* that," he muttered, letting the anger fuel him as he ran, faster than he could without armor, leaping over the corpses that he hoped Arator, not Sarothar, had made. It was not that he did not understand her desire to find Arator as quickly as possible. Light knew he shared that desire, and the fear behind it. Nor was it that he was directionless. The path Arator had taken could not be clearer.

Once again, Alleria had made a decision that involved both of them—involved all of them—without so much as a word. Once again, she had left him behind, determined to take care of everything herself. In the past, he understood her reasoning and often agreed with it. But not now.

He tightened his grip on his sword, alternating between asking the Light to help him blast Sarothar to pieces, in truth this time, and asking it to *please, protect my son, protect my love.*

Turalyon jumped over a pile of imps and was about to clear the spiny body of a felguard when something seized his ankle just as he left the ground. He twisted, drawing his sword, the Light limning his body. The demon hissed but clung on stubbornly. The paladin struck the ground with his shoulder, the Light shielding him from much of the pain, rolled, and slashed with his glowing sword.

The felbat shrieked. Its hand clamped down in its death spasm, and Turalyon struck it again. He kicked the corpse off, disgusted, then looked around.

"Behind you!"

Turalyon whirled on pure instinct, his body reacting to the warning before his mind flooded with joy and relief. An unusually brave imp, wounded, was summoning what energy it had left to attack, but Arator sliced it neatly in two.

"Not sure you could have handled that," Arator joked.

Heedless of his fel-spattered, sodden clothing, Turalyon shifted the sword to one hand and roughly embraced his son.

"Thank the Light you were here, then," he said, tears stinging his eyes.

Arator hugged him for a moment, then pulled back. "Where's Mother?"

"We found the trail of bodies, and she portaled ahead," Turalyon said.

Arator looked confused. "Wait . . . why did she leave you behind?"

Turalyon's head jerked, recalling a flash of impossibly bright light, Alleria reaching up to him—

The words he had said to her then, and long ago, the promise he had made her: *I will never leave you behind . . .*

"Oh," Arator said. "Right. Because that's what she does." Pain flickered across his features for a moment, and he looked away.

Anger stirred in Turalyon again. *She should not do this to him. To us.* He took a breath and said, forcing himself to keep the conversation light, "Well, in this case, it was because she was trying to reach *you* as soon as possible. Why did you backtrack?"

Arator scoffed. "Backtrack? From what? *I* didn't kill these." He nudged an imp with his toe.

I knew it. Alleria . . .

Turalyon forced back the fear and the fury. "Then your mother may be portaling right into a trap."

CHAPTER NINETEEN

Felsoul Hold Ruins, Suramar

BROKEN ISLES

Alleria was bizarrely reminded of a game she and her sisters used to play as children. It involved jumping from one circle on the ground to another. The challenge was that the circles grew farther apart with each step. It was supposed to be a part of their training, but it was so much fun they played it often.

I won because I was the eldest, so my legs were always longer than theirs.

The eldest Windrunner daughter was playing a dangerous version of that game now, teleporting from spot to spot. She never "jumped" farther than she could see. There was no sense in opening a Void portal right into Sarothar's path, nor did she wish to accidentally move ahead of her son, but she chafed at how slow it felt. *At this rate, Turalyon will beat me here,* she thought. There did not seem to be any dangers that would be any threat to him, and with the trail of bodies, there was no danger of him becoming lost.

The way was familiar now, after twice traversing it with her family. There was the sealed-in chamber, where a rat had gotten lucky enough to avoid her arrow. Up ahead was the boulder she had crouched behind, to assess the danger.

She did so again now, moving soundlessly to it and sinking down. She let her gaze go soft, augmenting her senses with the Void. She could smell the demon; its fel odor was strong. A sound: slow, heavy footsteps. Not hooves, nor boots. A felguard, most likely. Only one. Skittering, squawking . . . one, two, perhaps three imps. Laughter, then the familiar sound of one of them preparing then releasing a firebolt.

"Aah!"

Arator . . . !

The smell of burning cloth and flesh—

Alleria invited the Void in, accepted its gifts, and wove it around her as she charged forward.

The wrathguard met her head-on, bellowing, its voice wet and gurgling, as if it screamed through its own blood. Alleria thrust one hand toward the demon bearing down on her, the other toward the cluster of imps. A purple cloud descended upon them, and they dissolved, shrieking and steaming.

The wrathguard's fel-kissed blades cut the air in two swift strikes, but she was not there. It stumbled off-balance for an instant, but that was enough for her to send tendrils to snatch both its blades from its clawed hands. Undaunted, it lowered its head, pointing the metal spike atop its helm at her, and charged like a bull.

Alleria didn't move.

It was fast, as demons went, but she was faster. When the spike was but a few inches away from her unprotected chest, aimed directly for her heart, Alleria dropped, seized the wrathguard's protruding horns on either side, and summoned Void strength to flip it and wrench, hard.

The muscles about its neck and shoulders were thick, but she did not need to snap its neck. She simply needed it to choke. It flailed and struggled, its eyes wide in shock, and finally, she formed a spike out of black smoke that plunged itself into the base of its skull.

Alleria rose. There was no sign of her son.

"Arator!" she cried, heedless of who heard her.

A whisper. She looked up.

Her son was encased in fel chains, suspended from a rock formation that jutted out above her. Choking back a sob, she summoned tendrils of Void matter, using them to snap link and twine about his freed body, carefully bringing him down to the stone floor.

"Arator," she whispered, her heart breaking to see the burns from the gleeful imps and other signs of torture.

He reached up to her and she embraced him, rocking him as his arms went around her, mindful of the wounds that—

—the wounds—

The arms around her clamped down like iron bands, became white hot. In an instant, she was no longer holding her son, but was in the clutch of Sarothar. He uttered a word, and she was encased in fire.

■ ■ ■

The pain was all there was. Aching, sharp, throbbing. A dream, a vivid dream, but he opened his eyes, and it was still there.

Arator took a breath, winced at the pain in his chest, and inhaled more carefully, staring at gray stone a few inches from his face, feeling its hardness below his battered body. He tried to move—

"Ah!" he hissed, his body jerking in reaction, and he realized he was bound hand and foot.

"He's awake," someone said.

It came back to him in a flood of memories, in a disorderly rush, layered and interwoven with one another. Demons, so many of them, but he had held his own. Wandering, hiding. Finding the back way in, trying to unlock the soul engine's secrets. Then without warning, horrible pain, paralysis, then he was lifted and slammed—

He whispered a prayer, and the Light poured healing into him, warm and gentle. Another prayer, and he twisted the ropes at his wrists and pulled, breaking them with a satisfying snap.

Better. He rolled over and sat up, looking at his fellow captives. They stared back at him, bound as he had been, hope in their eyes as he removed the broken rope and set to work on his ankles. They were all nightborne, and Arator understood where he was and what was going to happen to them.

Before he did anything else, he wanted to know the immediate situation. He held up a finger to his lips, then rose and began to examine the area. It was not the same alcove where he had found the bodies. That would have been too small to house so many. This was essentially a small cavern, though not a natural one. A quick glance around showed a boulder wedged into the entrance, and that entrance itself was far too perfect a circle. Sarothar, or another demon before him, had ordered this area created. The air was, if not exactly fresh, not stale. They would not suffocate here, though Arator doubted Sarothar intended for them to live long enough for that to be a concern. He was not at all certain he could move the boulder, and it was far too solid to be able to determine if there was a demonic guard on the other side.

This wasn't going to be easy.

He closed his eyes. *Light . . . help me. Give me wisdom to do the right thing, and the strength to do it. Grant healing to these people and soothe their frightened hearts.*

He heard the soft murmurs and smiled to himself. The Light was still with him.

As Arator returned to the group, one of them asked, "Are you a priest?"

"Paladin," he said. "My name's Arator."

"The first arcanist's guest," one of them said. "Your parents got married today."

Arator realized they didn't know about what happened at the wedding. "Not quite," he said, kneeling beside the closest nightborne and beginning to remove her bonds. "Can someone tell me what happened to you, and when."

Arator knew what he would hear, and at first it seemed he was right. Felbats had descended upon various places in Suramar and borne them off. They had woken up here, in this cavern.

"When was this?"

"Just today," one of them said.

Arator paused and looked at him.

"What time?"

"Midday or thereabouts."

The time of the wedding. "And where is home for each of you? Do any of you live in isolated areas or encampments?"

Some did. But some didn't. "Did the felbats take everyone in your town or your camp?"

Heads were shaken, no.

Sarothar was no longer hiding. He had planned a coordinated attack at midday, did not care if anyone escaped, and as he'd obviously let his demons play with some of them, he planned to harvest their souls sooner rather than later. None of this was good news. They had to move quickly . . . but how?

Arator expected that Turalyon and Alleria, by now, had discovered he'd gone through a fel portal to the hold. Liadrin would have conveyed his message, but they, being who they were, would have ignored it. Sarothar had beaten them handily the first time they encountered him, but he'd had the element of surprise. The demon would not be met with such an easy fight this time.

He knew his parents had not yet attempted a rescue. If they had, he'd either be out by now, joining them in being sacrificed to the soul engine, or being paraded in front of them before being sacrificed to the soul engine.

He finished untying the last bond and rose, listening as a survivor spoke. "We are not unused to demons," one said as she finished her story. "But . . ." She looked at the others, who nodded. "We thought Felsoul Hold had been cleared of them. That there was no more danger."

Arator sighed deeply. "So did we."

"Is it another invasion?"

"Has the city fallen?"

"Can you help us get out of here?"

Others chimed in with their fears or questions, and Arator called for quiet. "Listen," he began, but then a thought occurred to him. On his own, he'd stand no chance to get them out of here, but with the others . . . "We're going to work together to move the boulder and escape."

"Escape?" a nightborne replied. "They'll kill us before we can take two steps!"

"They'll kill us if we stay here!" another shouted.

Arator gestured again for calm. "Any demons in the hold right now have one of two purposes. One—find and enter the portals to besiege Suramar City, or two—" he smiled ruefully. "Find me or my family."

"I'll create a distraction, slay the guards . . ." Arator gestured to the boulder. "That will give you an opening while I draw them to myself. Wait until I give the all clear to move."

He walked up and set his shoulder to the great stone, and they joined him.

▪ ▪ ▪

"I still can't believe that Sarothar was able to infiltrate the Duskwatch so easily," Arator said as he and Turalyon hurried toward the soul engine. "He was able to change into a lot of other people, too. Do you remember my friend Eadred?"

Turalyon frowned. "Don't tell me that was him, too."

"Yes," his son said. "It's . . . a little humbling, don't you think? How he was able to trick all of us?"

"I take some comfort in that Sarothar has been doing it for a long time," Turalyon said. "We are but a few of literally countless people who have been deceived by him. But you're right." He paused. "Humility is something we all need to be reminded of, from time to time."

"Are you worried about Mother?"

Turalyon glanced at his son briefly. Arator was a lively, inquisitive young man; he loved to jump into conversations. But this was not how he had behaved before, when the three of them were hunting and fighting demons.

This hunt, though, was different from any of their previous ones. This was the one they had been working toward. Was Arator rattled somehow? He had seen strong soldiers go into battle a hundred times, then one more, for reasons unknown, had broken them. Turalyon realized he had always understood what to do, or say, to those who struggled, but he had no idea how to talk to his own son.

"Your mother is smart and strong," Turalyon said. "She will be fine, but I admit, I too would feel better if we were all together."

"It's just like before," Arator said. "She did the same thing. If we'd had her with us when we summoned Sarothar, well . . ."

"You don't need to remind me." He slowed, stopped, and turned to his son. "Arator . . . I don't think I ever apologized for what happened in Dreadscar Rift. I hope you know I would *never* hurt you."

"I know, Father." Arator gave him a warm smile. "But you never should have been put in that position. That was Mother's doing. You deserve better."

In the space of a heartbeat, Turalyon had summoned the Light and placed the tip of his sword at his son's throat. "I'm in no mood for games."

The thing wearing Arator's face smiled. But Turalyon knew he would never see an expression so smug, so cruel, on his son's face.

"Took you long enough," the demon said, speaking in its own voice now. It uttered a word that Turalyon recognized as a spell dismissal, and now he saw its true shape. It continued to wear his son's wedding clothing, doubtless as an insult, although it left its hooves unchanged for Turalyon to see. "And Sarothar promised you'd be a challenge to convince. You really must be terribly distracted."

"You have my full attention now, sayaad," Turalyon growled. The incubus only smiled the more, unfurling its wings in defiance and tossing its horned head. Turalyon pressed the blade farther into its neck, and it hissed. "What have you done with my son?"

"Now, now, you'll learn nothing if you kill me, will you?"

The paladin could feel the sayaad trying to exert his power over him. He was one of the stronger ones Turalyon had run across, but the sayaad was wasting his time.

"Where is Sarothar?" Turalyon demanded, his outrage building. A vein throbbed in his temple. "*Where is my son?*"

"Remove your blade and I will tell you."

Turalyon wanted nothing more than to kill the creature on the spot, but it might say more if it thought it had a chance of surviving. He stepped back, knowing he was in no danger. He could now see that the demon had a small sack tied to Arator's belt.

"It's a difficult question to answer," the demon continued.

"I'm sure it isn't," Turalyon said. "Untie the bag and put it down."

The demon looked uneasy. "You don't need to see that," it said, making its voice soft and earnest, lulling and soothing. It was trying to use its power on Turalyon and he was having none of it.

"Put it down and step back," he ordered. The demon complied. "Now," Turalyon continued, stepping toward the bag. "Why is it a difficult question? And don't stall."

"Truly, it all depends," the demon said earnestly.

Turalyon listened, his gaze moving from the demon to the sack. Using the tip of his sword, he carefully began to move the flaps of fabric to the side, to see what it concealed.

"On which part of him you want to see."

Arator's face, eyes wide, bloody, stared up at his father.

■ ■ ■

"Where is my son?" Alleria demanded for the fifth time. The hundredth time. She had lost count. She was giving the demon nothing other than this question, doing nothing other than fighting the demons he sent her way, and he seemed to have no objection. In fact, Sarothar seemed to be enjoying himself.

"I don't usually participate in these stages," he said. "I'm well gone by this point, off on another world, sniffing out the possibilities, extinguishing anything that might blossom into problems. I confess I actually looked down on activities like this. Then again, I know many a demon that didn't live to be doing what I'm doing now. I would have preferred you had taken me up on my offer."

Alleria was silent. She sized up the newcomers he had summoned: a doomguard and another wrathguard. They joined the sayaad, felhounds, and felguards standing and waiting to be commanded. She had only seen doomguards and wrathguards on Argus before. They had been serving as honor guards to . . .

"Ah! I see the dawning realization. I am indeed an eredar lord. No one listens to you unless you are, and I do need an army. It was absolute chaos before I stepped up."

"Where is my son?"

"Ask another question."

"Where is my son?"

Sarothar sighed and inclined his head ever so slightly.

Alleria was ready. She decided to try another tactic. The eredar was stalling for time. What was he waiting for? News from Suramar City or another place in Azeroth? For word of Arator or Turalyon? Two could play that game.

"You killed Niandar and took his form. How?"

"Because I killed Mauvara and took hers first."

"Did you know we were tracking you?"

"Of course. See, isn't this better?"

"Where is my son?"

"I have him. He's not been harmed . . . well, not majorly, anyway. Nothing he can't clean up himself."

Alleria could kill him, if she tried hard enough. She could pull enough Void energy into herself to do it. Release it all and take him with her. The only thing Alleria did not know was if Arator and Turalyon would be casualties of the Void as well.

"How did you know we were tracking you?"

He grinned. It was not pleasant. And then, he was a vulpera in desert clothes. "Too bad we all never got together for that drink at the World's End."

"Maybe not *that* world's end," Alleria replied.

"Banter!" he exclaimed. "Excellent."

"Why haven't you killed me? If you even can."

"You are not a god," he said. "You know that. You've worn yourself down quite a bit. If you continue, that may change."

She had been fighting him and his demons for a while now, long enough to be weary. She needed to save her energy for when it mattered.

"My question still stands. Where is Arator, if you truly do have him?"

Before he could answer, pain shot through her. A shock, taking her breath, shuddering through her, the darkness in her reacting to the Light.

Turalyon . . .

The eredar lord was smiling.

■ ■ ■

With great effort, the boulder at last shifted. Their escape was not swift, but one by one, all the refugees emerged, scraped and bleeding but safe. Arator had gotten out first and done a bit of reconnaissance. He was not far from the soul engine, and he had found a route that skirted the walls of Felsoul, which would likely be the safest way out. To his surprise and amusement, he also discovered a pile where his sword, along with various weapons he suspected might belong to his fellow prisoners, had been casually tossed.

They were down to the last two people when Arator sensed the presence of the Light. It was strong and steady, not the Light of healing, but the Light of action, of war against the darkness, manifesting powerfully in this dark, fel-hued place.

Father . . .

CHAPTER TWENTY

Felsoul Hold Ruins, Suramar

BROKEN ISLES

Sarothar cocked his head as if listening, then smiled. He reached out a massive hand, creating a fel portal.

Alleria's heart sank. With the demons he already had here, if he was bringing in greater forces, she would not survive.

I would have liked to have seen Arator again, she thought. *One last time.*

She began to draw the Void close in to her, a second skin rather than an energy to be directed. What would it be, she wondered. Pit lords? Abyssals? They were all alike in death, and she would join them.

The portal swirled, fel-green writhing. Something was approaching.

Alleria leaped up, borne by the Void, and dove toward the very center of the portal. She, a missile of focused, harnessed Void power, and whatever horror the portal was about to unleash, would crash head-on, and nothing would remain.

Sarothar began to laugh.

And it was that—not her instincts—that made Alleria turn in midair, caused Turalyon to slow his charge ever so slightly, and alter their catastrophic course enough so a direct collusion became merely a brutal crash.

If a simple touch caused pain to each, this strike was agony. Alleria became a vessel of almost singular, pure sensation, and hit the stone floor hard. The wounded Void screamed in her mind, not in sadistic glee but in utter torment, for her to destroy the source of this pain, wipe it out of existence. And in that moment, as her physical heart raced and her lungs heaved, she wanted to yield to it, but she was not strong enough, not yet.

Turalyon lifted his head, the Light healing him as she watched, and their eyes met. For an instant, his eyes were golden brown. As Alleria saw him as Turalyon, and not the Light's Wrath, he saw her as herself, not the Void. It did not last, not here in the thick of battle, but it was there.

"You are an intriguing pair," Sarothar said. "You each command such power. And what abilities they give you. The boy would have been one to watch."

He strode over to them, his huge hoofs striking sparks from the stone, and gazed down at them almost sadly.

"I am appreciative. While I do not often enjoy inflicting pain . . . suffering has beauty to it. My Legion will cultivate the beauty in suffering, in destruction. Appreciation of the brevity of lesser things as they disappear. It's a shame, really, you can't stay and see it. The gratuitousness on display of our former leadership never appealed to me, but who else was qualified to fill the role? Demons like Varaskar? Do you think *she* would know how to organize an invasion? *Someone* has to see to it that all these worlds are destroyed properly!"

Something penetrated the Void's haze. A name. It meant something.

"Varaskar," Alleria said. Her voice was faint, but eredar ears caught it.

"Ah, yes, now, put it all together." The demon sounded pleased, as if he were a tutor encouraging a favorite pupil.

"The vulpera." Each word was an effort, but Alleria was stalling for time. The Void assured her that her strength would return, but now she was vulnerable, *vulnerable*—

"You," Alleria rasped. "You made sure we would find Lyana. To k-kill your rival."

"Exactly. One way or another, any obstacle on my path would be dealt with."

Vulnerable! The voices were terrified.

"We thought . . . Turalyon killed you. The soul engine . . . brought you back?"

"That?" Sarothar waved a dismissive hand in the direction of the soul engine. "This broken relic of the last invasion? I would not trust it for such things. Think, Alleria. Think how long I have been examining worlds. Do you think I have not observed the Light and its wielders under every circumstance imaginable? That is an old, old trick of mine. Preparation, illusions, and excellent timing. Turalyon's . . . enthusiasm at the moment certainly helped. Blinded by the Light, as it were."

A low, despairing groan came from Turalyon. He was still bathed in Light, but the wrath was not upon him. He was healing from the blow, but it would take time.

"Lord Sarothar." A wrathguard entered and knelt. "Suramar continues to close our portals. We require more energy if we are to claim victory."

Sarothar listened and nodded. "We have more than enough souls, for now," he said. "Go get them. Bring the paladin."

Alleria had not moved much. She was curled up in a fetal position, limp, barely responsive. The paladin.

Arator . . .

"You." It was Turalyon, stumbling to his feet, despite his injury. "W-we will stop you."

Despite everything, Turalyon still summoned the strength to stand against Sarothar.

"To what end?" Sarothar's voice was almost gentle. "The Legion is inevitable. Resistance is noble but doomed to fail. You will see your son again, to make your farewells, is that not kindness enough? Your deaths will be painless—physically, at least. I told you, I don't often enjoy causing pain, and you did me quite a favor in killing Varaskar."

"Lord Sarothar!"

Alleria had never seen a frightened wrathguard before, but this one was practically quaking.

"The captives have escaped!"

Sarothar's elegant features hardened to stone. He extended an enormous red hand. Fel chains shot forth, whipping about the wrathguard. The eredar yanked, and the huge demon slid across the floor. Sarothar planted a hoof on its chest.

"What. Happened."

"The paladin freed them. They are escaping through portals, and he is holding us off."

Sarothar pressed his hoof into the wrathguard's chest. There was a terrible hissing, sizzling sound, and the stench of burning flesh mixed with fel. The eredar removed his hoof and the chains dissolved. The wrathguard rose, the brand of Sarothar's hoof still smoking.

"Bring him," Sarothar said, and the wrathguard bowed, hastening to carry out the order. He turned to regard the prone figures before him. "Unfortunately, your son has now made it impossible for me to spare your souls. You three are my only supply for the moment, thanks to him, and I must set an ex—"

The wrathguard's roar, a short distance away, caused him to turn.

■ ■ ■

Arator leaped upward as the doomguard tumbled to the earth. Cracks snaked out from the stone as the ground shivered under the impact. He landed lightly, assessed the area, and began to run in the direction of the soul engine.

It had been close, but Arator, along with several courageous nightborne who had offered their considerable aid, had held off the demons attempting to halt the escape. By the time the last had stepped through the portal to safety, only a handful were left, easily dispatched. The lone wrathguard who had unexpectedly appeared had been his last obstacle.

As he drew near, he heard the familiar sounds of Light and Void in battle, and his heart surged. His parents were here, alive, and fighting. He began to see their magic, dark purple, golden Light.

Light, help us. Inspire my father, aid my mother's efforts. Grant me the ability to help them and save our world.

The fighting before Arator was fierce.

The bodies of demons, from wrathguards to imps, littered the floor—they must have been at this for some time. Only Sarothar and a few demons were left, and it looked like his parents were keeping the eredar busy enough that he could not call for reinforcements. Alleria sliced open a Void rift and vanished, only to reappear behind the single wrathguard, wreathed in black mist. A spike of black matter plunged deep into its eye. It stood for a moment, then toppled. He could see she was tired—her movements were slower than he'd ever seen.

Holy Light swirled around Turalyon, who seemed to be faring better. He spun off to sear a group of imps and felhounds who thrashed about, shrieking in pain. He swung his sword, slicing an incubus almost in half, and when the force of the strike brought him almost halfway around again, he raised his arm and called down a blast of golden fire directly upon Sarothar himself.

Sarothar hissed. "Remember, this was your choice," he growled, his voice low and deep as he raised his hands.

Before he could complete whatever he intended, a golden hammer struck. Alleria whipped around, meeting her son's gaze.

I'm here, Mother! he thought, watching relief spread over her face. He was almost giddy, memories of the three of them filling his mind. This time, they had the advantage, not Sarothar, and—

An enormous fel bolt struck his mother. She staggered, and then Sarothar unleashed fire upon her.

"No!" Arator shouted, horrified.

The demon's horned head turned and, before Arator could react, he was slammed back against hard stone. Taken by surprise, with no armor, he took almost the full impact. He couldn't breathe and slid to the ground, gasping like a fish. Unable to help, unable to move, he stared, helplessly, at the disaster unfolding before him.

Turalyon shouted in wordless fury, in a tone and timbre of voice that Arator had heard from him only once before.

Light flooded the area, the Light of retribution and rage. The Light that distinguished only between itself and the enemy. It slammed into Sarothar, who cried out. Arator's eyes closed reflexively against the brightness. He prayed that he would see a defeated, if not yet slain, enemy when he opened them.

He did not. Sarothar was staggering, badly wounded, yes, but still alive.

"You were so close to grasping certain truths, closer than I have seen in some time, but you cannot, you will not, grasp it. You've tried, expanded, but in the end . . . such powers will always take more than they give. You knew that already, and now . . ." Sarothar gestured at them, still trying to recover. The eredar lord laughed sadly, the way a parent might, when a child breaks a toy and weeps like they've lost the world.

"You were *never* a threat to me. Don't you understand?" His voice was almost kind.

Volleys of dark purple bolts assailed him. Flashes of gold struck him. Each did damage, but each was weakened by the other.

Words, spoken to him in his father's gently chiding voice, came back to Arator like a punch in the gut.

Teamwork is being aware of what others are doing. That's how you turn luck into strategy.

There was nothing of strategy from his parents now. Any strategy was on the part of Sarothar, who had recognized long ago what Arator had not wanted to see, and who was laughing at them now.

The Silver Hand protocol makes it very clear that a paladin must make contact, however briefly, with the senior paladin before just . . . jumping in.

Void and Light were powerful. But applied at the same time, they were weakening each other. Now, when everything was at stake, his parents had leaned fully into their powers, and in so doing, had ceased to lean on each other. So intent was their focus upon the demon, Turalyon and Alleria did not strike in accord, but in a devastatingly ironic twist, were instead attacking at cross purposes. They could not see what their son saw, what Sarothar saw, and they only struck the harder.

An enormous wave of grief washed over Arator, leaving a horrible emptiness in his wake. He surrendered to it, helpless and hopeless, everything he had clung to his whole life dissolving into dust in a matter of seconds.

"Brave little soldiers. So busy trying, and failing, to not destroy yourselves, that you've done it for me."

No.

Arator screamed, a roar of pain and defiance, and called on the Light. It healed him, and he seized his sword and began to run.

Not to Sarothar, nor to his parents, but to the soul engine.

Other words, spoken to him by a warlock but not heard by his parents, drove him now. *That soul engine's sustaining the portals,* Jubeka had told him. *The fel energy it channels enables Sarothar to bring whatever forces he wants here, until we're overwhelmed. Those runes? They likely double that power.*

None of the three noticed him, for which Arator was wildly grateful, and he reached the soul engine unchallenged. It pulsed, the runes glowing green, its energy palpable. For just an instant, Arator hesitated.

To make it overload, you'll have to switch the current, so to speak. Overwhelm the fel with Light.

What happens then? Arator had asked.

Damned if I know, dear boy. But the engine will be destroyed. That's all I can tell you.

Tears stung his eyes. He wanted more time. Time with his family.

Time to grow closer. But he couldn't buy that time for them. Not now.

He *could* buy time for the world.

Arator filled his heart with love for his parents. For their strengths, and their weaknesses. For his family, and friends, and the innocents he didn't even know. For everyone who had suffered at the hands of the Legion. And he poured that love, his will, his strength, into his prayer to the Light.

It answered in kind.

He lifted his hands, and a stream of bright, pure, healing light poured directly into the fel machinery, Arator as its conduit. The outside world fell away until he could no longer hear the shouting of his rage-filled father, the bursts of Void energy, and Sarothar's voice, filled with scorn.

Arator heard only the Light's song of joy, the same he had shared with D'ore. Only heard whispers of thank you, from those he had healed. He could feel the battle between the Light and fel, but the Light was growing. He could see it now, as he opened his eyes. Green and gold swirled in combat, and somehow Arator knew that the moment was imminent.

With a final push, Arator shut down the flow. He sprang to his feet and ran toward his mother as his father fought on. He threw himself on top of Alleria, shielding her with his body.

Light slammed into him.

Then nothing.

■ ■ ■

Alleria awoke to the face of her son, who knelt next to her.

She pulled him into her arms, holding him tightly as she surveyed the wreckage around her. Turalyon was sitting up, holding his head. No Light enveloped him, but he was alive and awake. Her gaze traveled to where Sarothar had stood, gloating at them, and the Void rushed back.

"No, Mother," Arator said at once. "He's dead. Truly dead."

With a sigh, she relaxed, looking into Arator's face, thinking to see weary relief. Instead, he was tense.

"Arator?" she said. "What happened?"

"I flooded the soul engine with the Light. The runes amplified the explosion. Father and I were safe, but I wasn't sure you would be. So I shielded you."

She touched her son's face, deeply proud, even as Turalyon said, "That was brilliant, son. Well done."

Arator sighed and rose, letting his mother's hand fall.

Alleria glanced down at what was left of her beautiful gown and grieved. It had once been so lovely, graceful, light. It made her feel like air, almost floating rather than walking. The chains had mostly ripped off, and what was left dangled, stained and dull. She almost couldn't bear it. Not for the ruination of a thing—a gown could be re-created with a little time and coin—but for all it had symbolized.

She turned her gaze to Turalyon. There was a bizarre disconnect between the gore and fel that covered him, and the man himself; it was the armor that should bear the mark of the ugliness of battle. It kept him safe . . . like she had kept that inner innocence of him safe. Both had failed, today.

Arator regarded them for a minute, then seemed to make a decision. He was agitated, almost grim looking. "Let's all go sit together," he said.

Turalyon looked at him askance. "What is it? Another front of demons?"

"Just . . . sit, all right? Please?"

Turalyon looked at his son searchingly, then he and Alleria both obliged.

Arator paced for a bit, then said, "We're not . . . doing this again. We're not going to just pick up our weapons, make some jokes, wash up, and move on to the next fight. And the one after that. Not this time."

"Explain," Turalyon said.

"Did neither of you see what was going on?" Arator burst out. "You were out of sync, not communicating, in your desperation to destroy him! Father's Light dulled your strikes, Mother. And while you both pummeled him, thinking he was somehow impervious, he had used your fear to manipulate you, to distract you from the true source of his power: the soul engine. Something we knew all along.

"Sarothar didn't have to destroy us: you two were doing that all by yourselves."

He stopped pacing and planted himself, taking a deep breath. Alleria saw the Light settle on him, like dust motes in a sunbeam.

"I should *not* have to be the one saying this, either. But, here we are. You need to figure this out," Arator said calmly. "This . . . thing you do. You get close, then drift apart, get close . . . you isolate yourselves, convince yourselves it's down to *you alone* to save the world. This has to stop. Because until you do that, truly trust and rely on each other to *be there for you,* nothing can be done. And we will all keep performing this dance until one day, we miss a step badly, and then everything's over."

Alleria and Turalyon were silent.

"You need to find out, once and for all, if you can love each other without war and, and violence providing convenient excuses for you not to talk about the things that matter. Maybe you can't. But maybe you can, and if that's true, then let's do it right here, right now. Just . . . just talk. Whatever you need to say, say it, but just tell the truth. Because I *will not* watch both of you do this again."

A heavy silence descended on the family as Arator moved to lean against a ruined wall.

Turalyon cleared his throat. "I'll go first."

Alleria forced herself to turn and face him. She knew what he would say. And it would be the truth . . . at least as he saw it.

"Alleria Windrunner. You know you're the first and only person I've ever been in love with."

She allowed herself a smile. "I do. And same."

He smiled back for a moment. "I'm not sure you know that you're also the first to simply . . . *love* me. And that night, when, when you came to me . . . of anyone in the world, to *me* . . ." He shook his head slightly, still disbelieving, his face soft with remembrance. "That was it. I knew. I knew it the way I know I need to breathe. And even if you never spoke to me again, which," he said, more lightly, "you almost did. I still knew. Whatever else happened in that war, I vowed I would not regret it, because it brought me you.

"With the Sons of Lothar, I found brothers and sisters, and not too long after that . . . I discovered how much love a father can know. I've always felt blessed."

He took a deep breath. It had been some time since Alleria had thought of anything being sacred, but she understood that these moments, these words, truly were.

"Our paths brought us to the Light, and to the Void. I knew I was meant to become Lightforged. I thought you would be, too. But when you accepted the Void . . ."

Impulsively, Alleria reached for his hand. He clasped it tightly. "I left you behind."

"It wasn't your choice, love," Alleria said.

"But I still did it. What I said was, and is, true. I would rather die than see you fall to darkness. But now . . . I know you won't." Turalyon smiled gently. "I don't fear death, because I know we would find each other, wherever we were, in that other place. You know this, too."

Alleria nodded, mute. It was true. "Just as I know I need to breathe." Her voice caught on the last word.

"Because you are my Alleria, and the Void is part of you. Just as you love the scars on my face because they're part of me. It's just . . . *you.*"

Turalyon paused, took a breath, and continued. "This mission we've been on together," he said, looking at Arator, "for me, it feels like years have fallen away. It brought back so much of the joy, the play—how we were with each other, once. Alleria, we have spent more consecutive days together now than we have in years. And all it's done is make me look forward to more.

"When I had no one to love me, the Light was there. My whole life, it has given me a sense of purpose, a feeling that I'm making things better. Fighting the good fight. I know it and the Void are always going to be in opposition. But I don't think the Light can be *bad.* I understand that recently, it's frightened both of you." He looked at Arator. "But you asked for the truth, and I promise you both. I'm still me."

He ran his thumb over the back of her hand, along the scrapes and the dirt. "I've been thinking about how we used to be unable to do even this," he said. "But we both knew resigning ourselves to not touching was unacceptable, and so we figured out how to work with these energies we share our lives with." Turalyon slid his hand to the side and opened his fingers. Without even thinking, Alleria twined her fingers with his.

"You're everything to me," Turalyon said, simply. "My soul revolves around you like the sun. Nothing has changed. I want to marry you. I want to hold you in my arms. Every look, every touch across every day we've ever shared together, even this one. Nothing has changed any of it. We know more about who we are, Light and Void, than ever before. If we can claw back our ability to do this," he moved their hands together, "then we can place what we choose, what we desire, above forces that are merely a part of us."

Gently, she touched his cheek, tracing the old scars. "We do know much more now. But . . . the lessons we have taken are different."

"I don't understand."

Alleria had never wanted to be in this place. To be causing him pain. But she had done so, time after time. And she knew that this, too, was a lesson. "Yes, we can fight together, you in your Light, me in my darkness. But we cannot *be* together. For a long time, we have . . . adjusted appropriately. Learned to touch, learned to trust."

Now she looked at him. "Learned to master the Void. My relationship with the Void has changed dramatically. And now, so has yours. You were once afraid for me . . . and *of* me. And I understand that."

Turalyon could see where she was going with this. His scars stood out white on a suddenly pale face. "No, no . . . you never need to be afraid, my love. *Never.*"

"I don't know what you saw, or what knowledge was given you. But in Dreadscar Rift, with Sarothar . . . when you called upon the Light, you saw as simple that which is not. The world is not so clear cut. And there was a moment . . . where I thought *you—my* Turalyon—were never coming back."

She entwined her fingers with his. For the last time? She did not know. Alleria closed her eyes, gathering strength to say what her heart railed against.

"My love . . . there is terror there, in that place in the Light. There is no making peace with fear. Love and fear cannot coexist. And Light and Void cannot, either. I love you, Turalyon. I do. We may desperately want to be together, to stay in love, but there are forces that are part of us that will forever drive us apart. And we saw that play out today."

Alleria gently began to withdraw her hand. His grip tightened for just an instant, then he released her. She gazed at the engagement ring, then pulled it off, slowly.

"You chose these stones so carefully," Alleria said, emotion breaking through her mask of coldness. "You are the Light-catching diamond, and I the black spinel. You arranged the stones so the spinel would be protected by the diamonds. But the stone is alone, and it is trapped."

"Alleria, no . . . *no.*"

Alleria swallowed at the pain, the incomprehension in his voice. She had always been aware that she could destroy him with a handful of words. Shatter that innocence she once would have died to protect . . . but she was no longer able to spare him from it.

"I, too, thought we could recover what we once had, you and I. And here is something you might not know: That night, when I came to you, I began to heal, Turalyon, in ways you've never known nor would understand. We had endured so much together. But we're not those people, and we can't go back to that."

"Then let us go forward," he urged. "The past is done; the present is shaping itself now, with each breath and heartbeat. And the future can be whatever we decide it will be. I refuse to accept that the Void and the Light determine what we can and cannot be to each other. I know we can because we've done it before. I believe in us, Alleria. And if you do, too, then we *will* find a way."

Alleria's sorrow and pain had gone beyond the speaking of them. She got to her feet, and he did, too. She took his hand and pressed the ring into his palm, folding his fingers over it. Bringing his hand to her lips, she pressed a soft kiss upon it, then released it and turned away.

■ ■ ■

Turalyon stood for a moment, gripping the ring tightly as the great love of his life left him. Then his knees gave way, and he half sat, half fell to the stairs. Out of armor, the exquisite doublet soiled and torn, High Exarch Turalyon appeared startlingly small and vulnerable to his son, the weight of grief bending his back, breaking his heart.

Arator was torn, his heart full, his head spinning. Then he turned, racing after his mother and grabbing her arm.

For an instant, darkness clouded her glowing eyes, then it subsided.

"My turn," he said. "The speech I made today—I didn't get through it. So I'm going to finish now. *My* truth. And you are *not* going to walk away from me till I've said it."

She nodded without speaking.

"I've been searching for something my whole life. I wasn't sure of what it was until recently. Vereesa, the twins—they love me and I them. They've been *good* to me. But Silvermoon, Dalaran, that house . . . it was never my home.

"So *I* kept looking. For this . . . *piece* that I was missing. I began to train with Lor'themar and Liadrin, hoping I might know *you* through them. And when that failed to fill this ache, I became a Knight of the Silver Hand, just like Father. And they, too, were good to me. There was a kinship on the battlefield, but otherwise, I still didn't really belong. Silvermoon? My little house is nice. But I'm not elf enough to be sin'dorei, and not human enough to feel trusted among the Silver Hand."

His brow furrowed as he searched for the right words in the right order to make her understand.

"I've been looking for belonging my entire life. I've been looking for *you,* for *Father,* my entire life. For—for *home.*" His voice cracked on the last word.

Still Alleria was silent, her full attention on him, listening with all her being.

"And these last few days . . . I found it. I finally found it. Home is you, me, and that man over there, the one who drives us both crazy and whom we love so much." She inhaled swiftly, and he saw her eyes fill with tears. "That's *my home,* Mother. And maybe I only get to be home when we're all in battle. All risking our lives, all chasing some world-ending threat, but together, watching one another's backs. Maybe that's all it'll ever be. Maybe this family will never have anything more than the next war, but that doesn't mean I'll stop fighting. That I'll stop . . . trying. Because if we all give up on one another . . . then my home is truly gone."

She broke then, like a fine piece of porcelain shattered by a child's carelessness. Alleria flung her arms around him and held him tightly.

And for a moment, Arator—soldier, paladin, demon slayer—let himself be the boy of his past, and he buried his face in the crook of his mother's neck and wept with her.

They parted after a time, wiping at their faces. "We are broken, perhaps beyond any mending," she whispered, brushing a final tear from his face. "But oh, my child, there is such love in the pieces. And I see it in you as I never have before. The hope that, one day, those pieces might build something new."

"Then don't leave," Arator said simply. "Please. Have the courage to stay here and build it. With him. With *me.*"

She found herself unable to tell him no. And so, instead, she pressed her lips to his forehead, as she had done when he was a baby, and put all her love into that.

Then Alleria Windrunner straightened and was gone.

EPILOGUE

Light's Hope Chapel

EASTERN PLAGUELANDS, EASTERN KINGDOMS

Not for the first time, Arator found himself amused that a place dedicated to the Light and the hope it offered . . . was underground. He'd made a joke about it once, and it had not gone over well. He'd endured a five-minute lecture about how the Light was everywhere, within everyone, there was no place it couldn't reach, et cetera, et cetera. He'd been younger then and so hadn't protested, but Arator had made a promise to himself that if he ever achieved a high rank in the Knights of the Silver Hand, he would strive to instill more imagination in its members.

He pressed his lips together so as not to smile; levity would not be welcomed, not now, at this solemn moment: the induction of three new knights to the Order of the Knights of the Silver Hand. Arator wouldn't spoil the moment for them.

These occasions, those of deep, sincere ceremony, Arator had little quarrel with his order or its protocols. The words of the service were meaningful—even if he did disagree with certain turns of phrase that struck him as overbearing or outdated. The site was beautiful, the formal robes and regalia striking, the fragrance of incense emanating from gently swinging censors pleasing, and the emotions and the efforts of those being honored sincere. The order could use more of this, stiff and formal as it was—things that celebrated what the knights endured, and the truth at the core of what they stood for: helping others.

Certainly the three knights-to-be were moved. They knelt before Lord Maxwell Tyrosus at the altar: heads bowed, hands clasped, eyes closed.

Three clerics approached the altar, draping each soon-to-be-knight with a blue stole, a match to those worn by all the knights present, and anointing their foreheads with holy oil. Three knights then offered their blessings. Each placed a hammer at the feet of their initiate and a ceremonial plate upon their shoulders.

"Arise and be recognized," Lord Tyrosus said, and the three got to their feet. "Do you, Malani Sullivan, Diarmid Stonehammer, and Jayse Langley, vow to uphold the honor and codes of the Silver Hand?"

"I do," they said in unison.

Arator thought about the lessons of Tirion Fordring. He'd been accused of violating the codes of the Silver Hand, but he'd lived them better than anyone. Honor and codes had their place, but real heroism, the kind that Lord Tyrosus had talked about what seemed like a lifetime ago, manifested in actions, not adherence to rules.

"Do you vow to walk in the grace of the Light and spread its wisdom?"

As far as Arator was concerned, this vow was essentially meaningless. Staying in the Light's grace wasn't necessarily one's choice. It felt—*arbitrary* to him and so did needing mortals to verbally extol it. Everyone knew about the Light, and it selected those it wished to have as its champions. The zealots of the Scarlet Crusade were quite certain they were in the grace of the Light, and their "wisdom" was to wipe the Forsaken off the face of Azeroth.

Jubeka Shadowbreaker is not in the grace of the Light, nor does she spread its so-called wisdom. She gives it no lip service, yet she acts in accord with what it supposedly embodies.

A second time, the three initiates replied, "I do."

"Do you vow to vanquish evil wherever it be found, and to protect the innocent with your very life?"

This . . . this one is the only vow that really matters. Evil was not always what, or where, one thought it might be. Paladins should fight whatever showed itself to be evil, not what someone told them it was. Good, too, sometimes showed up in surprising places. Even a demon could become a paladin. *I will gladly strike the one who dares say that my mother doesn't serve the cause of good.*

And protecting the innocent . . . that was everything. Greater than codes or personal honor. Fortunately, it was the final vow for a reason, and the voices of the three, strong before, reverberated with passion and commitment that rang through the chapel.

"By blood and honor, we serve!" shouted the new knights.

"Brothers and sisters—you who have gathered here to bear witness—raise your hands and let the Light illuminate these three."

Arator felt the warmth nestle into his hand and welcomed it. These three had good hearts. They knew themselves to be worthy, as he had known, and yet were awed, as he had been—and, he admitted, often still was.

Like in this moment.

Light wrapped around his hand, and he raised it in a blessing as so many others did. The hairs on the back of his neck lifted, and he felt the fullness in his heart as the Light drifted, like dust in a shaft of sunlight, to settle around the three new Knights of the Silver Hand.

As the Light about them began to fade, the three new knights stepped to the side.

"In days gone by, this would be the end of our ceremony," said Lord Tyrosus. "But the challenges facing the Silver Hand have come fast in more recent times. Heroism is demanded more than ever, and after the end of the Fourth War, our order decided to recognize deeds that went above and beyond what is asked of a knight. Such deeds are sometimes right in front of us, but we may not see them. That is why we chose to name them after humble herbs or flowers. The Golden Thorn is one such. One must climb hills to find it, and the thorns themselves often exact the price of the harvester's blood. It is versatile and can be used in many potions. It increases the ability to defend and protect. It promotes fortitude, agility, and insight. It heals and restores.

"For his demonstrations, in the past and recently, of all of these qualities; for preventing another incursion of the Burning Legion and eliminating its leader; for finding common ground among uneasy allies; and for his unwavering protection of the innocent: the Order of the Knights of the Silver Hand recognizes Arator the Redeemer."

Arator straightened and approached the altar. Lord Tyrosus was solemn, but his eyes crinkled ever so slightly as he stepped forward and pinned the commendation to Arator's blue stole. Quietly he said, "Well done. Well done, indeed."

Now the other three knights came forward to stand beside Arator. The four turned to face those assembled.

"Blessings on these four, and on all who are present to honor them. Light be with us all!"

The formality dissolved into cheers and applause. Arator turned to his new brother and sisters in the order, shaking hands, hugging, clapping backs. The little crowd moved out to a more open area, where food and drink awaited the celebrants. Most of the attention was on the new knights, of course, and this troubled Arator not at all. He was proud to have earned the Golden Thorn, but he realized, now that it was glinting on his chest, that it provided none of the validation he had been craving when he had spoken with Lord Tyrosus the last time.

He felt a tugging on his stole and looked down to see young Winthrop. The boy was beaming, his smile wide and free. "Congratulations, Sir Arator! I still can't believe you helped me with Lord Grayson's armor."

Arator laughed and ruffled the boy's red hair. "Now, now, I'm sure that one of these days I'll be congratulating you and calling *you* sir!"

"Oh, not for a while, I don't think, but Lord Grayson just learned that his old squire's going to be knighted in a few months! That's him over there! Doesn't he look happy?"

Arator turned to where Winthrop had pointed. Lord Grayson Shadowbreaker stood talking to a younger man who did indeed look very happy. Arator recognized him; this had been who Lord Grayson had been chatting with while Arator worked on his armor and Winthrop had been chatting a mile a minute.

He was glad for the former squire. He was not so glad to see Lord Grayson. "I'm sure it's well deserved," Arator said, remembering a promise.

Grayson looked up, and his gaze met Arator's. With a final word to his former squire, the older man made his way through the crowd. "Congratulations, young man," he said, speaking more loudly than normal to be heard above the buzz of excited conversation. "The Golden Thorn, eh? Went right past the Bloom of Peace and the Silver Leaf. You prevented a Legion incursion? I'm sure we'll all be briefed about that, but perhaps I can hear some of it from the man who did it himself?"

"As Lord Tyrosus said, I couldn't have done it alone. Others helped me at every step. I'm particularly grateful for the assistance from your sister, Jubeka."

The blood drained from Lord Grayson's face.

"You're mistaken," Grayson said. His voice was icy, but it trembled, and he spoke softly, for Arator's ears only. "I have no sister. Tragically, she was slain the awful day that Lordaeron fell."

Arator feigned confusion. In a louder tone, he replied, "No, I'm pretty sure it was Jubeka Shadowbreaker. I found her to be wise and courageous, with a wonderful sense of humor. And," he added, "someone worthy of compassion. You might want to talk with the founder of our order about her. You know. Alonsus Faol, the Forsaken priest?"

Grayson's pale countenance suddenly flushed red. His dark brows came together, and a vein stood out on his temple. Arator stood his ground calmly.

"Let's go outside, Winthrop," Lord Grayson said stiffly. "It's getting a bit stuffy in here."

Winthrop's eyes had grown enormous, and he looked anxiously from Arator to his master, then dutifully followed. Arator watched him go.

"Grayson's going to have a lovely time trying to explain to his squire how you met his dead sister," came Liadrin's warm voice, bright with suppressed mirth.

"It's probably very unbecoming of me, but I really don't care," Arator said. He tapped the Golden Thorn. "'Finding common ground among uneasy allies.'" He smiled.

"And something about preventing incursions, killing demonic leaders, and protecting the innocent," she added.

The chatter and bustle around them stopped cold. Then, soft murmurs arose. Arator caught whispered words:

. . . It's him! . . . Really? . . . I've never . . .

Arator closed his eyes, gathering his patience, then took a deep breath and turned.

The high exarch, the last living original human paladin, the man who had defeated Orgrim Doomhammer, who had gone through the Dark Portal to help protect countless worlds . . . he, the legendary Turalyon, had arrived.

He towered over most of those present, his gold-white hair bright, his shoulders broad and powerful even without armor, trying to smile politely and make his way through a throng of wide-eyed admirers. Arator noticed, though, that the smile was forced, and there was a clipped flatness in Turalyon's voice as he addressed them.

Arator glanced around, wondering if he could escape before his father noticed him, but it was too late. "Excuse me," he heard the smooth baritone voice saying, "I must congratulate my son."

Even at a ceremony where Arator had been honored for exceptional service to the order, where he might reasonably be expected to be at least part of the focus, his father had simply walked in, and every head had turned. Even Liadrin's. She watched the venerated paladin approach and said to Arator, "I'm sure you'll want to talk with him; I'll just say hello and leave him to you." She left before Arator could request that she stay.

"Arator," Turalyon said.

"Father." Arator inclined his head stiffly.

"I'm glad I caught you. I wanted to attend the ceremony, but thought that might be, ah . . . distracting."

"Apparently you simply coming into a room is distracting," Arator said.

"I almost didn't come . . . but I didn't want you to think I didn't care."

Arator was silent.

"We . . . didn't leave things very well."

Arator scoffed. "No one did."

"No." Turalyon started to say something, then appeared to think better of it. "Well, then. You've earned this acknowledgment, Arator. I'm proud of you. And I know your mother is, too."

At that, Arator turned to face his father. "You've seen her?"

Turalyon's expression didn't change. "No. But I asked your aunt Vereesa to make sure she knew about it."

Silence, awkward and lengthy, fell. Arator poured two cups of tea and handed one to his father. Arator drank his swiftly and plunked the cup down.

"Well, thanks for coming, Father. I have duties to attend to." He tried to push past Turalyon, but his father caught his arm gently.

"You're not as used to this as I am," Turalyon said.

Arator sighed. "No, I'm not. It's not something I want to get used to."

"As I told you, this isn't anything unusual for her."

Standing before Turalyon now, Arator was reminded more of his father's statue than the vital man brimming with life who'd fought by his side what felt like a lifetime ago. "Who are you trying to convince? Me . . . or yourself?"

"She'll make her way back, when she's ready."

"How do you *know*?" Arator asked, dully. He looked into the gold-brown eyes that, for the first time, seemed to hold not pain, not hope, but . . . resignation.

"Because she always has."

Arator heard the final word, the unspoken one. The one neither of them dared say.

. . . *before.*

Acknowledgments

To say that 2024 was a rough year for me is laughably inadequate. But thankfully, to say I simply had "support" is equally insufficient, and for this, I am so grateful.

It's a pretty wild coincidence that when each of my parents passed, I was actively writing a World of Warcraft novel. In 2024, as in 2011, I was shown nothing but kindness, compassion, patience, and care.

My Random House Worlds editor, Tom Hoeler, with whom I've worked off and on for a decade on *Star Wars* and then Blizzard books, was a source of steadfast support and an apparently endless well of gentle patience. It meant the world.

My editor at Blizzard, Chloe Fraboni, is an angel. Her care for this story and my approach and thoughts created a place of safety during a time when little in my life felt safe or stable. Her feedback was invaluable and made the book so much stronger, and often a little margin note from her made my day.

Chris Metzen, a friend for a quarter of a century (unreal!), reminded me of a great truth: We both dearly love creating for this game, and it's pure dopamine when we get to do it together.

Sean Copeland, another old friend, caught the lore errors and conflicts with his customary deep kindness and respect. Few people are so gracious.

Raph Ahad, I so appreciate your professionalism and attention to both small details and large, overarching themes. Thank you for thoughtfully considering all angles, approaches, suggestions, and impacts, and for being all-in during every part of the journey.

To Peter Molinari, thank you for your steadfast stewardship of our books and for always supporting me. It means a lot.

Thanks as always to my agent, Lucienne Diver, especially this year. Writers, get yourself an agent who can be fierce in your defense and have faith in you when your own is tenuous. Double win if they become a trusted and loved friend.

Out in the real world, I must acknowledge my friend Robert Brooks, who has helped me find strength when wobbly, given sound advice, and just been an all-around magnificent human.

To Amelia Savery, you are a soul of bright colors and big heart; so glad we met by the orc so long ago. And Freya Jackson, thank you for too many kindnesses to list.

To these wonderful individuals and many others, thank you for helping me rediscover my footing, and my voice, both in my writing and my life.

Finally, always, to my readers. This is a book of thorns and tears and laughter and love, and I hope you turn the last page with a heart as full for this family and their journey as mine is.

For Azeroth!

ABOUT THE AUTHOR

Christie Golden is the award-winning, *New York Times* bestselling author of nearly sixty books and more than a dozen short stories in the fields of fantasy, science fiction, and horror. Her media tie-in works include her first novel, *Vampire of the Mists,* which launched TSR's game line; more than a dozen *Star Trek* novels; and the Fate of the Jedi novels *Omen, Allies,* and *Ascension,* as well as the stand-alone *Star Wars* novels *Dark Disciple* and *Battlefront II: Inferno Squad.* For Blizzard Entertainment, she has contributed five StarCraft novels, including the Dark Templar trilogy, and the Warcraft books *Lord of the Clans, Rise of the Horde, Arthas: Rise of the Lich King, Before the Storm, War Crimes, Exploring Azeroth: The Eastern Kingdoms, A is for Azeroth,* and *Sylvanas.* In 2017, Christie Golden was awarded the International Association of Media Tie-in Writers Faust Award and named a grand master in recognition of thirty years of writing.

christiegolden.com
X: @ChristieGolden

ABOUT THE TYPE

This book was set in Caslon, a typeface first designed in 1722 by William Caslon (1692–1766). Its widespread use by most English printers in the early eighteenth century soon supplanted the Dutch typefaces that had formerly prevailed. The roman is considered a "workhorse" typeface due to its pleasant, open appearance, while the italic is exceedingly decorative.